The Nut Shop Years Series
The Nut Shop
Gathering Nuts
In A Nutshell

Visit Christine's website at www.christinemelvillekenworthy.com

"A great read, I couldn't put it down"

"The Nut Shop is a very human story about neighbours, friends and family and how they work together through the shop's good times and bad times. It is a joy to read out loud, with a smile, if not a laugh, on every page. Even through the bad times, the love at the heart of the book shines through."

"A funny and fabulous book which I read in one sitting. Move over James Herriot – Christine has stolen your crown!"

"If you like Maeve Binchy then this is for you. A great book with a definite feel-good factor to it. Funny in places but thought provoking at times."

"Many laugh out loud moments once again in this down to earth insightful book."

"A charming, witty and warming book. Once started it was impossible to put down – thought provoking mixed with laugh-out-loud funny!"

Dedicated to my Mam
Rachel Oliver Melville

Thanks to Sues Dodd, Juliet Freel and Audrey McIntyre for reading
and giving feedback on the first draft of In A Nutshell. Thank you
Anna Kenworthy for all the editing help and to Rose Kenworthy,
Carol Walker and Jess Fairfax for helping to organise the book
launch. Artwork by Simon Fawcett, thanks Simon.
Thank you Joe Melville, Andrew Moy, Peter Elliot and Andrew Tye
of 14th Emperor for rocking the launch!

In memory of Rita Sidney
Fly high with the angels Rita xxx

IN A NUTSHELL

CHRISTINE
MELVILLE KENWORTHY

Christine Kenworthy :)

CHAPTER ONE

I looked at the contraption made from cereal boxes and cardboard tubes and struggled for something to say.

'Well?' Aileen asked. 'What do you think?' I contemplated the porridge boxes that had been cut and taped together to form a large container. Emerging from the top was a long tube crafted from two kitchen roll inner tubes.

'Ah, yes,' I said, playing for time.

Lorraine was less hesitant, less polite. 'What the hell have you made now?'

Luckily Aileen was not easily offended. 'It's to keep the used till rolls in,' she said triumphantly. 'Let me demonstrate.' She took a till roll from the box beneath the till and secured it with an elastic band. 'You simply pop the roll into the tube where it falls into the box below, like so. At the end of the month, the tube can be taken off, the box taped and labelled and there you have the till rolls ready to store.'

Lorraine sighed loudly and rolled her eyes.

'Right,' I said. 'Very good.'

'And of course the tube can be re-used by connecting it to a new box.' Aileen smiled proudly.

Our present system of storage was to remove the used till roll each night, scribble on the date and chuck it into a box beneath the counter. When the box was full, we threw it through a hatch to a storage space at the side of the roof. We were required to keep them along with other paperwork for three years in case of a tax inspection.

I couldn't really see any advantage to this new system but to please Aileen I said, 'Oh how clever,' as she assembled it beneath the counter and Lorraine went off to serve a customer mumbling about not encouraging her to make any more of her shite.

It was January 1995 and my sister Lorraine and I had been running our health food shop for three years with the help of our part-time assistant Nadine.

Nadine was an old friend of Lorraine's, and although I'd been wary of employing her after hearing tales of friendships being ruined by such arrangements, she was worth her weight in gold. Whenever we told her this she would laugh and say 'That's a lot of gold!'

But she was. She made sure she was knowledgeable about all aspects of our business and often worked beyond her paid hours. We knew we were lucky to have her.

Business was good and life was hectic. My husband Peter worked at the local high school but also helped out as much as he could, mostly behind the scenes, keeping our accounts and tax returns up to date, and acting as a general handyman. We also shared the responsibility of looking after our twenty-two month old daughter Rosie, and keeping on top of the house and garden, which meant we didn't have much spare time for anything else. So when Lorraine suggested maybe we should take on a second assistant to work a couple of days a week, enabling us to have a day off, I'd agreed unreservedly.

Aileen had joined us a few months ago and was cheerful, hardworking and honest. The only downside was her passion for excessive recycling that compelled her to hoard every type of rubbish that came her way. I didn't mind when she swept up stray crumbs and sesame seeds from the bread shelves to take home for her bird table, or collected our used tea bags and vegetable peelings for her compost bin. Nor did I mind her taking packaging and empty boxes away. It was bringing them back converted into some ridiculous doodad she'd made that was the problem.

We tried to indulge her when we could, drinking her tea that she'd made with one teabag between six cups, and using her pan scrubbers made from knitted plastic string bags that had contained oranges, but there were times when we really had to reject her ideas, such as wrapping bread in newspaper and using her husband's old underpants as dishcloths.

Aileen finished arranging her Till Roll Holder and went off to put the kettle on for one of our many tea breaks.

Our morning routine after setting up the till and opening the blinds, was to sort the morning deliveries of bread and bakery products, and then prepare the sandwich fillings and salads. We usually completed this by around ten, when we would be joined by our local postman, Nige, and our favourite customer, Georgina for a tea-drinking-and-gossip session.

Nige arrived first, gambolling in with a fistful of mail.

'Morning me hearties. By, it's chilly out there.' He handed me a bundle of envelopes. He settled himself on a stool near the counter and took his mug of coffee from the tray proffered by Aileen.

Georgina followed not long after, dressed in some sort of enormous colourful pillow-case.

'Morning.' She took the camomile tea waiting for her. 'What do you think of this? Original 1960s kaftan from the vintage clothing store on the Quayside.' Although Georgina was approaching sixty she looked years younger with her piercings and tattoos and her unique style of dress.

'I'm saying nowt,' Nige said.

'It looks a bit bulky,' Lorraine said. I'd been thinking that but hadn't liked to say.

'That's because I have three jumpers on underneath,' Georgina said. 'In the summer it'll be great.'

'Suits you,' Lorraine said. 'Although I wouldn't wear it, like.'

'I think it's a great idea wearing second hand stuff,' Aileen said. 'I get loads of my stuff from jumble sales.' Georgina turned to her.

'Excuse me. I got this from a genuine vintage and antique clothing store. I paid nearly fifty quid for it. It's not from a jumble sale.'

'You can get some amazing bargains at jumble sales,' Aileen said, realising she'd annoyed Georgina.

'Fifty quid!' I said. 'Blimey, you could have bought a duvet cover from Woollies for a fiver.'

'That's a bit steep,' Lorraine said. 'I mean it's your style, but fifty pounds? For an old poncho thing?'

'Kaftan. It's a *vintage* piece. I keep telling you, it's an investment.'

'Eeh, I can't believe you paid that much to look like a pair of old curtains,' Nige said.

'I thought you said you were saying nowt?' Georgina snapped.

'I got an old jumper at the church jumble sale last week for twenty- five pence,' Aileen said.

'Twenty-five pence? Now that's more like it,' Nige said. 'That's what I call a bargain. Not fifty quid for some old hippy's nightie.'

Georgina was rattled now. 'It's a vintage kaftan. There's no comparison. I mean, twenty-five pence for a jumper? It must be minging.'

'Well it is a bit worn in places,' Aileen admitted. 'And the colour's a bit faded. But I'm planning to unravel it and knit it up again.'

'And then you'll have a worn faded jumper exactly the same as the one you started with.'

Lorraine, who had been sorting through the mail held out a flyer.

'Fancy doing this anyone? It's a sponsored abseil for Children in Need organised by Richardson's Travel.'

Richardson's Travel Agency had recently opened a branch at the top of the bank and the staff were good customers of ours. One of the assistants, a fresh-faced, attractive young girl, came every day with a list of lunch requirements for her colleagues. She was dark skinned with striking almond-shaped eyes and we'd all remarked how beautiful she was.

'When is it?' Georgina asked.

'Not until July. We have months yet. Anyone up for it?'

'No chance,' Georgina said. 'I have a morbid fear of heights.'

'Me too,' said Aileen.

Nige exhaled noisily 'You won't catch me jumping off a bridge voluntarily.'

'It's not jumping,' Lorraine told him. 'It's abseiling.'

'I don't care what kind of sailing it is, I'm not doing it.'

Lorraine looked at me. 'What about you?'

I hesitated before answering. I had secret hopes I might be expecting our second child, although it was still early to be sure. I'd had a few of the usual early symptoms, feeling queasy in the mornings and the odd dizzy spell but I didn't want to mention anything until I was certain.

'Yeah, put me down for it.' I could always cancel later if necessary. 'Put Nadine's name down too, I'm sure she'll be up for it. We'll tell her tomorrow.'

Lorraine wrote our names on the form and I went to serve a customer. He looked to be in his early twenties and seemed uncertain as to why he'd come in.

'Hello, can I help?' I asked. He gave me a look of relief and moved towards the counter.

'Please, yes. I am arrived and living house on street and I am finding my wife Hanna has none of the electric.'

'Your wife has none of the electric?'

'Yes. I asking please to telephone for electric in house I am arrived and living.'

'Ah, you've moved in and the electricity is off?'

'Yes. I asking please to telephone for electric in house. Is very cold.'

The man, who told us his name was Tomas, had arrived from Poland with his wife Hanna to move into one of the flats above the shops. He explained to us that he'd been offered a job at the City Recycling Plant and had agreed to rent the flat without seeing it. He had a whimsical way of talking which sometimes made his statements ambiguous but although his English was erratic, it was a heck of a lot better than our Polish. I wrote down his details and Lorraine offered to go and telephone his landlord to see if she could find out what the problem was.

Meanwhile, Aileen, who had heard the magic words 'recycling plant' quizzed him about whether any good pieces of furniture ever found their way to the plant as she was looking for some drawers for her aunt.

'For your aunt you look for pair of drawers?' Tomas asked.

'Chest of drawers we call it,' Aileen corrected him. 'I wondered if I'd be able to come and have a look at the stuff that arrives and see if I can make use of anything.'

After a few misunderstandings, Tomas grasped that Aileen loved to make new useful items from things others had discarded and Aileen understood that Tomas had only been in the job for a week and would enquire for her but thought the public were not allowed into the premises and that anything brought to the plant remained the property of the company. He admired Aileen's Till Roll Holder although appeared a little perplexed by it.

Lorraine came to tell him she'd spoken to his landlord who said he had overlooked having the electricity supply connected and would sort it out as soon as possible. Tomas thanked us generously, telling us he would come back soon with Hanna.

'Will be best customer. Will be buying all the meats and the sausage every day,' he beamed.

I hoped he wouldn't be too disappointed when he discovered we were a vegetarian shop and he wouldn't be able to buy all the meats and the sausage every day.

CHAPTER TWO

The next morning, I arrived to find three crates of bread on the shop doorstep. I dragged them away from the door to enable me to open the shutter and after dumping my bag and keys on the counter, carried them through to the shop. I was checking the order against the delivery note when Lorraine entered.

'Bread here already?' she asked.

'Yes, it was dumped on the doorstep.'

'On the doorstep? It's a wonder it hasn't frozen.'

'I'm not happy about it. I've no idea how long it's been there. This is a busy street. It could have been stolen.'

'Or it might have started raining.'

'Or dirt could have blown onto it.'

'Or flies could have landed on it.'

'Or a dog could have weed on it.'

'Ugh! You'd better check it.'

'I did. There are no wet patches. But I'm still not happy about it having been outside.'

'Me neither.'

'So are we still going to use it?'

'Course we are,' Lorraine said. 'I'm not *that* unhappy about it. Not enough to lose sales.'

Later, Aileen told us she had a brilliant idea.

'Could you stick those eggs on to boil please Aileen?' I hoped if I distracted her she might forget. I'd heard lots of her brilliant ideas, enough to know that whatever the idea, it would not be brilliant. She began transferring eggs into a pan.

'I was thinking. I have an old dog kennel in my shed at home. It's a bit worse for wear mind, but that doesn't matter. I knew I'd find a use for it eventually.'

'You getting a dog?' Lorraine asked.

'No! I just had a thought. If I took half of the roof off like this,' she began scribbling a rough diagram on a paper bag. 'I could put a hinge on to make a sort of flap at the top.'

'And?' I had no idea where this was going.

'We could use it for the bread of course!'

'The bread?'

'You're not with me are you?'

'No.'

'We could put it outside the shop and the delivery man from the bakery could put the trays of bread in it.' She raised her hands and smiled widely. 'Problem solved.'

'Hardly,' Lorraine said. 'If we're not happy with the bread being left on the doorstep, why would we be happy about it being put in an old manky dog kennel?'

'It would keep the rain and dust off. And it wouldn't be manky because I could paint it. I've got some paint left from painting my bathroom, tangerine it is. Lovely.'

Before Lorraine could tell her that there was no way we were having an old dog kennel outside for our bread, tangerine-painted or not I said, 'Great idea Aileen but you know how strict Mr Reeves is about things like that. He wouldn't allow it.'

'Oh.' Aileen looked crestfallen. 'Never mind. I'll keep thinking. I'm sure I'll come up with something else.'

Edward Reeves was our local Environmental Health Officer.

He was a dour, humourless man who visited regularly to offer advice and demand changes to our working practice. We were always polite and complying as we were well aware he had the authority to restrict or even close our business, but I often wondered why he wasted both our time and his with his silly requests. I was sure there were food vendors who were much less conscientious, but Mr Reeves preferred to harass us with his petty demands. Lorraine had a theory that because we were so complying we made it possible for him to submit 'mission accomplished' files to his superiors on a regular basis.

We were always thorough about the cleanliness of our premises. The kitchen was cleaned every night before we left, as were the floors and the lavatory. The wooden shelves were systematically emptied, cleaned and polished, and as soon as we finished we immediately started again at the beginning. We did a 'deep clean' at the end of each week when we scrubbed the oven and cleaned the fridges and freezers, after heaving them forwards to clean the floor beneath them.

As for food preparation, we were meticulous about hand washing and food storage, our ethos being that we would never sell food we would not be prepared to eat ourselves. One summer, we had dismissed a temporary sales assistant when she sneezed violently and wetly over our workbench holding dishes of salads and fillings and then questioned why we felt the need to dispose of them, stating 'no-one would know'. Despite having been given our initiation training which gave clear guidance about the standards we expected, she had previously been spotted scraping up a spoonful of egg mayonnaise from the floor where she'd dropped it, intending to use it in a customer's sandwich. We'd spoken to her sternly, reminding her of our hygiene policies, but she obviously didn't understand as during the conversation she commented it was a shame that our kitchen and prep area was in full view of customers making it 'difficult to get away with'. When we'd told her it had been intentionally designed to enable customers to watch us prepare their food, she seemed to think we were missing a trick. The trick we missed was getting rid of her there and then instead of waiting until she'd contaminated our fresh fillings and salads with sneeze-fired mucus droplets.

'Edward Reeves is due to call this week, actually,' Lorraine reminded us. 'I wonder what nit-picky complaints he'll have for us this month.'

Aileen gave a sigh of disappointment at another 'brilliant-idea' rejection, so I thanked her for the idea and said it was such a shame we couldn't use it as it would have been an ideal solution and Lorraine looked at me and rolled her eyes.

The morning, as usual, was busy. Nadine and I set to work in the kitchen, Lorraine stayed at the till serving the queue of customers and Aileen began cleaning the therapy room ready for Maureen's appointments later that afternoon.

Maureen, or Mariana as she preferred to be known, was a local clairvoyant and psychic who rented our therapy room to give

13

readings to clients. Although I'd been sceptical at first, she proved to be popular and her appointment slots always filled quickly. I had to admit that sometimes her predictions and statements were very accurate, but she also gave a lot of general comments that could really apply to anyone. However, she had lots of devoted followers who returned time and again, which was also good for us as they would often stay to do some shopping after their appointment.

'Is she any good then, this psychic?' Aileen asked as she carried the vacuum cleaner into the therapy room.

'She's brilliant,' Nadine told her. 'She can look into your eyes and see right to your soul.' Nadine was one of Maureen's devoted followers. I wasn't.

'She's okay,' I said. 'A lot of the things she says are a bit vague but now and again she hits on something.'

'She was amazing with me,' Nadine said. 'She's told me all sorts of things that came true.'

'Like what?' Aileen asked.

'She saw travel ahead for me, and about a month later I went on the train to Hexham. And she said there was a surprise heading my way and I won a tenner on the lottery.'

'Like I said. Vague.'

'She also predicted a new man would bring romance into my life and he would be dark and intelligent and there's a new dentist at the clinic and he's black,' Nadine said, triumphantly.

'And has he brought romance into your life?' Aileen asked.

'Well no, not yet but I'm working on it,' Nadine admitted.

'I thought you'd had a lot of dental appointments lately,' I said laughing. 'I don't think dentists are allowed to have relationships with patients are they?'

'No, I think it's the same as doctors,' Aileen said. 'Not allowed.'

'Oh,' Nadine said. 'No wonder I've not been getting anywhere. I thought perhaps he was in a relationship or gay or something. Anyway, she was right about the dark, intelligent man bit.'

Maureen greeted us with tales of woe about her bus journey, carrying two large shopping bags, one containing her costume and make up, the other holding her pug, Billy.

She smacked her ample bottom onto one of our wooden stools which protested with a loud creak. At least I presumed it was the stool and not her bottom.

'How's everyone? Just the same? Eeh, things never get any better do they? I waited ages for that bus, me feet are killing. No doubt me corns will be playing up tonight. Bloody freezing out there. We'll have snow by tea-time, you mark my words.' Maureen's glass was always half, if not completely, empty.

'We're all fine, thanks,' Nadine said in an over-cheery voice she kept especially for speaking to Maureen. We'd all got into a habit of speaking to her as though we were presenters on Blue Peter, using bright voices that were optimistic and upbeat and more than a bit patronising. We all loved her, but she viewed life through mud-tinted glasses, and if not intercepted, her gloomy observations had the ability to suck the joy from any situation.

Nadine lifted Billy from his shopping bag and he snuffled and tried to lick her face as she cuddled him.

'He's getting a bit big for that bag, you're a heavy little lump aren't you?' Lorraine said as she took him from Nadine for her turn to cuddle him. We all loved Billy. He was a lovely little well-behaved dog who didn't seem to mind the indignity of being hauled about in a flowery shopping bag.

'Tell me about it.' Maureen kneaded the roll of flesh that lay around her hips. 'Little bugger's a ton weight now, my back is nearly broken carrying him around.'

'You should get him a pram.' I suggested. 'You'd love that, wouldn't you Billy, being pushed about like a baby!'

Maureen stopped kneading and looked at me. 'What a great idea. If I get one of those big old ones I could carry all my stuff around in it too.' I had meant it as a joke but she was so pleased with the idea I let it go as there weren't many things that put a smile on her face.

Billy had now been passed to Aileen who introduced herself to Maureen and asked if she could have a reading.

'Course you can my darling,' Maureen told her. 'In fact I'll go and get ready now, I'll do you before my first appointment.'

Maureen took her bags into the therapy room saying, 'I'll give you a shout when I'm ready.'

My first experience of a reading with Maureen had been bizarre and a little alarming. To get herself into the right frame of mind for contacting the spirits, Maureen would change into her alter ego, Mariana, by donning a black wig and thick make-up and affecting a deep, throaty voice. Her accent changed too, veering across the country and sometimes even crossing the channel so it was difficult to pinpoint the effect she was aiming for. She brought with her, long lengths of silky material which she draped around the therapy room and incense sticks that filled the air with a smoky haze. She even used poor Billy as a prop. He had his own little gold turban, worn stretched over his ears and a red velvet cushion to sit on. When a client entered the room, Maureen would launch into a dramatic performance of summoning the spirits.

I wondered what Aileen would make of it all. Local opinion was divided into those who believed Mariana to be an under-rated sensation and those who saw her as an over-rated sensationalist. Aileen was very down to earth and not usually given to flights of fancy so I guessed she would see through Maureen's dramatics and be unimpressed by her shenanigans.

'You don't mind, do you?' Aileen asked. 'After all, I am supposed to be working.'

'No, it's fine,' I told her. 'To be honest, I'm interested to hear your thoughts about it all.'

'Me too,' Lorraine said and we smirked at each other. Aileen flinched as a deep voice emerged from the therapy room.

'I am Mariana, seer of the unseen, perceiver of what is and of what is yet to be. Come to me, my child. The spirits are ready to impart their wisdom.' Aileen looked at us, from one to the other and back again.

'Off you go,' Lorraine told her, and we both smiled reassuringly as Aileen walked hesitantly towards the therapy room.

I looked at Lorraine and laughed. 'Well? What do you think? Is she going to come out bursting with wonder and awe or is she going to think it's a load of old tosh?'

'Oh I think she'll love it.'

'Nah, don't agree. I think she's too level-headed to be taken in by Maureen's play acting.'

'Bet she isn't.'

'Bet she is.'

'Okay then, bet you a bottle of wine she loves it.'

'Done.'

Aileen came out of the therapy room in raptures. 'Oh my word, she's amazing!'

Lorraine smirked. 'I'll have a bottle of Merlot thanks,' she murmured.

'She told me I'm very creative, not materialistic and have no interest in the superficial trappings of modern society.' To be honest, anyone could have deduced the same by a quick look at Aileen's 'recycled' outfit.

'Wow, what else did she say?' I asked.

'That I've endured difficult times in the past but have overcome many challenges by perseverance. Sometimes I'm not appreciated by others as much as I deserve to be and I have dreams and goals I've not quite achieved yet.'

'Amazing,' Lorraine said, glancing at me. I knew what her look meant. Maureen had a few stock phrases she used for all her clients. I'm sure we all think we've overcome challenges, are not always given the respect we warrant, and have goals and dreams yet to be accomplished.

'She also mentioned I've attracted a spirit and it now resides here.'

'A what? A spirit? Like a ghost you mean?' I said.

'Yes. Apparently, sometimes entities attach themselves to the energy a person emits without them knowing and one must

17

have attached itself to me,' Aileen explained. 'Then while I've been here, it's detached and now resides here, in the shop.' She smiled at us. 'It's incredible isn't it?'

'Well that's great news,' I said, but my sarcasm missed, and she continued smiling proudly as though she'd done us a great favour.

'Aye, well it can bloody well attach itself back to you and you can take it home,' Lorraine said. 'We get enough nutters in here without a flippin' ghost on the loose.'

CHAPTER THREE

The following morning, after we'd dropped Rosie at my mam's, Peter drove me to the shop. I told him about Aileen's attached entity and predictably he thought it was a hoot. He laughed so much he couldn't speak.

'What a load of tripe,' he said, once he'd calmed down enough to be coherent. 'I can't believe you've been taken in by that.'

'I didn't say I believed it. It's made me feel a bit uneasy that's all.'

'Uneasy,' was a bit of an understatement. 'Terrified' would be more accurate. Although my rational side told me it was ridiculous, I'd joined Lorraine in spooking ourselves up into such a state of fright we'd been afraid to be left alone in any part of the shop.

'Anyway, I thought you believe in ghosts and spirits and stuff? You're always going on about wanting to have a weekend at some haunted place.'

'I think a ghost hunt would be a laugh,' Peter said. 'I wouldn't mind a weekend in Chillingham Castle or that old hotel in Alnmouth or somewhere. I'm open minded about stuff like that, but I definitely don't believe Aileen has unknowingly piggy-backed some lost spirit into the shop and it's decided to stay.'

'You make it sound so ridiculous,' I laughed.

'Well it is!'

We were still joking about it as we approached the roundabout at the foot of the bank. As we were about to pull out, a van shot in front of us causing Peter to slam on the brakes. He muttered a few impolite words as the van sailed around the roundabout, the driver oblivious to the chaos in his wake.

'It's a wonder no-one's been killed on this roundabout, Peter said. It's ridiculous, it needs to be changed.'

I recognised the bakery's logo on the side panel of the van. It was our bread delivery.

The driver's elbow rested on the open window, one hand gripping the wheel, a lit cigarette hanging from his lips.

'He's smoking with a load of fresh bread in there,' I said. 'I think he needs some serious training on health and hygiene.'

We followed the van as it turned into the lane behind the shop and came to a halt at an angle. Peter pulled up behind him.

'What's the idiot doing now?' I said, as the driver jumped out and threw his cigarette butt to the ground. 'Is he leaving it parked there?'

Roughly, Peter moved the gearstick into reverse position. 'I'll have to back out. He's blocked the whole lane.'

'Let me out first.' I climbed out of the car and squeezed around the van ready to go and give the driver a dressing down. He had opened the back doors and was pulling out a stack of bread trays.

His face broke into a smile when he spotted me. 'Mornin',' he said.

'Morning,' I said, a little put off my stride by his cheery greeting. 'Did I just see you smoking as you were driving?'

'Smoking? Cigarettes? Filthy habit, never touch 'em.'

He lifted the tower of bread trays and carried them towards the shop, singing loudly and flatly as I hurried after him.

'I saw you smoking in the van,' I told him. 'You do know it's unhygienic, carrying fresh bread in a van filled with cigarette smoke?' He increased the volume of his tuneless song.

'I must ask that you refrain from smoking while our bread order is in your van...' I began as he carelessly deposited the trays on the pavement.

'...and please do *not* put our bread on the pavement...' I added as a couple of granary baps rolled to the ground. He quickly scooped them up, throwing them back onto the top tray and made his escape.

'There you go darlin', see you tomorrow.' He gave me another wide smile and a wink then resumed his enthusiastic singing as he strutted back to his van.

'Cheeky bugger,' I muttered.

Peter came around the corner as I opened the shutter.
'Did you tell him then?' he asked.
'Oh yes, I told him.'
'And how did he take it?'
'He didn't. He completely ignored me and sang out of tune.' I picked up the granary baps that had been on the ground and Peter lifted the pile of trays. I grumbled about the delivery man as I unlocked the shop door.

'It's not good enough. I'm going to complain to the bakery about him.'

Peter carried the bread trays into the shop as I put the soiled bread to one side for Aileen to take for her bird table.

'Must go,' he said as he left to go to work. 'See you at lunchtime.' The school was about a fifteen minute walk from the shop and he came most days for lunch.

I was filling the till with coins as Lorraine and Nadine arrived. We had a collective whinge about the bakery driver and called him a few names as we assembled our collection of chopping boards, knives and graters, ready to prepare the sandwich fillings and salads.

I loved this time of day in the shop. Although the morning routine rarely differed, I never tired of it. There was something reassuring about the cosy familiarity. After the first pot of tea had been brewed, our next task was to load the shelves with fresh bread. The bread was often still warm from the oven and impossible to resist, so we'd choose a granary cob or a soft poppyseed twist to tear apart and share. Warm, newly-baked bread and a pot of tea are still one of my favourite simple pleasures.

We'd discuss the hot dishes and soup we were to offer that day and one of us, usually Nadine, would go off to buy fresh produce from Derek the greengrocer. Derek was a good talker and sometimes it could be a while before she returned. However, he knew everything that was happening locally so she usually came back with a titbit of information.

News and gossip of the day would be discussed exhaustively as we chopped and grated. Crisp salad leaves, chopped

21

olives and peppers, slices of cucumber and juicy tomatoes, grated cheese, carrots, radishes and celery, and whatever else looked particularly tempting at the greengrocers that morning. Vegetables, herbs and lentils simmering in our huge soup pan filled the kitchen with a delicious aroma. Sometimes a pot of vegetable chilli or curry bubbled on the stove, or a lentil casserole or lasagne baked in the oven, ready for our hungry lunchtime customers.

The scent of garlic and lemon drifted into the air as chickpeas and tahini were whizzed into hummus and a tray of roasting peppers and red onions, laced with olive oil and herbs, added to the delicious fragrance. By ten o'clock, the fridges would be filled with bowls of creamy egg mayonnaise, mushroom pate, crunchy coleslaw, cheese savoury, hummus, three-bean salad and roasted Mediterranean vegetables, along with the pies, quiches and tarts that were delivered to us daily.

This would be when Nige would appear with our mail, often Georgina would arrive with him, and our daily tea-drinking-and-putting-the-world-to-rights session would begin. Today we were talking about our recently acquired lost spirit.

'That woman talks absolute rubbish,' Georgina said. 'I thought you were trying to promote natural therapies and help make them more acceptable? Using your therapy room for a medium or a fortune-teller or whatever she calls herself reinforces the view that people who are into natural food and therapies are weird.'

'Well they are, I mean look at you lot,' Nige nodded towards us.

'That's a bit harsh Georgina,' I said. 'She's very popular, she has loads of followers.' I had to admit I'd had reservations about including Maureen in our programme of natural health practitioners feeling that her services were unrelated to our business but the customers loved her. 'Her appointment sheet fills quickly every week.'

'Oh so it's about the money she pays you then?' Georgina said with a smirk. 'And I thought you were all about the ethics.'

'We're all about ethics *and* making a living,' Lorraine said. 'I don't believe a word the woman says but she's good for business.'

'Well I believed her as soon as she told me,' Aileen said. 'I'm sure I'd felt a presence in here. I just didn't realise what it was at the time.'

'She's a good psychic,' Nige said. 'She told me I attract men and women alike and even straight men find me attractive. I mean, I've always known but I never liked to mention it.'

'Sorry Nige, but you do nowt for me,' Georgina told him, the rest of us quickly echoing her sentiment. Nige looked disappointed.

'I think she's amazing,' Nadine said. 'And if she says there's a spirit here then I believe her.'

'I could have put money on that,' Lorraine said. 'I knew you'd believe it.'

'You were pretty convinced yourself last night,' I said to her, remembering how the two of us had worked ourselves into a state of panic each time we heard the slightest noise.

'I'm keeping an open mind.'

'That's what Peter said too. He's raring to go on a ghost hunt at Chillingham but I'm too chicken to go with him.'

'Let's have a séance!' Nadine said. 'Then we'll find out for sure.'

'Now hang on...' I began, but was drowned out by the enthusiasm of the others.

'That's a great idea!'

'I'm up for it!'

'It'll be a right laugh!'

Even Georgina, who minutes ago had slated us for allowing such things in our therapy room, was suddenly fired up.

'Count me in,' she said. 'It'll be a hoot.'

I continued to object but my voice went unheard amongst the excitement.

'Did she say what kind of spirit it is?' Nige asked.

'Don't worry Nige, I'm sure it'll fancy you whatever it is,' Lorraine told him.

Georgina nudged him and winked. 'As long as it doesn't give you the willies.'

'She didn't say anything about what it was like,' Aileen said. 'I suppose that's something we could ask it. I'm sure I'll have something at home to make a Ouija board with.'

'Now hang on a minute...' I said.

'Brilliant,' Nadine said, and the others all seemed to think this was a great idea too.

'Let us know when it's ready and we'll arrange a night to come in,' Georgina said. 'What about Peter? Will he be up for it?'

'Probably,' I said.

'We'll get some wine and nibbles,' Lorraine said.

'For the ghost?' Nige asked.

'For us,' Lorraine said. 'It'll be a fun night.'

Fun night? Sitting in the shop in the middle of the night trying to make contact with a ghost was not my idea of a fun night. I decided to try to change the subject, hoping they would forget all about the ridiculous idea. Before I had a chance to think of a distraction, Nige announced it was time for him to leave to continue his round. Georgina left with him so before Aileen, Nadine or Lorraine could say anything more about the subject, I turned to Nadine.

'I forgot to tell you, Nadine, we've entered you in an abseiling event for Children in Need.'

'A what? An abseil? Oh thanks, like. You could have asked first.'

'We thought you'd be interested,' Lorraine said. 'The Royal Marines are involved, they're doing the training.' Nadine's eyes lit up and she struggled to hide her delight.

'Well, I suppose it's for a good cause. I'll do it. Where is it taking place?'

'Tyne Bridge.'

'You're telling me I've got to jump off the Tyne Bridge?'

'Sort of,' I told her. Actually, I didn't know a great deal about it.

'Is it where they tie a bit of elastic to your ankle and you bounce up and down like a ping pong ball on a string and your head nearly dips into the river?'

'Blimey, I hope not,' I said, thinking of my potential unborn child. 'You're thinking of bungee-jumping. Abseiling is where you let yourself down on a rope. It's very controlled.'

'Ah that's okay then. I'll do that. Bungee jumping's too dangerous. I've heard about people's eyeballs popping and all sorts...what's wrong?' A wave of nausea swept over me at the thought of popping eyeballs.

'Feeling a bit queasy all of a sudden,' I said, sitting down and taking a few gulps of air.

'You pregnant again?' Nadine said jokily and when I hesitated she yelled, 'Oh my Lord, you are aren't you? Oh that's fantastic! You lucky thing!'

'No, I'm not...well I might be, I'm not sure,' I faltered.

Nadine was thrilled. 'Lorraine!' she yelled. 'Did you know? You're going to be an aunty again.' She hugged me excitedly. 'Oh can you imagine having another baby as lovely as Rosie? I wonder if it's a boy or a girl this time.'

Aileen, busy at the kitchen bench, gave me her congratulations as Lorraine hurried through from the office and joined in the hug.

'Really? When? How many weeks are you?' she asked.

'I don't know, I mean I'm not even sure...'

'Yay!' Lorraine cheered. 'That's great news, I'm so happy for you. And for me! Another little nephew or niece.'

'Look, you two. I might not even be pregnant, I don't really know.'

Lorraine stopped in shock. 'You don't really know...?' She pushed past Nadine and rushed into the office.

'Where are you in such a hurry to get to?' Nadine asked.

'I'm phoning the clinic to make an appointment for her. I can't stand the suspense, I have to know.'

'No you're not,' I said, hurrying after her. I squeezed in front of her and snatched up the phone before she could reach it. 'I don't want to go yet, I want to wait a bit longer.'

Lorraine stood in the doorway with her arms folded. 'Get dialling.'

I looked to Nadine for support but she crossed her arms too.

'Get on with it,' she said.

I called them a few rude names then picked up the phone.

CHAPTER FOUR

The next morning we were greeted at the door by Edward Reeves, our local Environmental Health Officer. As Lorraine unlocked the shutter and pushed it up into its casing, he told us he had called by to check we'd replaced a cracked wall tile he'd discovered on his last visit. Lorraine unlocked the door and he pushed his way ahead of her. I knew we had nothing to worry about – we always left the shop scrubbed clean each evening ready for the next morning, and the tile he referred to had been replaced by Peter.

I heard a van pull up beside us and turned to see our bread delivery. I hurried to intervene and took the trays from the driver before he had a chance to place them on the pavement. I struggled to carry them through the door and Lorraine came and helped me put them on the counter. Mr Reeves took a pair of protective gloves from his briefcase and pulled them onto his hands with a snap.

'Proceed with your business as usual,' he told us and I pulled a face behind his back as he mounted the steps to the sink area.

Lorraine set up the till while I arranged the bread on the shelves. As soon as Nadine arrived she took a basket and went to Derek's. It was not really business as usual. Normally we'd make tea and switch on the radio to allow Steve Wright to compete with our chatter and clatter as we joked and worked and welcomed the first customers of the day. But today we worked in silence, aware of the adversary in our midst.

Nadine returned with a full basket.

'Wait till you see these tomatoes I've got. They're as big as...'

'I'll take those thanks,' I said, cutting her off. I had no idea what she was about to say but knowing Nadine there was a high possibility it was something rude. 'He's still up there,' I muttered.

'Doing what?'

'Probably looking for something else to complain about,' Lorraine said. We served a few customers, aware he was still examining the wall tile, periodically glancing at the clock then at each other.

I had given a customer her change and was closing the till when I heard a deep cough behind me. I started, jamming my finger in the till, and turned to see Mr Reeves standing in the kitchen, unsmiling as ever.

'Everything okay?' I asked, shaking my throbbing finger.

'No. I am unable to locate the tile in question.'

'Well it's been replaced,' Lorraine told him. 'You can see there are no cracked tiles there.'

'I can indeed,' Mr Reeves said. 'But my objective is to check the tile has been replaced and I am unable to determine which of the tiles was cracked on my last visit.'

His absurdity fuelled the irritability I was feeling due to the pain in my finger and I snapped at him.

'Well does it matter which one it is as long as it's done?' A nudge from Lorraine came as a reminder not to antagonise the man and I changed my tone. 'I'll show you,' I said, and I climbed the short flight of steps to the sink area. I pointed to a random tile. 'It's this one.'

Mr Reeves thanked me and proceeded to carefully examine the tile, donning a pair of spectacles to peer at it closely while he ran his hand over the surface.

'Perhaps you could take a photograph?' I suggested.

'Good idea, Mrs Kenworthy. I will make sure I am equipped with a suitable camera on my next visit. Perhaps until then you would oblige me with paper and pencil to enable me to produce a diagram charting the tile in question?'

'I'll oblige him with a kick up the arse,' I muttered to Lorraine as I fished about under the till for a notebook. I turned to hand him it and noticed his usually vacant face was flushed and contorted as though struggling to control a tic. He snatched the book from my hand without looking directly at me.

'I need to have another thorough check over the premises, *Mrs Kenworthy*,' he said. My name was spat out like an obscenity.

Lorraine slapped my arm. 'Aw man! He heard you. Now he's gone off to find more pointless repairs for us to do.'

I silently berated myself. Me and my big mouth. I rearranged my features into my customer-greeting smile and turned to serve a woman waiting at the counter. My smile slipped for a second but I pulled it back, professional that I am.

'Caroline! Hello! What can we do for you today?'

Caroline was one of my least favourite customers. She had a snide way of wrapping up insults in pseudo-compliments. *'What an attractive skirt you're wearing. Such a lovely cut for the larger bottom.' 'That cardigan is such a beautiful shade of lemon. Delightful for spring. Such a shame you haven't the skin tone to carry it off.'*

Sometimes she didn't bother with the wrappings. *'Dear, dear. How tired you look today. Positively haggard.'*

'Good morning, Christine. I'm so distressed to have to come with a complaint.'

Bet you are, I thought.

I tilted my head into a sympathetic listening position, keeping my smile in place.

'I happened to pass by the shop yesterday morning and I noticed several trays of bread on the pavement outside. Yes, on the pavement. I could not believe my eyes. I thought, I know the girls are very casual in their approach to business, but surely they would not stoop to storing food on the roadside?' She shuddered and grimaced. 'I'm sure you must have attended food-hygiene training at some point, am I correct?'

'You are indeed correct, we have attended food-hygiene training. At several points actually.' I was aware of Mr Reeves moving about in the office, and I sent a silent plea for him to stay there until I'd got rid of her. 'The bread was accidentally left outside and was subsequently disposed of. So you see, there's no problem at all.'

'Oh I see. I did consider telephoning Environmental Health but I thought it was only fair to give you a chance to defend your actions first.'

'Excuse me, did I hear someone mention Environmental Health?' Shit. Edward Reeves slunk out of the office like a rat sniffing for a nearby dustbin. He extended his palm towards Caroline. 'Edward Reeves, Environmental Officer. Always happy to listen to the concerns of the public.'

Caroline beamed. She couldn't believe her luck.

'Thank you Mr Reeves! I came in to speak to the girls about a little problem but I think we may have got to the bottom of it.' I hate the way she called us 'the girls' like we were children playing at shops.

'Yes, all sorted.' I nodded at Caroline and then at the door, my body language subconsciously telling her to leave.

'And the problem you encountered was?' Mr Reeves asked.

'As I say, all sorted, just a misunderstanding...' I babbled. I looked to the kitchen where Lorraine quietly tidied kitchen utensils. I beckoned her with my eyes but she raised her eyebrows and shook her head. I could read her so well. I knew she was telling me I'd got myself into this one and I could get myself out. Nadine looked at me and shrugged to indicate she was unable to help. Or more likely, unwilling to help.

Caroline clasped her hands in front of her chest, her eyes bright with exhilaration. She looked like she was about to wee herself with excitement.

'Now you mustn't be too hard on the girls, Mr Reeves, they do try their best. It was just a little matter of food being stored inappropriately but I have spoken to Christine and she assures me it will not happen again.'

'No, no, that's not really how it was...' I started. I felt really hot, annoyed at Caroline's drama-making and also worried Mr Reeves might take her comments seriously.

'Incorrect food storage is a matter of great concern,' Mr Reeves interjected. 'In what way was the said food being incorrectly stored?'

I was sweating now. 'The said food, um...that is, the said bread, was left on a pavement,' I flapped. 'But not by us. By a third party.' I don't know why I said 'a third party.' I was beginning to sound as stuffy as he did.

'A pavement?' he repeated, with as much gusto as Lady Bracknell bellowing '*a handbag?*'

'I can explain,' I offered, and both Mr Reeves and Caroline turned their smug faces to me while I gabbled my justification. After having enjoyed witnessing my squirming, Caroline spoke.

'Mr Reeves, I feel a little leniency is needed. I cannot lie, the girls are often slipshod in their methods, however it is part of their charm. I believe rough diamond is the term used.' She lowered her voice. 'They grew up in *Walker.*' Mr Reeves nodded as though this explained everything. Caroline continued. 'This is a strong community area and I feel it is most important to support a small business such as this, especially when it is so obviously struggling.'

Mr Reeves turned to face me.

'On the reassurance this will not happen again, I am willing to overlook this lapse. However, I have found some areas of the shop that are not up to standard and must insist they are attended to as soon as possible.' He bade Caroline good day and requested I follow him into the office where he proceeded to tell me we'd have to replace the flooring and also board the ceiling.

Caroline was still hanging about like a bad smell when we came out of the office. As soon as Mr Reeves left she hurried over, presumably to give me the benefit of her wisdom so I turned on my heel and went to sit in the office until she'd gone, leaving Lorraine to listen to her put-downs, thinly disguised as advice.

I wasn't too happy with Lorraine and Nadine either, for leaving me to deal with it all, and although they apologised and fussed about, making me a cup of tea and offering me first choice of the day's cakes, my mood was set for the day.

Later, when the bakery rang to take our bread order for the following day, the poor girl on the other end of the phone got the vent of my spleen as I blasted her about the incompetency of the delivery man, stating that if their service did not improve I'd order from a rival company.

She apologised profusely and offered to make a deduction on our invoice.

'Apparently they have a new delivery lad,' I told Lorraine. 'She's going to have a word with him when he gets back to the bakery. Shouldn't happen again.'

'I hope not.'

'He's related to the owners,' Nadine told us. 'Jonathan told me.' Nadine had dated Jonathan, the previous delivery man for a while.

'Jonathan was furious. He got moved to a different delivery area because the boss's son wanted to have a go at delivering the bread. Jonathan said he's useless. Apparently he's messed up every role they've given him in the business. They don't know what to do with him so they've put him on the vans.'

'I thought I hadn't seen Jonathan for a while,' I said.

'No, he does the west end area now, over Fenham way. Just as well really. It was getting a bit awkward him coming in here, all puppy-dog eyes with his tail between his legs after I'd dumped him.'

I could clearly recall a day when for hours she'd alternated between indignant anger and heart-breaking sobbing, telling us she loved him and wanted him back and hated him and never wanted to see him again. I was under the distinct impression it was she who had been dumped but I nodded and agreed it had become a rather awkward situation and things had indeed worked out for the best.

CHAPTER FIVE

At Druridge Bay, the shore stretched ahead of us, unspoilt and seemingly endless. The sea was gentle, continually sweeping the sand with soothing ripples. We were wrapped in layers against the biting cold, although both sky and water were a soft faded blue, like washed out denim, the horizon almost indistinguishable.

'I love it here,' I told Peter as we walked on the sand, arms wrapped around each other. Rosie toddled ahead, splashing into a pool of seawater, delighting in her new red wellies.

'Me too. I don't think I'd like to live away from the sea.'

We were lucky to live within walking distance of the north east coast. A twenty minute walk from our home would take us to the seafront, where the locally famous Rendezvous Café served ice-cream sundaes and coffee as it had since the 1950s. A short walk south was the traditional seaside town of Whitley Bay, popular by day with families for its amusements, ice-cream and fish and chips, and at night by young revellers who came from far and wide to visit the many pubs and night clubs.

A couple of miles further along lay the old fishing village of Cullercoats, with its curve of Edwardian houses lining the crescent bay. Beyond that was Tynemouth, busy with coffee houses, wine bars and art shops.

If we wished to go further afield, as we had today, we would drive north, further into Northumberland, past the harbour village of Seaton Sluice, up to Cresswell, and on to our favourite, Druridge Bay.

The sky blushed pink as the sun began to set, and we turned back, enjoying the last of the light. Rosie came to a sudden halt as her attention was caught by a shell glinting in the sunlight. As she stumbled, falling over her feet, Peter dived to catch her, swooping her into the air as he saved her from landing bottom-first in a pool of sea water. Her tinkling laugh as he swung her around was the sweetest sound and I felt a surge of joy as I watched the two people I loved most in the world.

Peter swung Rosie up onto his shoulders where she hugged his head, her chubby fingers spread across his face as she giggled hysterically. I linked his arm as we walked.

'How do you fancy a holiday next year?' I asked him. 'A proper family holiday?'

'Sounds good. Just the three of us you mean?'

'Four of us.'

'Four? Who else do...oh...'

And suddenly it was I who was lifted from my feet and swung around as Rosie squealed with delight.

We dropped Rosie at my mam's and went out to dinner to celebrate.

'How long have you known?' Peter asked, as our drinks – lager for him, apple juice for me – were brought to the table.

'Since this morning.'

I explained how I'd inadvertently let it slip to Lorraine and Nadine and been pressured into booking an appointment

Peter grinned and took a drink. He looked as though he'd won the lottery.

'I wanted to tell you first so I've been avoiding Lorraine's phone calls. I knew I wouldn't be able to fob her off.'

The waiter arrived with two plates of wild mushroom and asparagus risotto.

'That looks delicious,' Peter said as he dived straight in. 'Aren't you hungry?'

'Not really.'

During my pregnancy with Rosie I'd been ravenous and had snacked constantly. Even the nausea I'd woken up with had not stopped my hunger and I'd happily eaten my way through each day. But this time food held no attraction. Even my favourite meals were tasteless and unappealing. I'd been eating because I knew I should, not because I wanted to.

I picked at my plate. Pushing asparagus and mushrooms to one side, I managed a couple of forkfuls of rice before nudging the plate towards Peter. I knew he'd be more than happy to finish mine off too, although he was concerned at how little I'd eaten. I nibbled on a slice of garlic bread to appease him.

'It feels so different to last time,' I said.

'In what way?'

'I have no appetite at all. I don't feel queasy or anything, I just don't fancy eating. And I feel...I don't know. Different.'

'Perhaps it's a boy this time,' Peter said and I smiled, imagining a baby boy with Peter's dark eyes.

'Perhaps. Although somehow I've always imagined us with two girls.'

'Would you be happy with another girl? I'd love another daughter.'

'Of course I would! What a daft question. Hey, what if it's one of each? Twins?'

'I was always told it skips a generation, or is that an old wives' tale?' Peter was a twin and before I'd realised how much hard work having one baby was, I'd sometimes hoped for twins.

'Don't know,' I said. 'Anyway, if it's a boy, I'm going to call him Maximillian.'

'Maximillian? Bit of a mouthful, where did you get that from?'

'From 'Rebecca'. I'll call him Maxim for short, like Maxim de Winter.'

Peter laughed. 'I'll call him Max.'

Our plates were removed and the desert menu discreetly placed in front of us. I could quite easily have done without, but I knew Peter's sweet tooth would be craving for satisfaction and he wouldn't order if I didn't, so I chose a lemon sorbet and he decided on apple crumble with custard.

'What about a girl's name?' he asked. 'Anything in mind?'

'I don't know. I can't find anything I like. Perhaps that's another sign it's a boy. Last time I could only think of girls' names.'

Peter smiled and squeezed my hand. 'So, Max it is then.'

The following morning, Lorraine greeted me with at the shop door with a hug.

'Congratulations!' she cried. 'Best news ever! I rang Mam last night and she tried so hard not to tell me, she thought you'd want to tell me yourself but I could tell from her voice.'

'Sorry sis. I wanted to tell Peter first.'

'Don't be daft. Of course Peter should hear the news first. How was he?'

'Like a pig in poop,' I said and we laughed. 'He didn't even know I had an appointment so it was quite a surprise.'

Nadine was thrilled at the news too, and the morning's conversation encompassed all things maternal.

Nige and Georgina congratulated me too, Nige uncomfortably (he hated hearing about what he called 'women's matters') and Georgina half-heartedly (she believed anyone choosing to experience childbirth more than once was insane) and so the conversation moved on. We were discussing whether it would be appropriate for Nadine to send her dentist a Valentine card when a commotion outside caught our attention.

'What's all that shouting about?' Lorraine asked.

'Parking again, probably,' I said as we moved to the door.

Our shop was on a corner and originally had two huge windows, one overlooking the main road and the other looking onto the side street which led to the lane behind the shops. The side window had been smashed a couple of years previously by a drunk on his way home one night, and was now bricked up. This suited us as we now had an extra wall of shelving inside and space for a huge advertising board outside. However, it meant our view was now restricted which was a great disadvantage for such a nosy lot.

Georgina reached the door first and stepped out to peer around the corner. 'It's the reps again,' she said, as loud voices and the revving of an engine were heard. 'They've blocked someone in and he's obviously not happy about it.'

We watched, brazen in our curiosity, as the red-faced man complained loudly to the reps strutting coolly out of the building to shuffle cars about like a giant jigsaw puzzle.

The lack of carparks was a big problem for the retailers on the bank. There were several bays on some of the side-streets, but the main road was narrow and double-yellow-lined. Sometimes a space could be found in the back lane, but as this was the preferred access for delivery vans, parked cars were often hemmed in by trucks. The often-repeated joke was that we had lots of passing trade. It literally passed by us.

Many of our customers came by car, as did the sales reps working for the vacuum cleaner business across the side street. Their flock of sales reps constantly arrived and departed, most of them in large flashy cars that they abandoned wherever they cared to, resulting in a constant parking battle, especially at lunch times when the shop was at its busiest. Customers often returned to their cars to find them barricaded, sometimes even pedestrians were obstructed from their route due to wall-to-wall vehicles parked across both the street and pavements. It was not unusual for an argument to break out.

Our extractor fan, set into the wall that bordered the side street, acted as a sound funnel, channelling outside sounds into the kitchen. Often we would find ourselves standing at the hob cooking a batch of veggie burgers to a background of effing and jeffing from an ongoing argument.

Recently the police had been called to deal with a particular fracas involving a man who'd been so fed up with being blocked in by the reps cars, he'd repeatedly driven into the back of the BMW parked in front, then reversed into the Audi behind, until the rhythmic banging of crushing steel aroused attention. Staff and customers from nearby offices and shops – including ours – had rushed out to join the crowd of spectators surrounding the three cars, but the disgruntled driver had continued his protest, paying no heed to the baying crowd, until removed from his vehicle by a police officer.

Today's argument came to a close as cars edged their way out of the gridlock, revving angrily as they made their escape down the back lane. As the spectators dispersed, I saw Tomas amongst them. He waved and came over, following us back into the shop.

'I am watching the brouhaha,' he told us.

'The what?' Nadine asked.

'Is this not correct word? Brouhaha?'

'It is,' I told him. 'But we usually call it a big barnie round here.'

'Big barnie,' Tomas repeated.

'Or a right rumpus,' Lorraine said.

'Right rumpus.'

'I'd say it was a canny kerfuffle,' Nadine put in.

'Canny kel...fluff...uffle'

We laughed as Tomas struggled with the word.

'Is difficult, the speaking of the English. I am learning not good.'

'You're doing very well Tomas,' Lorraine told him. 'We're pulling your leg.'

Tomas looked puzzled. 'You pulling my leg? Why you mean you pulling my leg?' This made us laugh all the more.

'It means we are teasing you. Having a joke,' Lorraine explained.

'Ah, I am seeing. You are having joke.' Tomas laughed good-naturedly.

Tomas told us he'd come for sandwiches for himself and Hanna, and after we'd explained we did not sell meat of any description (a concept he found strange and asked us to repeat several times, until he was satisfied he'd understood correctly) he asked us to choose something for him.

'What about our special of the day, nut roast with pease pudding?' I asked. 'Would you like to try some to see if you like it?' He took a piece of nut roast and after looking at it suspiciously, took a cautious bite.

'Yes. That is very nice.' He seemed surprised he liked it. 'And this is the roasted nuts?'

I explained that it was made with chopped cashews and vegetables with herbs and spices added, then roasted in the oven. I told him we sometimes served it with cranberry sauce or chutney, but today were offering it with pease pudding. I'm not sure if he

38

understood my explanation. He looked at the dish of freshly made pease pudding steaming on the kitchen bench and was not impressed.

'What is making pudding of the peas?'

'Pease pudding. It's a northern thing,' Lorraine told him. 'It's made from yellow split peas with a bit of vegetable stock and seasoning. It's usually eaten with ham but we serve it with our home-made nut roast.'

'Ah. I am not seeing this roasted nuts and pudding of peas in Poland. I will try,' he said bravely, as if he were volunteering for some dangerous feat.

'You'd better taste the pease pudding first Tomas,' I said. 'Not everyone likes it.'

In my experience, most non-northerners thought it was the most disgusting stuff ever. I gave him some on a teaspoon and after putting it in his mouth and swallowing, he closed his eyes and screwed up his face. He held his throat and coughed, falling to the floor as Nadine, Lorraine and I rushed forwards.

'Oh my God, he's choking,' Lorraine cried.

'Quick! Get him some water,' Nadine said, but as we panicked, Tomas let out a high pitched laugh.

'Ha ha ha...' He stood up, looking proud of himself. 'I too am having joke. I joking your leg.'

CHAPTER SIX

I was in the queue at Derek's when I felt a gentle tap on my shoulder.

'Excuse me, are you the lady from the health food shop?' I turned to see a man of around thirty, smartly dressed with large rimless glasses and a rather superior expression. He was extremely pale-skinned, to the point of looking unhealthy.

'I am, yes.'

The man looked me up and down. 'Now I wonder how I knew you worked in a health food shop, haha.'

I gave a smile. I wondered too.

'James McAllister.' He held out his hand so I took it. It was small and soft and slightly damp, like a rubber glove filled with jelly and I was pleased when I could drop it. 'We're new neighbours, so to speak. I've taken on the property above your shop.'

He explained that his business involved building as well as servicing computers. I didn't understand a lot of what he was saying. He kept mentioning PCs and I thought he meant police constables which made what he was telling me nonsensical. He also used the word 'tad' a lot. I was glad the building was to be used again and I told him so.

'It's great to have a new business on the bank,' I said. 'It's been standing empty for too long.'

'Yes. It's a tad dilapidated. Terrible state. As you can imagine there's a lot of refurbishment work needed so I'm afraid there may be a tad of noise for a couple of weeks.'

A tad of noise? That was an inadequate description for the type of noise builders usually made.

'No problem,' I said. 'It's great the building is being smartened up.'

'Ah yes. Glad you've mentioned that. I wondered if there was any chance of you doing the same.' He looked me up and down again. I was wearing faded jeans and my favourite Greenpeace t-shirt I'd bought when I was in sixth form and I was about to tell him he was being rude, a *tad* rude actually, when I realised he meant our shop's façade and not mine.

'The paintwork's looking a tad shabby, if you don't mind me saying. See if you can get it up to scratch before I open. Much appreciated.'

When he'd left and Derek was putting my order together, I tried to grill him about the new computer business. Derek was always first with any local gossip so I was sure he'd know all about it. However, this morning he was uninterested and distracted.

'You okay?' I asked him.

'Yeah. Just tired. Had a bit of a late night.' I guessed he was probably hung-over. He said he hadn't eaten breakfast and asked if I'd make him a toastie.

'I'll pay you now and I'll come up for it in a few minutes.'

I hurried back to the shop to tell the others about my conversation with James McAllister.

'Cheeky bugger,' Nadine said. 'Who does he think he is, coming along here, telling us to smarten up our business?' She was fiercely protective of the shop.

'He's got a point though,' I said. The shop front could do with a bit of a facelift.' The constant passing traffic threw up clouds of dust, and trails of dried dirt flecked the paintwork where rainwater had trickled down. In other places the paint, bleached by the sun, had blistered and peeled. 'Maybe we should have it painted.'

'Yeah, but because we think so, not because *he* thinks so,' Lorraine said.

'What's he like? Is he attractive?' Nadine asked.

'Not unless you like the pale, sickly type.'

'Ugh.'

'So he has a computer business?' Lorraine said. 'Seems to be the up and coming thing at the moment. They're opening everywhere.'

Lots of people were buying home computers but it wasn't something that interested me then.

I remembered in the eighties, my dad sending off for a ZX Spectrum advertised in the Sunday paper and waiting impatiently for it to arrive. I remember his excitement as he unpacked it and explained to us how it worked. My mam was first to lose concentration and went off to put the kettle on, but Lorraine and I feigned interest as he took out a small black plastic keyboard and connected it first to our television, and then to a cassette player. We listened to a stream of squeaks, hisses and buzzes as it loaded information which enabled us to play Space Invaders. I wasn't impressed to be honest, but then computer games have never grabbed me. I preferred our game of Pong we had in the seventies. Later, Peter bought a BBC computer that he used for game playing with friends. They would hold tournament nights, and I would join in a game of Defender or Chucky Egg, but quickly became bored and would slope off to read a book with a glass of wine and a bowl of crisps.

Peter disposed of his computer once the novelty wore off, but my Dad continue to upgrade and had recently given us his old Amstrad. It sat in the office, like some alien thing, ignored and untouched by all except Peter. He had invested in Payroll software that he used to print off staff wage slips, proclaiming it saved hours of time, although he still recorded the shop accounts by hand.

The media constantly warned us that computers were the future and that we should be prepared, but for most people, before the time of social media and mainstream access to the internet, they were simply expensive game-playing machines.

'Do you think he'd give us discount?' Nadine said. 'I fancy getting a home computer.'

'He may do,' I said. 'I'm glad the old gym has gone at last. It's been an eyesore for ages. The only downside is that it will make our shop look tatty in comparison.'

'We can't afford to paint the shopfront,' Lorraine said. 'It'll cost a fortune.'

'Not if we do it ourselves.'

'By 'ourselves' I take it you mean Peter?'

'Yeah.'

I had unyielding faith in Peter's ability to tackle any task I presented him with. He was my definitive Mr Fix-It.

I took Derek's toastie from the toaster as he entered the shop.

'Good timing,' I said as I slid it into a paper bag.

'Any chance of you making me a cuppa too?' he asked. 'I'm on my own this morning, wor lass is at home.'

'Did you two have a night out last night? Is she having a lie-in?' I asked as I put a teabag into a take-away cup.

'Nah. The cat died and she's been crying all night.'

'Oh, I'm sorry to hear that.'

'I'm not bothered, it was just a cat. It's wor lass I'm concerned about, she's right upset.'

'Right.' In my mind no cat was 'just a cat'. We'd adopted many rescue cats over the years and whenever we lost one it broke my heart.

'It was me that found her, like, when she was a kitten,' Derek said. 'I was down the allotments and she was behind the compost heap. Tiny and half-starved she was. Folk reckoned she was feral and she'd been left behind when the mother took the others away.'

'Ah, the poor little thing,' Lorraine said.

'I took her home for wor lass and we fed her up. I mean, I wasn't bothered like, but I knew she would like having a kitten.'

I poured hot water into the cardboard cup then Derek spoke again.

'She used to lie on the rug and I would tickle her belly with me toe.' He gazed into the distance and smiled. 'Aye, she used to like that. And she always came straight to me whenever she came in, jumped on me knee for a bit of a cuddle.'

There was a combined 'Aw!' from Nadine, Lorraine and me and Derek said, 'I'm not bothered like, it was just a cat.'

I gave him his cup of take-way tea but he didn't leave.

'Wor lass is devastated. Not me, like. At the end of the day, it's just a cat.' He gave a big sigh and picked up his cup. 'Aye the hoose won't be the same without her. She was a canny little thing like. Had a funny little miaow and when she wanted feeding she would pat yer leg with her little paw.' He turned to leave. 'But I'm not bothered like.'

'That's so sad,' Nadine said when Derek had gone. 'It's heart-breaking losing a pet.'

'He's not bothered like,' Lorraine said.

The next morning I arrived at the shop to find two posters lying face down on the shop floor. Lorraine had been last to leave and I wondered if she'd taken them out of the window and forgotten about them. She arrived a few minutes after me, while I was filling the till with coins.

'Why are these on the floor?' she asked. 'Are they for the bin or to go back in the window?'

'I was going to ask you. They were there when I came in.'

'Nothing to do with me,' Lorraine said.

'Strange.'

Nadine had an explanation.

'It's the spirit,' she said. 'It's moving things to get attention.'

'Don't be daft,' Lorraine told her. 'They've fallen off the window during the night, that's all.'

'Both of them together? And lain themselves down on the floor side by side?'

'I'm sure there's a logical reason for it,' I said.

'Oh look!' Nadine cried. She pointed to the kitchen shelf. 'It's another cry for help from the spirit.' Apparently, the cutlery had moved itself about in its box.

'I never leave knives crossed, it's bad luck,' she told me. 'And look at them now!'

'Don't be ridiculous,' Lorraine said. 'Someone else must have touched them after you put them away.'

'Did either of you touch them late yesterday afternoon?'

'I don't think so,' I said. 'I can't really remember.'

'You see! They've moved over night. Mark my words, there'll be more of this. It will keep happening until we acknowledge the presence of the spirit.'

I was beginning to feel a bit uneasy now. I didn't really believe what Nadine was saying, but it didn't take much for me to be spooked.

'I think we need to find out its name,' Nadine said.

'And how are we going to do that?' Lorraine asked. I could tell that although Nadine was deadly serious, Lorraine was taking it as a joke.

'We need to have a séance,' Nadine told her. 'But in the meantime we should ask for a sign.'

'What kind of sign?' I didn't want any signs. Not if it involved ghostly deeds. And I certainly didn't want to have anything to do with a séance.

'Like crossed knives?' Lorraine said, laughing. 'Or posters on the floor? Are they signs? Because if they are, I've no idea what name it's trying to get across.'

'They were to get our attention,' Nadine said. 'Now it's got it, we can ask it to be more specific and give us a name.' She looked up and held out her arms. 'Come to us spirit and give us a sign of who you are.'

A shiver passed over me and I shook it off, annoyed at myself for allowing such silliness to affect me. Lorraine grinned in amusement. She was finding it all very entertaining.

'Ah, don't be daft,' I said, and I turned to switch on the radio, aiming to bring a little normality back to the shop.

'...and that was Elvis with 'Way Down'...' Steve Wright told us and Nadine screeched.

'Elvis! Its name is Elvis! That's our sign!'

'Elvis?' Lorraine echoed. 'As in Presley? You think Elvis Presley's spirit is in the shop putting posters on the floor and mixing up the cutlery box?'

'You make it sound absurd when you say it like that,' Nadine laughed sheepishly.

'It *is* absurd,' I told her.

'It's absolutely ridiculous,' Lorraine said, then seeing Georgina and Nige coming in, called out 'Hey you two, come and listen to this.'

I went to make the morning's hot drinks as Nadine and Lorraine explained what had happened.

Georgina thought it was hysterical. 'I've heard it all now! Ha ha ha! Elvis haunting a wholefood shop!' She turned to face the shop floor. 'It's a bit late now darlin',' she called. 'You should have held off the burgers when you had the chance.'

Nige thought it was hysterical too. 'Eeh, that's brilliant. People will come from all over to buy nuts Elvis has haunted! You'll have to phone Look North and get them to come round. You'll be famous.'

'Don't be so disrespectful,' Nadine told them. 'It might not be Elvis Presley any way, it could be a different Elvis.'

'What like Elvis Smith?' Georgina sniggered. 'Elvis Brown? Elvis Jones?'

We tried out a few different surnames, finding each funnier than the last.

Nadine took it in good fun. 'It's a name the spirit wants to be known by, it doesn't have to mean it's Elvis Presley,' she told us.

'Our very own Elvis here in at Nutmeg,' Lorraine said. 'Who'd have thought it?'

'We definitely need to do the séance now,' Georgina said. 'We can ask him questions, find out if it's really Elvis or just a great pretender.'

Nige giggled hysterically. 'We need to do it soon. It's now or never.'

Nadine reached for a notebook and pencil. 'Let's write a list of questions.'

'I've got one,' Nige said.

Nadine looked up in anticipation, pencil at the ready.

'Are you lonesome tonight?' he crooned.

'You're not taking this seriously. A séance is not a joking matter.'

'I am taking it seriously,' Nige said. 'In fact I'm all shook up.'

CHAPTER SEVEN

Peter was happy to take on the job of painting the shop exterior and decided to start the following day to take advantage of the mild weather predicted. I wasn't happy to spend my Sunday off working, but knew we had to get the work done.

Rick from the tool hire shop loaned us some scaffolding free of charge, which he delivered and helped Peter to erect on the Saturday afternoon. We went to buy paint on the way home, intending to make an early start in the morning. Lorraine and I had chosen a rich cream but Peter wasn't keen.

'I would have gone for something darker,' he said.

'Cream will brighten up the shop and look fresh and clean,' I said.

'It will, but it will also show up every speck of dirt,' Peter warned.

'That's why I like light colours,' I said. 'Who know what horrors lurk on a black towel or dark sheets? If you have light colours you know that things are clean.' (I did regret this logic later when we needed to regularly scrub down the paintwork to remove dusty rain deposits and smears of dirt.)

We woke late and by the time we'd dropped Rosie at my mam's it was close to lunchtime when we arrived at the shop.

Peter got straight to work while I pottered about inside, changing a few displays and cleaning out the rubbish that seemed to accumulate beneath the counter. It didn't take long for me to become bored. Desperate for something to do, I unpinned the posters and cards from our noticeboard and rearranged them, matching up the coloured heads of the pins.

Through the window, I saw Peter climb the scaffold, and watched flakes of paint and dirt flutter to the pavement as he scrubbed the stone and woodwork with a stiff brush.

As he descended and opened the paint tin ready to start, I went out and asked if he had a spare brush so that I could help.

'I'd rather you didn't,' he said. Oh here we go again, I thought.

'I'm just pregnant, not injured,' I told him. 'I could climb up there easily.'

'No.'

'Well, I'll do the low bits then.'

'No. Go and make a cup of tea.' I wasn't used to Peter telling me what to do. I tried to be outraged about it, but actually felt pleased that his intent was to look after both me and our unborn child. So I made a bit of a fuss in protest then went off to put the kettle on and find something for our lunch.

I made tea and heated vegetable pies which I wrapped in kitchen paper and carried out.

Peter ate as he worked. I carefully picked up a brush and began to paint the bricks beneath the window. He realised what I was doing and told me 'Just the low bits, no climbing.' I planned on ignoring him but I soon discovered it wasn't a very satisfying task. The paint did not cover well and left a streaky finish. It was obvious another coat would be needed. I gave up fairly quickly and perched myself on a lower rung of the scaffold where I ate my vegetable pie and chatted to Peter.

'Max will be nearly three months by Christmas and Rosie almost three,' I said. 'Won't that be lovely? Two little Christmas stockings on the mantelpiece.'

I was so excited to have another baby. I loved Rosie desperately and a second child would complete our family and bring even more joy and love to us. Rosie's Moses basket was in the loft. Maybe I would make new covers in lemon or perhaps mint green.

Peter offered the occasional word as he listened to my prattling. He worked steadily and methodically. It was a time-consuming task, the building was old and tall and there was a lot to paint. Originally a department store, it had been divided into separate units. The exterior had been grand, with elaborate columns edging the large plate glass windows, the tops of which were sumptuously decorated with carved scrolls, each one topped with a sphere. These Peter painstakingly coated in paint, stretching from the scaffold as he clung with one hand.

I'd never seen the old store in its heyday but imagined it to be along the lines of the Grace Brothers' store and in my mind's eye could see Mr Humphreys gadding about offering to take inside leg measurements while Mrs Slocombe worried about her pussy.

The building was now shared by three businesses. Our shop covered most of the ground floor. A wall built at the back of our kitchen had created a self-contained retail area at the rear, currently used as a shoe repair and key-cutting business. The old gym took up the first and second floor.

On our shop floor, two large pillars stood as evidence of the long gone department store, a hint of an era when shopping was a more personal and luxurious experience. Once, these decorative pillars had flanked the large staircase that rose centrally from the back of the store, leading customers up to higher floors. Now the stairs were rudely cut off with a hardboard wall, leaving a slither of the steps leading to our washroom, the rest walled off in a storage area and stacked with boxes and sacks.

The afternoon light was fading fast and I pulled my coat around me. Peter finished the last area at the very top of the fascia and climbed down to examine his work.

The paintwork was mottled, the old surface showing through, giving the new cream a grey tinge.

'It looks a bit patchy,' I said.

'It will,' Peter said. 'The first coat never covers straight away. It will be fine when I get the next coat on.' I hoped he was right. It looked awful.

The last weak rays of the sun disappeared as Peter climbed the scaffolding to start painting again. He worked in the orange glow of the streetlamps but I knew he would not stop until the job was finished. I hated the dark, long evenings. I always looked forward to the clocks changing and the lengthening of the days as we moved towards summer but we still had a couple of weeks to go. I went inside and switched on the lights and heater. I decided I might as well make tomorrow's soup, and had a rummage through the vegetable rack.

At six I took Peter a hot drink and was glad to see he'd almost finished. As we stood with our mugs of tea, Mr Khatri arrived to open up the Indian take-away. Dressed in his long robes and hat, he bowed his head in his usual greeting. It was a while since we'd seen him. He opened for business after we'd closed so we rarely met. I told him I'd met James McAllister and about his plans.

'That is good,' he said. 'It will be a big improvement for the area. More businesses are good for us all.' He promised to send us a snack once he started cooking, and a little while later the smell of frying onions and warm spices began to drift into the street.

'That smells great,' Peter said and my stomach rumbled in agreement.

True to his word, Mr Khatri appeared with a tray laden with onion bhajis, vegetable samosas, vegetable tikka, spiced paneer, nan breads, rice and poppadums.

We thanked him, touched by his kindness, and taking the tray inside, put it on the counter and fell upon it like a couple of vultures.

The next morning, I walked around the corner to be greeted by our newly painted shopfront gleaming in the morning sun and I have to say I was impressed. It looked fresh and new and somehow made the business look more upmarket. I said as much to Lorraine.

'What you saying, like? That we aren't upmarket?'

'Of course we are. We were just starting to look a little jaded.'

'Speak for yourself.'

Lorraine was pleased when I told her I'd made up the fillings and also cooked a pan of soup the previous evening.

'Great,' she said. 'Just the salad to prep.'

Nadine wasn't so pleased. She fretted that there wasn't much for her to do.

'Have an easy morning,' I told her. But she decided it would be a good chance for her to give the coffee grinder a good clean, and after that, the insides of the windows.

I'd hoped the talk of Elvis the ghost would be forgotten, but no such luck. As soon as Nige and Georgina arrived, it was the first thing to be discussed. They bantered on excitedly, making plans and joking around. I didn't join in with the conversation, instead I took the used mugs to the kitchen to wash up. I really didn't want to have a séance. Although I didn't believe we had a spirit in the shop, I'm an imaginative person and I knew just the atmosphere of a séance would be enough to scare me senseless.

Also, I wasn't feeling at my best. Although I'd had no morning sickness yet, I felt constantly tired yet never hungry. Perhaps I'd use my pregnancy as an excuse not to attend the séance. Yes, that's what I'll do, I thought. I'd tell them it wouldn't be a good idea for me to be there, given my pregnant condition. Surely none of them would object. I felt a bit lighter knowing I'd be able to avoid it.

As we finished the prep early, I thought I'd use the time to give the office an over-due clear-out. There was a pile of old supplier catalogues under the desk that could be disposed of, and Aileen had collections of boxes and packaging stacked about that I'd like to get rid of. I was glad of my decision as I heard Val enter the shop complaining loudly about a blister on her foot that she claimed had the appearance of a sixth toe.

Val was possibly our most irritating customer ever. She stockpiled health ailments like other people collect family photographs, storing them in a mental folder, ready to be retrieved and shared at any time. She visited a couple of times a week to tell us of her latest acquirement - a torn ligament, a skin infection, a mysterious ache in some part of her body -and would ask for advice that she immediately disputed. We tried to be accommodating but sometimes bluntness was the only way to rid the shop of both her and her whining complaints.

I heard her ask for a seat so that she could remove her sock and show the offending deformity to anyone who'd like to view it. I smiled to myself smugly, knowing that Lorraine and Nadine would have to inspect the blister and offer sympathy and also suggest treatments that Val would dismiss.

By lunchtime, I'd cleared out loads of rubbish, most of which Aileen transferred to her car to take home, exclaiming joyfully at all her re-found treasure she'd stashed away and forgotten about.

Later that afternoon, when the lunchtime rush subsided, I went into the kitchen to do some cooking. I took some tofu from our display fridge and gathered ingredients together.

Lorraine grimaced when she saw my ingredients. 'Ugh, tofu. What are you going to do with that?'

'I'm not sure yet. I'm going to experiment with a few different flavours and see how it turns out.'

Although I'd eaten it in restaurants, I'd never cooked tofu myself and wanted to invent a suitable recipe to serve in the shop. I knew on its own, tofu could taste bland, but took on the flavours of other ingredients, so I made up various marinades to flavour tofu slices and then seared them on a hot griddle pan. I was using a spatula to turn slices of lime infused tofu with garlic and chilli when Tomas came in. Hanna stood silent but smiling, by his side. I smiled and called hello and continued cooking as Lorraine went to serve them.

'We come buy lunch foods,' he said. 'Nice foods in the breads for lunch.'

'Sandwiches,' Lorraine said. 'What fillings would you like?'

'I like roasted nuts and the pudding of peas and Hanna too.'

'Two nut roast with pease pudding.'

She took bread rolls from the shelf and joined me at the kitchen bench. Tomas chatted to us as Lorraine prepared his order. Customers would often talk to us while we worked in the kitchen, I think it pleased them to watch us assembling their sandwiches, knowing they were freshly made.

'I liking shop so much,' he said. Hanna nodded in agreement, then spoke to Tomas in Polish. 'Hanna is liking the foods very much, even no meats.'

'Ah that's good,' I said. I was pleased he'd enjoyed what he'd bought from us and hadn't been put off by the fact it was vegetarian.

'Would you like to taste this? It's tofu with garlic, lime and chilli.' I took a couple of forks and speared some pieces for them to try.

'Be careful, it's straight from the pan,' I said, and they took the forks from me and tasted my offerings. I gave one to Lorraine too.

'Is liking, yes,' Tomas said, and Hanna smiled and nodded. Lorraine liked it too.

'Really good,' she said, and Tomas agreed enthusiastically.

'I tell all peoples this is the best shop. I say, this shop sell good foods make from roasted nuts and no meats, and make the toe food with garlic, very nice.'

'Well that'll have them coming in in droves,' Lorraine said. 'It's called tofu, Tomas, not toe food.'

'Ah, is toe-foo. I remember.'

CHAPTER EIGHT

As James McAllister had warned, there was quite a bit of noise from upstairs over the next couple of weeks – more than could be described as a tad. Prolonged bouts of drilling and hammering pierced the day; we sighed with relief at each cessation only to groan as after a short interval the noise resumed. A skip was delivered, brought on a huge wagon that blocked the side street until the great metal container was lifted by a hydraulic arm and lowered to the ground. It stood to the left of the old gym door adjacent to the side wall of the shop. Not only was it right outside our business, but it also took up coveted car parking space. This, along with the billowing clouds of dust that hung in the air and coated our windows and ledges, proved to be very annoying, but we understood that with building work comes noise and dirt.

The day the building work commenced, we opened to find the kitchen surfaces dusted with grey powder, having found its way in through the extractor fan.

'It's supposed to blow stuff out not suck it in,' Lorraine grumbled as we set about cleaning the kitchen. We could have done without the extra work this morning. There were just the two of us, Nadine was at the dentist and not due to start work until eleven.

'We'd better keep it switched off all day then,' I said. 'And keep the door closed too.' It was our habit to leave the shop door open except in cases of bad weather, as we'd learned at a Retail Training event that a closed door acted as a psychological (and physical) barrier to customers. Apparently people are much more likely to wander in through an open entrance than make the effort to push doors open.

Once the kitchen was cleaned, Lorraine set up the till and I grabbed one of our wire shopping baskets and went to buy vegetables, turning the 'Closed' sign to 'Open' on my way out. The pavements were coated in dirt and bits of rubble and I stumbled on half a brick as I walked the short distance to Derek's shop.

He was picking through a box of tomatoes, throwing those past their best into a plastic tub.

'Morning,' I greeted him and he turned and feigned an exaggerated look of surprise.

'Hey! A visit from the big chief. I'm very honoured Madam. Sacked yer lacky have you?'

'If you mean Nadine she's at the dentist.' She'd had a lot of appointments lately, she was still trying her luck with the new dentist.

Derek put down the tub of tomatoes and came to serve me.

'What can I get you?'

'I'll have four pounds of tomatoes to start. And I hope you're not going to throw away those soft ones, they'd be great for soup.'

'Ah you can have them,' Derek said, putting the tub onto the counter. 'I'm sick of throwing stuff oot.'

'Great, that's today's soup sorted then.' I asked for four lettuces and a couple of cucumbers and as Derek went to get them I picked through his box of carrots pulling out the fresher ones. Most were soft and I doubted they would stand up to being grated for our cheese savoury. I was about to say this when a customer came into the shop. However, I needn't have been concerned about criticising his stock as the man immediately launched into a tirade of complaints.

'Here mate! Have a look at these carrots you sold wor lass. They're a disgrace.' He emptied a bag of sorry looking carrots onto the counter. 'They're like bliddy rubber, ah tell ye, I could've boonced them off the floor.'

He picked one up, and to demonstrate his point, flung it to the floor.

'Here man, there's nee need for that,' Derek said, snatching up the rest of the carrots before they too were bounced. 'I'll give you some more, these things happen, it's a one off.'

'It's not a one off though is it? Them Brussel sproots we got from you were like bullets, hard as hell they were.'

'Aye well, that depends on how they're cooked.'

I thought it best to mind my own business so moved away, although not so far that I couldn't follow the drama.

'Are ye saying wor lass can't cook, like? Cos you could've boiled them sproots for ever and they would've still been like ball bearings.'

'No problem,' Derek said. 'I'll give you another lot free of charge.' He bent and roughly scooped Brussel sprouts into a bag. His face was flushed and he scowled as he filled a second bag with carrots muttering 'Neebody's ganna accuse me of selling rubber carrots and hard sproots.'

'Make sure they're better than the last lot and you may as well hoy a cabbage in there as well because there was nowt left of the one you gave us yesterday. It was half eaten before we had a chance. It was full o' holes.'

This last comment tipped Derek over the edge. He grabbed an empty potato sack from a pile behind his counter and stuffed the bags of sprouts and carrots into it. He then picked up a savoy cabbage and rammed it in too.

'Right mate,' he shouted. 'There's your carrots and your sproots. And there's your cabbage. Here, have a cauli as well. And a few bananas, and a pineapple.' He strode around his shop, randomly seizing vegetables and fruit and stuffing them into the sack. The customer watched in silence. He caught my eye and I looked away as I glimpsed a spark of laughter in his expression.

Once the sack was full, Derek presented it to his customer.

'Here, take that. And divven't come in here again saying I sell rubbish or I'll sue you.' The customer appeared to be about to speak but thought better of it. He gave a nod, took his sack and left.

There was a moment's silence and I struggled for something to say but Derek had plenty to fill the void. He raged for a while about how difficult it was to replace unsold stock with fresh and have to dispose of boxes and boxes of wastage.

I felt rather guilty at this point for accepting the tub of tomatoes and offered to pay for them. But Derek was too wound up to hear my suggestion.

'The big supermarkets have put an end to people like me,' he said. 'How can you compete with that? At one time I had customers who bought all their stuff here every week. Now I only get folk coming in when they've forgotten something.'

I hadn't realised business was becoming so difficult for Derek and I muttered some platitude about being sorry he was finding things hard. I didn't know what to say. It was true small businesses were suffering due to the many 'superstores' that had opened recently. Fortunately for us, our stock mostly consisted of niche products that supermarkets could not sell in enough quantity to warrant stocking. Though we did have to be constantly checking what was available in the big stores in order to keep one step ahead with new health trends. We pioneered many products that when became mainstream were unable to keep in stock as we could not compete with prices offered by supermarkets.

'All I get in here,' Derek complained, 'are students wanting one baking potato to go with their tin of beans or pensioners wanting an onion and a carrot. How am I supposed to make a living out of that?'

'I'm sure it can't be that bad. There's plenty of places besides us on the bank doing sandwiches, don't you supply them? And this is a really affluent area, why don't you offer a delivery service to the big houses up near the high street?'

'I do, but the trouble with posh folk is they're never satisfied. If I have galia melons they want honeydew, if I have honeydew they want cantaloupe. I mean, melons are melons, I get whatever's the best buy at the market. It's the same with potatoes. Spuds are spuds. But they want two pounds of Maris Piper and a pound of King Edwards and some Charlottes for a salad...'

I was beginning to see his problem. If a greengrocer couldn't distinguish between different varieties and give advice on the best type for different flavours he obvious didn't love his stock, and to be successful at retail I really think you have to have a genuine interest in what you sell. Derek was still ranting.

'And then they want all this fancy stuff, mange tout and aubergines. I had one of them poshies in here the other day asking for kale. I said where do you think you are? The Ritz?'

A woman entered the shop and I picked up my basket. There was a possibility that this one sided conversation could run on for hours if I stayed to listen. I planned to take my leave as soon as Derek turned his attention to his customer.

She was well-dressed and left a faint waft of expensive scent as she looked around the shop.

'I need some grapes for my cheeseboard, but I'm after a particular flavour,' she said and Derek raised his eyebrows and gave me a 'see-what-I-mean' look.

'I've got green grapes and purple grapes,' he said. 'That's your choice.'

'Oh right,' the woman said. 'I'm pretty good at identifying what I want. I can tell by the smell. Could I possibly sniff them?'

Derek's back straightened and his eyes narrowed. Time to leave. I took my basket and made my escape, although I couldn't help hovering at the door to hear his reply. I'm sure most of the street would have heard it.

'What? What? Sniff me grapes? No you can't sniff me grapes. What a bloody nerve. I've heard it all now. Sniff me grapes? First it's me carrots being hoyed on the floor and now you want to sniff me grapes? BUGGER OFF!'

I scuttled back to our shop to make my tomato soup.

When we were having our morning putting-the-world-to-rights- session, Georgina mentioned that Derek didn't seem himself.

'I've been in there for a few bits and pieces and he had a face like a fart,' she said.

'I think business has been a bit slow lately,' I told her.

'I asked for a couple of plums and he said if I asked to sniff them he'd throw me out. I don't know what he meant, I hadn't said any such thing.'

'It must be difficult,' I said. 'All that fresh stuff, must be hard chucking it out when it doesn't sell.'

'I was thinking about stocking vegetables ourselves, organic stuff, but I don't feel we can now,' Lorraine said.

'Hmm. Well business is business. We have to do what's best for us.'

'I hope it picks up for him,' Lorraine said. 'There are too many little businesses going under.'

'I see the wool shop is having a closing down sale,' Georgina said. 'That'll be another one gone.'

'Oh, really?' I said. 'I always thought they did well.'

'Well nobody knits these days do they?' Nige said. 'I wouldn't be seen dead in a hand knitted garment.'

'Yeah they do actually, Nige.' Georgina said. 'I hand make lots of my stuff.'

'Aye, and like I say, I wouldn't be seen dead in any of it.'

Georgina ignored him and turned to me.

'I was thinking,' she said. 'I thought I might make something for the baby if you like?'

'Gawd help the poor little bugger,' Nige muttered.

'Nige!' I said, and he mumbled an insincere apology. 'Georgina that's really kind of you. I'd love that.'

Georgina smiled. 'I have something in mind.'

Apparently Derek's mood did not improve. Val arrived at the shop in a state of distress complaining that he'd been very rude to her.

'I've just had a terrible shock,' she said as she shuffled in with the aid of a stick. I'd seen her walk and, on a few occasions, run without the need of a walking aid so I could only assume she used it for effect. 'I've just been assaulted by Derek in the fruit shop.'

'Assaulted?'

Val quickly modified her choice of words.

'Verbally insulted. I'm suffering from shock. I'm afraid you'll have to administer first aid. A sit down with a sweet cup of tea and a slice of cake should do it.'

Lorraine ignored her, but I carried a stool to the front of the counter for her and switched on the kettle. Lorraine gave me a swift frown but I wanted to find out what Derek had said to her. Val was the kind of person who would take delight in reporting the incident. I knew Derek's language could get a bit fruity, and I hoped he hadn't said anything too offensive.

I bypassed the fresh carrot cake Val pointed to and gave her a piece of slightly stale lemon cake left for Peter, our resident food waste disposal.

She seemed not to notice and ploughed into it, showering cake crumbs onto the counter as she spluttered her complaint.

'It was uncalled for. I hadn't even spoken. I just walked into the shop and before I could mention my heartburn, which incidentally I put down to those tinned peas he sells, he just launched into a verbal attack.'

'What did he say?'

'He told me to get out. He took one look at me and said...' - at this point Val drew herself up and grimaced, contorting her face to what she must have thought resembled Derek's ' – '..."Get out you whinging ninny."'

I sniggered unintentionally. I'd been expecting a lot worse. For some reason, the choice of insult really tickled Lorraine and she laughed till she cried.

'Sorry for laughing, Val,' she spluttered, but continued. I struggled to remain calm but the more hysterical Lorraine became, the more difficult it was.

'What's going on?' Nadine came from the kitchen.

'Derek called Val a whinging ninny,' I said gravely, trying to convey sympathy for Val but my voice wobbled and Nadine's face stiffened for a second then she too sniggered.

'He called you a whinging ninny? Eeh, Val that's awful '

'I wonder why he called you that,' Georgina said and she laughed her screechy laugh. Nige tittered, turning away from Val to hide his smirking face.

It was one of those situations where the more inappropriate it is to laugh, the funnier it gets and we gulped and snorted trying to swallow our laughter, unable to look each other in the eye. Eventually, we all calmed down and I apologised to a stony-faced Val who accepted another cup of tea and cake – this time of her choice - as a peace offering. Knowing we'd behaved badly, we fussed about her, Georgina even offering to accompany her home to carry her shopping, and she left surprisingly cheery considering she must have known she'd always be The Whinging Ninny to us.

CHAPTER NINE

Rosie's second birthday fell on a Saturday and so we decided to take her away for the weekend to celebrate. Peter booked us a couple of nights at a family-run hotel, so on the Thursday evening we had a family tea party then left for the Lake District the following morning.

Rosie loved the little cot-bed provided for her and made friends with the house cat who sat on a sunny wall in the hotel garden. We visited the Beatrix Potter Attraction which she loved, and took a trip on a steamboat.

The days were mild and sunny and we made the most of them, rising early and filling each hour. By around four o'clock, unable to stay awake any longer, Rosie would fall asleep in her pushchair. Taking advantage of her nap we would nip in to a tearoom and have a quiet pot of tea until she awoke, raring to go again and hungry for her tea.

Before driving home we had a look around the shops and Rosie chose a Peter Rabbit colouring set from a little gift shop.

There was a section displaying Beatrix Potter themed babywear and I examined the tiny outfits, touching the soft material, feeling a rush of joy knowing soon I'd be shopping for things like these again. I'd told myself I wouldn't buy any baby clothes until the baby arrived. A few people had questioned why I wasn't going to ask the doctor the gender of my baby at my scan but I preferred to wait until the big day. I don't know why but I was sure I was carrying a boy and we still referred to the baby as Max. I had plenty of little vests and sleepsuits of Rosie's stored away which would be fine for the first couple of days. It would be lovely to go shopping once the baby had arrived. But then I saw a blue, new-born sized outfit with Peter Rabbit on the front. It had tiny matching socks and I couldn't resist. I was so sure I was having a boy that although I've never really been into all that pink for girls, blue for boys stuff, I bought it.

Back at home, I tucked it away in my drawer. I would take it out and hold it to my cheek, imagining my baby boy wrapped in it, all snuggly and smelling deliciously of baby soap.

I also had a pair of bootees that Georgina had knit. They were not like the usual style found in shops at the time, being rainbow striped, and although the others had laughed at them, I loved them, and couldn't wait to be able to pull them onto Max's little feet.

I couldn't wait to tell Rosie she was going to have a baby brother - or perhaps a sister. Nine months is a long time for a child, especially when they are waiting for a new baby to arrive, so we decided to hold off telling her until it was closer to the delivery date.

I knew she'd be a wonderful big sister. She had such a loving nature and was full of fun. I watched her chatting to her toy rabbit as she ate her breakfast, and smiled when I heard her ask him if he wanted some toast.

Although she had many lovely cuddly toys, her favourite was a weird old rabbit I'd bought at a car boot sale. I'd been attracted to it because it was such a funny looking thing – furry head and paws and huge rabbit ears, and long legs encased in striped trousers. I'd put him through the washing machine and sat him on my desk but Rose loved him and claimed him as her own. He soon became known as Funny Bunny.

'Come on,' I told her. 'Coat on, ready for Grandad.' Some days Dad picked us up and dropped me at the shop before taking Rosie back home where he and Mam would look after her for the day.

Rosie chattered the whole journey, telling her Grandad about the two high spots of her weekend, the little bed she'd slept in, and the Mrs Tiggywinkle figure at the museum that she'd been photographed next to.

Today Dad had to circle the shop a couple of times as there were no parking spots, and eventually pulled up near the door so I could jump out.

'Bye!' I waved to Rosie and blew kisses. I laughed as she held Funny Bunny's arm and waved it, and I wished I was going with them. I sometimes felt pulled in two directions. I loved being at the shop developing our business, but I longed to be with my little daughter too.

The builders working on the gym renovation were already hard at work. They really put in some long shifts, busy when we arrived to open up and still labouring when we left at five-thirty.

Each morning more progress was apparent. At first it seemed only destruction and chaos were being created as the interior was gutted. I wondered how far a building could be stripped back without it giving way and collapsing and for a while feared for the safety of our shop. I expected at some point to arrive to see a heap of rubble where the shop had been. However, just when it appeared nothing else could possibly be torn from the structure, the builders began to replace and renovate, and slowly the stylish premises that were to be James McAllister's computer business emerged from the chaos.

His business opened with a flurry of activity that brought us extra custom too. He employed a staff of eight who found us convenient for snacks and lunches, and often he would recommend us to customers picking up or dropping off their mysterious bits of technology.

Although my first impression of James had not been favourable, we grew to like him immensely. He was fair, true to his word and always generous in sending business our way whenever he could, although I have to say I found his conversations boring. They rarely strayed from the subject of computers and were usually incomprehensible to us. He and I once had a very confusing conversation about installing windows. I thought he meant in the property upstairs but apparently he meant something completely different. He regularly came with orders for his staff and would stay to chat while we put together sandwiches and cartons of soup. We had a joke amongst ourselves that every time he used the word 'tad' we would use it back to him, although he never noticed.

He told us about how he'd spent so much time studying and working towards eventually opening his business he'd not had time to meet 'that special girl'. He often mentioned this to Nadine and we would tease her about him.

'It's such a shame he's so unattractive,' Nadine would say. 'He has everything else, intelligence, sense of humour. He's such a lovely man.'

'And of course he has money,' Georgina said.

'Well, yes. He has money too. But that's neither here nor there.'

'Of course not.'

'But he's so pale and weak looking, not very attractive all at.' It worried her.

'That is so shallow,' Lorraine said. 'Looks aren't everything.'

'Not everything, but something. It's so unfortunate. He's so close to what I want.'

'You could always feed him up,' Lorraine joked.

'He needs the love of a good woman,' Nige quipped. 'Or at any rate the love of a bad woman. I'm sure you could sort him out.'

'That is such a bad idea,' Georgina said. 'You should never go into a relationship intending to change someone.'

It bothered Nadine for a while, but in the end she dithered too long because he met someone else. As soon as she heard, Nadine concluded that actually he was a great catch and must have improved in the looks department as she now couldn't understand why she'd though him to be so unappealing.

'Strange how attractive a man becomes when he has another woman,' Georgina said cynically.

'You missed the boat there, girl,' Nige said. 'He's loaded. Computers are the future, he'll be raking it in.'

'I'm not a gold digger!' Nadine told him. 'I'm looking for my soul mate, I'm not interested in money.'

'Not much,' Georgina said. 'You're kicking yourself at what you've missed out on!'

'I am not.'

'So you won't be interested if I tell you he's dumped her then?'

'Really?' Nadine's face lit up.

'No, just kidding,' Georgina said, and there was an outcry from the others as they laughed at Nadine but also berated Georgina for her cruel joke.

They were loud and boisterous, Georgina's voice brash and Nadine's laughter shrill. I usually loved our morning get-together but today I found the rowdiness irritating. The radio was belting out a Blur song and the combined noise was too much for me.

When the phone rang I took the chance to go and answer it and distance myself from them.

A man introduced himself as Dermot and told me he was ringing to see if we were interested in hiring a stall at an upcoming Mind-Body-Spirit Fair at Gateshead Stadium, run by a group called First-Soul. We'd seen the fair advertised in the Health Food Retailer magazine and talked about possibly going, so it didn't take much persuasion for me to sign up. Dermot took our details and said we could pay the fee on the day, and that he was looking forward to meeting us.

I wrote the details in the diary and, reluctant to join the others who were still screeching and laughing, held my throbbing head in my hands.

'What's up?' Lorraine asked.

'I'm not feeling too good. I have a headache and the noise is getting on my nerves.'

Lorraine looked concerned. 'Shall I ask them to leave?'

'No, of course not. I just feel a bit groggy. Probably overtired. If you don't mind I'll stay off the shop floor and do some paperwork or something.'

'Have you seen the midwife lately? Are you eating properly?' Lorraine fussed.

'I'm fine, honestly. I'll just take it easy today if you don't mind.'

'Course not. I'll make you a cuppa and a bite to eat.'

I spent the morning in the office, filing invoices and telephoning suppliers with orders. I had difficulty concentrating and I had that awful detached feeling like when you are coming down with a virus. When Peter arrived at lunch time I stayed in the office with him and we ate together, although after a bite or two of my sandwich I'd had enough.

'Not hungry?'

'No. I feel really drained today. Early night for me tonight.'

After lunch I pottered about dusting shelves and tidying the stock but by three o'clock I was exhausted and my headache had worsened. Lorraine suggested I leave early and go home to rest.

'Sure you don't mind?' I asked.

'Don't be silly. I can manage here. You need to look after yourself. Go on, get yourself away. If you go now you'll miss rush hour.'

I didn't need to be persuaded.

I reached home, dropping my coat and bag on the floor and went straight to run a bath. After a quick soak, I sank gratefully into bed and before Peter got home from work, I was fast asleep.

The next morning I was awakened at dawn by a heavy, dragging ache through my abdomen. By eight o'clock that evening, after one of the worst days of my life, it was all over.

Without me ever holding him in my arms, Max had returned to heaven.

CHAPTER TEN

I cried for my baby until I could cry no more.

I questioned myself constantly. What did I do wrong? Why had my body rejected him? Was my diet lacking? Did I not rest enough? I had failed not only my tiny, growing baby, but also Peter, who, already consumed with love for his unborn child, had been betrayed; the joy snatched from him, leaving only shock and sadness. At least, that's how I saw it at the time.

For the first few days, nothing could make me smile. Even things of beauty appeared to bring with them a sweet sadness that triggered more tears. I knew I had a good life and so many things to be grateful for, but I could not feel it. The world for me was dark and harsh. I was fearful of how life could give such promises of joy then cruelly steal them away. Rosie's chatter and laughter made me ache for her, for the brother she'd lost without knowing. I was glad we'd delayed telling her, waited until the later months. The months that would now never come. He was gone.

I knew he was a boy, because I dreamt of him. I dreamed that no matter how tightly I held him to me, an invisible force would wrench him from my arms as I fought to keep him. I would wake hot and feverish, my face wet with tears. I'd fetch the little blue outfit from my drawer and break my heart weeping over it. Eventually Peter took it from me, gently telling me I needed to let it go, and disposed of it. I kept the rainbow bootees, I couldn't bear to part with them. I needed to keep a physical reminder of the baby I'd carried for such a short time.

Eventually the perpetual noise in my head subsided as a numbing blackness engulfed me and I sunk into a depression as I grieved for my child.

It was a dark time for us. I knew Peter was grieving too, but he stayed strong and supportive and I only once saw him give way to tears.

Rosie was a huge comfort to us. The simplicity with which she viewed life, and the delight she exuded at new discoveries every day, lifted us and reminded us to feel gratitude for the good life we had.

I was advised to take a couple of weeks off work, which I spent sleeping off my exhaustion and mooching about at home.

I was soon keen to get back to the shop. I had been declared physically fit, and told there was no reason I should not try for another child. However, I needed time to heal emotionally and I threw myself into work.

The first days back at the shop were difficult. It seemed that the whole country knew of my loss, and I was overwhelmed by customers coming to sympathise, bringing stories of other miscarriages, until I felt compelled to retreat and compose myself in the therapy room. I knew they meant well and intended to make me feel better, but it was all too raw, and hearing stories about mothers losing babies broke my heart.

But mourning cannot last forever. Life has a way of gradually enveloping you back into its bosom, and slowly the pain diminished as life, as ever, moved on.

And time passed, each day leaving me a little stronger and happier, and with a growing realisation of how much love surrounded me.

And there was one compensation for which I held gratitude. Aileen tearfully revealed that she'd made me a cot blanket from an old tablecloth she'd found in her garage which she now felt she could not give me, even for a future child, as I would associate it with sad memories. However, she told me not to worry over it as she could easily recycle it back into a tablecloth, so nothing would be wasted.

She also had something else to show us.

'It's in my car,' she told us. 'I'll nip out and get it.'

'Any idea what it is?' I asked Lorraine but she shook her head.

'I dread to think.'

The shop was slowly filling up with Aileen's 'recycled' efforts. Our paperwork was now filed in cornflake boxes that had been covered in with offcuts of wallpaper, the office chair had been re-upholstered with a piece of striped canvas from a defunct deckchair, and a row of jam jars decorated with gummed paper shapes held paperclips, staples, pens and other bits of office equipment.

A margarine tub, painted with the word 'teabags', stood next to the kettle as a receptacle for used teabags to rest for a few minutes before being tipped into the bin. We had holders for kitchen utensils, price labels, paper bags, receipt books - all made from discarded containers and labelled in Aileen's slanted handwriting. Even the kitchen roll holder had a holder.

The lavatory had not escaped the Aileen-treatment. Spare toilet rolls were now stored on a wooden pole taken from a sweeping brush we'd thrown away. It stood upright in an old Christmas tree stand and the rolls of paper were threaded on. Rolls were taken from the top, so the ones at the bottom were never used, and after a while became torn and ragged but none of us had the time or inclination to remove the whole stack when it was re-filled with new rolls.

Various discarded vests and pairs of pants lay folded in a bucket ready to use as cleaning cloths, and the soap on the hand basin was made of the ends of countless other bars, melted and pressed to form a new piece, which invariably fell apart when exposed to water.

Worse than all of this was the crocheted lavatory seat cover Aileen had hand made from an unravelled pom pom hat. I hated the bloody thing. It served no purpose at all, looked hideous and had to be regularly removed and washed. It was in shades of yellow and purple and she'd even re-used the pom pom by stitching it to the centre.

Aileen took home most of the cardboard boxes, packaging, cartons and tubs we tried to dispose of, the rest she squirrelled away under the counter, in the therapy room, or wherever she could squeeze them. The more unusual the item, the more she saw it as a challenge, and took great pleasure in finding a new use for it, often bringing her projects back to the shop for us.

At best her creations were inefficient and unattractive, at worst they were useless and unsightly.

However, she was such a kind and well-meaning person that I found it difficult to criticise the things she made. Lorraine was a little more inclined to give her honest opinion, but we both loved her and couldn't bear to hurt her feelings, especially when she showed such pride in her creations.

Aileen returned to the shop and presented us with a large piece of card cut from a box that had once held a television. A circle of individual letters cut from magazines and newspapers had been glued on to it. Some were capitals, the rest lower case. They were various colours, fonts and sizes, reminiscent of a ransom note from an old film. Sticky-backed plastic of the sort Blue Peter presenters were fond of using had been used to cover it.

'It's a Ouija board,' she announced proudly, although, with sinking heart, I'd already guessed.

'Shouldn't the letters be in alphabetical order?' Lorraine asked.

'Yes but I'd started sticking them on before I realised. Don't suppose it matters.'

'No.'

Lorraine was examining the letters, and began reciting the alphabet.

'...O, P, Q, R...there's no S.'

'There must be. I counted twenty-six letters.'

'There must be two of something else,' Lorraine said. 'There look. You've put M on twice.'

'Not to worry,' I said. 'It'll be fine. I'll put it in the office to keep it safe.' I pushed it beneath a pile of paperwork on the desk in the hope it would be forgotten.

Unfortunately it was unearthed and brought out to be shown to Georgina and Nige, who admired it and had started on the Elvis jokes again when Maureen, who had a day of appointments booked, arrived.

'What do you think?' Aileen asked proudly. 'I made it from old packaging.'

Maureen looked at it and sniffed.

'Well I've never seen a Ouija board like that before but it'll do,' she said with her usual apathy. 'Do you want me to come in and lead the séance?'

Oh heck, I thought. I'd assumed it was just going to be Nadine, Nige, Georgina, Lorraine and possibly Peter, bumbling about in the dark having a laugh, but now it was going to be the full shenanigans with Maureen in Mariana guise. However, everyone thought this was a great idea and began discussing which night would be best.

'Shall we dress up?' Nige asked excitedly.

'Dress up?' Georgina said. 'In what? Halloween costumes or something?'

It was getting worse by the minute. There was no way I would be able to keep my composure sitting in the dark with a collection of ghouls and zombies, while Maureen called up the dead.

'No, I was thinking of Elvis costumes. To make him feel more at ease. We could all wear them.'

The thought of Peter in an Elvis costume was scarier than the zombie outfits.

'We don't even know if it is Elvis yet,' Nadine said.

'We don't know if it's anyone,' I said. 'I mean, you don't all really believe there's a spirit in here do you?'

Just as I finished speaking, a terrific crash from the back of the shop caused us to jump in shock and clutch hold of each other. One of our big herb jars lay, luckily unbroken, on the shop floor.

Nige broke the silence.

'I do believe in spooks, I do believe in spooks, I do, I do, I do believe in spooks...'

CHAPTER ELEVEN

Attracting new customers was an ongoing mission. Over the past two years we'd built up a good base of regular customers, but learned there is no such thing as loyalty where shopping is concerned. When we'd first opened, it would unsettle us to see our 'regulars' buying lunch from other shops on the street.

'Look, there's those girls from the solicitor's buying their lunch from the baker's,' Lorraine said on a particularly quiet day. 'I wonder why they didn't come here.'

'Do you think there was something wrong with their sandwiches yesterday?' I asked. 'I mean, they usually come in here every day.'

'Well that's probably why then,' Peter said. 'If they come in here every day they probably fancied a change.'

'Hmm, yeah I suppose,' Lorraine said.

'They are allowed to buy from other shops, you know. After all, you two are hardly loyal to any particular stores. You shop anywhere and everywhere.'

Lorraine and I laughed at our own indignation.

'True, I hadn't thought of it in that way,' I said.

'But they're our customers,' Lorraine said. 'They're not allowed to shop elsewhere.'

It was one of the lessons along the curve of our learning. Customers did not have to shop with us, we needed to be grateful when they did and work to keep them happy.

Lorraine and I shopped at Nutmeg ourselves, with a generous discount of course, and topped up at SuperSavers. I called there each Thursday evening after closing the shop and often saw customers of ours there. I'd strike up a conversation to give me a chance to scrutinise their trolley, desperate to rake through the contents to see what they'd bought. If there was anything we stocked in Nutmeg, I would be irked and would then go and find the offending item on the shelves to check the price. It was not often we could offer lower prices than the supermarket so I kept an eye on any new products that appeared on display and tried to keep one step ahead with the latest 'healthy' food trends.

Today, I'd just about finished my shopping when I noticed a new range of vegan ice-creams in one of the freezers. I was examining the list of ingredients when I heard a familiar voice.

'Hello there, didn't think I'd see you in here! Checking out the competition?' I turned and the first thing that caught my eye was a trolley holding, amongst other things, a bag of red lentils and two tins of butterbeans.

As I saw the owner of the trolley, my irritation rose.

'Hello Caroline. Could hardly be classed as competition, a multimillion organisation and a little independent local healthfood shop,' I said, putting emphasis on the word local. 'Hardly a fair contest, haha. Which is why we need all the support we can get from the local community. Haha.' The 'ha ha's came out a little more sarcastically than I'd meant and I sensed the rise of her hackles.

'Well I have to say I'm surprised to see you in here. It's not a good advert for your business if you have to buy your own groceries from the very establishment you claim are destroying communities.'

'I'm certain I've never made such a claim. I just feel it's important to support small businesses. I seem to remember you saying a similar thing to Mr Reeves a while ago.'

'Indeed. I've always felt a sense of duty to help those less fortunate.'

As she spoke I flicked my eyes across the contents of her trolley and spotted brown rice, dried fruit and herb tea.

'I see you have blackcurrant tea there,' I beamed. 'And brown rice. Oh, and dried apricots. You didn't need to come all the way here for those Caroline, we stock them at Nutmeg. Much more convenient for you.'

Her features hardened. 'Yes I know. And at twice the price.'

I forced my features out of the scowl they'd involuntarily formed and into a strained smile.

'I think that's a bit of an exaggeration. Maybe a few pence more, but not double.'

'A few pence here and there soon add up.'

'But of course, money isn't the main priority is it? Not when it comes to helping local communities and the environment,' I said, with as much condescendence as I could squeeze into two sentences.

She craned her neck and I edged in front of my trolley to hide it from her view as I realised she was examining my purchases.

'Tell me. Those prepacked vegetables you have there. The ones in the plastic bags.' She nodded at my bags of courgettes and peppers, and feigned an expression of puzzlement. 'Plastic packaging is so damaging to the environment. Surely the loose ones would be a wiser purchase, yes? '

'Usually, yes,' I faltered. 'But unfortunately today they didn't have loose courgettes in the right size I need for a particular recipe.'

'Really?' Her face was so smug I was tempted to smack it. I peered into her trolley.

'May I suggest you consider buying bars of soap rather than bottles of liquid soap in future?' I asked. 'No plastic bottle to dispose of you see, and no waste.'

Caroline narrowed her eyes. 'I'll bear that in mind.' She nodded at the big bar of fruit and nut I'd bought to guzzle while we watched television. 'I hope you don't mind me saying, but it may be a good idea not to be seen in public buying *huge* bars of chocolate. You know how people can be. They may think it's a little hypocritical of someone who pushes health food for a living.'

I forced out a laugh. 'Yes, I know just what you mean. Like all those bottles of wine you have there. And the bottle of sherry. People could make wrong assumptions.'

There was a lull in our exchange as we now faced up to each other, our smiles scarcely disguising that we both knew war had been declared. She pointed to my tube of Immac.

'Oh, is that leg-hair remover? I've heard dark-haired women have such a problem with superfluous body hair. A woman on my church committee has terrible trouble with her legs, positively gorilla-like. I've never seen the need to use it myself, being fair.' Her voice was filled with false sympathy. I responded in the same manner.

'Really? There's a facial-hair remover too, it would take that moustache off for you in minutes,' I told her, smiling kindly.

For a moment I thought Caroline was about to set about me with a baguette but then she composed herself.

'It amuses me that brunettes are always so envious of blondes...'

'Envious?' I gave a little chuckle. 'Oh I don't think so. There are so many jokes about blondes not being clever aren't there? It must get very tedious.'

'The general opinion is that blondes are more attractive.'

'Even if it's not natural?' I nodded to a box of hair colourant in the corner of her trolley.

Caroline's jaw tightened. She reached into my trolley and picked up a pair of pink cotton pyjamas I'd found on the sale rail.

'Oh I do like these. I looked at them myself but unfortunately the smallest size was a twelve. I'm an eight. Lucky you, there were so many lovely things in the larger sizes.'

'I would hardly call size twelve large', I said, snatching them from her grasp.

'Pink is a good choice for you. I always think pink makes hefty women look so much more feminine.'

I threw the pyjamas back into my trolley, aiming to conceal two family size bags of crisps. But too late, she'd seen.

'Perhaps if you cut down on the crisps and chocolate...?'

'That's just rude. And ridiculous. Size twelve isn't exactly obese.'

'Not exactly obese, but getting close.'

'Excuse me! I am not obese!'

'And I don't have a moustache!'

'Actually you do.'

'And I am not an alcoholic!'

'I didn't say you were, but you know what they say about those who protest loudly...'

'And I'll shop where I damned well like!'

'Yes. You do that.'

'I will.'

'And I'll wear size twelve pyjamas and eat crisps and chocolate if I want to.'

'Well good for you.'

'Yes. Good for me.' I swung my shopping trolley about, my face reddening with embarrassment as I realised other shoppers had been enjoying the entertainment. Caroline swung hers in the opposite direction and we marched away from each other.

CHAPTER TWELVE

Lorraine and Nadine laughed hysterically when I related my conversation with Caroline and I laughed with them, although I felt a bit hollow about it.

'I wish I'd seen her face,' Lorraine said. 'It's about time someone gave her a bit of her own treatment.'

'Good for you. Sounds like you really out-bitched her, 'Nadine said.

To be honest, I felt disappointed about how I'd handled the situation. I knew I'd let myself down. 'Out-bitching' someone didn't feel like something to be proud of. Ultimately, all I'd done was allow Caroline to get under my skin and then retaliate with malice.

'I wish I hadn't bitten. I should have been more patient, less reactive.'

'Why?' Lorraine said. 'She deserved it.'

'I keep thinking about that Buddhist talk we went to,' I said.

'Ah, she had it coming,' Nadine said. 'I bet she could drive a Buddhist monk to lose his inner peace.'

'She probably did deserve it but like Rinpoche Chen-Chio said, I could have chosen to react differently.'

Lorraine laughed wryly. 'Oh here we go. Here comes the next fad. Looks like we're finished with angels and on to Buddhism.'

The previous week, Lorraine, Nadine, Georgina and I had attended a meeting where a Buddhist monk gave a talk about developing a peaceful mind. The presentation was hosted by an organisation called the Inspiration Group, who held events about various subjects on the first Tuesday of each month in the local community centre. We had been to several of the meetings and had learned about the work of Japanese artist Haruto Matsumoto, taken part in a macramé class, watched a vegan Indian cookery demonstration, and listened to a talk about angels.

Nadine and I threw ourselves into these events, joining in enthusiastically, buying books and merchandise and putting into practise what we learned. Lorraine was often sceptical, especially with what she called airy-fairy-happy-clappy subjects. She enjoyed the events, but enjoyed the chance to ridicule us more, teasing us about how earnestly we incorporated our new-found knowledge into our working day.

The presentation about angels really caught our imaginations. Nadine and I were enthralled with the whole concept and subsequently searched for angelic signs, which seemingly included white feathers, shiny coins and reoccurring numbers. Nadine was more enthusiastic and even started conversing with angelic beings as she worked, asking for help with her problems and confessing to things she'd done. This made for some confusion at times, especially when we answered her only to be told it was Archangel Raphael or Gabriel she was addressing. But the angelic thing waned a little as our interest in Buddhism increased.

The Buddhist talk was billed as 'A Journey into Peace and Mindfulness with Rinpoche Chen-Chio'.

We'd arrived at the centre and after being welcomed with herbal tea and home-made oat cookies, had waited quietly with the rest of the audience. I was so excited to meet a genuine Buddhist monk I could hardly swallow and choked on a crumbly bit of cookie, coughing and spluttering and generally making an exhibition of myself.

Before entering the main hall where the meeting was to take place, we were asked to remove our shoes and enter with heads bowed. We were to remain standing until Rinpoche Chen-Chio indicated we may sit.

The atmosphere was thick with anticipation and I could feel my heart beating as we waited. My eagerness must have shown because Lorraine nudged me and said, 'Calm down, it's just a bloke in an orange frock.'

A bell rang, the doors to the hall opened and we all shuffled forwards.

I walked slowly, following Lorraine with my head lowered and my hands clasped in front of me. We entered the hall silently, each of us taking our place next to one of the thin mats that lay in rows on the floor. The smell of burning incense filled the air and I could hear someone chanting quietly as we filed in.

I expected the evening to be a solemn and serious affair, but the monk (Chen, as he asked to be called) revealed a gentle, and sometimes mischievous, sense of humour.

He spoke to us of how we respond to everyday mishaps and problems, giving an amusing interpretation of human behaviour we all related to. He described how we react unthinkingly to problems, seeing them as disasters rather than challenges, meeting them head-on with anger, bitterness and complaint, rather than with determination and gratitude for the opportunity to learn and grow. He encouraged us to approach every situation from a place of love, explaining we are often too quick to judge the behaviour of others without knowing what is in their hearts.

'If someone steals your car,' he said, 'why be angry and miserable? You have lost your car, are you to lose your inner peace too? Have compassion for the person who has compromised his peace of mind to commit such an act, and have gratitude that you had something worth stealing. No-one can disturb your calmness unless you allow it. Rejoice! Although you have lost your car, you have so much left of value. Love, inner peace and compassion are worth far more than material things.'

Yes I know. When I say it, it sounds like a load of old rubbish, but honestly, when he spoke those words, they triggered an understanding deep within, and as I listened it was like a door had been opened slightly. I could see a little daylight beginning to shine through and I wanted to push the door wider.

Lorraine hooted when I told her this but Nadine agreed with me. She too felt the truth of his words and claimed to have seen a different way to dealing with life. Lorraine was her was usual cynical self, saying we were like a couple of dustbins ready to be filled with anything verging on the ridiculous.

'Didn't you take on board anything he said?' Nadine asked her.

81

'Some of it,' Lorraine said. 'I just think it's a bit unrealistic that's all. It's natural to want to fill somebody's face in if they nick your car. Imagine if we all started accepting everything, nothing would ever change or improve.'

'I don't think it's about accepting things in that way,' I said. 'My understanding was that you can still work to change things and improve them, but without the emotional attachment and upset.'

'Yes, I agree,' Nadine said. 'We should all detach from anger and judgement and approach everything from a place of love and compassion.'

'Especially those things that irritate and annoy us,' I added.

Lorraine nudged me. 'Aye, well. Here's Caroline coming. Go and show some understanding and compassion for something that irritates you.'

Caroline walked into the shop and as soon as I saw her self-righteous face, my hand itched to slap it. Deep breath. Love and compassion. I waited until she'd bought a loaf of bread and as Lorraine wrapped it, I moved forwards.

'Hello Caroline. How are you?'

Caroline looked at me with something between a sneer and a snarl. She took the wrapped loaf from Lorraine and put it in her basket.

'Oh, got over your fit of jealousy, have you?' she said.

I cleared my throat. 'If you are referring to our...um...exchange of words at SuperSavers the other day, then I must apologise.'

Caroline folded her arms, obviously waiting for a barb at the end of my apology. Nadine and Lorraine watched keenly, Nadine smiling encouragingly and Lorraine waiting in hope that I would fail her challenge.

'I said some harsh things and I didn't mean them,' I told her. I waited for her to apologise too but she didn't.

'You certainly did. Very harsh.'

'Yes. Well, as I say I'm sorry and I hope we can put it behind us.'

'It was an absolutely disgraceful display of jealousy.' She turned to Lorraine. 'I'm afraid to say your sister launched a spiteful and unprovoked verbal attack as I went about my shopping trip.'

Unprovoked my arse, I thought.

'Mmm. I heard about it.' Lorraine said, and gave me a reprimanding look. I gave her one back. Love and compassion, I reminded myself.

'I'm sorry for what I said, and hope we can forget all about it,' I forced myself to say.

'Jealousy is an ugly emotion and you really need to work on your issues,' Caroline said haughtily.

I clenched my teeth and kept quiet. I'd apologised three times, I wasn't bloody well going to say it again.

'Fortunately, I have a forgiving nature and I understand the motivation behind your behaviour. It must be difficult working in a shop, an occupation that is really little other than servitude, especially when you are called upon to serve successful women such as myself. I'm sure I can find it in me to pardon your behaviour. Have you anything else you wish to say before we put the matter to rest?'

Yes. I'd like to push your face in a dish of hummus, you pompous windbag.

I swallowed down the words and shook my head.

'Then let us speak of it no more,' Caroline said, and turned on her heel and swept out like she was auditioning for a part in a costume drama.

'Well!' Lorraine said as the bell on the door jangled violently. 'It seems Caroline was able to approach the situation with love and compassion. All that forgiveness and understanding...?'

I looked at her and gave the only reasonable response to her statement.

'Piss off.'

'Are you sure you're feeling up to this?' Peter asked. 'You don't have to do it if you don't want to.'

'Yeah, I'm fine,' I lied. I felt anything but fine, but I knew he was referring to my physical health not my anxiety. There were so many other things I'd rather be doing on a Saturday morning than learning to abseil. Even cleaning the house appeared attractive in comparison.

'It's just the training, not the real thing,' I said.

'You look absolutely terrified.' He put his arms around me.

'I am!'

'Then don't do it. No-one will mind if you back out.'

'I'll mind. I want to be able to do it. You know what they say, *feel the fear and do it anyway.'*

'If you're sure,' he said.

Rosie sang to herself as I strapped her into her car seat. It was such a sweet sound and I kissed her cheek, wishing I was taking her to Paddy Freeman's, her favourite park, rather than going to confront my fear of heights.

When we arrived at the Royal Marines Training Centre on Newcastle Quayside, I saw Lorraine's car parked near the river. Nadine waved to us from the passenger seat, and by the time we'd parked, they'd walked over to greet us.

'Ready for this?' Lorraine asked.

'Yeah, bring it on!' I spoke with more bravado than I felt.

Peter unfolded Rosie's pushchair and slid the bolts into place as I lifted her from her car seat. Her sleepy face broke into a huge smile when she saw Lorraine, and she held out her arms.

'Aunty Lain!'

'Hello beautiful.' Lorraine took her from my arms, and she and Nadine cooed at her. Rosie lapped up the attention. We walked towards the training centre, Lorraine holding Rosie's hand and Peter walking ahead pushing her empty chair.

'How are you feeling?' Nadine asked.

'Terrified to be honest. It seemed like a good way to confront my fear of heights when we were safely in the shop, but now...' I pulled a face.

'Ah, you'll be fine,' Nadine said kindly. 'Won't she?'

Lorraine grinned wickedly. 'Not sure if it's a good idea for Rosie to be here though.'

'Why not?' Nadine asked.

'Could have long term effects seeing her mother falling from a great height.'

'Get lost,' I said. 'That's not helping.'

Lorraine laughed and began paraphrasing a line from a silly song we used to sing when we were children.

'She landed on the tarmac like a lump of strawberry jam...'

I slapped her and hurried ahead to walk with Peter who I knew would be more supportive.

'I'm feeling really anxious now,' I told him. 'I'm sweating and my hands are shaking, look.'

'I'm not surprised. You're all mad. You couldn't pay me to do it.'

'Thanks for that. I feel much better now.'

He took Rosie from Lorraine and strapped her into her chair. She looked about excitedly, watching as groups of people made their way towards the huge building. I recognised a girl from the hair salon up the bank from Nutmeg and I waved. She waved back, her face taut and white, and it heartened me to think someone else looked more scared than I felt.

We entered the Centre and after signing in at reception were guided through a set of doors. As I followed the flow of people into the huge training hall, I felt the blood drain from my head. Situated about forty feet up on the far wall, accessed only by an elongated metal ladder, was a small platform about the size of a beach towel.

'Look at that,' I said, nudging Nadine, but she was too busy checking out Marines who were sorting equipment at the left-hand side of the hall.

Peter left me with a kiss and a murmured 'good luck' as he pushed Rosie's chair to go and find a space amongst the crowd of spectators sitting on designated benches along the right-hand wall.

Once all the participants were gathered in the hall, one of the instructors welcomed us and gave a short talk about safety procedures. At least I think that's what it was about, I was too absorbed in trying to keep breathing normally to listen. When he'd finished speaking, harnesses, helmets and gloves were given out. I picked up my harness and attempted to work out how it was worn. My heart pounded in my chest and I resisted an urge to take to my heels and run for the door. Lorraine took the harness from me and held it so I could put my feet through the straps.

'Weren't you listening?' she asked and I shook my head, wondering whether I should leave now before I passed out with fear.

'Neither was I,' Nadine admitted. 'He's gorgeous, I went a bit weak at the knees, couldn't focus. And look at him over there!'

Lorraine helped me secure the harness and made sure I had my helmet on while Nadine gawked at the Marines.

'You okay, sis?' Lorraine asked.

'No. I'm really panicking here.'

She looked at me with concern. 'Take a deep breath,' she said. 'Sorry if I freaked you out before, I was just joking. I didn't realise how bad your fear was or I wouldn't have teased you.'

'Neither did I until I got here.'

'You don't have to do it, you know. A few people have changed their minds.' She nodded towards two girls who had given back their equipment were shuffling off to the spectator area and although I knew there was no shame in doing so, I did not want to join them.

'No, I'm going to do it,' I said and Lorraine smiled and nodded.

A Marine was now stationed on the platform. I hadn't seen him get up there, but now the first eager participant was climbing the ladder to join him. I forced myself to watch as he shinned up, making it look easy.

'Doesn't look too bad,' Lorraine said, trying to reassure me.

'Mmm.'

The man had now reached what appeared to me to be the most perilous part of the procedure - stepping from the ladder onto the platform across a gap of about twelve inches - although he had no problem. He strode across competently as if he were hopping over a puddle. He was steady and confident as he stood next to the instructor, who checked his harness and fastened it to the ropes. I watched him descend effortlessly, using his braking device to control his speed. There were calls of encouragement as he plunged downwards and a round of applause as his feet touched the floor. The whole thing had taken less than a couple of minutes.

I can do this, I thought. It's just a matter of a few minutes. Then it will be over.

The next person in line, a small blonde woman, was now halfway up the ladder.

'I think we'll be fine,' Lorraine said reassuringly. 'It looks straightforward.'

It was a fairly quick process and the queue ahead of us shortened steadily. I watched as abseilers made it to the ground one after the other without a hitch until I realised it was nearly our turn. Once again a wave of dread flushed over me. I turned my head away and took some deep breaths. I'd managed to calm myself a little when a piercing scream caused me to clutch at Lorraine as I looked to see the girl from the hair salon descending horizontally. She had somehow leaned too far back and had toppled over in mid-air so her head was lower than her feet. She yanked at the braking device, interrupting the flow of her descent and shrieked loudly at each jolt.

'Remember not to lean too far back,' Lorraine reminded me as I uttered a few swear words that I don't usually keep in my vocabulary.

And then we were at the front of the queue. I was tempted to push Lorraine and Nadine ahead of me, but a surge of adrenalin propelled me forwards. I had waited in fear long enough. If I had to do this thing I wanted to do it as fast as possible and get it over with.

'Me next,' I trilled.

Lorraine and Nadine watched in astonishment as I cantered off towards the instructor and gripped the base of the ladder. A curved safety rail arched behind me giving me the feeling of climbing up a tube as I slowly stepped on the first rung. I knew it was there as a safety barrier and that should have made me feel reassured, but being enveloped in the tubular steel framework made me claustrophobic. I suddenly felt hot and sickly. I began to stumble up the ladder as fast as I could, trying to escape the feeling of suffocation that was making my head spin. My heart clattered in my chest and I could feel a prickle of perspiration on my forehead. My foot faltered on one of the rungs and slipped down to the previous one causing me to bump my chin. My panic increased and I battled to climb higher, as if I were in one of those dreams where you're desperately trying to run but your feet are unexplainably rooted to the ground, giving maximum effort but making no headway.

'Steady there, lass,' the instructor called up to me. 'Where's the fire? Take your time.'

I made it to the top, my t-shirt damp against my back and my whole body shaking. The instructor waiting on the platform realised I was not going to step across to him and held out his hand.

'Reach across and I'll help you,' he said. 'Don't look down.'

Too late. I'd already looked. The upraised faces of the spectators swam about far below, waiting to see the spectacle I was about to perform. I saw Rosie in her pushchair and Lorraine's lyrics about strawberry jam pushed into my mind. The instructor, impatient at my hesitation called 'one, two, three, JUMP,' and I had no alternative as he pulled me firmly towards him.

I can still feel the shame now as I remember how I threw my arms around him, clinging limpet-like and whimpering as he fastened my harness to the rope.

'Step to the edge of the platform,' he commanded, peeling me from him.

I peered down below. The floor appeared to be a live thing, veering up towards me then sinking down, like the surging waves of a heaving sea. He held me by my upper arms and guided me so my back faced the crowd below.

'Now take a deep breath,' he told me.

'Deep breath...deep breath...'

'Lean back and let the device click into place.'

'Deep breath...deep breath...'

'Then let yourself fall backwards.'

'Deep breath...deep...' Let myself fall? From a forty foot high platform? Was he mad?

I could hear a murmur of voices below, and the realisation that the spectators thought I was going to chicken out spurred me into action. I took a deep breath, closed my eyes and jumped. I swung like a conker on a string, crashing back into the platform with a resounding clang as my knees collided with the metal edge. There was a collective gasp of horror from below and amongst it I heard the hysterical laughter of Rosie. Ignoring the pain in my knees, I used the braking device to control my speed and suddenly I was rushing through the air to the ground. I was high with relief when my feet touched the floor.

Peter came forward to hug me.

'Well done. You did it!'

'Yes I did, and I loved it! I loved swooping through the air, it was amazing!'

Rosie giggled. 'Mumma!' she said, and I lifted her from her chair and hugged her.

"Did you see what Mammy did? Yes, Mammy's clever isn't she?'

'Mumma funny,' she said and I laughed. I was flushed with the sense of invincibility that comes when you achieve something you never thought you could. It is worth experiencing the horrendous fear just to have that amazing sensation afterwards.

'Here's Lorraine coming down,' Peter said and I turned to watch her descend.

'That was fantastic!' she said.

'I know! I loved it!'

'Let's do it again.'

I didn't love it that much. I hobbled off to examine my bruised kneecaps, leaving Nadine and Lorraine to have as many turns as they liked.

CHAPTER FOURTEEN

We were always coming up with ideas to attract new customers, so when we saw a lecture advertised in the 'Healthfood Retailer' magazine which promised to show us 'easy and effective ways to increase sales in the health trade' we signed up immediately. The course was apparently formatted specifically for our business, although I'm sure most small shops could use the ideas. We returned full of enthusiasm to put the things we'd learned into practise.

Some were as simple as recommending additional items to customers when they purchased a product. I'd always felt a bit pushy doing this, but it worked well and customers were often pleased we'd taken the time to pick out things we thought they'd like.

One idea that appealed to us was to hold a children's drawing competition.

We'd been assured by the speaker at the retailers' event that this was the easiest, low-cost, minimum-effort way to promote our business and attract more customers. The idea was to invite local children to design 'healthy eating' posters which we should display in our window. Local schools and groups should be contacted and encouraged to take part. Prizes would be given for each age category. These we would obtain by asking for donations from local businesses, the incentive being that their services would be advertised in our window and mentioned in any press releases and radio stories covering the competition.

We managed to collect an impressive collection of prizes including toys, art equipment, swim vouchers and cinema tickets— I was surprised at how willingly items were donated.

Posters began to trickle in and I incorporated them in a window display. We contacted a local radio station and they mentioned our competition in their 'What's On' slot. It seemed the idea was working. The competition created a lot of publicity for our business.

Parents who brought children to deliver their entries often bought shopping. Many hadn't visited us before and were interested to find the delicious foods we stocked and no sign of the sawdust-type cereals and solid loaves of brown bread they expected.

But then a customer with connections to Newcastle United FC offered to get us a voucher for a tour of St James's Park and that's when the trouble started.

News of the NUFC prize spread, and entrants came thick and fast. The window space filled quickly, and I resorted to pegging the extras on lengths of string stretched across the shop walls.

A pack of one-hundred and fifty posters arrived from the local primary school.

'Where the hell am I going to put these?' I asked Lorraine.

'In the bin if I had my way.'

I'd used every possible area of wall space, there were posters strung along the counter front and on the sides of the fridges and back of the door. The shop looked a mess. The posters distracted from our stock and on breezy days fluttered to the floor with each opening of the door. I would put them to one side until I had a minute to peg them up.

'Just hoy them out,' Lorraine said.

But I couldn't. Behind each poster was a child hoping to win.

We were constantly harassed by parents asking, pleading and sometimes demanding their child's poster should be a winner. Some gave sob stories as to why their child needed to win, some gave veiled threats about ceasing to shop with us if the results were not pleasing. One woman even tried to bribe us with a bottle of wine, which I'm happy to say we refused (although I was tempted).

'You do know there'll be a riot when we eventually announce the winners?' Lorraine said. 'We'll be mobbed by unhappy parents.'

'I know. It's getting out of hand.' I fretted about how to choose the winners. There were so many entries. 'There are going to be a lot of disappointed children.'

'It's not disappointed children we have to worry about, it's angry parents.'

It was Peter who came up with a solution.

'Get someone else to judge. Someone with a bit of standing in the community who would relish the importance of making the decision.'

'Caroline,' Lorraine said.

'Caroline?'

'Yeah. She'll love it. She's a member of every busy-body committee around here, she's perfect.'

After protesting unconvincingly, claiming she was too busy, Caroline accepted the role and was obviously delighted. And so at the end of the month, the posters were stripped from the shop and sent to her. Her winning choices were exhibited in our window with her name as the judge clearly displayed. They were also featured in the local paper, alongside a photograph of Caroline, puffed up with self-importance as she posed next to the winning designs, meaning the losing parents knew exactly who to aim their complaints at.

Another idea that did not go well was producing healthy packed lunches for children. The idea sounded so simple when it was explained to us. Each day we would make up boxes containing a sandwich, a flapjack or similar 'healthy' cake, some raw vegetable sticks, a piece of fruit and a bottle of water. The type of sandwich filling and vegetables/fruit would differ depending what was in season and to give variety. Customers would subscribe to this service, paying upfront for a week at a time, the idea being they would collect the lunchboxes on the way to school.

Initially a rush of parents signed up to the service, happy their children would be eating a nutritious lunch and delighted it would save precious time in the mornings.

But then the requests began.

'If it's bananas can Alfie have an apple please because he doesn't like bananas? But only red apples, not green. He doesn't eat green food.'

'Megan needs to have white bread on Tuesdays because she goes to gym club after lunch and wholemeal bread gives her indigestion.'

'Joe likes green grapes but not red, and would you cut the crusts off his sandwiches because he doesn't like them?'

If I'd thought some of our customers were fussy they were nothing compared to our younger customers – or perhaps their parents.

Lettuce not shredded small enough, raisins too small, cherry tomatoes too large, hummus too lemony, paté too lumpy, carrot sticks too crunchy, not enough celery, too much celery, peaches too furry, satsumas too juicy, apples too appley... Needless to say it became too time consuming and complicated so after a short trial run, we ditched the idea.

The idea that lost us the most money was offering something free along with a best-selling item, the theory being that it is easier to increase sales of something already popular than build up interest in a little-known product.

At the talk, the speaker asked random audience members to name their best-selling product. He then suggested a suitable item to pair with it for a free offer. When we told him our sandwiches and lunchtime food constituted for about thirty percent of our sales, he immediately suggested we give away a free drink with each lunch purchased.

We put this into practice hoping our sandwich sales would increase. They didn't, although our expenses and work load did as we had to run about brewing drinks as well as making sandwiches. Most of the free drinks went to customers who shopped with us anyway, so nothing was gained there. We learned a lesson though. And that was to always take great care in the wording of our offers.

Our poster declared 'Free hot drink with every lunch' which we interpreted as 'You are entitled to one free hot drink with every sandwich purchased.' However, customers tried every possible variation of the poster's meaning. Several people claimed they were entitled to two free drinks as they were sharing a sandwich. Some bought a twelve-pence bread roll (our cheapest item at that time) and argued the poster did not state what constituted as a 'lunch'. Some people asked for a bottle of Purdey's or fruit juice instead of a hot drink, or even a cake or packet of crisps. One cheeky bugger said he couldn't face eating anything but could he have four free hot coffees for him and his mates who were suffering from hangovers?

From then on we abandoned the 'easy and effective ways to increase sales in the health food trade' and developed our own ideas.

We continued to offer free items, but only when suppliers gave us promotional materials to give away. T-shirts with the logo of a herbal tea merchant were awarded when ten boxes of herbal tea had been purchased and the relevant receipts presented to us. Other give-aways included cotton tote bags with organic cereal, hair combs with tea tree shampoos and conditioners, and chopsticks with packs of ramen noodles. The promise of a free gift prompted customers to buy extra items.

Give-aways were a great opportunity to design a window display. I could faff about for hours arranging and rearranging stock and props. Our window was an effective advertising tool. Facing the main street, it had a large platform with movable shelving giving lots of scope for different schemes. I built up a collection of baskets, wooden crates, boxes and sheets of coloured fabric so could assemble a themed design for any occasion.

We installed an electric socket at the side so we could put lamps in the window, or drape fairy lights across the shelves. Once we had a huge light-up globe we'd borrowed from a customer during a 'world foods' event, and another time had a miniature railway circling the window platform, the trains pulling trucks loaded with lentils and dried beans.

I always looked out for anything eye-catching I could include in a display, and over the years made windows displays incorporating a giant polystyrene snowman, a dolls' house, pots of growing bamboo, a tent and camping accessories, an old mangle and once a couple of dustbins to illustrate our recycling campaign.

The displays attracted a lot of attention and we received many comments - not always complementary – and were always a talking point on the bank. In fact, I reckon it was the most talked about shop window in Newcastle. After Fenwick's of course.

The current window had a 1970s theme. The others questioned the reason behind this and I'd had to admit there wasn't one except that my mam had recently cleared out the attic and found some of our old things and I really wanted to use them. I'd draped the display area with lots of orange fabric and aluminium foil as a background for Lorraine's old space hopper and set of weebles, my stylophone, the pairs of clackers that had bruised our wrists and a pair of hideous platform sandals I'd whinged for until my mam finally gave in. Reproduction posters from the decade and signs in bubble writing completed the look.

I confess the display had very little to do with our business, but it was bright and eye-catching and the customers loved it. We even had people bringing us memorabilia to add to it – a lava lamp, a plastic tomato-shaped ketchup dispenser, a sunflower-patterned coffee set, copies of Jackie magazine and various LP covers and posters.

Caroline however, was not impressed and came in especially to tell me.

'Oh my goodness, I saw all that junk in your window and I just had to come in to see what on earth had happened.'

'The only thing that has happened, Caroline, is I've changed the window display,' I said.

'Thank goodness for that. I thought you must have closed down and one of those awful charity shops taken over the premises. I didn't know what to think. Whatever possessed you to put a pile of old rubbish in your window?'

'It's just a few pieces of memorabilia.'

'In memory of what?'

'The seventies.'

'Christine, my dear, you must forgive me. I completely fail to see the link between the seventies and your establishment. I'm afraid I'm being terribly dim.' She gave a fake laugh so I gave one too. It was rather more enthusiastic than hers and her face immediately dropped into an expression of hostility. 'Perhaps some good sound business advice from a professional may help?' she suggested.

'Caroline, it may surprise you to know there is more to life than business. Our shop is about community and that window display has given people a lot of pleasure.'

'Really?'

'Yes, really. It's just a bit of fun. Fun Caroline. Do you know what that is?'

'Not seventies fun I'm afraid. I'm too young.'

That was such a blatant lie, I struggled to remain quiet but the awareness that this could so easily progress into another nasty argument stopped me from biting back, and taking the higher moral ground, I thanked Caroline for her concern.

I turned to the elderly woman who was now waiting at the counter.

'Hello, how may I help?'

The woman lifted a black binbag onto the counter. 'Just dropping off some old clothes for you to sell. I've plenty more to bring. I was going to take them to the RSPCA shop on the High Street but this is much more convenient.'

CHAPTER FIFTEEN

Lorraine and I loved ordering new products. If we got wind of something new in the health food trade we had to have it. The Karma catalogue, mailed to us four times a year, featured a 'new stock' section. Often, there was an offer of free stock to allow customers to sample before buying, and we would take advantage of this as we aimed to hold a tasting event every Saturday morning.

A table would be set up at on the shop floor with the new product displayed along with the free samples. Posters in the window and our chalkboard outside let customers know which products we were offering that week.

Reaction to the tasting would vary, activating a discussion amongst customers. We noted that when it came to trying something new, people were very sheep-like. Sales would ebb and flow depending upon the remarks of the tasters. A comment such as 'that's delicious' would produce a scramble of customers eager to hand over their money, whereas a 'no, don't like it' would deter people from even taking a sample. If we heard a negative comment, we'd nudge each other muttering 'bad sheep' and subtly move in to divert the customer away from the product, distracting their attention to avoid losing more sales. 'Good sheep' were customers who encouraged other shoppers encountered on their morning errands to pay us a visit for a free sample. On a good day with a popular product, word would spread and other sheep would flock in to make sure they didn't miss out. Sometimes we'd sell out of stock, which made it all the more desirable and we'd start an order list, taking payment in advance.

One of our customers, Mr Boothby, was meticulous in his scrutiny of our free samples. He would arrive early each Saturday with a notebook, eager to examine the goods. He was a rotund man, always dressed in a checked three-piece suit and cravat. He had a waxed moustache, carefully curled at each side of his face which gave him a comical look, although I'm sure it wasn't his intention.

He was a jovial man and I found him pleasant and enjoyed his conversations, but his flowery language and flamboyant mannerisms irritated the life out of Lorraine.

It was impossible for him to arrive unnoticed. Even the bell on the door jangled louder than usual as he entered, announcing his arrival with a loud, cheery greeting.

On this particular Saturday, I was setting up the table with cartons of rice milk and sample glasses when he arrived.

'Aw gawd, here he comes, the big buffoon,' Lorraine said as he marched past the window, cane in hand and notebook tucked beneath his arm.

He entered the shop with vigour, bursting through the door and traumatising our poor shop bell, looking like the villain from a pantomime as he twiddled the end of his moustache. I always half expected him to say something like 'Mwah-ha-ha! At last I have you in my clutches,' or some such thing, but he'd invariably say the same words.

'Good morning ladies. And what fine offerings do you extend this glorious morning for my perusal?' He strode to the counter where he graced us with a small bow.

Lorraine gave a 'harrumph' of annoyance.

'Good morning,' I said. 'We have rice milk today, a new alternative to dairy milk.'

'Excellent!' It's difficult to explain how much expression he managed to put into one word. I found it amusing but Lorraine snorted and went off into the kitchen to find something to do to avoid having to speak to him.

His first undertaking was to thoroughly examine the packaging, taking out an eye-glass which he held in place by squinting his eye. This had the effect of lowering a bushy eyebrow on one side of his face, and raising the swirl of moustache on the other. It suddenly came to me that he reminded me of Hercule Poirot, and I stifled a giggle.

He nodded and mumbled to himself as he made notes in his book. Occasionally he'd look up and announce his findings.

'Perfectly acceptable salt content,' he said, prompting a couple of customers to join him in examining the rice milk. 'Organically produced, now that's the ticket.' The two women bought a carton each and after taking the money, I whispered to Lorraine:

'See! He's a good sheep.'

'Yeah I know, but he gets on my nerves.'

He stayed for ages, studying items on the shelves and asking questions. He always made a few purchases but only after 'finding out the far ends of a fart' as Lorraine put it.

'I wish he'd bugger off,' she muttered, as he stood at our bookshelves, making a note of the book titles in his notebook.

'Ah, leave him alone, he's harmless.'

The morning was busy, lots of people came to do a 'big shop' on Saturday mornings and customers would call in to collect things they'd ordered through the week.

Customers had more time to browse and ask questions, and we welcomed this, knowing that if they felt unrushed and relaxed, they'd be more likely to try something new. We also tended to sell less cold sandwiches as most of the local offices were closed, but more of the hot ones as people treated themselves to a breakfast sandwich, so one of us would volunteer to stay at the hot plate to do the cooking.

The demand for breakfast sandwiches slowed down as we approached midday, by which time the aroma of hot food and fresh bread would make our stomachs rumble, and we'd take the largest wholemeal stotties we could find from the bread shelf and fill them with veggie sausages, fried egg, tempeh 'bacon', mushrooms, tomatoes, home-made hash-browns and baked beans. A swirl of ketchup finished off what came to be known as Stuff-Ya-Kite Stotties.

I never liked to eat in the shop front while customers were browsing, but Mr Boothby was hanging around as usual, so I sat in the kitchen and try to nibble daintily on my huge sandwich without dropping bits on the floor or down my front. He was still working his way through the books when Maureen called in.

Dressed in an old raincoat with a headscarf tied beneath her chin she looked far from the exotic Mariana who contacted spirits and foretold the future.

'Hi Maureen,' I said. 'We weren't expecting you today.'

'No. I'm on me way to the chemist for some haemorrhoid ointment. Eeh, I'm in agony. I thought I'd pop in to say I'm free this Friday evening if you want to go ahead with the séance?'

I was about to mumble some excuse as to why it wouldn't be a good time, but Lorraine got in first, telling Maureen she'd let everyone know and asking what time we should start.

'I'll get here at about ten-thirty,' she said. 'Spirits are always more active after midnight so that will give me time to tune in and familiarise myself with any entities before we start.'

I wish she wouldn't say 'entities'. That sounded even worse than ghosts or spirits.

'Everyone else can get here a bit later and I'll start the sitting at about twelve. Well I say sitting, although I don't know if I'll be able to sit, might have to be the first séance I do standing up. I tell you, I've never felt pain like it.'

Mr Boothby, who I'd noticed had become less interested in the books and more concerned with listening to our conversation, stepped forward, dipped his head and spoke.

'Excuse me, madam. I may be able to help you. I have a great deal of experience in this area.'

'Piles?' Maureen said loudly. 'Suffer from them too, do you dear? I tell you, mine are horrendous. Like a protruding bunch of grapes...'

'No, no, no!' Mr Boothby held up a hand to halt Maureen in her tracks. 'I meant in the area of supernatural activity. If I heard correctly, I believe you are going to host a séance?'

'That's right,' Maureen said. 'We have a lost spirit in this very building, possibly going by the name of Elvis, although that has yet to be clarified. We're going to contact it on Friday evening to see if we can help.'

Mr Boothby held out a hand to Maureen and gave a little bow.

101

'Then let me introduce myself. Gerald Boothby, retired civil servant and part-time paranormal investigator.'

Maureen took his hand, 'Oh how lovely.'

I'd never seen her so flustered and I'm sure she even blushed.

'My dear lady, let us retreat to the Saffron Café and discuss the matter over a refreshing cup of tea.'

Maureen looked him up and down, then up and down again.

'Don't mind if I do.'

He opened the shop door and with a tip of his hat, escorted Maureen out.

We watched them cross the road, arm in arm, Mr Boothby strutting along like a peacock and Maureen treading gingerly, presumably because of her grape-like protrusions.

'Did you know he was a paranormal investigator?' Nadine asked.

'No,' Lorraine said. 'But then I never speak to him if I can help it.'

'Well you're going to have to speak to him on Friday, it looks like he's going to be part of this bloody stupid séance,' I said.

'Bloody stupid séance?' Nadine said. 'That's not very encouraging.'

'I don't want to encourage it. I'm dead against it.'

Nadine looked shocked. 'This is our chance to help Elvis find the light,' she said.

CHAPTER SIXTEEN

I awoke on Friday morning with a vague sense of anxiety niggling in the back of my mind and then I remembered. Today was the day of the séance.

I don't remember much about what happened that day, except it passed slowly, the way it does when you have a dental appointment looming.

We eventually closed and cashed up, planning to meet back at the shop at eleven.

'I'll pick Maureen up on the way,' Lorraine told us.

'Keep an eye on her,' I told her. 'Make sure she doesn't plant any false evidence or anything.'

My mam had eagerly agreed to have Rosie for the night. She made it quite clear she was against the idea of a séance, but jumped at the chance for her and my dad to have their granddaughter overnight.

'Hello Rosie Posie,' she said, holding out her arms to take her. Rosie smiled, her face lighting up.

'Mommar!' She reached out, Funny Bunny grasped tightly in her fist and wrapped her arms about her grandma's neck. Peter carried in the huge bag of paraphernalia necessary for a small child and my dad took it from him.

'So what's this carry-on you're doing tonight?' Mam asked me as Peter removed Rosie's coat and chatted to Dad. 'Some sort of a séance?'

'Sort of,' I said, trying to play it down. I knew she thought it was ridiculous, and to be honest a part of me agreed with her. 'Maureen's doing it, we're just going along to watch.'

'Maureen? Is that the daft bugger who thinks she can talk to dead people?'

I hesitated, but she didn't wait for me to answer.

'Well I think you all must be off your heads, sitting in a shop in the middle of the night when you should be in bed. A séance! Pah! What a whole load of rubbish.' She continued in this vein for a while, trying to draw my dad into joining her, and when he eventually said that although he didn't believe in those sort of things, we were old enough and daft enough to do what we wanted, she changed tack and agreed with him, saying she wasn't one to interfere.

'Just be careful,' she told us. 'There could be strange people out and about at that time of night.'

'Yeah. Like us' Peter told her.

At home I went into the kitchen to prepare dinner although I wasn't sure if I'd be able to each much. My stomach was gnawing with dread.

'Why are you so worried if you don't believe in any of it?' Peter asked as we chopped vegetables for a curry. 'It will just be us lot sitting in the dark, mucking about and having a laugh. I can't see us taking it seriously.'

I wasn't so sure.

'I think Mr Boothby will take it seriously,' I said, and Peter laughed.

'Yeah, you're right, he will. I can't wait! It's going to be a right lark.'

'Stay next to me. And no pulling any tricks either.'

'I did think of it,' Peter said. 'But we've all promised Maureen.'

Maureen had been clear about what she expected from us.

'I don't want any arsing about,' she'd told us. 'This is a serious matter. We have a spirit in distress who needs our assistance. I want no-one making silly noises or knocking sounds and no deliberately pushing the glass or trying to lift the table with your knees.'

Peter had looked disappointed. He'd probably been going to do all of those.

I served the curry and put the plates onto trays so we could eat in front of the television. I thought it might take my mind off the ordeal ahead.

'Blimey, how much garlic have you put in here?' Peter asked as he took the first forkful.

'Loads. I thought it might be a good idea for tonight.'

'It's a ghost we're going to be meeting, not a vampire.'

'Yeah, well. I'm not taking any chances.'

We sat in front of the television and I flicked through the channels, nothing really taking my interest. There were just the usual soaps or yet another documentary about the OJ Simpson trial.

'Load of rubbish on here,' I grumbled. I eventually settled for a comedy with Pauline Quirke. Normally, I found her funny but I was too anxious to concentrate. I watched it half-heartedly until Peter looked at his watch and said we'd better be making a move.

I switched off the lamps, leaving only one burning near the window and plumped up the cushions. My sofa had never looked so warm and inviting. I'll be back soon, I told it silently.

The shop had a different atmosphere at night time. During the day, light poured in through the large window, reflecting off the clean white walls and giving warmth to the wooden shelves and counter, but now, beneath fluorescent light, the shop had lost its personality. There was an unfamiliar muteness, gone were the daytime sounds of chattering, whirring kitchen implements and the constant blare of Radio One. The door and the shop bell were conspicuous in their silence, the till lying with its cash drawer empty and still.

'Brr! It's cold in here,' I said to Lorraine and Georgina, who were standing in the kitchen, their hands wrapped around steaming mugs of tea. 'Been here long?'

'About half an hour. Maureen's in the therapy room getting ready.'

I took 'getting ready' to mean putting on her wig of wild black curls, thick layer of make-up and rings of black kohl around her eyes, as well as draping herself in layers of floaty fabric and scarves.

'She'll terrify any ghosts for miles around in that wig she wears,' Georgina said.

'You're on your best behaviour, remember,' Lorraine told her. 'Be nice and if you can't be nice, be quiet.'

'I'll try. But it's bound to be a load of tosh.'

'So why are you here?'

'Wouldn't miss it for the world. If it's as hilarious as the reading she gave me it'll be a scream.' The fact that Georgina was so down to earth about it all quelled my fear a little.

'Behave yourself,' I told her. 'And don't start sniggering and giggling.'

Georgina grinned but didn't answer.

'Anyone for another cuppa?' Lorraine asked.

Peter had a cup of tea but I declined. I didn't want to have to climb the stairs to the lavatory once the séance had started and Elvis was lurking about in the shadows.

The shop had been set up in preparation for the séance. The shelves had been pushed back and a circular table stood in the centre of the floor, surrounded by nine seats made up of the two tub chairs from the therapy room, four shop stools, the office chair, an upturned wooden crate and the space hopper from the window display. Aileen's Ouija board was in the centre of the table with a glass tumbler, and a few unlit candles were dotted about.

I made a mental note to be fast to the table so I could purloin a comfortable seat, preferably the office chair and definitely not the space hopper.

Mr Boothby was next to arrive. After greeting us all in his usual portentous way, he proceeded to place three tennis balls on the floor.

'This is a little test I like to set up,' he told us. 'I'm going to draw a chalk circle around these balls. Then if anything moves them, we shall be able to detect it.'

'Are you expecting them to move?' Lorraine asked him.

'I live in hope, my dear. One day a spirit will indulge me in my whim and disturb my balls.'

Peter suddenly developed a choking fit and rushed into the kitchen to get a glass of water.

'I also have an audio tracking device that I will set in action at the beginning of the séance.' His audio tracking device looked to me very much like the radio cassette recorder I'd used during my teenage years to record the top twenty from Radio One.

I could hear Peter, still coughing and clearing his throat, so I went into the kitchen.

'You okay?'

'Yeah.' He didn't look it to me. He was red in the face and kept spluttering and his eyes were watering.

We joined the others in the shop front to find Aileen had arrived. She was practically quivering with excitement.

'This is amazing,' she said. 'I really hope we're able to make contact, do you?'

'Let's just say I won't be disappointed if we don't,' I told her.

Nadine arrived next, I saw she was wearing a crucifix and I was about to make a joke when I noticed her expression. I'd expected her to be in a similar state of eagerness to Aileen, but she was subdued, looking close to tears.

'You okay?' I asked.

'Yeah,' she said uncertainly. 'I've changed my mind now I'm here. It sounded like a fun idea earlier but now that it's dark...' She looked around the shop and shivered.

'Nothing to be scared of,' Aileen told her. 'Nothing at all. The dead can't hurt us. And after all...aaarrghhhh!' Her scream of terror was joined by one from Nadine as they stared with expressions of horror to the window behind me. I turned, filled with dread at what might have caused such a reaction, and involuntarily found myself joining them in their screeching as a ghostly apparition of Elvis lingered at the door.

'What the hell...' Peter said, stepping forward to open the door.

'Wella howdy folks, how y'all doin'?'

'Nige! What do you think you're playing at? You scared us all senseless.'

'Am I the only one who's made the effort? I thought we were all dressing as Elvis.' He looked around, checking out our outfits. 'I feel ridiculous now.'

Lorraine and Georgina, who had come to see what all the screaming was, fell about in hysterics. Dressed in a black wig with his bony wrists protruding from a too-small flared white suit, Nige looked like an emaciated Elvis impersonator. His trousers were far too small, embarrassingly tight at the crotch and ending mid-calf, revealing stick legs and oversized blue suede shoes.

'I bet I look like a proper ninny,' Nige said.

'More like an improper ninny in those trousers,' Peter said, and we averted our eyes.

'Blimey Nige!' Georgina said. 'You'll do yourself a mischief in those.'

'Where on earth did you get it from?' Lorraine asked.

'I borrowed it especially for tonight, actually,' Nige said tetchily.

'Who from? A midget?' Georgina laughed.

Mr Boothby did not find Nige's outfit amusing.

'I hope you realise this is a serious matter. It's not a fancy dress party.'

Nige was offended by this and became petulant, mincing about and justifying his choice of outfit in a very theatrical manner. This rekindled Peter's choking fit which only worsened when Mr Boothby complained that Nige had accidently kicked his balls.

'Pull yourself together,' I told him as he sniggered and snorted. I wished we could get started and get the whole thing over and done with.

'Maureen's almost ready,' Lorraine called. 'She's asked us to turn off the lights and light the candles. We all need to take a seat at the table.'

Mr Boothby lit the candles and Lorraine switched off the overhead lights. The candles cast a weak light across the table, everywhere else was black. I clutched at Peter's hand. I felt the steady pounding of my heart and I wondered why on earth I'd allowed myself to be part of this.

Nadine, who'd given a small yelp when the lights went out, moved closer to me.

'I've changed my mind, I don't want to do it,' she whispered. I could feel her shaking and could almost smell the fear radiating from her. Strangely her panic gave me courage and I took her arm.

'Don't worry it'll be fine, come and sit next to me and Peter.'

She huddled close to me and we shuffled towards the table. It was suggested the office chair should be left for Maureen so I headed for a tub chair. Peter took the tub chair next to me with Nadine next to him perched on the upturned crate. The others settled themselves on the stools, leaving the space hopper for Nige.

None of us spoke. We made a strange group sitting around the table in silence, candlelight illuminating us from below, giving us weirdly shadowed faces.

I'd done some ridiculous things in my life but this was probably the winner. I looked around the circle, Nadine shaking visibly and mouthing a silent prayer as she held her crucifix, Aileen with her eyes closed in some form of meditation, Georgina and Lorraine waiting expectantly, Mr Boothby's expression concealed in shadow, Peter still coughing spasmodically to hide his mirth and Nige in his Elvis wig, perched on a space hopper.

To top it all, the therapy room door flew open and 'Mariana' appeared, her wild wig and upheld arms in silhouette, looking like a cross between Cruella de Vil and Siouxsie Sioux.

CHAPTER SEVENTEEN

We all turned to look at Maureen who held her pose a little longer, to be certain of maximum impact. With a sweep of her arms and a billowing of silk scarves, she walked majestically towards the table.

'I am Mariana, seer of the unseen and perceiver of what is and what is yet to be,' she announced, in the deep voice she used when portraying Mariana. Unfortunately the effect was blighted somewhat as she stumbled on Mr Boothby's balls and yelled 'Eeh shit'.

Peter, who had never seen Maureen as Mariana, collapsed over the table in muffled hysteria until I kicked his shin beneath the table, a little harder than I meant to, making him swiftly come to his senses.

Mr Boothby, however, was in awe.

'My word, the woman is magnificent!' he gasped, and Maureen shushed him, although I'm sure she was delighted at his reaction.

She took her place at the table and slowly looked around. She stared each of us in the eye, nodding her head slowly in an unsmiling, rather sinister manner. I found it quite menacing to be honest. When she came to Nige, she did a double take but quickly regained her composure.

I regretted choosing a tub chair now, as they were fairly low and I felt like a child who'd been allowed to sit at the dining table with the grown-ups. It was better than the space hopper though, which was even lower. Nige was straddled over it, his knees pointing upwards, making his rhinestone-studded flares rise even further up his legs.

'Let us join hands and begin,' Maureen instructed and we did as she said. I was between Peter and Lorraine and I grasped their hands tightly.

'Friends, we are here to communicate and assist a brother or sister from the spirit world,' Maureen said. 'We ask for protection as the souls of the past move among us. I ask all seated at this table to visualise a white light surrounding and protecting us.'

Maureen paused. I shivered and silently asked the spirits not to bother visiting us tonight. I looked around the circle. The atmosphere was grave, faces solemn. Nadine looked positively terrified and so did Nige. Aileen's eyes were wide in concentration and even Lorraine and Georgina looked serious. From where I sat, Mr Boothby's face was just a black shape but I could see Peter's clearly in the candlelight and was surprised to see how intense he now looked. Seemingly, he was over his coughing fit.

'And now I ask any souls present to move among us...' (At this point, in my head I yelled 'No! please don't') '...and be guided by the light and love of this world.'

Maureen paused then asked the million-dollar question.

'Is there anybody there?'

I alternatively strained my ears for sounds of ghostly activity and then sang loudly in my head to block out any possible noises I knew would scare me senseless.

After a couple of seconds, Maureen repeated the question. We sat, tense and silent, and as the seconds passed, relief relaxed my body as no answer came to Maureen's query. I had just given Peter's hand a sneaky little squeeze when I stiffened in fear as a low buzz sounded across the table. There were sharp intakes of breath as we strained to listen.

'Come forward O Spirit, reveal yourself to us' Maureen said and Mr Boothby cleared his throat apologetically.

'Ahem. Afraid that was me. Hearing aid battery appears to be depleted. So sorry, awful timing.' He fiddled with his ear, removed the device and put it in his pocket. 'Don't have a spare unfortunately, but I'll manage. My right ear is fine but, I'm afraid I'm as deaf as a post on the left.'

'Not to worry,' Aileen said, and we all muttered that it was no problem, even though we'd all nearly pooped with fright. We all settled down and once again Maureen asked if there was anyone present.

After the third repetition brought no results, Maureen told us she was sensing nothing at all from the spirit world.

'Although I am sensing the smell of garlic.'

'Me too!' Aileen said, and the others muttered in agreement.

'Sorry, that'll be us,' Peter said.

'Oh,' Maureen said. 'I thought perhaps it was a sign from the spirit. Nothing at all then.'

Great, I thought. Time to go home to my bed. I was about to feign great disappointment but Maureen had other ideas.

'Let us join energies across the Ouija and call upon our spirit friend to communicate.' She told us to each rest one finger lightly on the base of the glass that stood in the centre of Aileen's home-made board. Maureen closed her eyes and took a deep breath.

'Is there anybody there?'

'Pardon?' Mr Boothby said, and Maureen explained, not too patiently that she was calling out to the lost soul in our midst and added that this was the second time he had interrupted the proceedings.

'I'm so sorry, my dear lady. Perhaps I should sit on your left and then I can take advantage of my working auricle.'

'Perhaps you should.'

There was a bit of shuffling about as seats were moved and places swapped and once again we all settled down.

'Right. Are we all ready?' Maureen snapped, forgetting for a moment to use Mariana's voice. She closed her eyes and took a deep breath and was about to commence when once again Mr Boothby spoke.

'I say, I'm so sorry, I completely forgot to switch on my audio tracking device.' He rose from the table and held onto the counter for guidance as he stumbled across the shop floor, while Maureen huffed and puffed her displeasure.

'I'm afraid I'm a little unfamiliar with the layout out of the premises... oh dear, I believe I've nudged my balls with my toe.'

'Never mind your balls, hurry up, it'll be morning soon at this rate,' Maureen said, except she pronounced it 'baahlls' with a Geordie infliction. It was unnerving the way she fluctuated from Maureen to Mariana without warning.

After a bit of fumbling about, his voice came out of the darkness.

'Testing, testing, one, two, three. This is Gerald Boothby, reporting from Nutmeg Wholefoods, Station Road. The time is precisely...oh, I say...what is the time precisely?'

'Get back over here, man,' Maureen barked.

Oh dear. I'd been hoping there might be a bit of a romance between those two but he seemed to be irritating the life out of her. Although, then again, maybe that was a good sign for a lasting relationship.

We waited in silence, our fingers touching the glass. Reaching from my low position in the tub chair was uncomfortable and my arm began to ache. This is ridiculous, I thought. How long were we going to sit like this waiting for something to happen? I changed my position so I could use my other hand to support my elbow.

Suddenly, Maureen took a great intake of breath, threw back her head and in a booming voice said something that sounded like 'Haawassa manna manna. Berrigus originus, haawassa wassa.'

We looked at each other in confusion, then Mr Boothby whispered 'She has spaketh in tongues.'

Maureen's head lolled about alarmingly.

'Haawassa manna manna. Berrigus originus, haawassa wassa.'

Christ, I thought. You couldn't make this up.

And then, to my absolute horror, slowly, the glass began to move.

CHAPTER EIGHTEEN

'It's moving!' someone whispered, I'm not sure who. My heart moved up my chest into my throat, I'm sure I could feel it pulsating in my gullet.

Terrified, I tore my eyes from the glass that was circling slowly in the centre of the ring of letters and looked at the faces staring with disbelief, excitement, and in Nige's case, absolute horror. Maureen was puffed up like a prize chicken.

'We welcome you to our gathering, O Spirit. Please give us your name.'

As we watched, the glass ceased its circling and began to move back and forth amongst the letters.

'What is your name, O Spirit?' Maureen asked again. We read the letters in unison as the glass moved steadily across the board.

'B...L...A...M...P...T'

The glass stopped moving.

'Blampt?'

'Blampt? What does that mean?'

'Is it a foreign word?'

'Trust us to get a dyslexic ghost.' This from Georgina.

'Blampt. Does that mean anything to anybody?'

'Isn't it a lampshade from Ikea?'

'Maybe it spaketh in tongues?' This from Peter.

'Silence!' Maureen demanded. 'Please remember, it is I, Mariana, seer of the unseen and perceiver of what is and what is yet to be, who is leading this interaction.'

We fell silent and replaced our index fingers on the glass.

'We mortals did not understand your message O Spirit,' Maureen said. 'Please try again. Please tell us your name.' The glass set off again, moving so swiftly it was difficult for me to keep my finger in place.

'E...L...V...I...T...H.'

'Elvith?' Maureen repeated.

'I knew it!' Nadine said. 'I knew it was Elvis.'

'Actually, it's Elvith,' Peter said. 'He seems to have developed a lisp since he passed over.'

'Is your name Elvith?' Maureen asked.

'Y...E...T...H.'

'Yeth? Do you mean yes?'

'Y...E...T...H.'

'Why's he speaking with a lisp?' Aileen whispered, and a thought occurred to me.

'There's no 'S',' I said.

'That's right!' said Aileen. 'I missed it out and put two 'M's on didn't I?' Her face glowed in the candlelight. 'Ask it! Ask it if it's because I've missed the 'S' off.'

Maureen breathed deeply.

'O Spirit who giveth the name of Elvith. Are you saying yeth instead of yes because Aileen missed an 'S' off the board and put two 'M's on instead?'

It occurred to me that if we were genuinely making contact with someone who had died and come back in spirit form, it was a ridiculous question to be wasting time on.

'Y...E...T...H.'

'Yeth,' Aileen repeated. 'You see, it is Elvis after all.'

'Ask it what its other name is,' Georgina said, and before Maureen had a chance to repeat the question, the glass was off.

'P...R...E...T...H...L...E...Y.'

'It is!' Aileen hissed, excitedly. 'It's him!'

'Elvith Prethley?' Peter said.

'It really is Elvis, here in our shop!' Aileen whispered. 'I really can't believe it.'

No. Me neither. I didn't have a clue what was going on but I knew for certain we were not in the presence of Elvis Presley's spirit.

'Shouldn't we be asking more meaningful questions?' I asked in a hushed voice. 'I mean, if there really is a spirit here it's our chance to find out about the afterlife.'

'What would you like me to ask?' Maureen asked.

'Ask what Heaven is like,' I said. Maureen puffed herself up again with a great intake of breath.

'Oh Spirit, in preparation for our eventual demise, we humbly and respectfully ask, what is Heaven like?'

We watched eagerly as the glass stirred.

'N...I...C...E.'

Nice? I'd been hoping for a bit more than that.

'The energy will be dropping soon,' Maureen said quietly. 'I need to ask for messages before he has to leave.' She raised her voice. 'I humbly ask, O Spirit, do you have a message for anyone present?'

'Y...E...T...H.'

We were all jittery now, even the more cynical amongst us were on the edge of our seats. (Or space hopper as the case may be.)

'And who, O Spirit, is the message for?'

'C...H...R...I...T...H.'

Shit. I took my finger off the glass and was immediately ordered by Maureen to replace it so as not to break the circle of energy.

'Chrith? Oh it means Chris...'

'Chris?'

'It's Chris...'

'Chris, it's for you...'

My name was repeated around the circle as I was told what I already knew. I was the chosen one. Elvith had a message for me.

'I don't want a message,' I gabbled. 'I'm fine just to say hello, and I'm touched it was me you wanted to talk to but...'

'Silence!' bellowed Maureen.

I was silent. Eight pairs of eyes turned to look at me, some filled with envy and others with relief and I broke out in an instant sweat.

She's loving this, I thought as Maureen rolled her eyes to the ceiling.

'What is the message, O Spirit?'

There was a simultaneous movement as everyone - except me - leaned forwards expectantly. I shrunk back into my seat forcing myself to keep my eyes on the glass. Slowly it began to move, forging a route from letter to letter.

'R...I...T...H...E.'

Rithe? I thought. What's that supposed to mean? What was Elvith trying to tell me? Did he mean writhe? Or right? Or maybe rise? I was about to ask if anyone had any clue as to what it meant when the glass took off again.

'E...V...E...R...Y...O...N...E.'

'Rise everyone,' Maureen said, and we all obeyed and got to our feet. 'No, no, I was just repeating the message,' she said and so we all sat down.

'Then again, perhaps that's what he wants us to do.' Once again we all stood.

'Do you wish us to stand, O Spirit?' Maureen asked. The glass shot across the circle from N to O.

'No,' we chorused, and sat. As I settled into my seat, I felt something brush my leg and I screamed.

'There's something under the table,' I shrieked, causing everyone to stand once again. Georgina looked at Mr Boothby accusingly and I must admit I'd had a similar suspicion but both of his hands had been above the table.

'I felt it too.' Nadine's voice was shrill. 'It touched my knee.' She cowered and clung to Peter as we all stood back from the table in fear. Georgina was braver.

'I'll find out what *or who* it is,' she said and thrust her hand beneath the table only to withdraw it with a shout. 'What the hell is *that*...?' She shuddered as she shook her hand and wiped it on her coat it as if to rid it of some unspeakable thing. 'It felt like a big...ugh...'

'Like a big what?' Nadine squeaked.

There were gasps of horror and confusion and then Nige spoke.

'Don't panic, it's me. It's my spacehopper. It rolled off.' He retrieved it from beneath the table, dragging it by one of its horn-like rubber handles.

'Nige man!' Nadine said. 'You nearly scared me to death.'

'Keep hold of that thing, would you?' I said, as he was berated by the group for scaring us all.

'It's not easy you know, sitting on a spacehopper in a pair of tight trousers,' he said huffily.

Once we had settled down, Maureen addressed Elvith in her deep Mariana voice.

'We apologise for the interruption, O Spirit. Is there anything else you wish to tell us?' The glass remained stationary so she tried speaking in tongues again, accompanied with some head lolling and eye rolling.

'Haawassa manna manna. Berrigus originus haawassa wassa.'

'It's moving,' Aileen announced excitedly.

'N...O.'

Thank God for that, I thought, although I heard sighs of disappointment from Aileen and Mr Boothby.

'Are you sure, O Spirit?'

'Y...E...T...H... M...A...N'

'Yes man? He seems to be getting irritated with us,' Peter said. 'Elvith Prethley, the irritated Geordie ghost.'

'SILENCE!' Maureen bawled. 'I need to guide him to the light before the energy goes.' She closed her eyes. 'I need you all to keep your fingers on the glass and concentrate. Imagine the spirit moving towards the light. Keep concentrating as I make contact.'

We waited in silence as she composed herself.

'We thank you for your message, O Spirit, and we ask you to look to the light and move towards it.' At this the glass began to rotate, circling the ring of letters as it built up speed.

'Look to the light, look to the light,' Maureen repeated as the glass hurtled round and round, until suddenly it shot across the table and over its edge, hitting the floor and shattering into fragments.

A hush fell over us, and then Maureen opened her eyes. 'Mission accomplished. Elvith has left the building.

CHAPTER NINETEEN

The next morning I had several false starts before I finally managed to get out of bed. We'd returned after two o'clock last night, and I'd been so hyped up I'd been unable to fall asleep. I'd lain in bed going over and over the events of the night, putting forward questions and ideas to Peter, without waiting for his response. My head was full of conflicting theories, jumping from one to another, trying to order my thoughts and make sense of it all.

What had caused the glass to move? A message from a spirit or some sort of explainable phenomena? Vibration of some sort? Had we been jointly responsible for subconsciously moving it? It had been difficult to maintain the right amount of pressure, perhaps we'd each unknowingly pushed from different directions, causing the glass to travel from letter to letter. But then again, if it was a message from 'the other side' what did it mean and who was it from? Why had the name Elvis been used? And what did 'Rise Everyone' mean?

Peter finally told me to shut up and I eventually fell into a restless sleep plagued with strange dreams.

The morning cast a different light on it all. I was now more intrigued than scared. I'd always been open-minded about Maureen's supposed 'gift' but also felt I needed evidence before I would fully believe. Last night had not dispelled my doubts. If anything, I was more convinced that something other than a spirit had moved the glass.

As expected, it was the first thing Lorraine and I spoke about as we opened the shop.

'I don't believe it was a spirit for a minute,' Lorraine said as she dropped coins into the till. 'There must be a logical explanation.'

I stepped into the window to open the blinds before turning the sign on the door to 'Open'.

'You gave the impression you did last night. You were as scared as the rest of us.'

'Exactly. It was all psychological. In the dark with Maureen doing her heebie-jeebie antics, we all got so hyped up and scared we were ready to believe anything.'

'So how do you account for the glass moving?'

'I don't know. But I sure as Hell know it wasn't the spirit of Elvis Presley moving it.'

'Elvith Prethley,' I corrected.

Nadine arrived, and went into the office to take off her coat.

'You okay?' I asked.

'Yeah,' she said, although she looked tired and was very subdued, definitely not her usual chirpy self.

'We're talking about last night,' I told her. 'What did you think of it all?'

Nadine shook her head. 'I don't know.' She sighed heavily then climbed the steps to wash her hands.

Lorraine and I looked at each other.

'You sure you're okay?' Lorraine asked. 'I thought you'd be dying to get here to talk about what happened.'

'I was hoping we could forget about it,' Nadine said. She descended the steps and went to the till. Taking out a couple of notes, she picked up one of our wire baskets and headed to the door. 'Just the usual from Derek's?' she asked, and went off to buy salad and vegetables.

'What's up with her?' Lorraine said as the door closed behind her, the bell jangling noisily.

'No idea. She was very scared last night, I think she regretted coming. Maybe it was too much for her.' The door opened and I looked up. 'Hi Aileen, what are you doing in this morning?'

'I know it's not my shift today, but I was so excited after last night, I just wanted to come in to see what you all had to say about it.' Her eyes were bright as they darted between us. 'I'll put my things away then I'll make us a brew.' She put her coat and bag in the office then set about making tea. She hummed to herself as she poured hot water into the teapot.

121

'You're happy this morning,' I said.

She handed me a cup of tea.

'I am. I'm thrilled at the evidence we got last night. I knew as soon as I started working here this place was haunted. I could sense it. And then last night, well, who would have believed it? We've had solid proof of the existence of the after-life! The more I think about it, the better it gets.'

'That's probably because every time she thinks of it she exaggerates it in her head,' Lorraine whispered as Aileen greeted a customer.

Aileen stayed at the counter while Lorraine and I assembled utensils and dishes. As she chatted to a customer, I heard her describing a scene which I took to be from a ghost film until Lorraine nudged me and I realised Aileen was giving her highly embellished version of our séance.

'Just you wait,' Lorraine said. 'The story will grow and grow until we've had poltergeists flinging bags of lentils about and Beelzebub showing up to barter for our souls.'

I wasn't happy about Aileen discussing it with customers, whether it was the true version of events or otherwise. Maureen's psychic readings had caused enough controversy locally – several customers had objected, saying we were messing with things we didn't understand and there'd been a one-woman protest accusing us of 'cavorting with the devil'. If it got out we'd held a séance in the building, there'd bound to be more trouble.

I spoke to Aileen and tactfully suggested it might be best if we didn't mention the séance to anyone as it might affect business.

'I have to warn you,' I told her, 'Nadine is a little upset this morning, it might not be a good idea to scare her with talk about supernatural activity. Perhaps we need to play it down a bit and think of some rational explanation for what happened.'

'Oh but there is a perfectly rational explanation,' Aileen said. 'It was a trapped spirit and we freed him. Simple as that.'

'You don't really believe that do you?' Lorraine said.

'Yes I do. What else could it have been?'

I had no answer to this but was saved from responding by the arrival of our bread order and I signed the delivery note as Aileen transferred the loaves and rolls to the bread shelves.

'You'll need to pay me,' the delivery lad said.

'Oh right,' I said. 'I usually send a cheque at the end of the month.'

'New system. If you don't mind.'

I took the cash from the till and gave him it along with the invoice. He took a biro from behind his ear and wrote 'PAID' across it, then signed his name with a flourish. When he'd gone the conversation picked up from where it had left off.

'Do you think someone in the group deliberately pushed the glass?' I asked, at which Aileen gasped.

'No! Who would do such a terrible thing?'

'The thought crossed my mind,' Lorraine said. 'But I can't imagine who. I know I didn't do it...'

'Me neither,' I said.

'And I certainly didn't,' Aileen said.

'...so that leaves everyone else,' Lorraine finished.

'It wasn't Peter,' I said.

'Are you sure? It's the sort of thing he'd do,' Lorraine said.

'Yeah I know but I asked him. And anyway, he'd have had the glass telling cheesy jokes, he wouldn't have been able to resist.'

'That's true,' Lorraine said. 'The message was a bit weird too. 'Rise Everyone.' What's that supposed to mean?'

At this point in the conversation Nadine returned with a basket of vegetables, placing it on the kitchen bench before lifting out salad which she took up to the sink to wash.

'We're discussing the possibility of someone tampering with the glass last night,' Aileen told her. 'Christine thinks it could have been someone messing about, but of course that's ridiculous. It was definitely a ghost.'

'I don't really want to talk about it,' Nadine said. 'Someone hand me that bag of tomatoes and I'll do them while I'm up here.'

'It's really freaked her out,' I whispered. 'I think we should change the subject.' I took the bag of tomatoes to her and she went to speak then hesitated. 'What?' I probed.

'I need to speak to you. I've been awake half the night going over what happened last night. I was dreading coming in here today. Could I have a word with you when we've finished the prep?'

'Course you can. Don't worry. In a few days we'll have forgotten all about it and moved on to something else, you know what we're like for our fads!' I smiled but she didn't smile back.

She was really spooked. I'd never seen her so quiet. I wondered what she wanted to speak to me about. It occurred to me that maybe she didn't want to work here any more. I hoped that wasn't the case. We couldn't lose Nadine. She was the best worker we'd ever had. And we loved her.

Lorraine and Aileen were still talking about who may have moved the glass.

'Could have been Georgina,' Lorraine suggested. 'She's always up for a laugh.'

'Did I hear my name being taken in vain?' Georgina came through the door, carrying her wicker basket that she deposited on the floor near the counter.

'They don't believe there was a spirit here last night,' Aileen said. 'They think someone messed about with the Ouija board.'

'Oh and you think it was me, do you?' Georgina said.

'Possibly,' Lorraine said.

'Well it wasn't. If it had been, I've have given a better message than 'rise everyone.''

'What about Nige?' Lorraine said, at which Georgina laughed mockingly.

'Huh! There's no way it was Nige. He was in a right state last night. I had to walk him home, he was scared fartless.'

'If someone did do it, I reckon it was Mr Boothby,' I said. 'After all, we know nothing about him.'

'Mmm, I don't know. He took it very seriously. He was thrilled by the results we were getting. And all that fussing about with his balls and his recording machine,' Lorraine said.

'It's obvious who it was,' Georgina said. 'Maureen.'

'Not Maureen!' Aileen said, shocked. 'She's genuine. I don't know how you can say such a thing.'

'Pah!' Georgina said. 'I'd bet my life on it, if it wasn't paranormal activity then it was Maureen.'

'She wouldn't!' Aileen said. 'And I don't believe anyone pushed the glass anyway.'

'Course she would. She'd do it to make it look like she was a proper medium.'

'She is a proper medium!'

'Proper medium, my arse. She's a charlatan. All that speaking in tongues and carrying on...'

'It was a spirit!' Aileen cried.

There was a crash from the sink as Nadine threw down the colander of tomatoes.

'Stop it!' she shouted. 'Just stop it!' She stomped down the stairs, and into the office slamming the door behind her.

We looked at the closed door in silence, none of us sure what to do.

CHAPTER TWENTY

I was about to follow Nadine into the office when a loud hiss caught my attention.

'Psst! Over here. It's me.' Nige was beckoning from the door. 'I've got mail for you. Come and get it.'

'Aren't you coming in?' Lorraine moved to the counter to serve waiting customers.

'Is it safe?' Nige came in warily, looking about as though something was about to jump out at him at any moment. 'Any sign of him this morning?'

'Who?'

'Elvith.' He peered around the door.

'Yeah, he's upstairs having a pee,' Georgina said. 'Don't be so stupid.'

'Well you never know,' Nige said. 'Sometimes spirits get left behind after a séance and if he did he'd be madder than ever.'

'He's definitely gone,' Aileen told him. 'The smashed glass was proof of that.'

'Pah! It was Maureen doing it, Nige. There was no ghost,' Georgina said.

'Really?' Nige looked so relieved, I immediately crossed him off my mental list of suspected glass-pushers.

Suddenly Aileen's knife clattered to the floor. Her face was flushed and her eyes bright with tears as she shouted at us.

'I will not listen to another word against Maureen! This is how gossip and rumours start. Before we know it, word will spread and people will think she's a fraud.'

The fact that she was so upset inhibited us from pointing out that, actually, a lot of people already thought Maureen was a fraud.

The customers who'd been served, stopped and watched us in the kitchen until Lorraine moved forward and ushered them out, closing the door behind them.

As I moved forward to comfort Aileen, the office door opened and Nadine stepped quietly into the kitchen.

'It was me.'

We were silent except for Aileen's intermittent sniffing.

'What?'

'Look, I moved the glass, okay?'

'*What?*'

'You're joking!'

'*You* did it?'

'But why?'

'I thought having a séance would be fun. But when I got here last night I was terrified. If that glass moved I wanted to know it was me who moved it.'

Aileen was the first to speak.

'But the messages and everything! They were from Elvis.'

'No. They were from me.'

'I can't believe you did that to us,' Aileen said. 'I'm shocked.'

'Well y'bugger,' Lorraine said. 'You were the last person I thought it would be.'

'I'm sorry. I really am. I haven't slept all night. I was dreading coming in here today because I knew I'd have to confess.'

Aileen sniffed loudly. 'Yes, well I think I'm owed an apology from someone else too.'

Nige nudged Georgina. 'That's you.'

'I don't owe you an apology. I never accused you. It was Maureen I accused.'

Nige nudged her again and she looked at our disapproving glances.

'Oh okay, I'm sorry,' she said, in an unapologetic voice 'Anyway. Never mind that. I want to know why she did it.'

'I've told you,' Nadine said. 'I was so scared of the glass moving I decided to move it myself. That way, I knew exactly who was moving it. Mind it took a while to get the hang of it. It was all over the place at first.'

'Blampt was the first message if I remember correctly,' Nige said. 'What was that supposed to mean?'

'It didn't mean anything. I was just moving the glass about. It was really hard to direct it. Plus I couldn't find the letters. They weren't in alphabetical order. I had to look and try to find them before I started the glass moving so I knew which way to nudge it.'

'Well I must say you made a good job of it,' I said. 'I had no idea you were pushing it.'

'It would have been easier if we'd used a proper Ouija board instead of that load of old rubbish.'

'Excuse me,' Aileen said. 'Don't try to put the blame on my Ouija board. You're the one who deceived everyone.'

'I'm just explaining how difficult it was. The letters were jumbled, there was no 'S'. I think I did well under the circumstances.'

'I'm so sorry. If I'd known I was making the board for you to use, I would have made it simpler,' Aileen said. Her eyes glittered with tears.

'I think Nadine did very well, considering,' Georgina said, and we had to agree.

Nadine gave a sudden snigger. 'I couldn't believe you all fell for it. I was sure that at any moment you were going to call me out.'

'Elvith Prethley!' Georgina said. 'Haha! Quite funny really.'

'I don't think it's funny,' Aileen said. 'I think it shows a huge lack of respect for all of us, especially Maureen.'

'I'm just relieved we've solved the mystery,' I said.

'Me too,' Nige agreed. 'I was so spooked last night. I was worried Elvith had been offended by my outfit and followed me home.'

'We were all offended by your outfit Nige. It bordered on the obscene,' Lorraine told him.

'Your description of Heaven was a bit underwhelming,' I said. 'Was that the best you could come up with?'

'Yes it was. I didn't think it would go on for so long. You kept asking such stupid questions, I got quite irritated by the end.'

'Aye, we noticed,' Lorraine said.

128

'So am I forgiven?' Nadine asked. We assured her she was and Lorraine, Georgina and I hugged her but Aileen was still annoyed. It would take a while to get over her disappointment.

'I couldn't believe how gullible you all were,' Nadine said, which further fuelled Aileen's anger.

'Not gullible. Just trusting. We didn't think anyone in the group would be so callous. You made fools of us.' She turned her back on Nadine and continued preparing salad.

'Yeah, well I'm sorry,' Nadine said. 'It wasn't planned. It was fear that made me do it.'

'It's Maureen you need to apologise to,' I said. 'She believes she helped a lost soul.'

Nadine shook her head. 'I can't tell Maureen.'

'You'll have to.'

Nadine looked at us imploringly. 'No please. Maureen doesn't need to know.'

'I think you need to tell her,' I said. 'She'll be disappointed but she deserves to know the truth.'

But I was outvoted. The others agreed adamantly it would be cruel to tell Maureen that she'd been hoodwinked.

'She's so thrilled,' Lorraine said. 'I think we should let her believe she saved a lost soul. She doesn't have much pleasure in her life, we can't take this away from her.'

'Let's leave it as it is,' Nige said. 'Why upset her?'

Georgina agreed, but she had a different motive. 'She'll moan about it for weeks if she finds out. She'll drive us all mad.'

Surprisingly, even Aileen was of the same opinion. 'Yes, I think it would be far too cruel. She would be devastated. And she does have genuine psychic powers, they just weren't needed on this occasion.'

So it was agreed Maureen would not be told of the real events of the evening and Nadine went to buy cream cakes all round as a way of making it up to us.

Later, when Aileen, Nige and Georgina had gone, and Lorraine was serving customers, I remembered something.

'What about my message?' I asked. We were standing side by side at the kitchen bench, making up sandwich orders. 'What did it mean, Rise Everyone?'

Nadine looked a little shame-faced and laughed sheepishly. 'It was a hint for a pay rise. We haven't had one since the shop opened. I hoped you might be able to look at the figures and see if it was possible. I mean for everyone, not just me...'

I had to laugh. I'd racked my brains all night trying to come up with a meaning and although I'd thought of lots of possibilities this one hadn't even crossed my mind.

'I'll see what I can do,' I promised. 'Providing that next time you think you're due a rise you speak to me instead of pretending to be Elvith Prethley!'

CHAPTER TWENTY-ONE

Nadine had a valid point. We'd been running the shop for three years and were still on the same rate of pay.

Nadine and Aileen were on an hourly rate, but Lorraine and I paid ourselves a salary. Tasks such as visiting local wholesalers, laundering towels and doing the accounts were completed out of shop hours. I guess if we were ever to work out our hourly rate, it would be a lot less than we were paying our staff.

It wasn't that I'd deliberately kept the wage cost down, it just hadn't occurred to me to increase it.

I had little interest in the financial side of the business. Although I recorded sales and invoices when necessary, I never pored over them, analysing trends and keeping an eye on profit levels. I loved the everyday running of the business – interacting with customers, displaying stock and inventing new recipes. I knew I did not have a good 'business head'. I was just having a ball doing what I loved.

Peter was forever questioning us about what we had ordered, telling us the shop was overstocked. It was true. The shop was bursting with goods. The fridges and freezers were stuffed, the shelves loaded, and filled baskets and tubs were squeezed in every place possible. When the shop first opened, we stocked a moderate range of natural foods with a small selection of environmentally-friendly cleaning products. Since then, our food range had increased vastly, and we now sold a comprehensive range of herbal remedies and food supplements, as well as essential oils, soy-wax candles, cooking implements, organic cotton clothing, books, cruelty-free cosmetics and crafts from local artists. Lorraine and I somehow lost all sense when we were presented with new products and could not resist ordering new lines.

When deliveries arrived, we were like two kids on Christmas morning, ripping the boxes open and shrieking with delight at what was revealed. Peter repeatedly suggested we should limit the number of lines we stocked by focussing on our best sellers and products with the highest margins. He also nagged us constantly to keep on top of the book-keeping, and we did try, but every time a VAT return was due, we would realise we'd let it all slip again, and it would take a full day - which became known as V-day - to sort through invoices and till rolls and get everything up to date.

It has to be said that without Peter the accounts would never have been sorted and our VAT returns never completed. Occasionally, Lorraine or I would make a start, but after fiddling about half-heartedly, we'd lose interest and Peter would offer to finish the job.

On V-day, he would hide himself away in the office to pore over piles of invoices and scraps of paper while we enjoyed ourselves in the shop front, serving and chatting with customers.

He spent hours sifting through mounds of paperwork, sorting it into piles and recording figures in the hefty shop ledger. I think he gained great satisfaction from seeing the pages of neatly recorded information and would scrutinise the columns of figures if they dared to be even a few pennies off balance.

As he worked, I would take him little treats, a cinnamon cookie, a leek and potato pie, or his favourite – a cherry bakewell tart. As long as he had a regular supply of tea he was happy, coming out of his cave occasionally to ask us to decipher our handwriting or to request a missing document, reproaching us for our lax organisation as we scuttled about, pulling out forgotten price lists and junk mail from beneath the counter as we hunted for the missing paper.

When he'd finished, Lorraine and I would be summoned to the office to hear his outline of the state of affairs. We'd listen as he reeled off lists of figures, increases and decreases, percentages of this and that. All we were interested in was to know we were still solvent but we listened meekly, aware of his satisfaction at having everything in order. His greatest pleasure however, was the walk to the post box with the completed VAT return, knowing it was off his back for another three months. The process was made slightly less tedious when my dad upgraded his computer and gave us his old one. It was early days for computer skills and as Lorraine and I had very few, we edged the paperwork towards Peter, happy for it to be taken off our hands, especially as he did the task so thoroughly.

We all had our own skills and talents which, combined, made us a good team.

Lorraine had great management skills. Staff hiring and firing was always left to her, as well as any tricky negotiations with suppliers and providers. Her down-to-earth style cut through any nonsense and she could arrive at the crux of a matter and have it sorted while the rest of us would still be pondering on how to approach the problem.

Nadine's main skill was in sales. She had a knack of making people feel at ease and could draw even the most dour shopper into a conversation, remembering their names and little snippets of information to make them feel special. She did this with no ulterior motive. Her bubbly personality naturally charmed and attracted people, and many left our shop delighted with the service they'd received, regardless that they'd spent twice as much as they'd intended.

Although Aileen's penny-pinching ways were sometimes obsessive, her methods helped us keep running costs down. She had an eye for a bargain and often came with news of where she could get us packs of teacloths, pan scourers or paper bags for a discounted price. She was also good at finding ways to make more money - buying candles, rice-steamers and tea-infusers in bulk to sell separately alongside appropriate stock, mixing and bagging our own mueslis, spice mixes and teas, and growing cooking herbs from seed to sell in pots.

My talents lay more towards the creative. As someone who was easily bored, I loved setting up new systems and routines, then leaving them for the others to monitor as I moved on to my next project. As well as the window displays, I organised the shelves, enhancing the stock with props and posters. I often arranged food tastings, cookery demonstrations and customer events, but my favourite endeavour was producing our monthly newsletter filled with recipes and details of new products.

Updating the look of the shop was an ongoing project. My latest plan was to improve the therapy room.

We now had a good team of therapists on our books and our tiny therapy room evolved to suit the treatments on offer. The room was well used and I had decided it was time for a re-vamp.

'What colour scheme do you think I should go for?' I asked as the day's food preparations were in progress.

'I like it as it is,' Lorraine said. 'Blue and lavender. It just needs freshening up.'

Her answer did not please me. I'd spent the weekend collecting paint charts and material swatches.

'What about you two. Nadine? Aileen? What do you think?'

'Paint is expensive.' This from Aileen.

Nadine's response wasn't what I wanted to hear either. 'The therapists love the lavender colour. They all say purple is a very spiritual colour. And blue is calming. I'd say it was an ideal combination.'

'She's not interested in the effects of colours on the psyche, are you?' Lorraine said. 'You just want an excuse to buy some new stuff and have a faff about.'

Lorraine knew me too well, so of course I denied it and dismissed her comment.

'The correct shade is important,' I said. 'It needs to be suitable for the clients and it needs it to look professional.'

The jangling of the shop bell interrupted our conversation and I went to greet the arrival.

'Hello Dana. What can we do for you?'

Dana Quinn was a hypnotherapist who hired our therapy room to treat patients for various problems, ranging from eating disorders to unwanted habits. She'd successfully helped a client to quit smoking, and word had spread, causing a rush of interest in her services.

'I have a few more appointments to add to my list,' she said. 'I was passing so I thought I'd call in and collect something for dinner while I'm here.' Someone else may have said they could kill two birds with one stone, but Dana would never have used such a phrase. She smiled her delicate smile, her pale blue eyes clear and wide. Her slight frame was draped in a pale, loose-fitting dress, her silky hair falling over her shoulders. She looked like an art-nouveau painting of a nature spirit.

'We're discussing what colour to paint the therapy room,' I told her, as I hunted beneath the counter for our appointments diary. 'We think it needs freshening up but can't decide.'

'I love the colours in there,' Dana said softly. 'So relaxing and calm. But if you were to change, I'd suggest orange, it's an uplifting, energising colour. Think crocosmia petals,' she said dreamily. 'Marigolds, California Poppies. Beautiful.'

Hmm. Not sure I fancied orange.

'Or green. Grey-green like pine needles on a blue spruce. Or the soft fresh green of new fern fronds beginning to uncurl in a shady wood.' I'm sure she was a flower fairy in a previous life. 'The silvery-green of sage leaves would look beautiful next to the lavender you have in there, much warmer than the blue.'

I liked the sound of that, and so did the others.

'Lavender and green sounds good to me,' Lorraine said.

'Okay, the blue goes,' I agreed.

Dana updated the appointments diary and chose olives and salads from the fridge, which she bought along with a loaf of crusty herb bread.

Once she'd left I took the paint charts from my bag.

'What do you think?' I spread the charts on the counter and Lorraine came to look. 'There's loads of shades of green.' I pointed at the row of squares that began with 'Rich Emerald' fading to 'Forest Mist'.

Squinting at the colour sample card held against the wall in the therapy room, I could see Dana was right. The pale green against the lavender did give a warmer look than the blue. We agreed on 'Pistachio Cream' and decided some new cushions and candle holders would be good too.

'I'll make a list,' I said excitedly.

'Don't go wasting money on paint,' Aileen said, when we showed her the shade we'd chosen. 'I have loads of half empty paint tins in my shed. There's bound to be some green amongst it.'

My heart sank. The chance any of Aileen's leftover paint being the same shade as 'Pistachio Cream' were slim. The wrong green could ruin the look.

'Same with cushions and stuff, I've got loads of old blankets and things I can recycle. Don't buy anything until I check what I have at home.'

I wanted the therapy room to look contemporary and professional, which it wouldn't if Aileen put her stamp on it. I thought about some of her past home-decorating projects. A standard lamp made from an old budgie cage came to mind. She'd made it when her aunt's bird died, covering the cage in fabric to act as the shade and running a cable up the stand to a bulb holder fixed to the abandoned bird swing. It stood in her lounge next to an old radiogram painted pink with its innards removed which served as a television stand. The television had to be lifted off to access the video tapes stored inside. I couldn't let her loose on the therapy room, not unless we were intending to enter it for some bizarre modern art competition. I would have to let her down gently before she got her teeth into it and started making plans for recycled furnishings.

'Thanks Aileen, but there's really no need. I'm going for the paint tonight, I want to get started.'

'No problem,' Aileen said. 'I'll go and have a look as soon as I finish here at two and bring back what I've got.'

'Don't start if you're not going to finish it, mind,' Lorraine said. 'I was speaking to a new therapist and he's going to call in and have a look. I don't want him to see it half painted.'

'Of course I'll finish it!'

'New therapist?' Nadine said. 'How exciting. And a man too? Is he nice? Do you think he'll give me a sample treatment?'

Lorraine and I laughed.

'What are you like?' I said. 'You don't even know what the therapy is yet.'

'He's an Iridologist,' Lorraine told her. 'And he sounded very nice but we haven't seen him.'

'What's an Iridologist?'

'Someone who studies the iris,' Lorraine told us. I'd never heard of it. Neither, it appeared, had Nadine.

'What've flowers got to with anything?'

'Not iris as in flowers,' Lorraine told her. 'Iris as in your eye. The belief is that you can tell a lot about a person's health by studying the colours and patterns in the iris of your eye.'

'I've never heard of it' Nadine said. 'But they do say the eyes are the windows to the soul.'

'So how's it supposed to work?' I asked.

Lorraine explained it was based on the theory that the iris contains nerve fibres that correspond to various parts of the body, and can change colour depending on diet and state of health.

'How come you know so much about it?' I asked.

'I didn't until Kyle explained it to me on the phone.'

'Kyle?'

'Kyle Hendrick. The Iridologist. He's coming next week so you'd better get cracking if you want the therapy room finished for him.'

'I might come in at the weekend to do it,' I said. 'Shouldn't take long if Peter helps. We can bring Rosie in with us then call in at Paddy Freeman's Park on the way home.'

'You do know it's the abseil this weekend, you hadn't forgotten had you?' Nadine said, and I groaned.

'Aw, yes I had to be honest. It was so far off, I was hoping it would never arrive.'

'I'm worried about my outfit. What are you going to wear?' Nadine asked.

Clothes were the least of my worries.

'Ballgown and stilettos.'

'I was thinking more flippers and swimming goggles,' Lorraine said.

'Oh har har. I'm serious. I don't know whether to go for a casual look, you know, jeans and a t-shirt or a sportier look.'

137

'Is it for that Marine's benefit?' Lorraine asked.

'No,' she lied. 'I just want to look right for the task.'

'Wear what you wore for the practise,' I told her. 'That's what I'm going to do.'

'Mmm. It's just I've bought this cute little top with a dark red trim and I was going to get my nails done in the same red...' Lorraine and I laughed.

'Eeh, Nadine! Only you could turn a jump from a bridge into a fashion show.'

CHAPTER TWENTY-TWO

Late afternoon, Aileen arrived loaded down with carrier bags. I hoped she'd forgotten so I could go and buy paint this evening and then greet her tomorrow with 'oh what a shame, I've bought the paint now, never mind you can keep your leftovers for another time.'

'I don't have time to stay,' she panted, 'so just have a look through and take what you need.' She struggled in and released the heavy bags into a heap on the floor, sighing with relief as she straightened up, rubbing the small of her back.

'Thanks Aileen, that's very good of you,' Lorraine said as she saw my face fall at the sight of a rusted paint tin rolling out from one of the bags.

'Yes, thanks,' I mumbled.

Aileen smiled. 'I thought I had half a tin of green paint, but I haven't so I've brought an old tin of grey.' She headed for the door. 'Sorry, have to dash. I passed a skip on Hunter's Avenue yesterday, full of wood. I need a bit to mend my fence so I'm off to see if it's still there. Oh, and remember to save my carriers, I'm crocheting a carpet from plastic bags for my outhouse. See you tomorrow.'

'See you.'

'Bye Aileen.'

As soon as she'd gone I picked up the dented paint can.

'I wanted fresh green not manky old grey,' I grumbled. ''Pistachio Cream' to be exact. Not...' I peered at the label on the dented paint can '... 'Sheer Cloud'.' There were dribbles of pale paint down the side of the tin. I held it up to the light. Actually it was quite a pretty colour. Soft grey, like, well yes, okay. Like a sheer cloud. And it might look all right with lavender. Perhaps.

I carried the paint and the bags through to therapy room, leaving Lorraine to serve a customer who I remembered as being confrontational, but couldn't recall details of her complaint.

Against the lavender, the 'Sheer Cloud' grey looked gorgeous. I rooted through the carrier bags, and found some striped

139

purple cushion covers which I threw over our cushions to see how they looked. I was still faffing about when Lorraine came through, moaning about her customer.

'What a pain she is,' she said. 'She'd come in to complain about the parking outside. Mrs Stern her name is. Suits her. I told her it was nothing to do with us but she went on and on saying we should do something about it.'

'Ah, yes. I remember now. She's been in before complaining about the reps from the vacuum cleaner place.'

It had been an afternoon when I'd been in the shop alone. She'd parked in the side street and returned to find her car blocked in by a badly parked BMW. I explained the offending vehicle did not belong to me or my customers but she still decided to take her frustration out on me. I felt it was a bit unfair, especially seeing as she hadn't parked to visit Nutmeg, she'd stopped to collect a suit from the dry cleaners.

'I don't know what she thinks I can do about it,' Lorraine said. 'I told her we can't always get parked ourselves and we have a business to run.'

'Never mind that,' I said. 'Have a look at this grey paint. What do you think?'

We both agreed the grey worked beautifully with the lavender, and that the cushion covers were perfect.

'Oh ye of little faith,' Lorraine said, as searching through the contents of Aileen's carrier bags, I exclaimed in delight at finding a candle holder made from driftwood and a pair of framed botanical prints.

'They'll look great,' I said, holding up the white-framed pictures.

'Looks like Aileen's come up trumps,' Lorraine said. 'What else is in there?'

I pulled the last bag towards me and began to unravel layers of newspaper.

'I feel a bit bad about how I pre-judged her,' I told Lorraine. 'I was expecting her to bring in a right load of rubbish.' I removed the last layer. Contained in the newspaper was a garden gnome holding a bunch of lavender. His face was crudely painted, giving him a squint and a leer. I turned his smirk towards Lorraine, one lumpy fist offering her his bunch of gaudy flowers, the other positioned in a rather unfortunate manner on his groin.

'Blimey,' Lorraine said. 'I take it all back.'

'That's horrible,' I said and Lorraine sniggered. 'We can't have him in the therapy room, not if we want people to be able to relax in there.' I put him on the desk on top of a couple of invoices. 'There. We'll use him as a paperweight.'

Like usual, once I'd got an idea in my head, it was full steam ahead. I couldn't wait to get started. As soon as I arrived at the shop the following morning, I opened the 'Sheer Cloud' and spent the morning obliterating the blue walls. Lorraine and Nadine were happy to leave me to it as they whizzed through the food prep and looked after business.

I worked happily, feeling a sense of fulfilment as I watched the fresh grey paint cover the scuffed blue walls. By the time I'd given both walls a couple of coats, Lorraine called to me that the Nutmeg Express was coming in, so I quickly washed my hands, put on a clean apron and went to help. At around twelve each day, a huge queue of customers would materialise as though they'd been dropped off by a tour bus, hence our term 'The Nutmeg Express.'

I'd had an idea I'd not yet mentioned to the others. I was going to paint words in a border around the top of the room in silver script. Words that inspired me; words of beauty. I was pretty certain Nadine would love it, but I guessed Lorraine would pooh-pooh it as another of my airy-fairy ideas so I'd decided to paint a couple of the words and then ask their opinion. It took me ages to finalise my list to just fourteen words.

Love, Joy, Faith, Peace, Courage, Kindness, Gratitude, Clarity, Serenity, Grace, Forgiveness, Happiness, Inspiration and Harmony.

At home I'd spent ages making stencils of the letters I needed. Now I had to transfer them to the wall in silver paint.

141

When the lunchtime rush was over, we sat down together to have a sandwich, then I was keen to give my stencils a try. The lavender walls had been left, so as they were the only two dry walls, I decided to have a go at applying the words on those. I began tracing the letters onto the wall. This was much more difficult than I'd anticipated. There wasn't much space to manoeuvre the stepladder and at times I had to lean precariously, holding the ladder with one hand and wedging my bottom against the wall to reach the area I needed. I managed to outline the words 'Courage' and 'Harmony' in feint pencil lines. Taking my silver paint and fine paintbrush I began to painstakingly fill in the letters with light strokes of paint.

It was a difficult process because of my perilous balance on the stepladder, and because the pencil lines were invisible unless I held my head close to the wall. I managed to complete half of each word then climbed down to check how it looked from the floor.

The silver, flowing letters looked really effective. I was admiring my handiwork when Lorraine called me through to the shop front where she said a police officer was waiting to speak to me.

CHAPTER TWENTY-THREE

It's incredible how many disaster scenarios race through your mind during the few seconds you wait to hear what a police officer has come to tell you. Visions of car accidents, media coverage of child abduction and headlines reporting disasters flashed before me as I waited. In my heightened state of anxiety I heard words and phrases and tried to make sense of them.

'...situation has become intolerable...several complaints...not acceptable...parking spaces...'

Gradually it became clear the officer had come because a member of the public had reported the regular disruption caused by bad parking, and he was hoping to alleviate the problem by speaking with local business owners.

I sighed, relieved he had not come to tell me that my loved ones had perished in an unprecedented disaster. Lorraine and I told him of the problems we'd experienced, especially when delivery vans were unable to park near the shop, and on a couple of occasions left without leaving our stock, to keep to their schedule. He explained that although he could not allocate parking spaces for us or our customers, he was able to give us a set of six traffic cones we could use to reserve a space when our deliveries were due.

'Put them out an hour or so before you're expecting them, and make sure you retrieve them afterwards,' he told us.

I stacked them in the office. 'I'll put them out tomorrow for our Karma delivery,' I said. I was looking forward to being able to assert my new authority.

Aileen returned as we were busy with our end of day tasks. The kitchen had been cleaned and the floors swept and polished. Lorraine counted coins into money bags and I tidied the shelves. Aileen was thrilled that she'd not only retrieved from the skip enough wood for her fence but also a large, cracked mirror.

'What are you going to do with that? It's knackered,' Lorraine said.

'I'm going to smash the glass into small pieces and use them to mosaic a table top,' she told us. She asked if the stuff she'd brought had been useful and I took her to see the revamped therapy room.

'Wow! You got that done quickly,' she said. 'It looks great.'

'It does, thanks to you.'

'No problem. You know how I love to see things recycled.' She looked around trying to spot something.

'Where's Arnold?' she asked.

'Arnold?'

'The gnome. Ah, there he is, on the desk. I think he'll look great here.' She stood him on the shelf where he leered down at the therapy bed.

'I was going to use him as a paperweight,' I told her.

'Don't worry, I'll find you something else for that. Look how lovely he looks with his lavender flowers against the grey wall.'

'Yeah,' I said. 'Lovely.'

'What's that horrible thing?' Peter asked later. He picked up the gnome and examined it.

'That's Arnold.'

'Look where his hand is. It looks obscene.'

'I know, Aileen brought it.'

'We could accidently smash it,' Lorraine suggested.

'No, we can't do that!' I said. 'Put him back and I'll just have to hide him when the room is booked.'

Peter replaced the gnome on the shelf above the therapy bed.

'You'll have a good view from there, Arnold. For your strange hobbies.'

'Strange hobbies?' Lorraine said.

'Pink Floyd.'

'Ah yes, of course. Arnold Layne.'

The next day we had the first opportunity to use our cones. We were expecting a delivery from Karma - our primary supplier - so at twelve o'clock, full of self-importance, we went out with the cones to put the new plan into action. A car was pulling away, leaving a space outside the shop, so I immediately stepped onto the road with my cone, only to almost suffer a heart-attack as a car horn sounded behind me. I jumped in fright and saw behind the steering wheel, Mrs Stern, the woman who'd complained to Lorraine the previous day about the parking problem.

She gesticulated for me to move out of the way, blasting her car horn angrily so I held up my cone and made a performance of determinedly placing it on the road in front of her, at which she promptly ran it over.

'Here! What's your game?' I yelled. 'You've squashed me cone.'

She opened her car window.

'Move out of my way. I intend to park here.'

I bent to retrieve my flattened cone from the kerbside as Lorraine made a point of hurriedly setting down the remaining cones.

'Look what you've done to it, I just got it this morning,' I said, trying to pull the cone back into shape. A van emerged from the lane behind the shop and came to a halt behind Mrs Stern's car. A man's head appeared from the window.

'Hey! Are you parking there or what, love? I can't get through.'

'I am indeed parking here,' Mrs Stern said.

'No she's not,' Lorraine said.

'This space is reserved,' I said, as she reversed her car a little, then changed gear to move forwards.

'Don't you dare squash another cone!' I shouted at her. 'These are police property and I'm authorised to use them.'

'Don't talk such nonsense,' she said and edged forwards.

Lorraine immediately moved so she was almost touching the front of the car.

'This space is reserved. You'll have to move on.'

'Move out of my way!'

'No.'

'I tell you, I am parking in that space whether you like it or not.'

'No you're not. Unless you're going to squash me like you squashed the cone.'

The workman in the van began to lose patience and sounded his horn. Mrs Stern opened her car door and climbed out.

'Get these cones out of my way at once!' she yelled, making a grab for the nearest one, and flinging it to the pavement.

'Don't you touch my cones,' I shouted. She made her way to each cone, picking it up and tossing it to the side as I retrieved and replaced them. She realised what I was doing, and began to move faster, so I too picked up my speed. Lorraine joined me, and the three of us participated in a shouting match while we flung the cones from pavement to road and back again, accompanied by loud honking from the builder's van.

'You are not parking here!'

'Oh yes I am!'

'Oh no you're not!'

'This is a reserved space!'

'Shut up, you stupid woman!'

'No, you shut up!'

'Here, man!' the workman yelled from his van. 'I'm waiting here to get by while you lot are playing silly buggers with a load of traffic cones. Get out the way!'

'You shut up as well,' Mrs Stern told him, and threw a cone in his direction. It narrowly missed his windscreen and he got out of his van and picked it up.

'You nearly had my window out, you silly cow,' he yelled, throwing it back towards Lorraine.

'Here! You can pack that in,' Lorraine yelled. 'I didn't throw it, it was her.'

'Don't you call me a silly cow, you ignorant man,' Mrs Stern shouted. 'I'm trying to solve the parking problem around here.'

'Well it doesn't look like it to me,' the man said. 'Hoying cones around isn't helping.'

I realised people had stopped to watch, some laughing and some, obviously aware of the local parking problem, adding their opinions.

'It's a bloody disgrace, the parking provision round here.'

'Not good for business.'

'We need a carpark.'

There were now two cars behind the workman's van. In the first, a man in shades and a leather jacket shook his fist and thumped his steering wheel in frustration. I couldn't see the driver of the second, but could hear the car horn parping, tentatively at first, then the blasts becoming louder and longer. As other cars joined the queue I saw a figure cycle around the corner and wobble his way towards me. It was Mr Boothby. He made a comical sight on his sit-up-and-beg bike, dressed in tweed with bicycle clips at his ankles, his moustache flamboyantly curled and a cycling helmet perched on his head. After dismounting and making sure his bike was stable as it leaned against the wall, he marched over to us with an air of authority.

'I say. What seems to be the problem here?'

Mrs Stern turned to him, smiling alluringly, in hope of recruiting him to back her up.

'Oh I do hope you can help me. I'm trying to park here you see.'

'Ah, not to worry Madam.' He gave a cough and smoothed his facial hair with his fingers. 'Allow me.' He held out his hand and Mrs Stern looked at it.

'Your car keys?' he asked.

Mrs Stern's smile dropped. 'I can park my own car,' she snapped. 'I need these cones out of the way.'

'The police gave us them, we're authorised to reserve a space for our deliveries,' I said and the cone flinging resumed.

Mr Boothby looked on in confusion as Lorraine and I frantically placed the cones on the road and Mrs Stern and the builder hurled them back to the pavement.

'I've had enough of this,' the builder said and he kicked out at a cone I'd replaced near Mrs Stern's car. It hit her wing mirror with a clang, knocking it askew.

'You stupid man,' Mrs Stern yelled. 'You've hit my mirror.'

'It won't be the only thing I'll be hitting if you don't all get out of my effing way and let me through.'

'Language, please!' Mr Boothby exclaimed. 'We are in the presence of ladies.'

'Bugger off, Colonel Blimp,' the man yelled at him and Mr Boothby stuttered his indignation, huffing and puffing beneath his moustache.

'How dare you, sir! I've never been so insulted...'

Some of the bystanders voiced their objections about the profanities being used, others joined in, effing and jeffing, either at the builder, or at Mrs Stern, as several arguments erupted simultaneously. A bunch of reps from the vacuum cleaner shop were finding it all amusing, laughing and jeering and joining in with the cone throwing, while more cars joined the gridlock and were using their car horns as well as their voices to object.

Nadine, who had been watching from the shop door, called to us.

'Chris! Lorraine! Quick, in here!' We stopped in our tracks and hurried inside where Nadine quickly locked the door then hurried to pull down the blinds. The shop was empty.

'What's up?' I asked.

'Someone must have called the police, look.' She moved to the huge front window and held open the slats of the blind for us to peep through. A police car was parked opposite the shop, and as we watched, two officers began making their way towards the scene.

Poor Mr Boothby stood near our door looking completely out of his depth as chaos reigned around him.

Lorraine unlocked the shop door and opened it. She leaned out, grabbed Mr Boothby's arm, yanked him into the shop and relocked the door, completely unnoticed in the hullabaloo. And we watched quietly as the officers walked around the corner and into an ongoing fracas of cone throwing, shouting and swearing, which had nothing whatsoever to do with us.

CHAPTER TWENTY-FOUR

I was awakened by Peter, who brought me tea and toast. Rosie padded in with Funny Bunny dangling from her hand. She looked delightful in her Tots TV pyjamas, her curls tousled and her face flushed. She climbed into bed and sat with her feet on the pillows chewing a piece of toast.

'How are you feeling?' Peter asked. I hesitated before answering. Today was the day I would plummet from the Tyne Bridge.

'Nervous. But it's a good nervous. Anticipation, not crippling fear like I had at the practise.'

'That's good,' he said. 'You'll be fine. Just remember to keep calm and fall back gently.'

'Yes I know.' I rubbed my knees in memory of the most spectacular bruises I'd ever had. The surface of each kneecap had evolved daily through shades of purple and blue, before developing patches of yellow and green, resembling watercolour paintings. The bruise on my right knee was shaped like a man's face. The changing colours gradually revealed (with a bit of imagination) the majestic features of a male Native American. Nadine suggested I should have a tattoo artist capture the image forever and, on a particularly quiet afternoon, we even accentuated the face with a felt tip pen to highlight the features.

We parked the car near the old Spiller's flour mill and walked along the river to the bridge, Peter pushing Rosie in her pushchair.

It was a glorious day. I loved this walk along the river - the area was different each time I came as more of the ongoing renovation was completed. I remembered my dad driving me along the Quayside when I was a teenager in the 1970s, past the old warehouses, over cobbles and rail tracks, telling me this ancient part of the town would soon be gone. Most of it was derelict, branches sprouted from what was left of rooftops and many windows were glassless, but its Dickensian appearance had fascinated me. It was easy to imagine Bill Sykes and Fagin skulking in the shadows behind one of the dilapidated wooden staircases.

Many of the warehouses remained, and the iron tracks along the road. We followed the river, between the market stalls and into the shadows beneath the Tyne Bridge, avoiding the piles of bird droppings staining the pavement. It was colder here, a breeze blew from the river and there was a sour smell of guano. I shivered as I glanced up at the arches looming high and foreboding above.

Back out in the sunshine, we crossed the Swing Bridge and I wished we were out on a Sunday stroll, enjoying the weather and choosing where to have lunch, rather than preparing to throw ourselves from a great height.

A crowd had gathered on the riverside in the carpark of the Tuxedo Princess floating nightclub, which was to be our landing point. I spotted Lorraine and Nadine and we went to join them. Peter's sister Susan had come along to watch and take photos, and a few of the locals from the bank were there too.

I saw my parents waiting, Dad looking relaxed as he watched the river traffic and Mam looking about anxiously, trying to spot us. She'd been unwilling to come to watch at first, saying she forbade us to take part. The conversation had gone along the lines of many of our family discussions, with Mam reluctant to let us do anything in the least bit adventurous and Dad urging us to go out and do whatever we wanted, with his famous proviso 'as long as it's not hurting anyone else.'

'I'm not having my daughters jumping off the Tyne Bridge, and that's that,' Mam said.

'It's not a jump, it's an abseil.'

'I don't care what it is, you're not doing it.'

My dad continued reading his newspaper, pretending he couldn't hear the conversation.

'Mam, it's perfectly safe.'

'You could end up in the river.'

'Well that's just silly.' We never took our mam's objections seriously.

'Jimmy, tell them.'

'There'll be loads of people doing it,' I said.

'So if loads of people jumped in the river, would you do the same?'

'We're not jumping in the river, we're abseiling from the bridge.'

'It's the most ridiculous thing I've ever heard.' Mam was prone to exaggeration.

'Mam, we're doing it. We'll be fine.'

Mam turned to Dad who was trying to read, unnoticed. 'Jimmy! Tell them.'

'I'm telling you,' my dad said from behind his newspaper.

Mam gave him a look of exasperation. 'Right. I'm putting my foot down. You're not doing it. I forbid it.'

I sighed. 'It's all arranged, we can't back out now. We're doing it, it's perfectly safe.'

'Jimmy, tell them. They'll do that jump over my dead body.'

As usual Dad had the final word. 'Well, if they're jumping over your dead body, at least they'll have a soft landing.'

An official registration table had been set up beneath a gazebo, and I decided to register for the abseil before speaking to Mam in case she tried to talk me out of it. Now I was standing below the bridge, my nerves were beginning to kick in and I knew it might be possible for her to succeed.

'Aren't you going to go and see your mam and dad first?' Peter asked.

'No. I don't want to be talked out of it at this late stage. Go and distract her with Rosie while I sign up.'

After collecting my helmet and harness, I went to reassure Mam it would all be fine. She was unusually quiet, I think she was genuinely anxious about us.

'Val's here,' Lorraine told me and I groaned.

'That's all I need. Where is she so I can avoid her? I can do without her tales of doom today.'

'Don't worry. She's got the St. John's First Aid man pinned up beside the burger van. Poor bugger's being forced to listen to her medical history.'

Peter bought coffee for himself and Dad, and juice for Rosie from a van selling drinks and snacks but the rest of us were too nervous to eat or drink. Rosie had somehow lost her sunhat, I remembered her wearing it as we walked along the river but it was nowhere to be seen and I began to fret she'd burn or get sunstroke.

'I'll run down to the market and get her a new one,' Peter said.

'But you'll miss the abseil.'

'I won't,' he said, hurrying off. Lorraine and Nadine collected their equipment and we began to get ready.

'I've never been here in the daytime,' Nadine said as we stepped into our harnesses and helped each other fasten our helmets. 'Everything looks so different.'

The Tuxedo Princess, anchored beneath the Tyne Bridge, was silent. In the evening, strung with lights and filled with music and voices, it was one of the city's brightest nightspots. This morning it lay quietly in the shadow of the bridge, a chain across its gangplank. Beyond it, Newcastle's famous bridges spanned the river. I watched a couple of gulls as they swooped across the water, their cries carried by the breeze, and I wondered why on earth I'd let myself in for this. Facing up to your fears always sounds great in principle until you actually come to do it.

I let my eyes travel up the huge metal structure, our beloved Tyne Bridge, to the parapet silhouetted against clear blue sky. I was sure it was growing in height. Around me, people stood in groups, drinking coffee as they waited. The air was filled with chatter and laughter, the atmosphere as warm as the rays of sun playing on the back of my neck. But a chill of fear caused my whole body to shiver and I played through various excuses in my head - reasons I would have to suddenly rush home.

I saw Peter making his way towards us, a pink hat in his hand. He plopped it on Rosie's head and she immediately removed it to examine it.

'I'm sweating,' he said. He pulled his t-shirt away from his body. He'd run there and back so as not to miss us, but we were all still waiting. Anticipation buzzed through the crowd and my anxiety erupted, panic churning in my stomach. I turned to Peter to tell him I'd changed my mind and couldn't do it, but before I could speak he took hold of my shoulders and looked me in the eye.

'Yes you can,' he said, and his words quelled the fear. He put his arms around me and pulled me into a bear hug. 'You'll be fine. It'll be over before you know it.'

And then our names were called. It was our turn to make our way up to the bridge. Peter gave me a last hug and I made my way out of the carpark and up the steps past St. Mary's Church like a condemned man on the way to his death. Nadine and Lorraine hurried ahead as I dragged myself after them, up Bottle Bank and along to the Gateshead end of the bridge where a Marine was stationed. I trudged along with my head down, trying to conquer my nerves.

Glancing up, I saw Nadine and Lorraine crossing the road to the other side of the bridge and picked up my pace to follow. A screech of brakes brought a van to a halt, the driver blasting his horn and yelling, missing me by inches as I leapt in fright. Vehicles behind him sounded their horns too as they were forced to come to a sudden stop. I raised my hand in a wave of sheepish apology as I hurried to the other side of the bridge where Nadine and Lorraine looked on in shock.

'Oh my God, I thought you'd had it then!' Nadine said as Lorraine pulled me onto the pavement. To be honest, in the state I was in, being squashed on the road presented itself as a better fate than falling from the bridge.

The wind was stronger up here, whipping our hair around our faces and snatching away our voices as we walked towards the queue of abseilers waiting near the descent point. A Marine was instructing a man on how to climb onto the parapet. He held the man's harness as he lowered himself over the edge.

Not wanting to watch, I turned my head and looked across the river to the Quayside where the Sunday market was in full swing. Two lines of brightly coloured stalls snaked along the riverside as music, voices and traffic noise drifted up, along with the smell of chips and doughnuts, carried on the wind that threatened to overbalance us at any moment.

'It's a lot higher than at the training,' I said to Lorraine.

'Yeah but the principle is the same. Once we're over the edge it's just a case of controlling the speed on the way down.'

'Yeah, once we're over the edge. That's the bit that's worrying me.'

The view was spectacular and one I love. Even though my fear was increasing by the second, I couldn't help being moved by the sight of the grey-blue river, flowing beneath bobbing, tethered boats, past the Baltic Flour Mills, bending away into the distance where the Byker Wall dominated the skyline. As I watched, the sun emerged from behind a cloud, its rays sharpening the scene and intensifying its colours.

'Just look at that,' I said. 'How gorgeous.'

'Can you see the tall, dark one?' Nadine said.

'Tall, dark what?'

'You know the one that I liked.' Her words brought me back to the present.

'You liked them all,' Lorraine said.

'Yeah, but I can't see my favourite.'

The queue of people waiting ahead of us decreased surprisingly slowly. Now I was up here I just wanted to get it over with. I glanced at the clock on St Mary's Church tower, and was sure the hands had not moved since the last time I looked.

'It's us!' Nadine said, and we moved closer to the descent point where a Marine checked our harnesses were secure. This involved quite a bit of physical contact, and when it was Nadine's turn she winked at us over his shoulder as he bent to pull her harness tighter.

'Mmm, very nice,' she whispered when we moved to the next Marine who waited to help us begin our descent. 'Very nice indeed. What do you think?'

155

I didn't think anything. Frankly he could have looked like Quasimodo, I had no interest in anything except getting back to the safety of the Quayside.

Nadine went first. We watched her smiling and chatting while the Marine fastened her harness to the rope. I couldn't hear what she was saying but it was clear from her body language she found him more than a little attractive. She climbed up onto the parapet and gave a cry as she fell backwards until her braking device locked in and she hung over the parapet, swaying like a pendulum. I turned away, unable to watch.

'She's off!' said Lorraine, and when I turned back she had gone. I heard her squeal as she descended, followed by applause. She'd evidently landed safely.

The Marine turned and beckoned to us.

'Who's next?'

'Me? Or you?' Lorraine asked.

'Me.' I was afraid if I waited any longer I'd chicken out. I walked to where he waited a short distance away but it seemed to take me forever. My legs felt as though they didn't quite belong to me, they were determined not to move and I had to force them towards the descent point.

The Marine attached my harness to the rope. 'Up you get.'

He waited and as I didn't move he put his arms around me and hoisted me up, which would probably have been very pleasant if I'd been in a different frame of mind. I clung to the rail, trying not to think of the sheer drop to the Quayside, my arms and legs wrapped tightly like I was about to take my chances on a Bucking Bronco.

'Climb over.'

'I can't, I can't.' I clung to the bridge as though my life depended on it. Which at that point, I was certain my life did depend upon it. I could see the Tuxedo Princess below, and the waiting crowds in the carpark. A gull was toddling along a ledge a few feet below me and I wished I had his confidence. I tried to move but had apparently lost the use of my limbs. I closed my eyes, feeling the wind brush over me, my stomach churning.

'Get yourself over to the other side,' the Marine said sharply. I opened my eyes, about to refuse again when he cupped his hand around his mouth and leaning over the bridge, yelled down to his colleague.

'John! Got a quitter here. Send someone up to assist.' I lifted my head and loosened my grip on the bridge a little.

'Excuse me, I'm no quitter! How dare you yell that! Everyone down there will have heard.'

The Marine shrugged. 'Up to you.'

I slung my leg across the parapet, still holding on for dear life with my hands and he smiled encouragingly.

'Lean back, I've got you.'

'You certain?'

'I'm certain.' I leaned back and sure enough the breaking device locked in and I sat in the harness with my feet against the stone side of the bridge.

The Marine looked at me with a grin that would have rendered Nadine senseless.

'Off you go.'

Remembering not to jump this time, I leaned back and after adjusting the braking device, sailed smoothly downwards. The sound of the crowd grew closer as I plummeted and adrenaline surged through my body as a delicious draught of cool air rushed by. I landed on the tarmac to a round of applause and a cheer from Peter and Rosie.

'I did it!' I yelled as I was unclipped from the rope by a Marine.

Peter came to kiss me. 'Well done, I knew you could do it.'

'I did it!'

'Yeah, well done. You were great.' He lifted Rosie from her chair and I hugged her.

'I did it! I DID IT!' I jumped excitedly, and Rosie giggled as she bounced with me. 'I DID IT!'

'Yeah, yeah. Okay,' Peter said. 'You're missing Lorraine, look.' I turned in time to see Lorraine land and ran to hug her along with Nadine.

'We did it!' we yelled to each other. Rosie was still in my arms, squealing at the excitement and joining in our group hug.

Peter's sister Susan had photographed us descending, and now she came over to take more pictures before we returned our equipment.

We were given certificates and as we were leaving I couldn't help feeling smug as we passed a group of girls who had been called to make their way up to the parapet.

On the way back we stopped at a pub for lunch. We found an outside table and sat in the sunshine, looking out over the river. After she'd eaten, Rosie climbed onto my knee for a cuddle and soon fell asleep, clutching Funny Bunny to her chest. Peter lifted her from me and we settled her into her pushchair, pulling down her new hat to shade her face.

'Let's have another drink,' Lorraine said.

'I'm going to have another dessert.'

'Aren't you full after that huge lunch?'

'No, I don't know what's up with me but I'm famished.'

Two days later, I discovered what was up. I had not abseiled from the Tyne Bridge alone. Unbeknown to me, I'd made the descent accompanied by our second child.

CHAPTER TWENTY-FIVE

'If I'd known you were carrying my grandchild, I would never have let you jump off that bridge,' my mam repeated, many times. 'Especially after a miscarriage. I don't know what you were thinking.'

'I didn't know, Mam,' I told her again and again. But she was worried for me and she chided me, urging me to stay at home and rest.

I was thrilled to be carrying another child, but also fearful it could be taken away from me at any moment. At night, unwanted thoughts circled my mind leaving me tired and anxious through the day. Peter, as always, was loving and supportive but I could not shake off the constant fear that lay with me.

I was saddened by the reaction of friends and relatives when they heard of my pregnancy. The news was received with great solemnity, there was none of the usual joy and excitement. I was met with grave looks of apprehension and pleas to take care of myself, and had to continually reassure everyone I was fine. Knowing they were so concerned about me intensified the feeling of dread that waited nearby to penetrate my mind at quiet moments.

I tried to keep such thoughts from taunting me, but my slender thread of confidence was worn ever thinner as even customers advised me not to get my hopes up, nor to make any preparations until at least the fifth month. One woman even suggested I should try to forget about my pregnancy, so that it would not be such a great loss to me if the worst happened.

It was my lovely, darling dad, who brought peace to my mind. With his usual straightforward and optimistic outlook on life, he hugged me and told me this was the best news he'd heard since he'd been told Rosie was on her way. He radiated delight at the anticipation of another grandchild and it lifted my spirits. At once I threw off the cloud of pessimism that had become my constant companion, and resolved to face whatever life held in store for me with confidence.

Okay, so I might not carry this child full-term, but I was his mother and he deserved my best. Even if fate decided he was not to live in this world, he was alive and growing inside me right now and I would love him with all my heart for however long he was with me.

I began talking to my child daily, surrounding him with love, telling him to stay strong, and assuring him that together, we could do this.

I followed my mam's advice and took a few days off work, although I soon became bored. I hunted out Rosie's old baby clothes and toys and had a lovely few days to myself, sorting and washing the little vests and sleepsuits I'd forgotten were so tiny.

By the end of the week I was chomping at the bit to get back to the shop.

'What have I missed?' I asked as we settled down for tea and tattle as Nige called it.

'Nowt,' Lorraine said.

'Oh come on! Something must have happened in the last week surely!'

'Well, we sold some lentils,' Lorraine said.

'I washed the dishes,' Nadine said.

'Obviously the excitement only happens when I'm here.'

'No more excitement for you,' Lorraine said. 'We're keeping you safe for the next seven months.'

Nadine nodded in agreement.

'No lifting, stretching, straining or general jumping about allowed,' she said. 'So that means no more climbing up ladders to paint either.'

You can both get lost, I thought, but I smiled and kept quiet.

'No more carrying heavy boxes either. We'll be sorting all the deliveries, you're not allowed to touch them.'

'And no standing at the kitchen benches for hours on end. We'll do all the prep and the cooking. You can sit behind the till.'

'What? All day?' I said. 'I'll go off me head. I need to keep busy, you know how easily I get bored.'

160

'It's only for a few months,' Lorraine told me.

I decided to take their new arrangements with the same importance I'd taken of my mam's ban on abseiling. None at all. No need to tell them though.

'Okay. Well, I'll go and give the therapy room a quick clean before the Iridologist arrives. Kyle, isn't it?'

'No vacuuming or cleaning allowed either.' Lorraine said. And with no choice in the matter, I was given a chair behind the counter where I was allowed to serve customers, while Lorraine and Nadine prepped the food, carried bread trays, filled shelves and cleaned the therapy room.

Kyle Hendrick was tall with dark shoulder-length hair carefully styled to look un-styled, and surprisingly vivid green eyes which were possibly enhanced with a smudge of eyeliner. He wore expensive jeans, faded enough to look stylish but not so much to look shabby, and a white linen shirt, left open at the neck to reveal a silver and leather pendant lying against tanned skin. As he turned his white-toothed smile to each of us in turn, I almost expected to hear a 'ping' and see the Colgate ring of confidence appear.

'Hi. Kyle Hendrick. Lovely to meet you.' He shook hands with each of us, repeating our names alluringly, prolonging each handshake as though he couldn't bear to let go.

'Wow,' he drawled. 'Such beauty.'

Nadine gazed at him, her eyes wide and face flushed. She was obviously captivated but I was already irritated by him. He was a good looking man, but far too sure of himself for my liking. He was obviously used to receiving attention from women. He acted like he expected us to throw ourselves at his feet, and I did not want him to think I was about to join his fan club.

'The therapy room is through here,' I told him, intending to treat him politely but indifferently, but Nadine squeezed by me and stood with her back against the therapy room door like some sort of movie queen about to make her entrance.

'I'll show you everything,' she said, then turning scarlet at her unintended innuendo, scurried into the therapy room ahead of him.

'What do you think?' Lorraine whispered.

'He's a bit full of himself.'

'Gorgeous though.'

'Hmm. He obviously thinks he is.'

'Ha ha. Aye he's a bit of a fat head, like. But he'll be popular with the customers.'

'Yeah. Oh Lord! Wait till Nige sees him.' We both laughed imagining Nige's reaction.

Nadine led Kyle back through twittering excitedly as she explained our appointment system.

'Everything okay for you?' I asked.

'With the room,' Lorraine added.

'Yeah, cool.' He threw us another of his smiles. 'I'll leave you some of my business cards and if you could get me some appointments that would be great.'

I took down his details and said we'd get a poster made up for the window.

'Would you tell us a bit more about what you do?' Lorraine asked. 'I know you gave me a few details on the phone, but we'd love to know more about it.'

Kyle brought out a folder of charts showing diagrams of various irises, pointing out variations in colour and telling us which area of the eye related to parts of the body.

He told us the story of a therapist who spotted a specific mark in the eye of a television newsreader which indicated he had a dangerous heart condition. The therapist contacted him, advised him to seek medical help and consequently saved him from certain death.

Kyle sensed that I thought his tale was a load of hooey.

'I can see you are not convinced,' he said.

'Wow! Does it show in my eyes?' I asked. I found him conceited and more than a touch irritating.

'Let me show you. For example,' he turned to Nadine. He put his hand beneath her chin and lifting her face to his, looked into her eyes.

'Ah. Now this tells me your kidneys are an area you need to pay extra attention to. Would I be right in thinking you suffer from frequent water infections?'

'Yes,' Nadine squeaked. 'I do. It's amazing you can tell that by...'

'Shush darling,' said Kyle and Nadine shushed.

'Hmm, it's apparent you suffered from some sort of back injury, a few years ago?'

Nadine nodded, her eyes filled with adoration.

'Even when conditions have healed, they leave a record in the iris.'

Nadine nodded again.

'And you have quite a lot of water retention.'

The enthusiasm of Nadine's nodding increased. If he'd said her eyes revealed she was an alien who'd had surgery to become more human-like she'd have carried on nodding. Kyle released his grip on Nadine's chin and she reluctantly tore her eyes from his.

'Anything you want to ask me about?' Kyle asked Nadine. I'm sure there were lots of things she'd have loved to ask him.

'Well, yes. About my weight. I've been on diets for years and nothing works.'

'That's because you're not overweight, darling,' Kyle told her.

Nadine momentarily lost her balance and put her hand on the counter to steady herself and possibly to stop herself from floating into the air with bliss.

'I'm not overweight,' she repeated. 'He says I'm not overweight.'

'Your problem,' Kyle told her, 'is water retention. Your tissues are flooded, which gives you a bloated, puffed-up appearance,' – at this point Nadine's smile wilted -'so you need to increase your water consumption.'

'Won't that make her more puffed up and bloated?' Lorraine asked, and the remains of Nadine's smile melted away completely.

Kyle shook his head. 'Funnily enough, the body sometimes retains water when it's not getting enough. Drinking more will get the flow going, clear out toxins and ultimately lead to weight loss.'

It all sounded a bit too simple to me.

'So drinking water helps you lose weight?' I asked. 'What about restricting fatty foods and doing more exercise?'

'Well of course these things go hand in hand,' Kyle said. 'But actually, most people don't drink enough water. They live in a constant state of dehydration. The body needs a minimum of two litres of pure water a day for optimum health.'

'That's a lot,' I said, thinking of our two-litre bottles of mineral water. I'd spend most of my day on the loo if I drank so much.

Kyle turned to look at me.

'You could do with drinking more water too.' He instructed Lorraine to look into my right eye. 'Can you see that line on her iris there? It indicates the body is crying out for water.'

That's ridiculous, I thought. I drink loads of tea. Tea has water in it.

'And you are deficient in some of the B vitamins. Do you drink a lot of caffeinated drinks? Coffee, tea, cola? Caffeine in large amounts can deplete B vitamins.'

'Well I do drink tea sometimes.'

'Gallons of it,' Lorraine added.

'You need to cut down and think about taking a vitamin B-complex supplement, especially considering you're pregnant.' Blimey. I hadn't told him about that. 'Or if you'd prefer not to take tablets, increase the amount of foods containing B vitamins in your diet.'

Lorraine was not to be let off the hook. Kyle leaned towards her and peered into her eyes.

'Yep. Same problem. Not enough water. The three of you need to drink more of the good stuff. Every function the body performs needs water. One of the easiest and quickest ways to improve your health is to increase your water intake.'

I have to say, Kyle was pretty accurate about our health. I didn't really understand how he did it, but he was able to tell all of us about past and current ailments, and advised us on diet changes and supplements.

'Looking forward to seeing you lovely ladies again soon,' he said as he prepared to leave. Nadine watched him walking to the door then blushed as he suddenly turned and saw she'd been watching his bottom.

'Just one thing,' he said. 'Any chance of covering up those words on the wall in the therapy room? I feel they are not really conducive to a healing environment. I'd appreciate it if you could get rid of them before I return.'

'What's he on about?' Lorraine asked when he'd gone. 'What words?'

'He means my angel words,' I confessed. I was so disappointed. I'd thought they'd be a lovely touch to the room, I couldn't believe he thought them inappropriate.

'Angel words?'

I sighed. 'I had this idea to paint a border of inspirational words. I started them last week when I painted the walls. He's obviously seen them and doesn't like them. I forgot all about it, haven't you seen them?'

'No,' Lorraine said. 'I haven't been in there.'

'I've been in to do a quick vacuum and I didn't see any words,' Nadine added.

'Didn't you see them when you showed Kyle the room?' I asked. Silly question. She'd have been too busy goggling at Kyle.

'No I didn't. What do they say?'

'They're words like 'Love' and 'Serenity' and 'Joy'. Things like that. But I'd only just started painting them.'

Lorraine went through to the therapy room and I heard her laugh.

'Angel words you say?' she cackled.

Nadine and I hurried through to see what had caused her such amusement. In the corner, at the top of the room, were two words beautifully painted in silver script, the first being the last four

165

letters of 'Courage', and the second, the first four letters of 'Harmony'.

CHAPTER TWENTY-SIX

There is a saying, *"The customer is always right"*.
Although we tried to adhere to this concept for the sake of our business, Lorraine and I did not have the personality traits to carry this idea through. Basically we were two bolshie Geordie lasses and however polite and patient we tried to be, at times, our true nature was unleashed when pushed to our limits by what we called 'toxic customers'.

Although it was clearly displayed on our signage that we were a vegetarian wholefood shop, we often had customers asking for meat products.

During the lunch time rush sometimes a customer would ask for a ham or chicken sandwich and we'd explain all our food was vegetarian, which was not always well received. One man studied our menu board for a couple of minutes then asked Lorraine for a pork and stuffing sandwich. I wondered if he was unable to read so had just ordered what he'd fancied.

Lorraine politely explained our no-meat policy and he grumbled a bit.

'I'll have chicken then.'

'Sorry, we don't have chicken, like I say we don't serve meat.'

'I'll have effin' ham then,' the man shouted.

Lorraine hesitated so I decided to chip in.

'Look, we don't do meat, but we can make you a cheese salad, or vegetable pate or...'

'I don't want effin' cheese, man. I want a proper sandwich.'

'Would you mind not swearing.'

'I'm not effin' swearing, I just want an effin' pork sandwich.'

'You've been told, we don't sell meat.'

'That's effin' stupid that.'

Lorraine drew herself up to her full height.

'You're effin' stupid!' she shouted. 'WE DON'T SELL MEAT!'

The man looked a bit shocked at being spoken to in his own manner. He looked down at the contents of our display fridge.

'Just give us one of those spicy chicken and pea pasties.' He pointed to a plate of spicy chickpea pasties.

I hesitated, waiting for Lorraine to tell him.

'Hot or cold?' she asked.

From then on, he returned once or twice a week for a 'spicy chicken and pea pasty'.

Another woman came regularly to buy flour, and would complain that it was organically produced.

'Haven't you any normal flour?' she would grumble.

'Just the organic,' I would tell her.

Each time she visited she'd stand grumbling to herself at the shelves before throwing a couple of flour bags on the counter and bemoaning that we had no 'normal' flour in stock. I sometimes wondered why she continued to buy it as there were a couple of grocers on the bank where she could have shopped.

Once she caught me at a bad time and when she whinged yet again that the flour was organic, I snapped and yelled. 'Look, I'll order in a can of DDT and spray your flour specially.' She still came back for her flour but never complained again.

Plastic bags were another bone of contention. We wrapped our loaves in tissue and used paper bags for items such as bread rolls, pies and cakes. For larger purchases we used American style grocery bags which were more eco-friendly but were not popular with customers who complained they were awkward to carry and became soggy in the rain. We did at one point have some biodegradable plastic carrier bags printed with our shop name and logo, but were loath to give them away because they were so expensive.

We kept the cardboard boxes our deliveries arrived in, and offered them to customers who bought lots of shopping, rather than trying to cram their purchases into paper grocery bags (or -

heaven forbid -give away several of our ultra-expensive customised carrier bags).

One time I gave a large box to a man who'd spent nearly fifty pounds with us, a good sale in those days. I placed it on the counter and we packed it with cans, bottles and jars.

'Thank you, see you again,' I said, placing the loaves of bread he'd bought on top. He lifted the box and managed to take three steps towards the door before the bottom flaps of the box opened and everything fell out. There was a great crash as cans and bottles rolled across the floor and a jar of beetroot exploded, splattering the man in purple vinegar. He stepped back in shock, stood on a bottle of carrot juice and fell backwards, hitting his head with a loud crack on the corner of a shelf. As he fell, he clutched at a shelf and knocked down a pyramid of honey jars which shattered spectacularly, leaving splodges of glass-speckled honey across our parquet floor.

I watched in horror as he got to his feet, a trickle of blood from his forehead mingling with beetroot vinegar. His clothes were streaked with purple and the jagged base of a honey jar was stuck to his shoe.

For some reason I could not react. I was frozen to the spot. With hindsight, I know I should have rushed over to assist him but I didn't. I eventually opened my mouth to speak but the man spoke first.

'I am so sorry,' he said. 'Please let me pay for the damage.' He opened his wallet and took out three ten pound notes and put them on the counter. He then stooped and picked up the undamaged items from the floor loading them into his arms, immediately retrieving them as they slipped from his grasp, hitting the floor once more.

'Please forgive me,' he murmured. 'So sorry.' He walked unsteadily out of the shop while I stood rooted to the spot unable to speak.

Lorraine returned to the shop to find me clearing up the sticky mess of honey, beetroot and glass.

'What on earth has been going on? I've only been out for ten minutes.'

I told her what had happened.

'*He* left *us* thirty pounds? We should have been paying him thirty pounds...at least! He could have sued us.'

'I know, I was so shocked I didn't know what to do.'

'So what did you do?'

'Nothing.'

'Nothing? You must have done something, did you offer him first aid?'

'No.'

'Did you replace his shopping?'

'No.'

'Well what did you do then, you must have at least apologised?'

'No I didn't. He apologised to me.'

Lorraine looked at me blankly.

'I know, I know,' I said. 'I don't know why I just stood there, I feel really bad about it.'

The shame stayed with me a long time and even now thinking about it, I am cringing at my crassness.

Over the years we were asked for everything from knitting needles to mealworms. I think for some the concept of a wholefood shop was difficult to comprehend. Others had quite definite ideas about what they thought health food shops sold and we were often asked for cannabis.

Occasionally we had men coming in to ask for 'twenty Regal Kingsize' or 'ten Benson and Hedges' and would be surprised we didn't sell them.

'What kind of off-licence is this?' a man asked when he'd asked for a box of Marlboro.

'A crap one,' Lorraine told him.

Relationships with our customers varied. Some visited rarely, so we didn't get to know much about them. Some travelled across town to buy a particular product they'd been advised to use by their GP. Many lived or worked locally and called in several times a week.

We had our favourites – those we looked forward to seeing and had long conversations with, often inviting them to stay for a cup of tea.

Then there were the customers who made our hearts sink when they entered the shop. This could be for a variety of reasons, complainers being the most tiresome.

We always took complaints seriously and strived to rectify problems as quickly and smoothly as possible. However, some people are natural born moaners who are not interested in solutions. We learned to dismiss their grievances and not waste time trying to please them.

Talkers could be useful on a boring afternoon. Sometimes, when customers were sparse and I was clock-watching, waiting for closing time, I welcomed a browser who was fond of a chat. The problem was, they didn't know when chatting was inappropriate. Often, someone I'd had a lengthy discussion with the previous day would return when I was up to my wazoo in boxes of new stock, or struggling to work my way through a long queue of customers, and would launch into a continuation of our previous conversation. Hints that I was busy would fall onto stony ground, and I would struggle to give my attention to customers whilst trying to fend off a debate about the benefits of organic food, or what I thought of Laurence's design on Changing Rooms or whether the woman in the chippy was having a fling with the window cleaner. I suppose looking back it was rather callous of me to one day encourage conversation to while away my boredom, and the next to rebuff the very same customer.

Eccentric customers could be entertaining, but often caused chaos. We had an elderly lady visit us once a week on a mobility scooter. She insisted on driving it right into the shop, knocking things from shelves, and generally causing an obstruction. It didn't help that she was not very adept at using the controls and often shot backwards over someone's feet as she attempted to move forwards. She once flattened a case of rice cakes I'd left open and ready to price on the floor near the crackers and crispbread shelves, and it was not unusual to see her victims hopping about in pain.

She kept a walking stick hooked over her handlebar, and used it dislodge items from the shelves, and also to poke people who got in her way.

We called her Lady Muck because she would trundle in, calling for people to get out of her way, then demand one of us act as her personal shopper. This entailed removing items trapped from beneath her wheels, and replacing stock she hooked from the shelves but never wanted to buy. She had an abrupt manner and could be very rude, getting especially belligerent when she backed into the counter or shelving units.

'Who put that there?' she would yell, waving her stick. 'Get it out of my way!'

When we saw her approaching we would run to remove obstacles from her path and advise people to stand back. I often wished I had the courage to tell her to stay out, but I worried about being accused of discriminating against elderly people, as were the others, so we all did a lot of complaining when she'd gone, but none of us ever told her not to come in.

When we had a pushchair or two in the shop, then Lady Muck arrived, there would be a total gridlock, and often an argument would break out.

I was in two minds about people bringing prams and pushchairs into the shop. They were cumbersome and caused an obstruction but I understood why parents would not want to leave a child outside while they shopped - something I never did - but we really didn't have room for more than two at a time. Sometimes they were parked too close to the shelves and a little hand would reach out and grab anything in reach which would then be flung to the floor or chewed. However, we all loved babies and would stop work to coo and fuss around a pram or pushchair.

Another of our eccentric customers was a hulk of a man with a grey, bushy beard who sometimes came to browse at the shelves, picking up items and systematically transferring them to a different shelf. This irritated all of us, but especially Nadine who wouldn't wait until he'd left the premises, but followed him around the shop, saying 'Excuse me!' as she snatched items from his hand and returned them to their correct place. She carried a damp cloth and would wipe anything he'd touched as his hands were always ingrained with dirt and his nails edged with black crescents. His long grey hair lay greasy and lank down the back of his grimy overcoat, and an unpleasant odour hung over him, a mixture of unwashed body and dirty clothes. It would slowly contaminate the space in which he stood, leaving a trail behind him as he weaved his way around the shelves. Nadine called him 'Auld Reekie,' and made no pretence of hiding her disgust of him.

Sometimes he would shuffle about for half an hour or so before finally buying bread. He was a forlorn and lonely figure and I felt sorry for him, but was relieved when he ambled off with his single bread roll in a paper bag.

A reminder of his presence lingered long after he'd gone, which Nadine dealt with by apologising to subsequent customers with the explanation that we'd had a smelly visitor. We kept a scented candle on the counter that we would light as soon as we saw him, but its perfume mingled with his sourness rather than eliminating it, creating a pong that stung the nostrils and turned the stomach.

Peter hated the smell and tried to stop us using the candle.

'Trying to cover a bad smell with a pleasant one never works,' he would complain. 'Mixing two smells always makes a worse smell. It's like fried fish and air freshener, or toothpaste and fart in campsite shower blocks. It makes the original bad smell worse. I'd rather smell a stinky old man than a highly scented stinky old man.'

Most of our customers were pleasant and friendly. Although we interacted regularly with them - some daily - we knew little about them. We had a tiny part to play in their lives, and they in ours, although they kept our business going and roofs over our heads.

These people were woven into the fabric of our working week, their faces and mannerisms as familiar as our own. We learned snippets of information about their lives and grew to recognise their shopping habits. Some faces I have forgotten, others I can see clearly in my mind's eye.

The slight, chirpy young woman who called every Friday for her weekend treat of mango juice. The long-haired, bearded lorry-driver who bought a week's supply of bread rolls to store in his freezer. The family with four dairy-intolerant children who twice a week stocked up on soya milk. The teacher who bought a large bottle of vitamin tonic at the end of each school term that she swore restored her energy after battling to teach French verbs to unruly teenagers. The man who left his motorbike leaning against the shop wall before carrying his bike helmet like a shopping basket, filling it with vitamin C that he force fed family and friends. And of course the many office workers who queued daily to buy lunch. They were all, even the awkward ones, cogs in the running of our business and we relied on them for our survival. Each one was valuable to us, whether they spent pennies or pounds, we were grateful for their support.

There were, however, a couple of exceptions...

CHAPTER TWENTY-SEVEN

There was a man who shopped with us regularly. He'd come in once or twice a week to buy fresh bread and sometimes vitamins and herbal remedies. He was a quiet spoken man, but pleasant enough. He'd mentioned he was a teacher, and his conversations involved unremarkable comments about looking forward to half-term, or about how much marking he had to do that evening. So when he stopped visiting, I didn't notice. Not until he came back in, about eighteen months later.

Lorraine had nipped out to the post box and I was holding Rosie who was bouncing in my arms to a song on the radio. While the shop was empty, I'd been whirling her about as she laughed and squealed.

'Hello there!' I said to him. 'How are you?' He smiled wanly and nodded, and I thought perhaps he'd been ill.

'Hello!' Rosie yelled at him. 'Hello!' He turned away from her and she frowned, not used to being ignored. She watched him awhile but lost interest and went back to bobbing about and singing.

I sat her on the counter, holding her steady while the man wandered to the supplement shelves and began browsing. She continued laughing and singing as I served a couple of customers, glowing in the attention they gave her. As I wrapped a loaf for a woman, she nodded towards the man and scowled. She mumbled something to me, something about 'the bairn', motioning I should lift Rosie from the counter. I couldn't make out what she was trying to tell me, but as Lorraine entered the shop the woman caught her eye, and nodded towards the man. Lorraine swooped Rosie from the counter and pressed her into my arms.

'Take her in the back.' I did as she said, the gravity of her tone halting my questioning.

Once the man had left she called me back into the shop.

'What was all that about?' I asked, at which Lorraine faltered until I pressed her to explain. She reluctantly told me the man had been arrested for offences connected to child pornography, the reason for his absence being that he'd been in prison. The details of his case were vile. I found it hard to believe at first, but as I listened, I felt heat flush over my body and the room tilted. I reached for a stool and sat, pulling Rosie onto my lap as I digested the words.

'You okay?' Lorraine asked.

'Yeah. Just shocked.' Lorraine got me a drink of water. 'When did you find out?' I asked.

'A while ago,' Lorraine admitted. 'But we kept it from you because you'd just lost the baby, and well, we know how sensitive you are about stuff - especially about children - and I knew it would upset you.'

'I've stood and chatted to him...I mean, Rosie was here in the shop.' I felt sick she'd even been in his presence.

'I know. I felt the same. That's why I got you to take her into the office.'

'So when you say 'we'...does Peter know?'

'No. It all blew up when you were dealing with the miscarriage, the whole of Newcastle was talking about it. I expected you to find out through the media but when it seemed apparent you hadn't heard about it, I thought it best not to tell you. Sorry, I felt you both had enough to deal with at the time.'

'And he's been in prison for eighteen months?'

'Yes, but no-one knew much about it until he was released. Then the story got out and it was the favourite topic of gossip. Seems to have died down now.'

'I can't believe he only got eighteen months.'

'That's what most people think. I think it was shortened for good behaviour or something.'

'Good behaviour?' I said. 'You mean he managed not to harm any children in prison? It's outrageous.'

We discussed the inadequacy of his sentence, and of sentences for violent crimes as opposed to less serious offences, and the conversation changed to other topics, but the revelation had left me shaken.

I was glad they'd tried to protect me. The facts Lorraine told me made me nauseous, disgust whirled around the pit of my stomach, rising up my throat. I guessed she had probably sanitised the facts to protect me from the worst, but I'd heard enough. I felt horrified that anyone could take pleasure in such things, and frightened that there were people out there who could enjoy hurting a child. But most of all I felt a huge weight of remorse bearing down on me. Why hadn't I recognised this man as a threat to my child? As a mother, shouldn't I have known? Shouldn't some intuition of danger have kicked in, an instinct to protect my young?

Opinions were divided in the community between those who shunned him, and those -albeit a much smaller group of people- who felt he had served his punishment and now needed support from the community to deal with his problem and make sure he never offended again.

Personally, I didn't want him in my shop, or near my family, although I didn't feel I could refuse to serve him. When I saw him enter, I would snatch up Rosie and take her into the back of the shop. His visits became less frequent, and after a while I heard he'd moved away, causing me to consider whether those who thought he needed support and understanding were perhaps right. Maybe we should have sought to keep him where he was known, where he'd be watched. In a new town, anonymity would enable a new start, but would also allow depravity to crawl back into his life if he allowed it.

Unease stayed with me for a while, I felt nervous and jumpy, my confidence in humanity tainted. I found myself suspicious of everyone I met. Who could be trusted? How could you possibly know that a quiet, polite, apparently harmless man, working in a position of trust with young children was not harmless at all, his public persona of a decent human discarded at his own front door as he went home to indulge his perverted desires?

Selfishly, I was glad when he moved away, as each time I saw him, the fear in me was rekindled until even a glimpse of him cast a dark shadow over my day. Looking back, I suppose I reacted with the over-sensitivity of a new mother afraid of the seemingly unending dangers skulking nearby. Of course he needed support, and I hope in his new town, he found those qualified to give the right help, although I can never pretend to even begin to understand such behaviour.

There was one woman we had quite a heated row with.

She was a short and stocky, with a heavy guttural accent, and came occasionally to buy rye bread. I'd never had a particularly long conversation with her, most of our exchanges concerned the bread she was buying.

One morning, I was serving a man who was buying bags of spices and she complained I'd served him before her. I'd honestly thought he was before her in the queue, so apologised saying I hadn't realised she was first.

'I am not first,' she told me. 'But I do not appreciate being made to wait for that type of person.' Her face twisted into an expression of contempt.

Taken aback by the venom in her words, I thought at first she meant because he was young and flamboyantly dressed. He lived in one of the student flats above the Saffron Cafe, and shopped with us regularly. I knew some members of the local community were not happy about the student housing, being of the opinion that it brought down the value of local property, but I always found him to be a polite young lad. He had a passion for environmental matters and would often discuss issues with Peter.

'He should go back to where he came from.'

I realised with a jolt that her problem was his skin colour. I don't know why I was so shocked. Perhaps because I'd never encountered such prejudice before. My experience of racist language was confined to unfunny comedians of the 1970s, and the rantings of a certain politician of whom my dad refused to allow screening time in our home. And because, due to the white privilege I'd unknowingly lived with for thirty-odd years, I'd never experienced racial prejudice personally.

'He *is* going back to where he came from,' I said, as the young man, who either hadn't heard or was choosing to ignore her, walked to the door. 'He lives up the road.'

Lorraine, who had heard the comment, came over and stood, arms folded, next to me.

'I meant back to his own country,' the woman said.

'This is his country,' Lorraine said. 'He was born here. He's a Geordie.'

I didn't know if she knew this to be true but I sure as Hell wasn't going to question it. There was an awkward silence then Lorraine spoke again.

'Actually, aren't you German? As in, from Germany?'

The woman did not answer so Lorraine repeated her question.

The woman shrugged. 'Austria or Germany, depending on who is asking.'

'Neither of which are in Britain. So this isn't your country is it?'

'Yes it is. I have been here for many years. He has no right to be here, getting an education.'

'He's got more right than you, he was born here, he's British.'

'Oh, but that is different,' said the woman.

Lorraine and I stood and faced the woman, waiting for her to speak. She looked at us, from one to the other and smiled.

'My dears, we three are the same. We are white. That is the difference.' She smiled slyly, as though we were in agreement. Her smugness repulsed me.

I heard Lorraine's intake of breath and her face reddened. She spoke loudly.

'We three are not the same. In any way.'

'But really, you misunderstand. We have to stick together, we should not allow these people into our country to be educated.'

Before we could answer, a voice spoke.

'May I suggest Madam, perhaps it is you who is in need of education?' The student had not left the shop, but had been hidden from view by our shelving.

The woman responded with a tirade of xenophobic abuse, the likes of which I had never heard before, nor have heard since.

It was hideous. How someone could hold so much hatred for someone they knew nothing about was beyond comprehension. I could not listen to such bilge a second longer - and neither could Lorraine.

'GET OUT!' she yelled. 'GET OUT OF MY SHOP!'

The woman flung her last insult at us, words I shall not repeat but which alluded to us 'lying with the enemy'. She left and never returned.

Afterwards, when we spoke about the incident with the others, there was disgust expressed, but also laughter as the story was related. I did not laugh. I could not find anything remotely funny about it, and as I recall the events today, I can still remember her vile words, and will never understand what human beings are capable of doing to each other.

CHAPTER TWENTY-EIGHT

The summer was long and hot that year. We did not have a holiday, but were happy to stay close to home enjoying the sunshine. We spent a lot of time at Seaton Sluice beach, taking beach towels and a picnic and setting up camp for the day. Rosie loved digging in the sand, making castles that she decorated with shells, while we lay in the shade of our beach umbrella, reading and sipping cold drinks. She had a bright orange and blue beach ball that we'd all play with, running down to the sea to splash in the waves. Rosie would squeal when the cold water lapped at her toes, a sign for Peter to swing her up high. They were happy days and I have many photographs. Rosie with a huge ice-cream cone, laughing at the camera. Peter dozing, unaware of the little pink sunhat Rosie and I had placed on his head. Me, lying on my front reading, my bump cradled in a hollow I'd dug.

Days in the shop were busy and hot. We had fans and a meshed window in the kitchen which gave a good flow of air, but after the lunchtime rush, we were all ready for a sit down with a long cold drink.

Lorraine, Aileen and Nadine kept an eye on me, making sure I was not doing anything too strenuous. I know they were looking out for me but it irritated me to be restricted.

Nadine offered to paint out the fragments of my angel words before Kyle Hendrick was due to use the therapy room but I refused.

'Thanks Nadine, but I want them left.'

'They'll have to go,' Lorraine said. 'It's a nice idea but we can't have people treated in a room with 'rage' and 'harm' painted on the wall.'

'No,' I said. 'I mean it. I'm going to finish them.'

Lorraine and Nadine tried persuasion, wheedling and downright bullying to stop me climbing a ladder to finish painting the words but I resisted it all. They even embroiled Peter to help stop me, but after a half-hearted attempt, he left me to it, knowing I was determined to finish my project.

181

It didn't take me long to finish, and the end result looked great.

I smiled smugly, as Nadine and Lorraine admired my handiwork.

'I really like that,' Lorraine said.

'Ha! You made enough objections,' I said.

'We didn't say it wouldn't look good,' Lorraine said. 'We were concerned for you, climbing up the ladder in your condition.'

Since Kyle Hendrick had gazed into our eyes and told us we were all dehydrated, we'd taken up the challenge of drinking more water. We each had a two-litre bottle of water stashed in the fridge that we would drink during the day, then refill the next morning. In the heat it was easy to drink our way through the bottles. I wondered if we'd fare so well through the winter when constant cups of hot tea fuelled our days.

We became competitive, comparing the levels of our bottles and pointing out who was in the lead. As well as our water intake, our water output also increased and we took turns at trotting up the stairs to the lavatory.

'I'm sick of piddling,' Nadine said. 'I spend half my day running up and down the stairs to the toilet.' She hated anything that disrupted her workflow. Lorraine and I used it as a way to get out of doing anything we didn't want to. As soon I saw a sales rep or customer I didn't want to deal with, I'd make my excuses and disappear up to the loo for a while.

Lorraine also used it to get out of answering the phone. We were getting lots of nuisance calls from businesses trying to sell us insurance or offering to secure a tax rebate or a business rates reduction. Each time the phone rang she'd disappear upstairs for a wee. If this coincided with the arrival of an unpopular customer, Nadine would be left to answer the phone and serve behind the counter while Lorraine and I fought to be the first up the stairs.

After a couple of days, we agreed we did feel better. I felt my energy levels had increased and I hadn't had one of the blinding headaches I sometimes suffered after a hectic day. We all concurred our skin looked smoother, and Nadine even claimed she'd lost three pounds.

After I'd set up the till and opened the blinds, I took our water bottles from the fridge to rinse and refill. I noticed Nadine's was still about half full and I smiled self-righteously to myself. I'd drank all of mine.

I'd served a couple of customers and was transferring the new bread to the shelves when Lorraine arrived.

'Sorry I'm a bit late,' she said. 'I've been speaking to the girl from Richardson's Travel Agency.'

'Which girl?'

'You know, the dark-haired girl. The one who organised the abseil. She asked if we had a catering service. They're looking for someone to provide lunch for a big meeting they're having in a couple of weeks so I told her we'd get some menus and prices to her.'

'But we don't do catering.'

'We do now.'

When Nadine arrived I goaded her about her water drinking.

'Oh by the way. Nadine. I refilled the water bottles this morning and I noticed yours was still half full. You're supposed to be drinking the full two litres each day,' I said piously.

'I finished all of mine,' Lorraine said.

'Me too,' I said.

'I drank all of mine too,' Nadine said. 'I refilled the bottle yesterday lunchtime so I actually drank three litres yesterday.'

'Oh. Right.' I instantly resolved to increase my water drinking.

Lorraine must have had a similar thought because she immediately retrieved her water bottle from the fridge and poured her first glass of the day.

'I'll put the kettle on,' Nadine said. 'What are you having?'

'I'll stick to my water thanks,' Lorraine said. So I did the same, even though I was dying for a cup of tea, and I too poured a glass. Lorraine drank hers and refilled her glass, so I did the same.

183

We worked side by side in the kitchen, taking turns to go and serve customers, swigging as much water as we could. After a couple of glasses, the lavatory visits began and I returned to the shop floor to find Lorraine in discussion with the girl from Richardson's Travel.

'It's a good opportunity for you,' the girl said. 'They have these meetings once a month and the budget is eight pounds a head for twenty five people, so that's two hundred pounds a month for throwing a few sandwiches on plates.'

'They know we don't provide meat?' Lorraine asked.

'That hasn't been mentioned. I've been given the job of finding a caterer and I immediately thought of you. Your sandwiches and pastries are delicious and I'd love to get them all onto veggie food.'

Lorraine turned to me. 'I think we should go for it,' she said. What do you think?'

I nodded in agreement, but my attention had been diverted by the girl's name badge which displayed her name in four typed letters. ANNA. A pretty name that suited her perfectly. I looked at her smooth dark skin and her beautiful almond eyes with their almost black irises and I suddenly felt I'd been given an answer to a question I'd never asked.

Anna, I thought. Anna. My daughters, Rosie and Anna. Perfect. If my baby were a girl, I would name her Anna, and I knew she too would be beautiful.

'That's great,' Anna said. 'I'll tell them to expect it in around an hour.'

'Expect what in an hour?' I asked Lorraine as Anna swept out of the shop.

'The lunch buffet. Weren't you listening?'

'No, not really. What do you think of Anna?'

'I think she's great. Very attractive and a lovely girl but we need to get started.'

'No, I mean the name Anna. Get started with what?'

Lorraine sighed. 'We've agreed to send a free lunch to Richardson Travel with the hope of them ordering a buffet for twenty five people each month. We have to deliver by eleven.'

'But we haven't planned anything...we don't know what they want...we don't have enough bread for sandwiches for twenty-five people.'

'It's not for twenty-five this time. It's for six. Just for the bigwigs. If they like what we do, then it will be for twenty-five on Tuesday, and afterwards, the first Tuesday of the month.'

'So how many is it for then?'

'I've told you! Six. Weren't you listening?'

'Yeah,' I said. But I wasn't. I was off in a daydream about my baby girl named Anna.

CHAPTER TWENTY-NINE

Nige and Georgina arrived to a scurry of activity. Aileen was at the counter dealing with customers and Nadine was on duty at the kitchen bench, simultaneously making sandwiches, cooking veggie burgers and wrapping cakes.

Lorraine and I left them to it and worked on getting the lunch buffet ready. Nadine suggested her aunt's recipe for curried eggs. She instructed us to hard boil some of our free-range eggs, mix the yolks with mayonnaise and spices and a little grated cheese. The egg whites were filled with this mixture and garnished with parsley. Lorraine and Nadine assured me they were delicious, but pregnancy had again brought with it an abhorrence of eggs and the sulphurous smell repulsed me. I covered the tray of stuffed egg halves with two layers of clingfilm in an attempt to contain the smell.

Our food processor made pastry-making a doddle, so I'd whipped up a quick batch to make vol-au-vont cases that Lorraine was now filling with a creamy mushroom and tarragon filling. The rest had been transformed into veggie sausage rolls that were baking in the oven, the aroma making us salivate. I made sandwiches using a variety of our fillings in thinly sliced granary and wholemeal bread, cutting them into triangles and fingers – a little more delicate than our usual stotties. Squares of carrot cake and lemon poppyseed cake looked tempting arranged on a platter with some fresh fruit.

'Sorry, you'll have to make your own coffee today,' I told Georgina and Nige as I grappled with a roll of clingfilm.

'I'll do it,' Georgina said, and joined the chaos in the kitchen, pulling mugs from their hooks and squeezing past Nadine to get to the sink with the kettle.

'Ooh nice,' Nige said, picking a sausage roll from the tray Lorraine had removed from the oven. Lorraine slapped at his hand as he juggled the hot pastry and it fell to the floor.

'Aw, now look what you've done,' he said.

'No, look what *you* have done. You shouldn't be touching. They're for an order.'

'One won't be missed,' he said, reaching for another and I snatched the tray from his reach.

'Gerroff!' I snapped. My stress levels were rising rapidly, the pressure to get the food ready along with the eggy smell had created a headache that was creeping up the back of my neck and spreading its way across my skull.

Aileen was doing her best to keep up with the sandwich orders, but she was not used to our high-speed way of working and so Nadine became frustrated she was not getting through the queue quickly enough.

'Give me another,' she kept yelling at Aileen, whose method was to deal with one customer at a time, waiting until they'd received and paid for their order before turning to the next in line. Usually we took payment with the orders then moved swiftly to the next customer, knowing they would not leave once they'd handed over money. Aileen became flustered as Nadine tried to hurry her, and confusion reigned as she called out incorrect orders and gave sandwiches to the wrong recipients.

'For God's sake...' Nadine muttered, her face growing redder and her handling of dishes more violent.

Lorraine and I were trying to load the prepared food onto a bread tray while costing it at the same time (not a recommended way to do business). We'd made far too much food for six people but wanted to impress them with the variety we could offer. Georgina was carrying hot teabags to the bin, one at a time, leaving a trail of drips across the floor. The telephone began to ring and Aileen moved towards it but Lorraine, Nadine and I yelled 'LEAVE IT!' in perfect unison.

'I'm so sorry...' Aileen began but Nadine cut off her apology.

'The queue! Just get the orders, will you?' she yelled and Aileen, in her attempt to comply lost her composure and pleaded to a man in the queue.

'What do you want? Quick! Quick!'

'Are you the owner?' he asked. 'I have a range of slimming products to show you. If you'd kindly give me a moment...' He opened his briefcase and began unloading bottles of pills onto the counter.

'No, I'm the owner,' I called to him from the kitchen. 'And I'm not interested, thanks.' I'd managed to get a piece of clingfilm wrapped around my arm and was struggling to remove it.

'D'you think that will do?' I asked Lorraine as we surveyed the tray of food we'd prepared.

'Yeah,' Lorraine said. 'Hoy some crisps on and it'll be fine.'

'Excuse me, I've been waiting ages,' a woman complained, and other customers joined in the general grumbling. Nadine left her position at the kitchen bench and began vigorously taking orders and ringing sales into the till.

'Here!' she said, pushing a couple of rolls at Aileen. 'Cheese, pickle and salad on the wholemeal and hummus and tomato, no butter, on the granary.' Aileen took the rolls from Nadine but by the time she'd reached the bench had forgotten the orders.

'Did you say cheese on the wholemeal?' she asked timidly.

'Cheese, pickle and salad on the wholemeal, hummus and tomato on the granary,' Nadine yelled, as she threw a veggie burger into the pan with one hand and a leek and potato pasty into a paper bag with the other. Her face had progressed from red to purple.

'I SAID NO BLOODY BUTTER!' she yelled as Aileen picked up the butter knife and threw it down again like it had burnt her fingers.

'Sorry...sorry,' she whimpered.

Nadine grabbed the bread rolls from her and began frantically stuffing them with fillings. 'GO AND GET THE NEXT ORDER!,' she yelled at Aileen as she threw the sandwiches into paper bags and gave them to the customer. Aileen was now in a blind panic, dithering helplessly around the kitchen while Nadine, shouted at her.

'GO AND TAKE AN ORDER, MAN! YOU'RE LIKE A FANNY IN A FIT.'

Nadine then turned to the sales rep who had arranged his bottles on the counter and was delivering his sales pitch, telling her the Daily Mail had run a feature on the slimming pills and that William Shatner used them to shed pounds, as though either of these facts could be pivotal factors in a decision to stock them.

'I DON'T CARE IF MR SPOCK LOST TEN STONE, WE'RE NOT INTERESTED!'

I began to feel concern for Nadine. Her face had the hue of a damp aubergine and she was panting, trundling back and forth, taking orders, grabbing up bread rolls and attacking the till keyboard as she hammered in sales. Aileen fluttered about nervously, trying to help but constantly getting under Nadine's feet. There was a lot of grumbling from customers who had paid for sandwiches but not been given them.

'Is Nadine okay?' I whispered to Lorraine, and she stopped to look, her head moving like a spectator at a tennis match as it followed Nadine's path from counter to bench and back to counter. I feared she was going to give herself some sort of heart attack or at the very least hyperventilate, neither of which would be good for business. Or for Nadine.

'Nadine, calm down,' I said stepping towards her, but Aileen, trying to slip behind me, caught my foot with hers and I stumbled, tearing the seam of my skirt with a loud ripping noise.

'Oh!' I cried, clutching my buttocks with both hands, at which Nadine, Lorraine, Aileen, and most of the customers in the queue turned to me in shock, believing I had just let off the most thunderous fart. Their stunned expressions – especially that on Nadine's sweating, blotched face, triggered an inherent reaction as I realised what they'd thought, and I sank to my knees, laughing uncontrollably while trying desperately to protest my innocence.

For a couple of seconds there was silence except for my gabbling laughter. Nadine was the first to crack, joining me in my hysteria.

I don't know if you have ever been in such a state, but it renders you helpless. I crouched on the floor, tears running freely down my face. Nadine clutched the edge of the bench, arms stretched, and head hanging as she sunk to her knees, gulping and snorting. An instant later, the hysteria hit Lorraine, her laughter hearty and irrepressible as she slid to the floor.

A woman in the queue finally lost patience and slamming her fist on the counter yelled at us.

'This is ridiculous! I have never seen such behaviour in all my days!'

Unfortunately, this flamed our hilarity, and we lay roaring on the floor as she stormed out shouting that she'd never had such bad service in her life.

Aileen hurried to the counter, apologising and attempting to placate customers, although most had turned and headed for the door in exasperation, passing Peter who had arrived for lunch. He looked at us, perplexed, which seemed to be the funniest thing yet and after ineffectively questioning us as to what on earth was going on, joined Aileen at the counter and even made a couple of sandwiches as we laughed by his feet.

Later, when the shop was empty and we'd dried our eyes and calmed down, I swivelled my skirt about on my hips to examine the damage, and found the seam was torn from waistband to hem.

'Aw, would you look at that!' I said. 'It's ruined.'

'You'll have to take it to the invisible menders,' Lorraine suggested. 'There's a place near the High Street. Have you been there before?'

'Yeah,' I said. 'I went once but I couldn't see them.' It was a truly rubbish joke, but it rekindled our hilarity, and off we went again.

'I'm going back to work,' Peter said. 'I don't know what you've all been on this morning but I hope it soon wears off.' He kissed my cheek and headed off, leaving us to spend the rest of the day giggling and snorting until we'd exhausted ourselves.

CHAPTER THIRTY

Summer gave way to autumn and I became more confident about the viability of my pregnancy. My regular check-ups showed that the baby was healthy, and each passing day was a day closer to a safe delivery.

Business was good, the therapy room was booked most days and at last we felt that we were beginning to reap rewards for all our hard work.

The catering experiment was a success. The travel company liked our food and asked us to provide lunch for their monthly meetings. We added catering to our repertoire, and soon we were delivering lunches to several local businesses on a regular basis. Two of us would prepare the buffet food while the others dealt with the usual morning's business, then Dad would deliver it for us. He declined payment for this, refusing even a token amount for fuel, but would return with the empty trays to sit and join the morning chat with a cup of coffee and an apricot flapjack.

News spread, and in the run up to Christmas we took bookings for party buffets, and also for gluten-free cakes, puddings and mince pies.

Often people would ask us to cook dishes for a dinner party they could pass off as their own by re-heating at home. Although we never got the credit for these culinary masterpieces, it became a popular service as the idea was whispered from friend to friend.

At the time, few caterers offered vegan and vegetarian food so although our market for this was niche, we had lots of repeat business which added nicely to our overall income.

I was approached by a man who wanted to arrange a surprise party for his wife's birthday.

'It's Poll's fortieth after Christmas and I want to do something special for her,' he told me. 'I'm going to get all her friends together. I've even contacted people she's not seen for years, school friends and workmates.'

'How lovely.' What a nice man to arrange all that for his wife. So thoughtful.

'We are both vegetarian, as are most of our friends so it would be great if you could do the food,' he said.

'We'd be delighted. If you give me the date and an idea of what you'd like, I'll get back to you with some prices.'

'It's not until February but I wanted to get everything organised before Christmas.'

I put a note against the date in the diary and asked what sort of spread he wanted.

'I was thinking of the usual, you know, cheese sandwiches, some sort of veggie sausage rolls, crisps?

'Right,' I said, although I had no intention of supplying such an uninspired spread for the poor woman's special birthday. 'Why don't I put a few ideas together and you can see what you think.'

'Great. And would you be able to deliver straight to the venue?'

'Yes, providing it's local.'

'It is. It's at the swimming pool.'

'Swimming pool...?'

'Yes, you see, my wife used to love swimming years ago,' he told me excitedly. 'She hasn't been for years. So I thought it would be a lovely surprise. I've thought of everything. It's a public session but I've booked a private room for the buffet afterwards. My plan is to not tell her where we are going, then I'll present her with a new swimming costume and when she comes out of the changing room all her friends will be there to surprise her.'

Christ, I thought. I couldn't think of anything worse to happen on your fortieth birthday. Not only having to wear a swimsuit chosen by your man, but having all your friends there to witness your shame. And not even being given a warning to get your legs waxed and lose a few pounds before the trauma. And then to top it off, being given a cheese sandwich and a sausage roll to celebrate with afterwards.

'And you're sure she'll enjoy that?'

'Yes, she'll love it. It will be the last thing she'll expect.'

'Yes, I'm sure it will.' I toyed with asking him if he'd like us to do the catering for the divorce party too, but refrained.

'There should be around fifty people coming.'

'Okay. I'll get some menus and prices ready for you. Would you like me to ring you with the information?'

'No, you'd better not. Poll might answer the phone. I'll call back in a couple of days, would that be okay?'

'Great.'

Nadine was horrified when I told her.

'My God,' she said. 'That's awful. Imagine the poor woman standing there in a horrible swimming costume with a pot belly.'

'And hairy legs,' I said.

'And a white winter body.'

'What if she hasn't painted her toe nails and they're all manky?'

'Or if he chooses a really awful costume that makes her bum look bigger?'

'And her boobs look droopy.'

'Honestly you two!' Lorraine said. 'You don't even know the woman and you've decided she looks like some kind of yeti. How do you know she'll have a pot belly and droopy boobs? You're thinking of how you'd feel. She may be gorgeous.'

'You saying we're not?'

'No. I'm saying she might feel confident about her body, whatever it's like.'

'Would you feel confident? Wearing a swimming outfit a bloke picked out that you'd never seen before, then being paraded about in it in front of everyone you know with no warning?'

'No. I'd hoy him in and drown the bugger, but we're not talking about me are we?'

'No. I supposed you're right,' I said. 'It's none of our business, we'll make the food and take the money. But I do feel sorry for poor old Poll.'

'Poll?' Nadine asked. 'Do you mean Poll who comes in here?'

'I don't know, he mentioned her name a couple of times. Who is she?'

'You know her! She's got loads of kids, four boys and two girls I think. Youngest is about seven. All really well behaved. She comes in every Friday morning.'

'Greyish hair and glasses?' Lorraine said.

'Does her own baking, buys a lot of fresh yeast and flour?' I asked.

'Yeah, that's her.'

'Oh no!' I said. 'She'll hate it!'

Poll was a pleasant, slightly nervous woman who shopped with us, often bringing her children who were polite and helpful, offering to carry shopping and not making a fuss if they were sometimes refused things they'd asked for. I'd vaguely recognised her husband when he'd called to arrange the buffet, but had not realised he was 'Dad' who they often spoke about while they chose cakes and treats for him.

The thing was, we all knew Poll was not a confident woman. Although lovely, it was apparent by her demeanour, and by the way she spoke about herself that she suffered from low self-esteem. She often made self-deprecating remarks about her weight and appearance, joking that after six children she was ready for the scrap heap.

'I think we'll have to tell her,' Nadine said. 'She'll absolutely keel over and die with embarrassment. She and I have loads of conversations about how many diets we've tried, there's no way she'll enjoy it.'

'And she's had a couple of appointments with Dana Quinn for hypnotherapy for her self-confidence issues. We'll have to warn her,' I said.

'And what are you going to say to her? Thought you should know your husband's planning to get you half naked in front of everyone you know to humiliate you?' Lorraine said.

'Can't we give away the secret as if by accident?' Nadine suggested. 'You know, mention it casually and then act mortified that we've given it away?'

'I don't know,' I said. 'We'll have to think of something.'

Peter had a totally different take on it.

'I don't know why you're all making such a fuss. It's nothing to do with you. Your only involvement is to provide the food. He's not doing it to humiliate her. He's doing it because he loves her and he wants her to have a great time.'

'But what if she hates it? It's her birthday, her special day,' I said, and Nadine and Lorraine murmured in agreement, shaking their heads with worried expressions.

Peter laughed.

'You know the problem with you three? You're too fond of sticking your noses into other people's business. You spend far too much time standing at that bench discussing the ins and outs of other people's lives.' He pushed his arms into his jacket. 'Anyway, I have to get back.'

'Aye go on, get lost,' Lorraine told him. 'So we can stand at our bench and talk about you.'

CHAPTER THIRTY-ONE

The last two weeks of trading before Christmas were frantic. Aileen and Nadine kept the daily business of the shop running smoothly as Lorraine and I prepared buffets, baked Christmas goodies and dealt with the many telephone queries we always got at this time of year.

'Why do they leave it until the last minute?' Lorraine grumbled, as she took a call from another customer needing to cater for a vegetarian guest and with no idea of what to serve.

'If they'd asked earlier we could have made something to put in the freezer and there'd be none of this last minute panic,' I said.

Consequently we had a few late nights in the kitchen putting together nut roasts and mushroom and chestnut pies for some poor unsuspecting vegan who'd otherwise have ended up with Brussels sprouts and parsnips for their festive dinner

Christmas passed by in a jingle, and before we knew it, the last of the mince pies had been devoured and the tinsel stored away and we were into 1996.

The Health, Body and Mind Show was coming up and we'd made no preparations. I was determined to make our stall look really eye-catching, I was not going to miss out on a chance for some major faffing about, and had already thought of creative ways to dress up our stall.

'What sort of stuff should we take?' Lorraine asked. 'A bit of everything? Or should we focus on one type of product?'

'Let's find out who's going and what they will be selling,' I suggested. 'Then we can decide.'

Most things appeared to be covered. Several stalls would sell essential oils and there would be natural therapists of every sort offering treatments and related products. Local gyms and fitness clubs would be represented, and also various companies offering water filters, yogurt makers, yoga mats, exercise equipment and bamboo cooking pots and steamers.

Beauty was well represented with exhibitors offering everything from herbal hair colours to seaweed skin treatments to vegan cosmetics.

'What about food?' Lorraine suggested. 'We could take a selection and have a 'healthy' grocery stall.'

'There's already lots of food stalls listed,' I told her, reading from the information we'd been sent. 'Gluten free, dairy-free, vegan, herbs and spices, sugar-free cereals, organic chocolate...'

'I don't suppose it matters if there's more than one stall selling similar stuff. There's bound to be crossovers.'

'Okay. Let's make a lovely grocery stall, lots of little packs of dried fruits, chutneys, patés, stuff like that,' I said. 'I'll make a list.'

Peter was not keen to attend and said he'd be more than happy to spend the day with Rosie, leaving Lorraine and I to man the stall.

'Do you need me to come along?' Nadine asked.

'No it's fine,' I told her. 'You enjoy your Sunday off.'

Nadine looked disappointed but it wouldn't be cost effective to pay her to work when there were already two of us there.

'I didn't mean you'd need to pay me. I'd just like to come along to help out and to have a look around at what's there.'

'Me too,' Aileen said. 'I'd be happy to come and help too, without being paid.'

'We couldn't do that,' I said. 'You can't work for free, we'd feel awful, wouldn't we Lorraine?'

Lorraine hesitated. 'Why not come along with us in the car and we'll all go in together then you won't have to pay an entrance fee. Maybe you could mind the stall for a while to let me and Chris have a wander about?'

'Aw thanks, that would be great,' Aileen said. 'It's a fiver to get in so that will be a good saving for us.'

'Yeah, thanks,' Nadine said. 'We'll have more to spend on stuff, won't we?' She and Aileen smiled at each other, both believing we'd done them a huge favour as they set about unpacking the Karma order.

I looked at Lorraine and was about to confess to feeling we'd taken advantage of them, but she read my face.

'They're happy, we're happy. What's the problem?'

As soon as our lunchtime rush was over, I carried our electric scales over to the kitchen bench and began making up packets of nuts and dried fruits, tying on little strips of parcel ribbon and sticking on our Nutmeg labels.

'Look at her,' Lorraine said, as I carefully arranged the packets in a basket lined with a piece of pale green linen. 'There's nothing my sister loves more than a bit of fannying about.'

I ignored her and continued rearranging my packets.

'Aw, they do look lovely though,' Nadine said. 'What about doing some of the organic coffee beans? Or some of our Nutmeg muesli?'

'Yeah, let's do both,' I said, and we had a lovely afternoon listening to the radio while we mixed up a great tub of our special mix muesli and packed it into bags while Lorraine served customers.

At about four o'clock, there was the usual busy spell of customers on their way home, stopping to buy the last of our bread or to pick up something for dinner.

Lorraine was busy ringing sales into the till when Val entered, puffing and blowing and making a drama in her usual irritating way. I put my head down and continued sticking labels on packets waiting for Nadine to go and greet her, but unfortunately the phone began to ring and Nadine, being nearest the office door escaped to go and answer it.

Reluctantly I put down my stickers and walked to the counter.

'Hello Val. How can I help you?'

'I don't think anyone can help me. I'm beyond help.' She slumped on the counter, knowing I'd go and get her a chair rather than have her draped near the till getting in the way of customers.

'There you go, have a seat,' I said, carrying a stool around the counter.

198

'Is that the best you've got?' she complained. 'It's not good for my spine, I need a chair with a back.'

Gritting my teeth I dragged the padded desk chair from the office from behind Nadine who was in full conversation on the telephone. I pushed it towards Val, and as she sank her heavy body into it, it rolled backwards slightly on its casters, and I was tempted to give it a shove and watch her go sailing out of the door and into the street.

'Now then, what's the problem?' I asked.

Val picked up at the anticipation of relating her latest list of aches and pains and shuffled in the chair to make herself more comfortable.

'Well for a start, I've got this nagging pain in my neck that keeps coming back.' Me too, I thought. 'And as for my feet, you've seen nothing like them. Do you want to have a look?'

I declined the offer and Val continued to update me about her various ongoing health issues. She did eventually get to the point of her visit.

'...so I thought it would be best if I came along with you and you could look after me.'

'Come along with me...? Sorry, I'm not with you.' Like usual I'd drifted off in the middle of Val's list of complaints and had no idea what she was talking about.

'The Health-Body-Mind Fair on Sunday. As you are going to be there anyway I thought you could give me a lift.'

I smiled at her while I inwardly searched through a list of possible excuses to find the most feasible. Lorraine answered before I had a chance to speak.

'I'm so sorry Val but we won't be able to do that.'

'Why not?'

'Because the car will be full, there are four of us going.'

'I'm sure I could squeeze in the back.'

'I'm afraid you couldn't, we'll be jam-packed with stock.'

Val thought for a moment. 'Couldn't you leave some of it?'

'No, we couldn't. That's the whole point of going.'

199

'You say there are four going? Who are they?'

Lorraine gave a sharp exhale of breath. I expected her to tell Val to mind her own business. 'Sorry Val, like I say we haven't room in the car.'

'I was going to suggest maybe one of you could get the bus or something?' Honestly, when it came to cheek, the woman knew no bounds. 'It's difficult for me to use public transport with all my problems,' Val whined. 'What with my back, and my knee and then I could have one of my dizzy turns.'

'Taxi?'

'Oh dear God, I couldn't afford a taxi!'

'Looks like a restful day at home then,' Lorraine said. 'By the sounds of it, you need it.'

'Derek from the greengrocers is going,' I said. 'Why don't you ask him for a lift? He closes soon, if you hurry you'll catch him.' Val hauled her body out of the chair and hurried to the door.

'Thanks, I'll go round there right now,' she said. I was impressed at the speed she managed to exit the shop in spite of her ailments.

'Must be feeling better, she's forgotten her stick,' I said to Lorraine.

'Is that true? About Derek? I didn't know he was going.'

'No I don't believe he is,' I said. 'But I'm getting revenge for potato-gate.'

Val shopped for vegetables at Derek's and had asked him if he would pre-peel her potatoes as it was too tricky for her. He told her he didn't keep a knife on the premises and said we would do it for her. Consequently she often arrived with a bag of potatoes or carrots for me to prepare.

'Has she gone?' Nadine crept out of the office, looking about. When she was satisfied Val had left she came in to tell us about the phone call.

'I've been speaking to a woman who would like to hire the therapy room.'

'Great, what does she do?' I asked.

'I can't remember what she said it was called, I've never heard of it.' She went back through to the office and retrieved the notes she written. 'Ah here it is. Amanda Wethering. Colonic Irrigation.'

'Colonic irrigation?' Lorraine said. 'In our therapy room? I don't think so.'

I shook my head. 'No, no, no.'

'Why, what is it? Nadine asked.

'It's what it sounds like,' I said.

Nadine looked puzzled.

'We did irrigation in geography at school. Something to do with water? But I don't know what colonic means. Something to do with a colony? Taking water to colonies? Doesn't make sense.'

'Ha ha, it's nothing to do with colonies! Colonic refers to your colon which is part of your intestines.'

'Ah. So is it drinking lots of water to fill your intestines?'

'Sort of, except you don't drink it. It involves shooting water up your bottom to clear everything out,' I told her.

'That's a polite way of describing it,' Lorraine said.

'Get lost,' Nadine said. 'What is it really?'

'It's what Chris said. It's a method of using a jet of water to clean out your colon.'

'Up your bum?'

'Yeah.'

'Like, with a pipe?'

'Yeah.'

'Ugh that's disgusting. I thought it was supposed to be a natural therapy? I mean, shoving a pipe up your bum doesn't sound natural to me.'

'It's really popular at the moment.'

'Why on earth would you want that done?'

'Apparently people say they feel really clean afterwards.'

'What's the matter with having a bath, like?'

'Well obviously this also cleans the inside.'

'Where does it go when it comes out?'

'I've no idea, I've never had it done.'

201

'Doesn't it come back down a pipe?' Lorraine said. Nadine looked horrified.

'You mean they shove two pipes up there?'

The conversation was beginning to put me off my lunch.

'However they do it, it's not happening in our therapy room. So one of us will have to call her and explain.'

'I'm sure she'd need access to running water and there's none in our therapy room so it's not really suitable anyway,' Lorraine added.

'And especially not in a food shop,' Nadine said. 'Imagine making sandwiches in the kitchen with that going on in the next room.'

'I think it's a sealed unit they use, but even so I don't think it's something we want happening in the back of our shop is it?'

'No, it's not. I'll ring her now,' Lorraine said. 'And don't mention it to Aileen or the next thing we'll hear is she's made us one from an old hosepipe or something.'

CHAPTER THIRTY-TWO

I was handing out hot drinks to Lorraine, Nadine and Nige when Georgina bustled in, holding a large carrier bag. Her face was bright with excitement.

'Hey wait until you see what I've got! I've been down to the new charity shop, it's amazing!'

Nige turned up his nose. 'Don't tell me. You've bought a load of dead people's clothes and you're going to wear them.'

'Don't be so horrible,' Nadine told him, although we all knew Nadine would rather be stuck in a lift with a wasps' nest than wear second hand clothes.

Georgina ignored Nige's remark and began to unpack her bargains. I was expecting some old kaftan, or a hideous 1970s dress, however, she brought out a fifties style dress, the skirt flared with net underskirts and a nipped-in waist.

'Wow, that's gorgeous,' Nadine said.

'Three quid,' Georgina said proudly. 'And have a look at this.' She pulled out a dark blue crushed velvet jacket. 'Laura Ashley. Fiver. And a pair of boots, three-fifty.' The jacket wasn't really my kind of thing, but the dress was beautiful and the boots hardly worn. In fact, all three were clean and looked new.

'Which charity shop did you get these from?' I asked. 'Whenever I've been in charity shops they always have a load of old tat and they usually stink of musty old clothes.'

'It's the old wool shop. It's just opened this morning, I was one of the first in. It's got some great stuff. You should go and have a look.'

We'd heard the wool shop was to re-open as a charity shop supporting a local hospice, and although it was a great cause, we were a bit concerned that having a charity shop on the block might make the bank look a bit downmarket. When we told Georgina this she'd told us not to be such snobs, saying the charity shop would help the community on many levels; by raising funds for the cause they supported, by offering employment to people with learning difficulties, and also by offering inexpensive clothing and toys for families on low incomes. I had nothing at all against second hand goods, or shops selling them. Our home was full of auction buys and vintage bargains - we'd had an antiques shop ourselves - but charity shops tended to be a bit like glorified jumble sales.

'Go and have a look,' she said. 'They've got loads of baby stuff.'

I hesitated and Lorraine said, 'Go on. If you don't go, I will.' So I grabbed my purse and headed off down the bank.

On opening the shop door I could tell this was different from usual charity shops of that time. The smell of freshly washed linen hit me and a CD of classical guitar music played. Clothes were displayed on rails by colour, with toning shoes, bags and accessories presented above each section. There were glass cases filled with jewellery, and scarves arranged on a rack from the softest, palest colours through the spectrum to dark indigos and violets.

There was a whole wall of books, crisp clean paperbacks as well as hardbacks, no dog eared, broken-spined volumes here. Sparkling glassware, household china, toys...everything was clean and displayed perfectly.

And then I saw them. A pair of Dolce and Gabbana six-inch heeled, leopard print sandals priced at five pounds. And, oh my word, they were my size. I didn't even try them on. They were so outrageously funky that even if they didn't fit, I would place them on a shelf and they would serve in an ornamental capacity. I loved them. I picked one up and turned it in my hand. The curve of the sole, moulded to caress the foot, the tapering heels. I admired it as others would admire a famous painting or piece of sculpture. I happily handed over a fiver and rushed back to the shop.

'What the hell are those?' Lorraine said. 'Stripper shoes?'

'These, I said, 'are a work of art.'

'I saw those,' Georgina said. 'They are pretty funky but not sure they are my kind of thing.'

'I'm not sure they're Chris's sort of thing either,' Lorraine said. 'When are you going to wear them?'

'I don't know. I just love them.' I slipped off my shoes and slid my feet into the sandals. I fastened the straps then rolled up the legs of my jeans to get the full effect. I lifted a foot and flexed my ankle to admire it from different angles.

'What do you think?'

Lorraine laughed. 'I think if they make you happy, go for it,' she said and Georgina told me I should wear whatever made me feel good.

I thought I'd try walking in them and held on to the tea shelves until I got my balance.

'I think they're really cool but I don't think it's a good idea to wear them when you're pregnant, you could fall,' Nadine said. I strutted across the shop floor clumsily.

'Oh yes, graceful,' Lorraine said. 'Very Tina Turner.'

'Simply the best...' I sang as I staggered about, jerking my knees and bending them at strange angles. Georgina and Nadine joined in the singing and Lorraine laughed as I sang into my invisible microphone pulling my best rock goddess face.

I was reaching a pivotal moment of frenzied dancing when it came to me that Georgina and Nadine had ceased singing and I stopped, knees turned out and face grimacing, to see a man with a black file tucked beneath his arm.

'Hello, I'm Mr Packer, manager at Brent Bakery. I've come to sort out the matter of your unpaid invoices,' he said. I slowly straightened up and lowered my pretend microphone.

'She's got an audition for Stars in Their Eyes,' Georgina told him and he nodded complacently, like this was a usual occurrence. 'See you later, Tina,' she said, and left us to it.

I turned to Mr Packer, aware of my dishevelled hair, rolled up jeans and six inch high leopard skin effect sandals, and tried my best to look and act professionally.

'Unpaid invoices?' I asked. 'I'm afraid I think there's been an error.'

Mr Packer placed a large file on the counter, and extracted from it a document listing our orders for the last two months.

'In light of the fact that we have not received payment from you for the last two months, I'm afraid I have to tell you that if the debt is not cleared in full today, we will cease to supply you and will begin action to recover the debt.'

For a moment Lorraine and I looked at each other, then she said, 'This must be a mistake. We're up to date with our payments.'

Mr Packer turned his sheets of paper so we could read them and pointed to the figure he claimed was owing.

'But we've been paying in cash every day,' I told him.

Mr Packer swallowed. 'Well I have only your word for that,' he said. Lorraine hastened to the office and returned with our copies of the invoices.

'These have been signed and dated by your delivery driver,' she told him.

He gave another nervous swallow and looked at the signature that Lorraine pointed out.

'Ah yes. I see. We have...had...eh...we have had a few...eh...problems shall we say with this member of staff before.'

'Problems?' Lorraine said. 'You mean like the problem that he's a thief?

Mr Packer neither confirmed nor denied this.

'Isn't he a family member?' Nadine asked, and Mr Packer gave a slight nod.

My anger surged, making me hot and reddening my face. I puffed myself up on the full height of my sandals

'How dare you!' I said. 'You knew before you entered this shop that your delivery driver, your *relative*, had stolen the money and yet you came in here and tried to get the money from us.'

'Not at all, not at all,' Mr Packer stuttered. 'I had to...eh...investigate first to make sure that was the case.' He was a short man, and in my heels I towered above him.

'I don't appreciate your driver pocketing the money we gave him, neither do I appreciate you coming in here trying to rip us off.' Mr Packer tried to speak but I cut him off. 'And while you are here, I can tell you I'm not happy about our bread being left on the doorstep, or that it is transported to our shop in a van full of cigarette smoke.'

206

'I can only apologise...'

'Well, you can keep your apologies. It's too late. We no longer wish to order from your bakery, so I'll return your crates...' I staggered to them and was about to pick them up when Nadine stopped me and bent to lift them.

'I'm sure there's no need for that,' Mr Packer said.

'I've nothing else to say about it. I would like you to leave. In future we will order our bread elsewhere.'

Mr Packer slumped, defeated. He picked up his papers and put them back in his file.

'If you change your mind we will be delighted to supply you,' he said.

'Goodbye,' I said.

'Goodbye. And the best of luck in the show.'

'Well you two didn't have much to say,' I said to Lorraine and Nadine who had stood silently throughout my outburst.

'You were amazing,' Nadine said. 'Magnificent. Wasn't she?'

'Oh yeah,' Lorraine said. 'Except we now have no bread supplier which means no sandwich sales tomorrow. And it will be all over Newcastle that the mad woman from the healthfood shop is going to be on the telly doing Tina Turner.'

'Aw shurrup, man,' I told her and I staggered off into the office to remove my sandals and tidy my hair.

It took a while phoning around, but I managed to find a bakery in Jesmond able to supply us and I placed an order for the next day. The whole thing turned out to be a blessing in disguise as the bread we received, although a little more expensive, was delicious.

Another result of my outburst, which was a great source of amusement to the others, was that word did spread that I was to appear on Stars in Their Eyes as Tina Turner.

'Let's go along with it,' Lorraine said, and the others agreed. So every time I tried to tell a misinformed customer it was all a misunderstanding, Lorraine or Nadine would chip in, telling the customer I was too modest to speak of it and that I should be proud of my singing talent. They got extra amusement at this, knowing that I couldn't sing for toffee.

And then, oddly, a girl did appear on Stars in Their Eyes as Tina Turner and a few people actually believed it was me and came in to congratulate me on coming second to Engleburt Humperdink.

CHAPTER THIRTY-THREE

Fridays mornings were always busy but this one portended to be more so than usual so I made an effort to get into work early. Lorraine had the same idea and we started the morning with a sleepy tea break.

Our Karma delivery was due, so the first priority would be to keep an eye on the side road and rush out with our cones when there was a space large enough to accommodate the enormous van. If we managed to place the cones, we usually found them kicked to one side and the space taken by the time the delivery arrived.

Often, at around half past eleven we would see the huge van pass the window several times as the driver circled the area looking for a parking spot. Sometimes, after several rounds, he would pull the van halfway onto the pavement outside our window. Traffic would back up as cars fought to pass the van from both directions, and our goods would be transported inside accompanied by yelling and car horns sounding. We would then hurry to unpack and price the stock before the Nutmeg Express came in.

Today, because we were so early, we managed to grab a space, laying out the cones we knew would be moved later when the sales reps arrived for work.

We also had Poll's party buffet to prepare. We had most of the ingredients in stock, I just needed to pick up some fresh vegetables from Derek's.

I made a shopping list while Lorraine checked the appointments diary.

'Maureen's fully booked again, she said. 'Jam packed.'

Whenever we advertised readings with Maureen, we were inundated with people asking for appointments. I didn't understand it, she was such an old ham, sitting in her costume telling people vague things about their past and future, but they loved it. Perhaps it was the spectacle of her performance they liked, whatever it was, her schedule always filled quickly. Usually when we took bookings for a therapist, we left fifteen minutes clear for a morning break, and then forty-five minutes for a lunchbreak, but Maureen was adamant we should fill all the available time slots. So consequently, she had a client every half an hour from nine till five.

By half past eight, the shop was already a hive of activity. Nadine grated and chopped salad, Aileen started on the pastry for the quiches and Lorraine filled the shelves with fresh bread as I served the first customers of the day.

Maureen arrived, as miserable as ever, pushing a pram. It was one of the new modern compact three-wheeler types and inside, stretched on a tartan blanket, was Billy. Shopping bags stuffed to bursting with Maureen's costume and props hung from the handles and it was to the credit of the designer that the whole thing hadn't tipped and launched Billy into the air.

We greeted Maureen and made a fuss of Billy, who lay contentedly in his pram. He was a placid little dog, the only thing that ever disturbed him was the sight of the Lollipop Man who appeared at set times of day to escort school children across the road at the top of the bank. It was not the man he took umbrage at, but the lollipop and had been dragged away in disgrace several times after snarling and snapping at the pole, trying to grip it in his teeth.

'Cup of tea, Maureen?' I asked.

'Aye, why not. It's one of me only comforts in life that is, a nice cup of tea. By, I don't have many pleasures but I do like a nice cup of tea.'

Lorraine rolled her eyes and sighed. We could do without Maureen's complaining this morning, usually we humoured her but there was no time for that today.

'Had any more trouble from Elvis?' Maureen asked.

'Not a peep,' I said. 'You did a good job there Maureen, sending him off on his way.'

Nadine looked away, embarrassed.

'Yes I did. Even if I say so myself, it was one of my finest moments,' she said. 'They're not always so straight forward. Have I ever told you about the time I was asked to deal with a monk haunting the Newcastle Breweries? My God, I was run ragged. The

210

bugger didn't want to leave. Had me running about, round the vats, up and down...' Maureen regularly related stories of spirits she had helped on their way, though I couldn't recall her telling us this tale. It sounded a bit more interesting than her usual yarns, however I assured her she had and taking her arm, firmly guided her through the gap in the counter.

'Go into the therapy room and get yourself sorted,' I told her. 'I'll bring your tea.' I wanted her ensconced in the back of the shop out of the way so we could get on with preparing the party buffet.

She left her pram, taking Billy and her two enormous shopping bags with her. While I waited for the kettle to boil, I pushed the pram around the shop floor, trying to find a convenient place to park it, but not finding one, eventually opened the door and pushed it outside. I stationed it near the window so I could keep an eye on it.

'Anyone else want tea?' I called to the others. Silly question. I brewed a pot and poured out five mugs.

'What about Nige and Georgina, they'll be here soon,' Nadine said.

'It's still a bit early for them,' Lorraine said. 'Anyway, they might have to do without, we're much too busy this morning.'

Aileen looked shocked and Nadine gave a gasp. 'I'll make sure I have time to make a pot when they arrive,' she said. Lorraine had obviously made a terrible faux pas by suggesting our morning gossip should be cast aside in favour of business.

I stirred three sugars into Maureen's mug and knocked on the door.

'Tea's ready, Maureen.' The door opened and Maureen stood, already kitted out in her black curly wig and a thick layer of brown make-up. She had not yet outlined her brows and eyes in black kohl or applied her bright lipstick so her face looked weirdly featureless and I started in shock, spilling a little of the tea.

'Oops, sorry Maureen,' I said.

'Mariana please.'

'Sorry. Of course. Mariana.'

Between the four of us - Lorraine, Nadine, Aileen and myself – we managed to prepare the day's hot and cold food, organise Poll's buffet, unpack the Karma delivery, escort Maureen's clients in and out of the therapy room and deal with a local drunk who came in looking for a fight, all by two o'clock.

The lunchtime rush over, Aileen and Nadine left as my dad arrived to collect the buffet and deliver it to the swimming pool. Once he'd gone, I made a well-earned lunch for Lorraine and myself. I made a sandwich for Maureen, ready for her to have a few bites between readings.

'I hope Poll's party goes well,' I said to Lorraine. 'I still wonder if we did the right thing by not warning her.'

Lorraine looked at the clock. 'She'll be on her way there now, completely unaware.'

'I hope she's okay.'

'Well, like Peter said, it's none of our business.'

'True.' But I couldn't help but wonder how it was going.

After the bustle of the morning we felt we deserved an easy afternoon, so sat at the counter drinking some new organic blackcurrant cordial we'd been sent as a sample, and took turns to serve customers. Maureen's clients arrived for their readings at regular intervals, and as they left, we tried our best to subtly interrogate them about their experiences.

They all thought she was wonderful.

'You know, I'm sure we could do this,' Lorraine said after a woman left the shop in raptures because Maureen – sorry Mariana –told her that her bad times were over and there were good times ahead. 'I mean, it's all rather vague isn't it? Ambiguous comments that could apply to anyone.'

'Why don't you give it a go then?' I told her. 'Get yourself a wig and a bit of face paint.'

'I think you'd be better,' Lorraine said. 'You're halfway there with the hair.'

'Cheeky bugger.' I pulled myself up into a pose that Maureen often used when calling upon spirits as Mariana. 'I am

Christiana, seer of sights and perceiver of…oh… Maureen… didn't see you there.'

'Any chance of another brew before the last punter?' she asked.

Maureen saw seventeen clients that day, surviving on countless cups of tea that we handed her between readings. Lorraine and I were more than happy to take Billy out for short walks at quiet intervals, although he had to be almost dragged away from his cushion, where he lay snoozing at his mistress's feet, his gold turban stretched over his head.

Maureen's last client left at five while we were finishing the end of day cleaning jobs. There were a couple of last minute customers browsing and while Lorraine tidied the shelves, I began counting coins into money bags ready to cash up while we waited. The customers realised we were waiting to close and hurried apologetically to the counter with their purchases. Once they'd left I turned the 'Open' sign to 'Closed'.

'Hey, looks like we've had a good day,' I said to Lorraine as I counted the stash of notes. I looked at the end-of-day print out from the till. 'Wow! Look at this. I didn't realise we'd been so busy.'

'Maureen brought a lot of custom in,' Lorraine said. 'Most of her clients spent a fair bit, and of course the buffet was paid for in cash.'

Maureen shuffled out of the therapy room carrying her huge bags with Billy at her feet.

'I'm fit to drop,' she complained. 'I haven't stopped all day.' She said this as if it were our fault even though we'd suggested having a limit on how many clients she should see in a day.

As was our policy, we counteracted each of her complaints with a positive statement.

'That's great,' Lorraine said. 'Glad you've been so busy.'

'I'm so hungry I could eat a scabby horse,' Maureen said. Nice thought.

'We've kept you some quiche and salad and a piece of apple pie to take home with you.'

'That's kind of you me lovelies. I only hope I can eat it. I suffer terribly with indigestion, you know.'

'I'm sure you'll be fine,' I said. I took one of her bags and Lorraine took the other as Maureen bent to lift Billy.

'Put them in Billy's pram,' she said. 'Where it is?'

'It's out here,' I said looking out of the window. My heart sank at the sight of a completely empty pavement.

I hurried to the door and ran down the side street. It was nowhere to be seen.

'Excuse me, have you seen a pram?' I called to couple on the other side of the street. They hadn't. James McAllister was locking up the computer shop. He hadn't seen it either. I ran to the back lane, hoping to see it tucked behind the wall, but no.

I trudged back to the shop to confess to Maureen that I'd pushed it outside and left it to be stolen. She was very gracious.

'Don't worry me darlin',' she said. 'These things happen. Especially to the likes of me. Terrible bad luck I have.'

'I'm so sorry Maureen,' I said. 'I'll report it, of course, but you know how it is. It's not often things like this reappear.'

'Oh, it's probably miles away by now. I only hope whoever has it is putting it to good use. Maybe it was some poor mother who couldn't afford to buy one.'

I was touched at how well she'd taken it, and how forgiving she was. She clipped Billy's lead to his collar and picked up her bags. I could see it was a strain for her to carry them.

'I'll give you a lift home,' I offered. 'We're about done cashing up.'

'No, no, I wouldn't dream of it,' she said. 'It'll do me and Billy good to get a bit of fresh air. I'll walk up the bank and get the Metro.'

'Are you sure?'

'Yes, we'll be fine. So long as the Lollipop Man isn't about. Billy makes such a scene when he sees him.'

'No, he'll be gone by now,' Lorraine told her. 'He's only there until half-past four. Look, there's his lollipop in the doorway of the newsagents. He leaves it there chained up overnight.'

We gave Billy a last cuddle and Maureen left laden down with her bags. I watched her making her way up the bank, past the newsagents, where Billy stopped for a moment to cock his leg against his nemesis.

CHAPTER THIRTY-FOUR

At six o'clock the following Sunday morning, I met Lorraine to load the car for the Mind-Body-Spirit Fair.

'Morning,' I mumbled and she yawned a greeting as she unlocked the door. I'd love to be one of those people who rise at dawn and by seven have cleaned the house, baked a week's supply of bread, run five miles and written a best-selling novel but I'm not. I'm not a lark. And unfortunately I'm not a night-owl either. I'm just really good at sleeping. It's one of my talents.

We worked quietly and quickly, loading boxes into the back of Lorraine's car. After checking the shop was securely locked, we went to pick up first Aileen and then Nadine.

Aileen was obviously a lark. She was wide-awake and raring to go, chatting about what time she'd risen, the chores she'd completed and what her cat had eaten for his breakfast. Lorraine and I listened, saying a few words when prompted, but generally happy to let her ramble on.

Nadine was waiting at her gate as Lorraine pulled up. She climbed in the car and we set off toward the city centre. I asked Nadine what time she'd risen and she didn't answer so I repeated the question and she looked at her watch and told me it was ten to seven.

Lorraine switched on the radio and Abba's 'Money, Money, Money' filled the car.

'That's a good omen,' Lorraine said, and Aileen and Nadine began to sing along.

Aileen was talkative, excited about the day.

'I've never been to a fair like this before. I used to go to the big trade show in Exhibition Park every year, because they gave out loads of freebies.'

'Boobies?' Nadine said.

'Freebies. Free samples. They're hardly going to be giving out boobies are they? I got all sorts of things and lots of free vouchers too.'

'There'll probably be free samples today,' Lorraine said. 'Although I think it would be impolite to collect free stuff and not buy anything. Why don't you treat yourself to a foot massage or something?'

'Butt massage? They do bum massage?'

'Foot massage,' Lorraine said. 'What's wrong with you today?'

'Sorry. I'm troubled with ear wax. I can hardly hear.'

'You might find something today to help,' I said. 'A natural remedy, maybe.'

'Pardon?' she said, and looked perplexed when we all laughed.

I was starting to feel a little more awake as we headed towards the Tyne Bridge. As always, the sight of the river lifted my spirits. On the quayside, the market traders were setting up their stalls, and early dog walkers and joggers were talking advantage of the fine morning.

We arrived at the stadium and after signing in at reception, were directed into a huge hall.

'Wow, this place is enormous,' I said, as we struggled in, carrying our boxes. A man dressed in a green t-shirt with 'First-Soul' in yellow came to greet us.

'Hi. I'm Dermot, lovely to see you. Now, if I can check you off my register...' We gave him our details and he flicked through his list.

'Nutmeg Wholefoods. Ah yes. You're over here. Between Butterfly Incense and the Aloe Vera stall.' He guided us to our table and we dumped the boxes on the floor. He gave us a floorplan showing where the fire exits and lavatories were and told us he'd pop back to see us when were set up. 'In the meantime, if you need anything, come and ask.'

'I take it the organisers are all wearing t-shirts like yours?' Lorraine said, although looking about, I couldn't see anyone else wearing one. But Dermot had rushed off to greet some more arrivals.

I've always loved markets and fairs, both as a customer and a trader. I love the enthusiastic bustling as wares are unloaded and displays begin to take shape. There is an air of expectation, and a collective optimism that the day will be successful. Furtive glancing at other stalls to see what is on offer as displays are tweaked and re-tweaked. New friendships made as a camaraderie is built between the traders of the day. At this point, it is all to play for. The dream of an unlikely sell-out lingers, with hopes of an empty table and a full cash tin. There is nothing more demoralising at the end of a long trading day than packing away mounds of unsold stock into your car. Piles of discarded boxes, and being able to point out the relative emptiness of the car boot are joyful signs of a successful market day.

My expertise in faffing about came into its own as we joined in the buzz of activity. Nadine and Aileen went off to find tea and coffee, and Lorraine unpacked our stock as I put together the look I'd planned. I covered our tables in crisp green fabric and pinned trails of ivy around the edge of the table. Our stock was displayed in wicker baskets and labelled with our Nutmeg logo stickers. I'd brought some herb plants to display, mainly for decorative purposes but also priced to sell, and the overall look was fresh and inviting.

We were packing the extra stock under the table, when the woman from the stall to the right of us came to introduce herself. She told us her name was Gail and she ran her own business selling aloe vera products.

'It's wonderful stuff,' she told us. 'I have everything you could possibly need, shampoo, skin cream, sun-lotion, lip balm...would you like anything?'

'Er, not at the moment, thanks,' I said. 'I'll come over and have a look later.'

'Well I would recommend the skin cream, fantastic for eczema, rashes, burns, anything like that.'

'Right. I don't actually have any of those...'

'How about you?' she asked Lorraine.

'No thanks.'

'How're your bowels?'

Lorraine didn't answer but gave the woman one of her withering looks so I mumbled: 'Fine thanks.'

'Because I have pure aloe gel here, marvellous for any sort of digestive disorders. Like to try it? Special price today only.'

'No thanks.'

'Oh look,' Lorraine said to her. 'You have a customer.' Gail hurried off to capture the unfortunate woman who had paused to look at her display.

'She's a bit pushy isn't she?' I murmured to Lorraine. 'Puts me off when people go on like that.'

We watched Gail bombard the poor woman with reasons why she needed to buy aloe vera products, and Aileen and Nadine returned with cardboard cups of tea.

'Sorry we've been so long,' Nadine said. 'There's loads to see. This is the main hall and that roped off area there...' she pointed '...is for displays and demonstrations. There's another hall to the right, smaller than this, that has all the take-away food stalls, and the hall to the left has therapists.'

'Do you know what the demonstrations are?' Lorraine asked.

'Here, have a look,' Aileen said. 'I picked up a timetable. 'There's one every hour, on the hour. Nine o'clock is Community Meditation, where everyone is encouraged to join in to start off the day. Ten o' clock is a yoga display. Eleven is 'Music for the Soul' whatever that is.'

'I hope it's not like those drippy relaxation CDs you bought for the therapy room,' Lorraine said.

'Apparently it's a 'Shangri-la of songs to calm the mind and soothe the soul by Dermot Langley, played on home-made medieval-inspired instruments',' Aileen read.

'Dermot Langley? Is that the Dermot we spoke to earlier?'

'Could be, it's an unusual name.'

'What else is happening?' I asked, and Aileen continued reading aloud from her program.

219

'Midday is a demo by the North East Weight Lifters and Body Building Club.'

'Ooh, I'll make sure not to miss that,' Nadine said.

'One o'clock, Tai Chi led by Dermot Langley. Two o'clock, poetry reading by Dermot Langley.'

'Dermot Langley again?'

'Then there's a Hypnotherapy demonstration at three o'clock. Oh, it's Dana Quinn.'

'Yes, I remember she said she was coming to do a talk or something.'

'It's entitled 'Demonstration of How Hypnotherapy Can Cure Phobias'. Then four o'clock is End of Day Community Meditation, led by no other than Dermot Langley.'

Our conversation was interrupted by Gail who tapped Aileen on the shoulder.

'Excuse me, are you interested in any aloe vera products today? I have several special offers. I have shampoo, skin cream, sun lotion, lip balm...come and have a look.' Aileen followed Gail to her stall and was immediately given a pot of cream to hold as Gail related its benefits.

'Keep away from her, she's dead pushy,' I whispered to Nadine. 'She's been over here trying to get us to buy her stuff.'

'Pardon?'

'I said avoid the woman on the next stall,' I hissed.

'She seems friendly enough to me. She keeps saying hello. Although I think she's mistaking me for someone else, she keeps calling me Vera.'

But there was no need to worry about Aileen being parted from her hard earned cash. Once she heard the prices of the products, she made it clear to Gail she wasn't interested and came back to tell us of her idea to make her own lotion with a plant her aunt had in her conservatory.

'It must be an aloe vera,' she told us excitedly. 'It looks exactly like the illustrations on those posters. I'm sure if I pulp a couple of the leaves and mix it with a jar of Vaseline it will be just as good and a fraction of the price.'

Meanwhile Lorraine had been speaking to the young girls at the stall to the right of us and called me over to join the conversation. Their names were Marnie and Alice and they were selling scented candles, oils and incense.

'Your stall looks great,' I told them. 'I'll come and have a proper look later. I love scented candles.' I half expected them to jump straight into hard sell mode but there was no such pressure from these two.

'Yours too,' Marnie said. 'I love the way you've draped the ivy, it looks lovely.'

'Watch out for the woman on the aloe vera stall,' Alice told us. 'She's very pushy. I made the mistake of picking up one of her bottles of lotion and she was like a dog with a bone.'

'Yeah, we've noticed,' I began, but was interrupted by a voice over a loudspeaker.

'*Welcome, my friends, to the First-Soul Mind-Body-Spirit Fair.*'

CHAPTER THIRTY-FIVE

'Did he say arsehole Mind-Body-Spirit Fair?' Nadine asked, and I must say, it did sound like that.

'*First* Soul,' Marnie told her. 'It's what Dermot calls his business.'

'Would that be Dermot Langley?' I asked.

'Yes. He's amazing. Runs this whole event single-handedly. There he is - look.'

Dermot, now dressed in black leggings and a tight-fitting black t-shirt stood in the centre of the demonstration area holding a microphone.

'Crikey, those leggings leave little to the imagination,' Nadine said.

'Before we begin our day of exploration and enlightenment, I ask you all to join me in a meditation to focus our minds and attract joy and success to us all.'

Dermot lowered himself to the floor into a seated position and asked us to do the same.

'Please sit in a comfortable lotus position.'

'Well there's an oxymoron,' I said to Nadine.

'There's no need for that. He's only trying to bring us all together and get us involved.'

'No, I mean I can either sit comfortably or in a lotus position, but not both.'

'I saw a stall selling ear candles, I'll take her over,' Aileen said. 'They might be able to help clear her ear wax.'

Harp music of the 'drippy' type that Lorraine disliked sounded over the loudspeakers, gently at first, then increasing in volume.

People around us began to sit so we did too, in front of our stall, legs crossed like children in a school assembly. We were instructed to close our eyes and concentrate on our breathing. I felt rather ridiculous at first, but the sweet, clear notes of the harp, and Dermot's rhythmic voice as he talked us though a relaxation sequence, induced a feeling of tranquillity. My mind, as well as my muscles, relaxed. I could smell the earthy scent of incense from Marnie and Alice's stall, and hear the gentle breathing of the others sitting next to me.

'I enjoyed that,' I said to Lorraine, after Dermot quietly counted down from ten, instructing us to return our awareness to our surroundings and open our eyes. 'That was great wasn't it?'

'No idea. I didn't do it.'

'Why not?'

'Well one of us had to keep our eyes open. Perfect opportunity for someone to nip about nicking all the handbags and cash while you daft buggers were all sitting there with your eyes shut, off in airy-fairy land.'

'You're so cynical,' I said, but I laughed because she was right. If anyone wanted to whip anything from one of the stalls they'd had the perfect opportunity.

'How about you two?' I asked Nadine and Aileen. Aileen still sat with her eyes shut, hands resting on her knees, palms up.

'Jeez, I can't get up,' Nadine said, struggling to straighten her legs. Lorraine moved to help her and I gave Aileen a nudge.

'Psst! Aileen! It's finished. You can wake up now.' I helped Lorraine yank a laughing Nadine to her feet.

'This aloe gel is fantastic for stiff legs and aching muscles,' Gail called over. 'Special offer, today only.'

'Wow, that was amazing,' Aileen said. She stood up, looking a little dazed.

Dermot now stood at the door greeting visitors and taking tickets. He had pulled his 'First-Soul' t-shirt over his black top which made the black leggings look even more indecent. The hum of voices and movement increased as customers trickled in, looking about excitedly at what was on offer. We assured Aileen and Nadine we'd be fine managing the stall and they went off to explore.

'There's a stall I want to show you, Nadine,' Aileen said, and I heard Nadine say 'Pardon?' as they walked off together.

'Where's she taking her?' Lorraine asked.

'Someone's selling ear candles, she's going to take her over.'

Lorraine snorted. 'Ear candles? They won't do anything. How can shoving a candle in your ear and setting it alight be good for you?'

'I don't know. I think the theory is that it's supposed to create a vacuum and draw up earwax.' Even as I said it, it sounded ridiculous.

'And do you believe it?'

'Well, some people swear by it,' I said. 'I've never tried it so I'm keeping an open mind.'

'There's keeping an open mind, and there's opening it so much your brain falls out.'

The hall filled with people, bringing with them a buzz of enthusiasm. Friends greeted each other, and groups stood chatting. Goods were bought and information exchanged. Our stock sold slowly but steadily and we refilled the baskets from our spares beneath the table. We spoke to many people who were familiar with our shop and some who weren't and said they'd call in.

At ten the yoga demonstration began. A group of around twenty men and women of all ages entered, carrying rolled mats.

'Oh look, I want to watch this,' I said. I fancied joining a yoga class again. I'd done yoga when I was pregnant with Rosie and it helped enormously, both with the delivery and with recovery.

'Go on,' Lorraine said. 'I can manage here, we'll take turns to man the stall.'

I was captivated by the yoga display. I resolved to start practising some gentle postures that very evening. With a bit of luck it would have the same effect and I'd have another easy delivery. As the yoga finished, I joined the other watchers in polite applause and as I scanned the crowd, noticed Val, propped up on two sticks, at the other side of the demonstration area. I dodged behind a couple of women hoping she would not spot me, although I knew she was bound to come across our stall. Maybe she would be keen to harass other exhibitors, after all, she could visit us daily if she so wished. There were plenty of fresh victims here to act as an audience to her rendition of afflictions and ailments she had suffered over the years.

Turning away, a book stall caught my eye and I wandered over to have a look. I had a lovely time browsing through the titles. There were so many interesting ones to choose from, it took me ages to decide which to buy. I pulled out a couple of vegan cookery books I fancied and one about angels. I added another about natural remedies for children, and another by the Dalai Lama. The stall-holder said he'd keep them for me until I had a chance to nip back with the money. He put them into a box beneath his table for me, adding a book about essential oils that had caught my eye. I was about to delve into a box of books I'd missed, when I heard Dermot announce over the sound system that he would perform his 'Shangri-La of Songs to Soothe the Soul' in ten minutes time. What! I'd completely lost track of time. Needless to say Lorraine was not amused.

'Where've you been? I've been stoved off here while you've been gallivanting about.'

'Sorry, I didn't realised I'd been so long. I saw Val over there, she's hobbling about on two sticks.'

'No doubt she'll be over to mither us at some point. What about the rest, what's it like?'

'I don't know, I've only looked at one stall selling books. It's brilliant. Loads of great books. I've put some to one side. I'm going to go back and pay for them.'

'Books? Where?' Lorraine looked about eagerly trying to spot the book seller. I took some money from my bag intending to go and pay for my books but she snatched it from me.

'I'll take it for you,' she said, and headed off in the wrong direction so I called to her and pointed.

I looked at the list of sales Lorraine had written in our notebook and was pleasantly surprised.

'She's been really busy,' Marnie said to me smiling. 'You're doing great.'

'How about you?'

'Oh not so bad. We've sold a bit, but not enough to cover our costs yet.'

'It's a bit slow for us at the moment,' Alice added. 'Hopefully it will get better later.'

'Why not light a couple of your joss sticks and candles?' I suggested. 'It might attract more people to buy.'

'Good idea,' Marnie said, and Alice took out a box of matches and selected a couple of candles to light.

'That smells great,' I said. 'Is it Neroli?' then we both turned in fright at the sound of an ear-splitting screeching. It was Dermot, making a variety of wails and squeals on an instrument that appeared to be a hybrid between a bassoon and a bagpipe.

'What the hell is that?' I said.

'That's Dermot's medieval-inspired instrument,' Marnie said and we listened to a cacophony of squawking and squeaking.

'Blimey, I thought it was supposed to soothe the soul not torment it.'

'Don't make me laugh,' Alice said, as we sniggered at the torturous sounds he managed to produce by squeezing the hessian-fabric sack with his foot whilst blowing into the huge tube protruding from the top. A line of holes were drilled into the tube. These Dermot covered intermittently with his hands, presumably to vary the pitch of the screech.

No-one else was perturbed by the noise in the least. People had either stopped to listen appreciatively or had continued about their browsing, unconcerned.

A ripple of applause broke out when Dermot eventually ceased his caterwauling and bowed to his audience. He picked up a small drum which he proceeded to beat with his fist.

Lorraine returned with my books and also a pile of her own.

'Great stall,' she said. 'But I couldn't stand there any longer. It was too close to that racket Dermot was making with that digeridoo thing. It was going right through my head. And that bloody noise is even worse.'

Dermot was now pounding his drum vigorously while he indulged in a strange dance which involved a lot of leg-jerking and face-pulling. There was something a bit manic about it. Slightly uncomfortable to watch but also compelling.

'It's quite entertaining in a strange kind of way,' I said.

But Lorraine didn't agree.

'Don't be so daft. It's ridiculous. Dancing about like Mick Jagger on speed. What's the point of it?'

I didn't know what the point of it was, but it became more frantic and I was relieved when it finished.

'Thank God for that,' Lorraine said but she spoke too soon. As the drumming ceased, another wailing began. It took us a few seconds to realise what it was.

'FIRE! FIRE! Run for your lives!'

'FIRE! Run! Run for your lives!' Val was shaking her sticks and yelling hysterically.

'Quick! The table's on fire!' Marnie yelled and I turned to see flames licking their way across the piles of incense sticks and consuming the paper table cover.

We all rushed to the table and began using whatever we could find to smother the flames. It was out in seconds. Val waved her sticks about wildly, shouting for help.

'Help!' she shouted. 'Fire! Help!' Remarkably sprightly for someone who'd previously needed the aid of two walking sticks, she rushed about, calling for everyone to evacuate the building and generally causing chaos. There was a mass movement of people heading for fire exits as the alarm wailed its warning.

'No panic, I've got it!' Dermot appeared with a fire extinguisher then realised it was not needed.

'Everyone back,' he yelled to the people exiting, and word filtered through the crowd that the fire was out and there was no danger.

'I'm so sorry,' Marnie said. 'The candle must have somehow caught the edge of the tablecloth.'

'Not to worry, all sorted' Dermot said, and although he smiled, it was clearly forced as he struggled to maintain his demeanour of peace with the world. He hurried off to reassure people there was no need to leave.

'I'm sorry, I feel awful,' I said. 'It was my idea.'

'No, no, my fault. I should have kept a better check on the candle,' Alice said.

'It's a good job I spotted that,' said a familiar voice.

'Val.'

'You're all very lucky I was so vigilant. I saw the flames and I managed to smash the glass on the fire alarm box with my stick, although it took some effort, I can tell you.' If she was anticipating gratitude, her expectations were not met.

'Was there really any need to be so dramatic?' Alice said bluntly. 'It was hardly a raging fire, merely a few small flames from a candle. If you'd alerted us at once I'm sure we could have smothered it.'

'Well of all the ungrateful, irresponsible, selfish...' Val took a great breath of air and shuddered. 'I feel quite faint. I have single-handedly diverted what could have been a tragic incident and I am met with such rudeness.'

'I think my friend means that breaking the glass was probably a little premature,' Marnie said. 'If you'd got our attention straight away there may have been no need to set off the alarm.'

Val was not interested in explanations.

'I am shocked,' she said. 'In my state of health, to have acted as I did, with no thought for my own safety...'

Gail, who'd been watching from the safety of the space behind her stall, called over to Val.

'I think you did the right thing.'

'Thank you,' Val said. 'I'm glad someone appreciates what I did.'

'Did I hear you say you had health problems?' Gail asked.

'I certainly do. You would not believe what I've been through over the years.'

'I may be able to help. I have aloe vera products for all sorts of conditions. I have shampoo, skin cream...' but she was cut off mid flow by Val, who settled herself on a spare chair beside the display of aloe vera products.

'Let me tell you all about it.'

'Serves her right,' Lorraine said and Nadine and I sniggered. 'They deserve each other.'

We helped the girls clear the burnt paper from their table and rearrange their stock.

The incident caused a lot of concerned visitors to make their way to the scene of the fire to ask if much damage had been done, which resulted in a rush of sales for Marnie and Alice, but also for us too.

I was manning the stall alone when a heavy-set man dressed in a sleeveless t-shirt, shorts and trainers approached the stall and swept his eyes over our table. He was bull-necked with biceps so huge his arms appeared to hang a foot away from each side of his body. His thighs were about as thick as my waist and I knew Nadine would find him attractive, although I did not.

'What crap ye selling then?' he said, to which I could not think of a suitable cutting reply.

'Wholefoods.'

'Av been having a walk aboot, there's people selling all sorts of rubbish.' He surveyed our stall and nodded to himself. The contents of our table obviously confirmed his statement. 'Ah'm starvin' for something to eat but I can't get a steak or a bit of chicken anywhere. It's aal that vegetarian crap.' Sighing loudly he picked up a packet of almonds and delved into his shorts pocket to retrieve some coins. 'Ta love,' he said. He handed me the money, then ripped the pack with his teeth and poured almonds into his mouth. 'Good protein these.'

I hoped he'd move on but he was keen to stay for a chat.

'Ah'm selling protein pooders for building muscles,' he told me. 'Well, ah'm trying to sell them but neebody's buying. I've selt nowt.'

I tried to look sympathetic as he showered me with fragments of chewed nuts.

'That's a shame,' I said. 'I think the people here are more interested in natural foods and therapies. There's a sports and fitness fair on next month maybe that would be better for you?'

'Aye, I might try it. Cos this place is mental. Ah've never seen so much shite in one place.' He took another mouthful of almonds which he chewed noisily.

'Ah mean, a while ago I saw this blond bird ower there, sitting with a candle in her lug, while some bugger set it alight. Mad or what? Ah tell ye, it's mental.'

Throughout the day, Lorraine and I took turns to wander off and have a look at what was on offer, returning with some gem we'd found. I added a box of granola to my stash beneath the table.

I'd bought mushroom pate, hazelnut carob cookies, seaweed hair conditioner, patchouli oil, a loaf of sundried tomato bread and a t-shirt for Peter with a screen-printed elephant from a wildlife charity. Lorraine had organic cider, date and walnut cake, coconut soap, a pendant made from sea-smoothed glass, and of course we both had a stack of books. And we'd only covered half of the main hall.

Nadine returned with Aileen to say she'd paid fifteen pounds to have burning candles put in her ears and was sure it had made a difference. Aileen showed distress that Nadine had paid so much.

'I wanted to watch how it was done. I've got some candles leftover from my auntie's birthday cake, I could have done it for her.'

'Aye, well I wanted it done properly,' Nadine said. 'Mind I felt like a proper narna sitting there with me head on the table and a candle in me ear.'

'And you say it's worked?' I asked.

'Pardon?'

'Blimey that's another hour gone,' Lorraine said as a voice on the loud speaker system announced the display by the North East Weight Lifters and Body Building Club was about to begin.

'Ooh I need to go and get a spot at the front so I can get a good view,' Nadine said and hurried off through the crowds, Aileen following behind.

There was a lull in sales, so Lorraine and I quickly totted up our takings and were both amazed at how much we'd made. Marnie and Alice were doing well too, and Gail claimed she'd had record takings. That was hard to believe considering all the customers I'd seen backing away from her after being harassed to buy.

'I don't think she's the type to admit to poor sales, do you?' I said to Lorraine. 'Unless her 'record takings' weren't much to beat.'

'I've only seen her sell a lip balm. And that was to a woman desperate to get away.'

'From Gail's sales pressure?'

'That and Val's whinging.'

Gail found herself unable to shake Val off. She sat behind Gail's table, giving everyone who passed, details of her various health issues. She'd even limped off to get a cup of tea and a sandwich at one point, which she brought back to her chair and devoured noisily while Gail did her best to convince shoppers they needed her products. It was a shame because aloe vera has so many great healing properties and the products she offered were pure and reasonably priced, but she scared people off by pouncing on them and clinging on until they could escape, in most cases by walking off, leaving Gail talking to herself.

'We've done really well,' I said, pleased. 'And we have another few hours to go.' I turned to watch the weight lifting display where the all-women group were demonstrating their weight-lifting skills. I nudged Lorraine.

'Look. Nadine will be disappointed!'

Lorraine and I had lunch in the food hall while Nadine and Aileen took care of the stall. There were lots of tempting options to choose from, but finally the fragrance of red peppers, spring onions and tofu stir-fried with garlic and ginger drew us to the noodle stall.

We carried our cartons of vegetable ramen to an empty table where we attempted to eat gracefully with wooden chopsticks. It was a messy but delicious meal, washed down with green tea.

'Do you think we have time for a quick look at the therapy hall? I'd like to see who's here,' I said.

'Yeah, we'll be quick,' Lorraine said, and dropping our cartons into the recycling bin, we made our way to the adjacent hall.

The hall was busy, most of the therapists were in conversation with customers and some were giving demonstrations.

A man lying face-down on a therapy couch was receiving a hot stone treatment, a group of onlookers asking questions as the stones were placed on his skin. I'd never heard of this before and fancied having a go, but I didn't relish the thought of lying half naked with a crowd around me asking questions.

We saw a stall selling beautiful crystals and semi-precious stones, where a woman was carefully placing pieces of amethyst and rose quartz on a girl's shoulders to demonstrate their healing powers.

'How does that work?' I asked Lorraine, and the therapist heard me and began to explain. She told us crystals hold and emit energy vibrations. Each type of stone resonates differently and will align with the subtle energies of the body. I was fascinated and wanted to hear more, but Lorraine thanked the woman, rather curtly I thought, and pulled me away.

'I was interested in that!' I said.

'I know you were, that's why I rescued you.'

'Rescued me?'

'Yeah. I know what you're like. You would have been there for hours and then you'd be buying crystals and rocks and off you'd go on your next big fad.'

'What a bloody cheek!' I was about to give her a piece of mind but caught sight of a treatment in progress at the facing stall. 'Ooh look. Let's watch this.'

'See what I mean?'

A therapist was giving an Indian Head Massage to a woman who I guessed to be in her sixties. She was an elegant, attractive woman, obviously skilled at choosing clothes and cosmetics to her best advantage. She sat, eyes closed, with a smile of superiority playing at her lips, completely unaware that the therapists hands, with the help of massage-oil, had moulded her hair into a shock that any punk would have been proud to sport, and that slithers of oil had run down her face, smudging her make-up like water-colours on cartridge paper.

We continued along the row of stalls and passed Kyle Hendrick's booth, where he sat facing a woman, their knees almost touching as he stared into her eyes. She gazed back, wide-eyed and flushed about the face. He took her hand to reassure her and the colour on her face grew darker and crept down her neck.

'Another victim falls for the Kyle Hendrick charm,' Lorraine said. A queue of people, mostly female, waited eagerly for a consultation.

'I didn't realise Iridology was so popular,' I said as we walked past the long line of fawning women.

'This is going to make his head even bigger. He already thinks he's God's gift to women.'

'God's gift to the world.'

We made our way back to our stall, skirting the other side of the hall and passing the brawny man I'd spoken to earlier. He stood with his enormous forearms crossed, his bulk dwarfing the pyramids of protein powder tubs in front of him.

'Hello darlin',' he said. 'How's it going?' Lorraine looked surprised he'd spoken to me.

'We're doing okay,' I told him. 'How about you?'

'Aye, deeing canny. It's picked up a bit since earlier, like.'

'Who's that?' Lorraine whispered as we moved on.

'Micky Muscles, my new friend. 'I'll introduce you if you like,' I said, to which Lorraine made a face I couldn't even begin to describe.

CHAPTER THIRTY-EIGHT

We'd returned to our stall when Dermot's voice announced the Tai Chi demonstration was about to begin. It was described as a 'remarkable, inspiring demonstration by a widely celebrated master of the art'.

There followed a loud blast of Chinese folk music, and after a couple of minutes, Dermot appeared wearing some sort of silver all-in-one suit.

'He looks like an oven-ready chicken,' Lorraine said, as the widely celebrated master of the art took to the floor to give his remarkable, inspiring demonstration.

It was disappointing to be honest. Perhaps those more familiar with the discipline may have appreciated the finer points of his performance, but to me it looked as though he was just wafting about a bit.

'It's a bit lacklustre,' I said to Lorraine. 'I expected something a bit more interesting, especially when I saw his outfit.'

'Aye, he's more dressed for doing a moon walk.'

'Music's nice though.'

'Suppose. If you like that sort of plinky-plonky stuff.'

'He's reading poetry next. I wonder what it will be like.'

'Probably of the same standard as his Tai Chi demonstration and his Soul Music.'

Nadine and Aileen were happy to sit at the stall drinking peach juice they'd bought, so Lorraine and I took the opportunity to go off on another jaunt.

We wandered about looking at the weird and wonderful products on sale, promising to boost our health and happiness. Some were more credible than others. Copper bracelets to ease rheumatic pain. Detox socks to extract impurities through the soles of your feet while you slept. Jewellery containing semi-precious stones that would boost energy levels and aid healing. Jars specially designed for growing edible sprouted seeds. Magnetic insoles that would relieve the body of pain. Juicers, yogurt makers and various implements for preparing vegetables and salads.

Many stall-holders advertised their product as 'the latest thing' or 'the new health craze' citing celebrities as enthusiasts of whatever they were selling.

'I wonder if Carol Vorderman has any idea of the products she's endorsing,' I said to Lorraine as we passed yet another stall displaying her image, this one claiming her svelte shape was down to the use of their cellulite oil.

'Who's that?' Lorraine asked, pointing to a poster of a blond, bird-like woman.

'She's Doctor Gillian Mac-something-or-other. I read about her in one of the health magazines the Natural-Wonder rep leaves. She's an up and coming health guru. She examines people's poo to see how healthy they are.'

'Get lost.'

'She does. She can tell how healthy a person is by examining it. And she gives advice about healthy eating.'

'Ugh, well that'll never catch on. Disgusting.'

The stall displaying her photograph was apparently selling trays of grass.

'It's wheatgrass,' the seller told us. 'It's full of great nutrients - it's the new wonder-food. Would you like to try some?'

'Yeah, go on,' I said, and was about to pull out a clump of stems to chew on, when the woman handed me a cardboard cup containing an inch of green liquid. I looked at it in surprise.

'Pure wheatgrass juice,' the woman told me. Lorraine declined the offer of a sample. I took a sip and immediately my mouth was filled with what I imagined chewing a piece of turf would taste like.

'It can be blended with other juices to make it more palatable if you find it unpleasant,' the woman told me as I tried not to grimace.

'Mmm, nice, ' I lied. I bought a tray of wheatgrass, not because I wanted it, but because I'm a salesperson's dream and feel obliged to buy things I've shown an interest in, especially when I've been given a free sample.

'What're you going to do with that?' Lorraine asked as we walked off, my purse eight pounds lighter. 'You don't have a machine to extract the juice.'

'I thought it would look nice in the kitchen,' I blagged. 'Or I might give it to the cats.'

We wandered about looking at stalls, stopping to chat and swap business cards with other stall owners. When Dermot's poetry reading was announced, we made our way to the demonstration area.

'He has quite a collection of weird outfits,' Lorraine commented as Dermot walked out dressed in a yellow-and-blue-striped all-in-one. It was elasticated at the wrists and ankles and reminded me of Andy Pandy.

He took the microphone and after explaining that he'd written his poems to explore the fragility of human emotion, hung his head in silence for a few seconds then suddenly burst into a loud, dramatic recital.

'When demons of the soundless night perform in all their raggedness
And the unholy tremors take flight into the endless abyss
When fleeing nightmares taunt the limpid soul
It is then my heart recedes.
My soul is tortured by vapours of distain hanging in the damp air
Never to be unbound in the heaving of the night
Within the clouds of desolation weighing on the rigorous threads of time...'

Lorraine nudged my arm. 'Howay, this is rubbish.' We squeezed our way past the listeners, some with eyes closed and an expression of rapture, some pan-faced and others in confusion as to what they were listening to.

'When it comes to poetry I'm more of a 'There was a young man from Bangkok' type,' Lorraine said.

'I think you must have to be really intelligent to understand stuff like that,' I said.

'Don't be so daft. You could write stuff like that if you wanted.'

'Really? Do you think so?' I smiled. I was always writing bits and pieces and hoped to be published one day.

'Yeah, course you could. It's shite.'

We bought fruit smoothies to drink as we made our way to a row of stalls we hadn't yet visited.

I was attracted to a stall displaying baskets of vegetables, and also to the stall owner who was tall and dark with a healthy 'outdoor' look. He told us his name was Nick and explained that he grew all the produce organically. He was very charismatic. We told him about our shop and discussed the possibility of starting an organic fruit and veg box scheme for our customers. We swapped business cards and agreed to get in touch.

I bought purple broccoli and celeriac and Nick told me about varieties of vegetables and fruit that were coming into season.

'And we'll have loads of lovely fruit later in the year,' he said. 'Strawberries, cherries, raspberries, plums – all sorts.' He wrapped some rhubarb stalks in paper.

'For you,' he smiled and to my horror I simpered like a fourteen year old meeting a pop idol. 'Beautiful cooked with a little sugar and ginger.'

'That will be lovely for your *husband,*' Lorraine said to me. 'Her *husband* will enjoy that,' she repeated. 'Nice to meet you, Nick. We'll be in touch but we must get back. As you can see, my sister is *pregnant* and gets tired easily. I must get her back to her *husband*.' She took me by the arm and led me away, non-too gently.

'What was all that about?' I hissed when we were out of earshot.

'He fancied you. It was obvious.'

'Do you think so?' I said, delighted.

'Yes. I was letting him know he had no chance.'

'I was only buying vegetables, there was no need to go on like that.'

239

'What about the way you were going on? Twittering like a budgie...'

'I was not twittering. Not like a budgie or like anything else.'

'I'm looking out for Peter.'

'Well there's no need. Crikey, anyone would think you were jealous!'

'I'm absolutely green with jealousy, he's gorgeous!'

I slapped her arm and we laughed. 'You don't have to worry about Peter,' I told her. 'You know how much I adore him. It's just nice to be admired by another man sometimes. So you really think he liked me?'

'Ah, shut up man.'

As we approached our stall, I saw a woman with her back to us speaking to Nadine. I recognised the slight frame draped in a floaty outfit.

'Hi, Dana. I see you're giving a demonstration this afternoon.'

'Yes, I'm on in about five minutes. I have a client who has a terrible phobia and she's volunteered to have a hypnotherapy session. I'm going to show how simply phobias can be cured.'

'Isn't that a bit risky?' Lorraine asked.

'Risky?' Dana looked puzzled. Lorraine opened her mouth to explain but changing her mind, closed it again and smiled encouragingly at Dana. Dermot's voice echoed over the loudspeaker, announcing a hypnotherapy demonstration would begin in a few minutes.

'That's me, I'd better go,' Dana said and she floated off in the direction of the display area.

'I hope she knows what she's doing,' I said. 'What if it doesn't work?'

'I reckon it must be set up,' Lorraine said. 'I bet she has a friend who's going to pretend to be scared of something then she make out she's been cured.'

'No!' I couldn't believe Dana would do that. Not Dana the flower fairy. 'She wouldn't. Not Dana. She's too...'

'Nice?'

'Yeah. Nice.'

'Just you watch. I bet it's a fix.'

Nadine watched me put my tray of wheatgrass under our table with my other purchases.

'That's a tiny piece of turf. Where are you going to plant it?'

'It's not turf. It's wheatgrass. It's the new superfood, packed with amino acids and vitamins.'

'It's for her cats,' Lorraine told her.

'Your cats? I know you like to pamper them but I've heard it all now. Why didn't you bring them along, they could have had a massage or some crystal healing.' They sniggered together at the thought of it and indulged themselves in pampered cat jokes until thankfully they were silenced by the announcement that the hypnotherapy demonstration was about to begin.

CHAPTER THIRTY-NINE

Dana introduced herself and gave a short explanation of the benefits of hypnotherapy. Her voice was as fragile as her persona and although she used a microphone, was difficult to decipher.

A nervous looking woman approached the demonstration area, her eyes wide with fearful expectation. She was welcomed by a ripple of rather indifferent applause from the audience.

'Ladies and gentlemen, may I introduce René. This lady has suffered terribly for many years, due to a morbid fear of snakes.' At the sound of the word 'snakes' the woman shuddered violently.

'She's putting that on,' Lorraine muttered. 'Told you it was fake.' People standing nearby turned and gave us disapproving looks and one woman hissed 'shush!' in our direction so I stepped away from Lorraine and joined in the shushing.

René was led to a chair where she sat, rigid and pale, facing Dana.

'Today I shall demonstrate how deep rooted fears such as these can be eradicated simply and safely by the use of hypnosis,' Dana said. 'I ask for you all to be silent please.'

The woman was instructed to close her eyes and Dana proceeded to speak to her in a soft lilting voice. It was a lengthy process, boring to watch, especially as Dana's gentle voice did not carry well. From the snatches I heard, I deduced that she was directing the woman to relax by tensing then releasing areas of her body. When this part of the process was complete, there were a few minutes silence then Dana began to speak rapidly. I struggled to hear but understood she was telling the woman, repeatedly in the same monotone sentences, that she was brave and confident and could deal with any situation without fear.

I looked around the hall to see the reaction of the onlookers. They stood in groups watching carefully, some in mild interest, some in fascination, and others like me - bored and waiting for something to happen.

And then something did happen. Two men appeared at the back of the hall, carrying a large item between them. Whatever it was weighed heavily, as it took some effort for them to bring it forward. It was large and lumpy and mottled brown in colour. As they walked towards the demonstration area, a scuffling broke out around them and several people began running towards the exit, some crying out in panic. The men moved through the hall, causing more people to take to their heels, one woman tripping, then screaming hysterically as she crawled along the floor before lifting herself up and darting for the door.

I could see now that the object was a huge snake, its coiled body supported between the men, one holding its triangular head, the other grasping its tail.

'Blimey, look at the size of it!' I said to Lorraine. 'It's enormous!' I turned to speak to Nadine and as I looked about for her, Lorraine nudged me.

'If you're looking for Nadine she's over there,' she said pointing, and I looked to see Nadine amongst a group of people hurrying for the door. I watched as she was herded along, like a sheep in the centre of a panicking flock, until, forced against a table she vaulted it and made her escape.

Meanwhile, Dana and René sat calmly in the centre of the chaos, René with her eyes closed, seemingly oblivious of the drama around her.

'Talk about in at the deep end,' I said. 'Wouldn't you think she'd have started with a grass snake or something?'

'Wouldn't have had the same dramatic effect though.'

A hush resumed as the hundred or so people who'd remained in the hall waited to see what would happen next.

The snake was brought closer to the woman, who sat with her eyes closed, unaware her greatest nightmare was about to manifest. The snake lay motionless, its massive body supported between the men, its unblinking eyes lying like opaque marbles in its flat head. It crossed my mind that the snake was not real, even the eyes showed no glint of life, but a sudden flick of its forked tongue, quivering as it probed the air, proved otherwise.

243

At Dana's direction the woman opened her eyes. For a moment she blinked in surprise, like she'd woken from a deep sleep. She looked about at her surroundings, scanning the waiting onlookers, her head moving slowly from left to right until her eyes came to rest on the snake.

I tell you, I have never in my life heard a scream like the one that poor woman gave.

CHAPTER FORTY

René's scream sliced the air, and I winced as the piercing shriek hurt my ears. The crowd parted, moving aside for the two men hurrying back through the hall with their monstrous load. They were sweating visibly, perhaps from the exertion of carrying the snake or maybe because of the distress they'd helped cause.

Dana huddled the unfortunate woman out the hall, her arms wrapped about her in an attempt to give comfort, apologising profusely as she guided her to the food hall.

The incident put an end to the day. Few of the people who'd fled at the first sight of the snake returned, although Nadine eventually did.

'Has it gone?' she asked. We assured her it had been removed from the hall and she resumed her position at the stall, but I could see she was still shaken. Many people left the fair complaining of how the woman had been treated and the hall emptied quickly. There were also those who found the whole thing hysterical, but after a man who guffawed loudly was berated by several people, there were many strained expressions as people struggled to contain their laughter.

A few browsers remained, and several stall holders began to pack up so I began to tidy our stall, gathering our remaining stock into boxes.

'Let's go and see if we can have a closer look at the snake before we go,' Lorraine suggested.

'No thanks,' Nadine said. 'I'll stay here and pack up.'

So Lorraine and I went in search of the enormous snake. In the food hall, René was sitting at a table nursing a mug of herb tea amongst a group of women, one of them Dana.

'She looks much calmer now,' I said.

'Let's go and see if she's okay.'

As we approached, Dana looked up and smiled.

'It worked!' she said, and René nodded in agreement.

'It did. I used to be absolutely terrified, it's diminished the fear I had.'

Lorraine and I did not speak. Possibly the same thought ran through both of our minds.

'Oh I know I reacted badly. But it got it out of my system you see. I feel like I could easy go and face that snake right now.'

Dana beamed with pride at her success. I don't suppose she'd yet thought about the fact that in the eyes of hundreds of people not only had she failed, but she'd also traumatised a phobic woman and half of the fair attendees too.

'Where is the snake now?' Lorraine asked.

'The owners have returned it to their van,' Dana said.

'Who owns it?'

'It belongs to an organisation called Creatures. They visit schools and events to educate people about animals often seen as unattractive or vermin.'

'We were hoping to have a closer look at it,' Lorraine said, and Dana smiled.

'Come on, I'll introduce you to the owner, I'm sure he'll be keen to show you.'

'I think I'll come too,' René said. 'I'm feeling brave.'

Are you sure?' I asked. 'You don't have to.' I was concerned she would take a second fit of screaming abdabs and I'm not sure my eardrums could cope with a second dose.

'Of course she's sure,' Dana said. 'She's completely cured. She's going to walk right up to that snake and look it straight in the eye.'

We followed Dana through the stalls to an exit at the back of the building. Most stall-holders had either packed up or were in the process of doing so. There were few shoppers about now. The snake had brought the day to a premature end.

Dana led us to a red van in the carpark, the word 'Creatures' cleverly depicted in pictures on its side. The letter C was formed by a green and orange striped snake, curved around the subsequent letters. Others were represented by various illustrations of other animals presumably owned by the 'Creatures' organisation. The back door of the van was open and a man sat on the ledge drinking coffee from a cardboard cup.

Dana asked if we could view the snake, and after calling his colleague to assist, the two men lifted it from its case.

The first man, the younger of the two, lifted the large flat head, holding it securely as the snake's body was hoisted up between them.

'There's my darling', he crooned. The snake's unblinking eyes were motionless as he murmured endearments. He told us she was a Burmese Python and her name was Nola.

The men held the huge body between them and we gently stroked the surprisingly firm and smooth skin.

'She's lovely,' Lorraine said as we admired the caramel and brown mosaic-like skin.

René, who had been watching, moved forwards and bravely stretched her hand towards the snake. At first she was hesitant, but as she slowly moved her fingers across the patterned surface she became braver.

'It feels much nicer than I'd imagined,' she smiled.

'Good girl, there's my pretty darling,' the man said, and at first I thought he was speaking to René, but I realised he meant Nola when he leant and gave the snake a smacking kiss on the head.

'Well done,' Dana said and patted René's arm. 'That's so wonderful. You wouldn't have been able to do that this morning! How amazing!' She was so pleased with the change in René. It was a shame the audience hadn't witnessed her contact with the snake and had left believing the hypnosis had no effect, except for perhaps making René's phobia worse.

We all congratulated René, and though she managed to touch the snake and her fear had diminished greatly, she was obviously still uncomfortable at being so close to the huge creature.

'Thank you,' she told the men. 'And thank you too Dana, I'm so grateful for what you've done.'

When she'd left, the older man asked if we'd like to hold Nola to get an idea of her weight.

'She a big girl, aren't you my pretty?'

Lorraine said she'd have a go at holding the snake, so I did too, knowing I'd never hear the last of it if I didn't, but somehow it was me the men brought the snake towards. My apprehension must have showed on my face because the older man began to reassure me.

'Don't worry, Harry here has her head and I'll keep tight hold of her tail. There's no danger.'

Although I had no fear of snakes, I was a little daunted. Nola was enormous, the girth of her body was the thickness of a grown man and I estimated her length to be at least fifteen feet. But I was not going to miss an opportunity like this. It's not often you get a chance to hold a giant Burmese Python.

The men unwrapped Nola's coils and laid her across my shoulders. Her weight was tremendous even though the men were supporting most of the snake's body. The younger man still held her head although her tail was free. As the men told us facts about her natural habitat and feeding habits, I felt the long body slowly wrapping around my torso. Although it was not an unpleasant sensation, I could imagine how it would feel to have those coils slowly tighten.

'Excuse me,' I said interrupting the flow of information coming from the older man. 'She's winding herself around me...'

'Ah, she's giving you a cuddle, aren't you my pretty? As long as she doesn't get her tail around you, you'll be fine. It's the tail that does the damage. Once the tail works its way around a body, that's it. The life will be squeezed out of you like toothpaste from a tube.'

'Yes well I think I've had enough now, thanks.' Thankfully, Nola was unwound from my body.

'Nothing to worry about, she could have swallowed you whole if she'd wanted to.'

Now he tells me, I thought.

'Your turn?' he asked Lorraine.

'No time unfortunately,' Lorraine said. 'We have to get back. But thank you so much for showing her to us. She's beautiful.'

While we talked, a grey cloud obscured the sun and the sky turned dark, except for a few shafts of light piercing through, shining like search lights. The day was cooler now and the first warning spots of rain that often prelude a deluge began to fall.

We hurried back through the emptying hall to where Aileen and Nadine were waiting for us, boxes packed and ready to go.

'I held the snake,' I told them proudly. Aileen was impressed but Nadine shuddered. 'Her name is Nola and she's a Burmese Python.'

'Don't want to know,' Nadine muttered.

'She's a beauty,' Lorraine said. 'Gorgeous markings on her skin.'

'Did you hold her too?' Aileen asked.

'No. Unfortunately Chris got in first so I didn't get a chance.' I raised an eyebrow but she smiled sweetly.

We joined the procession of traders carrying boxes out to the carpark. As usual, the others objected to my carrying anything of weight so I ended up carrying the car keys.

'I've just held a twelve stone snake,' I grumbled as they chided me for attempting to lift a box.

The downpour arrived and people covered their boxes in pieces of cardboard and plastic bags in an attempt to keep their goods dry. One woman wore a carrier bag on her head and another removed her shoes and walked barefoot through the puddles. We stood at the door debating our best plan of action.

'Let's run for it,' Lorraine said. 'We'll have to be quick. Try not to let the stuff get too wet.'

Aileen had a supply of plastic head covers, the type my grandma used to tie around her head if she had to leave the hairdressers in the rain. At first I thought she was suggesting we all wear them, but she spread them over the boxes to keep the rain off. Dermot was in the foyer, calling out to people and imploring them to return to the hall.

I tried to pass behind him but he turned and saw me.

'You can't go yet. What about the end of day meditation?'

I thought about making an excuse. I was tired, ready to go home and put my feet up, but he looked so dejected I found myself telling him we'd return after we'd packed the car.

'Put the keys in my pocket.' Lorraine lifted the box she carried to allow access to her jacket pocket. 'No point in us all getting wet. We'll go and dump this in the car then come back to join you.' I was pleased not to have to go out in the rain but I'd had enough now and wanted to be at home relaxing with Rosie and Peter, perhaps having a snooze on the sofa in front of the fire.

I wandered back into the hall, dodging stallholders carrying piles of boxes, some dragging trollies behind them. I made my way to the demonstration area where rows of yoga mats were laid, and sat down to wait for the meditation to begin. I realised I was close to the front so shuffled back to a mat in the row behind. Then I changed my mind and moved to the side. The hall was emptying rapidly. Most of the tables had been cleared, a few held boxes waiting to be collected and there was a pile of discarded cardboard boxes and rubbish bags near the exit that people kept adding to on their way out.

A woman returned to a table near to where I sat to collect the last of her stock. She turned and smiled.

'Excuse me,' I said. 'Are you staying for the end of day meditation?'

She shook her head. 'No, I'm in a bit of a hurry. Have to get off.' She took her bags from the table and headed for the door. I still didn't feel comfortable where I was so I crawled to another mat, but after realising it was in a draught, crawled back. There were only about twenty people left in the hall now. As I looked around, I realised I was in line with the Gent's lavatory and could see the row of urinals when the door opened, so I crawled to the front row again and sat on a mat in the centre. I wondered what was holding up Lorraine, Nadine and Aileen. Surely they should be back by now? I wondered where Dermot would sit to lead the meditation. If he sat front centre he would be directly in front of me. I shuffled along to the right a couple of mats, then two back only to land on the urinal-view mat again. I decided to go back to the mat I'd started at, front left. There was still no sign of Lorraine. I saw Micky Muscles heading my way with a box under each arm.

'Ye alreet darlin'? Av been watchin' ye, crahlin' aboot on the floor. What ye deein'?'

'I'm waiting for the meditation to start. Are you staying for it?'

'Am ah shite. Nee chance. Av seen enough weird stuff today to last me the rest of me life. See you round darlin'.'

Bugger this, I thought. They're not coming back and no-one else is staying. I got to my feet ready to head for the door when Dermot appeared, smiling and directing me to choose a mat.

In the end it wouldn't have mattered which mat I chose because as soon as I was settled with crossed legs, he sat on the mat in front of me after pulling it forward until he was too close for comfort.

'Oh dear. Only two of us,' he said. 'Never mind. Let's do a bit of meditative chanting together shall we?'

CHAPTER FORTY-ONE

'Nadine's late this morning,' Lorraine said.

'Not like her,' I said. 'I'd better go and get the salad so we can make a start.

Poll was in Derek's buying vegetables and when she saw me her face lit up. She hurried over to hug me.

'I was about to call in to thank you for the lovely birthday buffet. It was great - I had a fantastic day.'

'Really? Ah, great, I'm glad it went well.'

'I suppose you knew all about it? It was amazing. I thought we were going for a swim, but when we got to the pool Jack surprised me with all my friends. He'd even bought me a new swimming costume.'

'And you enjoyed it?'

'To tell the truth, I was horrified at first. I mean I'm not exactly Cindy Crawford am I?' she laughed. 'But then I thought to myself, you know what? If Jack was ashamed of me he wouldn't have arranged it. And when my friends saw me in my new cossie they all cheered.'

I was pleased it had gone so well for her.

'I'll never forget it,' Poll told me. 'It was a life-changer. We women waste so much time comparing ourselves to each other and worrying about how we look. All for nothing. I was surrounded by good friends and they didn't give a damn what I looked like. In fact, seeing them all in their costumes made me realise how we're all different shapes and sizes and it doesn't actually matter.'

She was right of course. I'd done a lot of it myself over the years and I resolved to take Poll's advice but it's a hard habit to break and I still haven't quite cracked it.

When I returned with the basket of vegetables Nadine still hadn't turned up.

'Do you think she's okay?' Lorraine said. 'She usually rings us first thing if she's poorly.'

'Let's give her a little longer then I'll ring her.' If she was ill in bed I didn't want to harass her with phone calls.

In the days before mobile phones, there was a lot of waiting to hear from people. It's hard to imagine, now we are instantly contactable, but there was a time when you had to take a guess at whether your other half wanted custard creams or rich tea because it was not possible to call them from the supermarket aisle.

Lorraine and I finished the food prep and were indulging in our morning gossip with Nige and Georgina when Nadine finally arrived, red-faced and panting.

'I'm fine,' she said in answer to our concerned questions. 'Let me get my coat off and freshen up a bit.'

Lorraine poured her a cup of tea, and when she returned, looking calmer and tidier, she picked it up gratefully and took a sip.

'Lovely.' She put down her cup. 'Sorry I'm so late. You will never in a million years guess what happened to me this morning.'

She took a seat with the rest of us at the counter and was about to begin her tale when a customer entered. Lorraine was busy handing out cups of tea so I had no option but to leave the group and go to serve the woman, who wanted to know about our bread.

'I want some nice bread to serve with smoked salmon. What would you recommend?'

I didn't eat smoked salmon or fish of any kind but a friend of mine always ordered smoked salmon with brown bread whenever we ate in a particular restaurant, so I pointed out a wholemeal loaf. I could hear Nadine's voice, low and intense, the others huddling round to hear her story. As Georgina tried unsuccessfully to stifle her laughter, I glanced over, straining my ears to catch what she was saying.

'Brown bread? Are you sure? Not white?' the woman asked.

'White would be fine too,' I said, replacing the wholemeal loaf and picking up an unbleached white.

'What does unbleached white mean?'

'It means the flour is natural. Some flours are treated with bleach to whiten them.'

'Really? I didn't know. I take it all your loaves are baked with organic flour?'

'Yes they are.'

I was itching to get back to the others to find out what they were discussing in such a clandestine way but the woman wanted to know all about how and where our bread was produced and the origins of the ingredients. Usually I was pleased when a customer showed such interest, it gave us a chance to spread the word about the quality of the products we stocked. But today I was glad when she finally made her choice and left with a brown loaf.

'Tell Chris what happened,' Lorraine prompted Nadine. Georgina sniggered loudly and Nadine reprimanded her.

'It's not funny Georgina,' she said. 'I'm traumatised by the whole thing.'

What thing?' I asked.

'It's hilarious, that's what it is,' Georgina said, then snorted loudly, unable to stop herself laughing.

'What is?'

'I don't think it's funny at all,' Lorraine said. 'It's disgusting.'

'I agree,' Nige said. 'I'm surprised at you, Georgina, carrying on like that about it.'

'About what?' I asked.

'Ah, stop being so old-fartish,' Georgina said to Nige. 'I bet you've done plenty of stuff in your time.'

'Excuse me!' Nige said. 'I would never do something so disgusting, I will have you know.' He was unusually stony-faced. Whatever Georgina was accusing him of, it offended him greatly.

'As disgusting as what?' I asked.

'That's a bit uncalled for Georgina,' Lorraine said and Nadine agreed.

'I think you owe a Nige an apology. That was out of order.'

'Ok I'm sorry,' Georgina said. 'I can't believe how po-faced you're all being about it.'

'About what?'

'I tell you, you wouldn't be laughing if it happened to you,' Nadine said. 'I'm still shaking.'

'For God's sake is anyone going to tell me what happened?' I yelled.

They all became silent then Nadine told me.

'I was flashed at.'

'Flashed at? You mean like...'

'Yes, I mean like flashed at.'

Again a moment of silence, then Georgina sniggered.

'Actually Georgina, they're right. It's not funny at all,' I said.

Georgina shrugged and rolled her eyes. 'I can't believe none of you can see the funny side.'

'There's nothing funny about a man exposing himself in public,' I told her.

'What makes you think it was a man?' Georgina said.

'It was a woman?' I asked.

'No it wasn't,' Nadine said, as Georgina cackled with delight. 'She's being ridiculous, she thinks the whole thing is hilarious.'

'Have you reported it?' I asked.

'Yes, I was going to wait until I got here, but I passed the phone box on Tragor Street, so I nipped and in and rang the police. They took all the details and said they were going to send someone straight to the scene to see if they could catch him.'

'So what actually happened?' I asked her. I realised she'd already related the story to the others as well as to the police, but she was happy to tell it again.

'I was early for the bus, so I thought, with it being a lovely morning and all that, I'd walk up to the station and get the Metro. It wasn't very busy and I got a seat straight away. Then this man got on at Benton and he caught my eye because he kept moving about from seat to seat as though he didn't know where to settle. He kept looking about like he was looking for someone.'

'Was he scruffy with an old mac on?'

255

'No, he looked really smart and respectable. He eventually made his way along the carriage and sat opposite me. He kept smiling and winking and at first I smiled back because I thought he was a harmless old man...maybe a bit confused or something but harmless.'

'Did he speak to you?'

'No. He sat smiling and winking. And then he starting doing this face...' she demonstrated by rounding her shoulders and widening her eyes. She contorted her face, lifting her cheeks into bulges and jutting out her chin, grinning widely as she moved her tongue across her lower lip.

'Christ, I thought you said he looked respectable,' Nige said.

'He did at first, till he started leering like Cosmo Smallpiece.'

'What did you do?'

'I turned away from him and looked out of the window, but when I got up to get off, he did too. He followed me out of the station. I knew he was tailing me because I changed direction and walked back the way I'd come and he did the same. Then I turned again and went into the park.'

'You shouldn't have gone into the park,' Lorraine said. 'Not when you knew you were being followed.'

'It's easy to say that with hindsight. It was broad daylight, I thought it would be okay. Anyway, I kept looking back, but then when I got near the bowling green I checked and he'd gone. I was so relieved. I kept walking along the narrow path at the back of the pavilion, you know where I mean?'

'Yeah, where it's all overgrown with bushes?' I said.

'Yeah,' Nadine continued. 'And then suddenly he jumped out of the bushes with everything on show.'

'Ugh.' This was from Lorraine.

'I tell you, the bugger must have legged it around the pavilion and got himself into the bushes, ready to spring out.'

'I thought you said he was old.'

'He was.'

'How old?'

'Old. Like eighties, or even older.'

'You got flashed by an eighty-year old?'

'Yes and I'll never forget it.' She shuddered. 'I can't get the picture out of my head. Ugh. You know when you find a mushroom at the bottom of the fridge and it's sort of all puckered and...'

'Ugh, no!'

'Aargh, stop!'

'Too much information, thanks,' Lorraine said. 'What did you say to him?'

'Well you know when you're put on the spot and you say something really stupid?'

'Yeah?'

'I said the first thing that came into my head.'

'Which was...?'

'Nice day for it.'

'Nice day for it? That's what you said to him?' I laughed.

'Hahaha, I bet he wasn't expecting that,' Lorraine said. 'It would have taken the wind out of his sails.'

'In more ways than one,' Nige said.

'Told you it was funny,' Georgina said.

CHAPTER FORTY-TWO

At around twelve-thirty a female police officer arrived to take a statement from Nadine. It was the most inconvenient time of day for this to happen, firstly because it was our busiest time which needed two in the kitchen and one on the counter. Also, a queue of nosy customers who pricked up their ears at the presence of a police officer didn't make a private conversation easy. I suggested they go into the therapy room away from curious ears.

Not having Nadine in the kitchen even for half an hour made a big difference in our productivity level. I worked in the kitchen, filling bread rolls and cooking veggie burgers while Lorraine stayed on the till taking orders and payments.

'What are they doing in there?' I grumbled as I tossed a couple of baked potatoes into cardboard trays and scooped coleslaw onto them. 'I thought it would take a few minutes.'

Lorraine handed me rolls, telling me which fillings were needed and I recited to myself *'cheese savoury salad on white, mushroom pate and coleslaw on granary, egg mayo and cress with tomato on wholemeal...'*

We often did this when trying to remember requests, Nadine was particularly good at memorising orders and could fill five rolls whilst frying burgers, topping baked potatoes and wrapping toasties. Sometimes there would be three of us in the kitchen mumbling away to ourselves, our combined chanting sounding like the drone of a beehive, which must have been a bizarre experience to observe.

Lorraine darted back and forth from the counter to the kitchen bench, wrapping sandwiches I'd made, and handing them over to waiting customers. There was a lull in the rush, and I finished assembling a veggie burger and took it to the customer.

It was Nick, the organic farmer we'd met at the Health Show.

'Hello there! I didn't realise it was you.'

He gave me a crinkle-eyed smile. 'Hi. I've been watching you cook.'

I felt colour rush to my cheeks and I became flustered. He was very good looking.

Lorraine snatched the wrapped burger from my hand. 'I'll take that, thanks,' she said, then handed me a wholemeal roll. 'Hummus and salad if you please.' She turned to Nick and handed him his burger.

'One-ninety-nine, please.' She held out her hand and he gave her some coins then turned to me.

'I have a proposition for you.'

'Yes?' I squeaked and my face reddened further.

'Would you be a collection point for my organic produce box scheme? It would involve taking orders for me and collecting payment from customers.'

'Yeah, I'm sure we could sort something out,' I said.

'Well, I don't know,' Lorraine said. 'We are very busy...'

'Of course I'll pay you a percentage for every box you sell.'

'...but I'm sure we'll manage,' Lorraine said.

'Great,' Nick said. 'It's quite straightforward. I've got some leaflets here,' he held them out to me and Lorraine seized them and gave me a smile.

'I'll sort it out,' she said to me. 'The customer is waiting for that hummus and salad. Chop chop.' She nodded to the kitchen bench and I gritted my teeth and went to make the sandwich.

When Nick left, I gave her a piece of my mind.

'What was that all about? Snatching the burger from me...and the leaflets. And then ordering me back into the kitchen. I'll bloody 'chop-chop' you. What is wrong with you?'

'He fancies you!' she announced.

'Good!'

'Good? You're a married woman! A very pregnant married woman!'

'So? It's still nice to be admired.'

'I'm looking out for Peter.'

'Peter doesn't need looking out for. I'm just selling the guy a burger or at least I was trying to before it was rudely snatched from my hand.'

'You two shouting about me?' Peter had arrived for lunch.

'Lorraine thinks I'm planning to leave you for a farmer,' I told him. I handed him the huge sandwich I'd made earlier.

'Nah, can't believe that,' he said. 'Now a chocolate maker or wine producer, yes. But not a farmer. She doesn't like wearing wellies.'

'He's very interested in her,' Lorraine said. 'I'm keeping an eye on her.'

'I think you're jealous,' I said. 'I can't help it if men find me irresistible.' I picked up the frying pan and sashayed exaggeratedly across the kitchen, waggling my bump, and Peter and Lorraine laughed. Our joking was interrupted by Nadine emerging from the therapy room followed by the police officer.

'I'll be in touch,' she told Nadine.

'Everything okay?' I asked and Nadine nodded.

'Yeah, they think they know who he is. He's been accused before but there wasn't enough evidence so they're hoping to get him this time.'

'That's good, I said. 'They need to get men like him off the streets. What if there'd been children in the park? They often use it as a short cut to school.'

'Mmm,' Nadine said. I could see she wasn't happy.

'You okay?'

'Not really,' she sighed. 'I have to go and identify him and I'm not looking forward to it at all.'

CHAPTER FORTY-THREE

We set up the box scheme, which worked well. Customers signed up to pay five pounds a week for a box of organic produce, of which four-fifty went to Nick and the remaining fifty-pence into our till. It wasn't a huge amount but added nicely to our weekly takings. The boxes were made up of whatever was in season and I looked forward to receiving mine. I never knew what it would contain and enjoyed the challenge of incorporating it into our evening meals.

Nick continued to call in to buy lunch and Lorraine continued to thwart any attempt of his to speak to me. He made a point of saying hello to me before Lorraine swooped in to serve him.

He began to bring me organic vegetables from his farm, a few leeks, some spears of purple broccoli, a bunch of radishes.

'I'm telling you, he's after you,' Lorraine said, after he'd left me a bag of spring greens.

'He's just bringing in samples of his stuff like any other sales rep,' I told her.

'So why does he never give them to me? Ay? Answer me that.'

'Well he probably thinks I'm the only one who cooks in here seeing as you banish me to the kitchen as soon as he appears.'

I must confess, I did love the attention. Especially as he was such an attractive man. But other than that, I had no interest in him at all. Anyone who knew me, knew my devotion to Peter.

Peter found it all highly entertaining. He made comparisons to the madman in Nicholas Nickleby who throws vegetables over Mrs Nickleby's wall as an attempt to woo her, and was particularly entertained when I was given a courgette with a slightly phallic appearance.

It always chuffed him when another man showed interest in me. I was the same with him, I loved it when other women noticed him. I've never understood it when people get annoyed when their partners are found attractive by other people. I'd much

261

rather women thought I was lucky to have a good looking husband than think he was an old minger.

The order list for Nick's organic produce scheme grew steadily as word spread and more customers signed up. There had been a lot in the press lately about genetically-modified crops and organically grown vegetables were becoming very popular.

Each Friday, Nick delivered the boxes which he would stack at the side of the shop, each one labelled with a name, ready to be collected. I loved to see what was included each week, keen to get cooking. I would come to look, prompting Nick to comment 'Some lovely artichokes for you this week' or 'Wait till you try those new potatoes' or some such. He would often suggest cooking methods and ask what recipes I'd tried with the previous week's produce. Lorraine would hover about with the sweeping brush, pretending to clean the floor, presumably listening to make sure he didn't overstep the mark and ready to attack him with her brush if he did.

Usually customers were happy with the selection supplied, but occasionally there would be a complaint there was too much variety, or not enough, or once that the cabbages were too large, but there were never complaints about the quality. We explained we had no control over the contents of the boxes but would pass the comments on to Nick.

One angry woman who telephoned to complain didn't even wait for Nadine to speak, but yelled her grievances about the price of the boxes. She had somehow discovered we were paid fifty-pence per vegetable box and was not happy about it. She vented her anger at Nadine, shouting that the whole thing was a scam and that we were ripping people off. Nadine was shaken when she ended the call and came to tell us.

'She was awful. She was really angry. I couldn't get a word in to explain, she kept yelling that if she'd known we were charging extra she would never have ordered in the first place.'

'We're not charging extra,' Lorraine said. 'We're a shop and shops need to make a profit. The fifty-pence is our cut. Does she think other things she buys don't have a profit margin?'

262

'I don't know, but she was horrible. She started by asking if I was the fat one who worked mornings.' She was struggling to hold back to tears and I felt a wave of protectiveness towards her. How dare she ring up and be so rude to Nadine! Our Nadine, who was so hardworking and loyal. How dare she shout and swear and even worse, make personal comments about Nadine's weight. 'She said she had a good mind to go to the police and make a complaint.'

'Pah!' I spluttered. 'Let her try it. We're hardly likely to be arrested for trying to make a profit.'

'Did you recognise her voice?' Lorraine asked.

'Yes. It's that woman from over Gateshead. I think she works at the Ministry. She comes in every Friday on her way up to the Metro station.'

I racked my mind to put a face to the description.

'Red hair, thirtyish?' I asked. Nadine nodded. Oh yes. I knew her.

'If she rings again, don't speak to her,' I told Nadine. 'Pass her on to me. And the next time she comes in, I'll serve her.' I'd have plenty to say to her.

I didn't have to wait long. The following Friday, at about four-thirty, as was her habit, she came in to collect her vegetable box.

I launched at her immediately.

'Oh. I'm surprised you've come in to collect that!' I said to her, and she looked at me questioningly.

'I was under the impression you weren't happy with the way we run our business.' She stared at me, frowning, but still didn't speak. Ah yes, I thought. I know your type. Typical bully. When someone stands up to you, you back down.

'Nothing to say, ay? Well I have something to say to you. We don't overcharge. We make a profit on things we sell. Such is normal business practice.'

'Chris...' From the corner of my eye I saw Nadine move from the kitchen into the shop.

'It's okay Nadine, you don't need to speak to her. I'll deal with it.'

'But…' Nadine started, and I cut her off.

'Go and have a break, Nadine. No-one is going to come in here and call you fat.'

Lorraine appeared and realised what was going on.

'Go on Nadine, in the back,' she said. 'Have a few minutes while we deal with this.' She pushed her firmly into the office, ignoring her objections.

'May I say…' the woman started.

'No you can't. I think you said enough on the phone.' Lorraine told her.

'How dare you upset a member of our staff, not only by shouting but also by insulting her! How dare you!' I said.

'And if you don't like the way we do business here then you can go elsewhere,' Lorraine said.

'Chris, Lorraine…' Nadine emerged from the office.

'Get back in there!' I snapped, and she did.

'Look here,' the woman said, 'I think it's time I said something.'

'You said plenty on the phone the other day,' I told her. 'I will not have my staff insulted. From now on you're barred.' I'd always wanted to say that someone.

'And you can go to the police if you like,' Lorraine said. 'I'm sure they'd love you to waste their time.'

The woman picked up her vegetable box and slammed a five pound note on the counter.

'Don't worry,' she said. 'There's no need to bar me. I won't be back. You're all nuts.' She turned and walked to the door, accompanied by Lorraine and me shouting 'good riddance'.

'That told her,' I said, as the door slammed behind her.

'We can do without customers like her,' Lorraine said.

Nadine skulked out of the office, white-faced.

'She's gone,' I said.

'Yeah. I heard.'

'Don't worry, she won't be back,' Lorraine said.

'Yeah. I heard that too.' She stood wringing her hands.

'It's okay Nadine,' Lorraine told her. 'You don't have to worry. She won't be back.'

'Yeah.' Nadine took a deep breath.

'It's just...'

'Yeah?'

'It's not the right woman.'

CHAPTER FORTY-FOUR

The next morning Nadine rang to say she'd slept in and would be late. She arrived just after Georgina, apologising as she rushed in. She was pale and her eyes had dark smudges beneath them.

'I haven't slept for worrying,' she said.

'Why what's up?' Georgina asked.

'It's my date today, you know with the flasher.'

'You've got a date with the flasher? Jeez, I knew you were desperate for a bloke but honestly...'

'She has to identify him,' I told Georgina. I wasn't sure if she was serious but if she wasn't, I didn't think it was a matter to joke about.

'Won't you view them through one-way glass? If he's amongst them, he won't be able to see you,' Lorraine told her.

'I'm not bothered if he sees me or not — he had a good look at me on the Metro anyway. I'm worried about picking the wrong man.'

'You do know it's their faces you'll be looking at?'

Nadine was not in the mood for jokes. She rolled her eyes.

'Yes, of course I do. I'm worried I don't recognise him, I don't want to accuse the wrong man.'

'He couldn't be convicted on that alone? There must be other evidence too, the identification is merely confirmation, surely?' Lorraine said.

'Yeah, that's right,' I said. Although I didn't have a clue it was pointless getting Nadine any more worked up about it.

'What time do you have to be there?' I asked.

'Half two. I'm going straight from here.'

We got on with our daily tasks, a little more subdued than usual. I was tired and my body felt heavy. The baby had turned and moved down and the pressure in my pelvis was uncomfortable. I also had a foot stuck up my ribs.

I tried to walk through the gap in the counter and found I had to squeeze through. When I was expecting Rosie I'd had a small neat bump which increased slowly. Depending on my outfit, I sometimes looked like I'd been at the pies a bit and I wished my shape was more defined as to be obviously pregnant. From the back it was impossible to tell I was carrying a child. I often noticed eyes scanning me surreptitiously, trying to decide if I was expecting a baby or just a bit on the pudgy side.

However, it was as if this baby grew overnight. Each morning my belly was more rotund, my bump spreading out to my hips so that there was no doubt from any angle I was definitely pregnant.

'Gawd!' Nadine said watching me wobble my way across the kitchen. 'You're enormous!'

'Thanks for that, Nadine.'

'What's your due date again?' she asked.

'Thirtieth of March. Two and a half weeks. Seventeen days to be exact.'

'I don't think you'll make it.'

'Me neither,' Lorraine said. 'You couldn't possibly get any bigger. You'd burst.'

'We should have a sweepstake, see who can guess the date.'

'Do you mind?' I said. 'I'm not a prize pig.'

'Could have fooled us!'

'Ah, shuddup the pair of you,' I told them.

'Sorry, from now on we will not refer to the elephant in the room.'

I was determined not to complain. I was so grateful to be carrying this baby and I would not have missed the whole experience for anything. I loved feeling my child moving in my womb, knowing it was safe and growing inside. It was just the last couple of weeks that were uncomfortable - running to the loo all the time because of the pressure on my bladder, and the terrible indigestion and heartburn that plagued me each time I ate. The midwife said these symptoms were normal and were due to my

267

organs being squashed by my growing baby. I was finding it increasingly difficult to bend, or pick something up from the floor. I couldn't reach my own toenails and had to persuade Peter to paint them for me. When I sat, my bump took up the whole of my lap, leaving no space for Rosie to squeeze on. It's a very strange sensation to be sitting on your own lap.

When I napped on the sofa, one of the cats would squeeze into the space between my boobs and bump and have a nap with me. Presumably it was the warmest place in the house.

I wondered if Lorraine and Nadine were right and I would not reach my due date. Rosie had been born a few days late, but maybe it was different with a second child?

I noticed Lorraine and Nadine were working twice as fast as I was, and it dawned on me I was not helping to ease the workload. They were humouring me as I waddled about completing the simple tasks they suggested I do.

At two, Nadine left to identify her flasher, promising to telephone us to let us know how it went.

We spent the afternoon, as usual on a Wednesday, putting together the Karma order that would be delivered on the following Friday. I made us a cup of tea first, and went to switch on the radio but Lorraine stopped me.

'I've got the Alanis Morissette CD you wanted to borrow,' she said. 'I'll put it on now.'

Usually we would speed around the shop with the catalogue, checking stock and noting down our requirements, but today, I sat at the counter drinking my tea while Lorraine checked the shelves and I filled out the order. We usually whizzed through the task but today I was unable to concentrate and kept making silly mistakes.

'Four cases of organic soya milk and two of the rice milk,' Lorraine called.

'Hang on, I haven't done the last one yet. What was it? A case of goat's milk?'

'No. I said we didn't need goat's milk. I said a case of soya cream.'

'Oh right.'

'And we'll need two cases of mushroom pate, two of herb pate and one of the olive.'

'To go back to the soya milk, how many did you say?'

I knew I was irritating and to Lorraine's credit she was very patient.

'Sorry,' I said after she'd repeated herself for the third time. 'I don't know what's wrong with me. I feel so groggy.'

'Go and put the kettle on and I'll finish off here,' Lorraine said. 'To be honest I think I'll be quicker without you.'

Nadine rang while we were cashing up, to tell us the identity parade had been quite straight forward.

'There was no mistaking him when I saw him,' she said. 'I'm so relieved. And there were other women there too who'd also had the misfortune of seeing his display so I knew I wasn't the only one.'

I was glad it had gone well for her, but found it difficult to focus on what she was saying. I'd found the day really tiring, my mind was foggy and I was straining to concentrate. Up in the washroom, I glanced in the mirror as I washed my hands. My skin was pale and my eyes rimmed with dark shadow. I was glad when it was time to close the shop and head home.

'Peter's late,' Lorraine said.

'Ah no! I've just remembered. He's going straight into town. I said I'd get the Metro.' It had to be today of all days when I was feeling rough. 'He's going to pick Rosie up first.'

'I'll take you,' Lorraine said.

'It's out of your way.'

'No arguing.'

For once I did as she said.

As soon as I reached home I went to run a bath. I decided I may as well make the most of the time to myself and have a bit of a pamper evening. I poured scented oil into the steaming bath water and lit a couple of tea-lights. I'd have at least an hour to myself.

Allowing myself to be drawn into the beliefs of old wives, I'd been afraid to buy anything new for the baby until last week when I had finally been talked into a shopping spree by Lorraine. We'd ordered a pram which Peter would collect tonight, and had a wonderful time buying new cot sheets and baby clothes, and a little square shaped teddy from Boots who became known as Square Bear.

I switched on the CD player, climbed into the bath, blissfully sinking my aching body into the warm fragrant water, and listened to Simply Red.

Two hours later, I was still lying there on my back like a portly black beetle. I'd tried to hoist myself up, but my body was too heavy and barrel-like to heave myself out. I tried turning onto my side, using my arms to push against the edge of the bath but I couldn't get out.

I was not in a good humour, having lain there, emptying and refilling the bath each time the water grew cold. Luckily our bath had centrally placed taps, otherwise my choice would have been to develop hypothermia, or else dexterity in my toes. The CD was switched to repeat and Mick Hucknall crooned his way through his selection for a fourth time.

'Shut up!' I yelled at him. I grabbed a towel and threw it in the direction of the CD player which I had placed at the bathroom door. Unfortunately, it hit the volume control and Mick's voice rang out louder.

Peter eventually arrived home, an hour later than expected having taken Rosie to Fenwick's toy department to choose a present for the new baby and a treat for herself, after collecting the pram.

'Where've you been?' I snapped. 'I can't get out!'

He laughed which enraged me all the more.

'I'm not surprised you're so irritated listening to him at full belt,' he said, stooping to turn off the CD.

'I can't get out,' I said again, he watched me struggling and laughed all the more. I kicked my legs like a trapped frog.

'Get me out of here this minute!' The angrier I became the harder he laughed, especially when I tried to stamp my foot which resulted in a splatter of water spraying my head and face and causing me to splutter.

'Shut up! It's not funny, I've been lying here for hours.'

'I've a good mind to leave you there for a few more hours,' he said amiably. 'Until you ask politely.'

Later, after we'd thoroughly inspected the pram, and practised pushing our cats about in it, and I was dry and warm, snuggled on the sofa in my jarmies, I did see the funny side.

'I should hire a crane in case it happens again,' Peter joked and I slapped him playfully as we laughed.

I pulled my fleecy blanket over my legs and tucked it in as I snuggled into Peter. I loved this time of the day. The house was quiet, work finished for the day and Rosie tucked safely in bed. The lamps gave a warm glow and my scented candles filled the room with the aroma of vanilla. I lay with my head against Peter's shoulder, half watching a programme about two friends who were renovating a holiday property in France.

'I'm so tired,' I said.

'Well go and have an early night.'

'I'm too tired to move.' I shuffled into a more comfortable position and dozed through the rest of the programme. When it ended, Peter got up to put the kettle on and I leaned against the arm of the sofa, stretched out my legs and flicked through the channels.

The BBC news was beginning and I froze in horror, unable to believe what I was seeing.

A gunman had entered a primary school and shot and killed sixteen children and their teacher before turning the gun on himself.

I remember hearing the remote control clatter to the floor, and I must have let out some sort of wail as Peter rushed back to the room. A huge wave of panic and nausea swept over me and I felt I was about to faint or vomit, or perhaps both.

271

Peter picked up the remote and pointed it towards the television set but I grabbed at his arm.

'No!' I cried. 'I need to know,' and he held me while I watched the footage of distressed parents arriving at the school to find out if their child were amongst the victims.

I could not process the information. I alternatively paced the floor then hung onto Peter, sobbing uncontrollably, my whole body shaking. This sort of thing could not happen in Britain. We had strict gun laws. And who... who could take a gun to a child? A class of children in a P.E lesson?

Dunblane. I'd been there many times. We always stopped there for a break on trips to Scotland. I remembered it as an attractive little town with a river running through it. I couldn't believe such a terrible thing could happen in such a lovely place.

Peter had known. The incident had happened during the morning at the beginning of the school day, and the unfolding story broadcast constantly. He'd contacted Lorraine and they'd colluded to keep the news from me, knowing how it would affect me.

It had been unusual for Lorraine to prefer playing CDs at the shop rather than listen to the radio as normal, but I hadn't thought too much about it. I was touched they'd tried to protect me, but there was no way I was not going to learn of it - the whole country was in shock.

Although I wasn't physically sick, I felt nauseous to my core. The horror replayed itself in my head like a loop of film I could not switch off.

I went to look at Rosie and my heart ached as I watched the rise and fall of her breath, her arms wrapped about Funny Bunny. Her rounded cheeks were flushed and her eyelashes dark and curling. I pulled the blanket up around her, tucking it in. Sobbing, I gave a silent plea to heaven to keep my baby girl safe and then immediately reproached myself. For some mothers it was too late. Their worst nightmare had happened.

Only hours ago they had prepared breakfast, filled lunch boxes and kissed their children goodbye in the schoolyard like any other school day. I imagined their mornings like ours – a chaos of missing socks, teeth brushing, cereal bowls... a normal family morning. If only they'd known, they would have wrapped their arms about their babies, held them close and protected them. But who could possibly know? Who could imagine such a terrible thing could happen? It was beyond comprehension.

I, like many others, did not sleep much that night. I kept thinking of the fear the children must have suffered, and of the parents who had lost their children. How must they be feeling at this moment? How could life go on after this? How could they eat and sleep and live and breathe after such a terrible evil had ripped their lives apart?

In the morning I was pale, my eyes red-rimmed and bloodshot. I couldn't eat, couldn't concentrate.

The shop was quiet, those who did come in were shocked and wanted to talk about the news. Going over and over the same details, the same observations and theories. Several times I had to leave the shop due to panic engulfing me.

'Sorry,' I told Lorraine. 'I just can't come to terms with it.'

Lorraine hugged me. 'It's understandable. Everyone is reeling from it. You're not the only one. You've always been so sensitive, especially when it comes to children and animals. Pregnancy makes you even more emotional.'

At her words my eyes filled again.

'Sorry,' I said again.

'Look, don't you think it's time to start your maternity leave?'

'No!' I said. 'What about the shop? You know how much there is to do.'

'You're due to give birth in a couple of weeks, you have to think about the baby. You've tired yourself out, I've seen you almost falling asleep behind the counter.'

'No I have not,' I said, jumping straight to the defence. 'I'm a bit tired that's all.' I felt tears spring to my eyes again and I shook my head, trying to ward them off.

'I'm worried about you. Peter is too.'

'Then why haven't either of you said anything to me? There's nothing to worry about I'm just...tired.'

'Since when did you ever listen to anyone telling you what to do?' Lorraine smiled. 'If you want me to be straight with you, I will. You're muddling about, making mistakes because you're so worn-out.'

The tears I'd been trying to hold back escaped and I roughly wiped them away with my hand.

'Chris, I'm not criticising you,' Lorraine said gently. 'You've been pushing yourself too hard, you're trying to do too much.'

'I'm tired,' I said again. 'And I'm upset about those poor children, I can't get it out of my mind.'

Lorraine hugged me. 'You're exhausted and stressed and this has pushed you over the edge. You need to get yourself calmed down. You have to be strong for the baby's sake.'

I took a tissue and blew my nose. I knew she was right. I had come so far in this pregnancy and done my best for my unborn child, I couldn't let it all slip now. Maybe the baby would feel my stress and anxiety and that would not be good for him. I needed to get a grip.

'Go home and get some rest,' Lorraine said. 'Put your feet up, read some of your favourite books or watch some old videos or something. No watching the news.'

'Okay,' I smiled weakly. 'I'll do that. Maybe I'll have the day off tomorrow.'

'No. I'm telling you to go home now. Get some rest and look after yourself. You can pop in if you feel up to it in a couple of days.'

'Okay,' I said.

'Now,' Lorraine said, handing me my coat and I put it on feeling lighter already.

CHAPTER FORTY-FIVE

Peter was pleased that I'd agreed to stop working, and fussed about bringing me breakfast and making sure I had something for my lunch. He had arranged to drop Rosie at his mam's to give me a day to myself.

I had a shower and pulled on a pair of joggers and a t-shirt. I mooched about the house, my brain whirring. The horror of the killing spree had tainted my view of the world. Everything – people, places, incidents, even the most innocent and joyful - seemed to have a sinister undertone and I could not shake off an underlying dragging fear. Whereas in the past I'd often been accused of viewing the world with rose-tinted glasses, the lenses now were shattered and murk coloured.

I did not know these were signs of a slowly growing anxiety disorder that was to later intermittently blight years of my life.

I took Lorraine's advice and re-read parts of my favourite books.

Books are life-savers, there to turn to in bad times, ready to escort the mind to other dimensions. I read of Ratty and Mole witnessing the Piper at the Gates of Dawn. I read of Scout and Jem Finch finally realising the truth about Boo Radley, and of The Black Rabbit coming to take Hazel to his new world. The words soothed and grounded me, and slowly the world came back into focus and the horror diminished and retreated to its rightful place.

I realised how exhausted I'd become, how I'd been pushing myself to live up to my unachievable expectations.

I recognised my fear of being out of control, of not being on top of everything and my inability to slow down and focus on my priorities. Another classic sign of anxiety. Striving to control micro-details of my life meant there was no space left in my mind for looming fears to creep in and take root.

I was due to give birth within the next couple of weeks, of course it was acceptable to take a step back. I needed to leave the business to Lorraine and Nadine while I rested and prepared for the arrival of my baby.

Peter rang me in the afternoon to tell me not to cook, he would bring a take-away home. He arrived with Rosie on one arm and a bag of Indian food on the other. I took Rosie from him and hugged her.

'How are you feeling?' he asked. We were in front of the television with our dishes of vegetable Balti. Rosie was sitting in her chair, chewing on a piece of naan bread, a dish of vegetables and rice on her tray.

'Much better, thanks. I missed Rosie, though. I'm looking forward to having a few days with her.'

'You sure?' Peter said. 'You know what a handful she can be. My mam is happy to take her.'

I watched her lean out of her chair to feed rice and vegetables to Funny Bunny, the sauce leaving a stain as she shoved it into his face with a spoon.

'Nice dinner?' she asked him, and I couldn't help laughing as I reached for a tissue to mop up the rice she'd manage to scatter on the carpet.

'Yeah, I'm sure.'

The next morning, Peter left us tucked up in bed with tea and toast.

'Look after Mammy,' he told Rosie as he kissed us goodbye. 'No cleaning,' he told me. 'Take it easy.'

'Okay,' said. As if that were going to happen with a toddler to look after. Anyway, I'd done enough resting. I intended to spend the time doing some serious messing about.

I had a lovely couple of days at home with Rosie, such special, valuable days I remember well. Reading my favourite books had eased my anxiety, but the time spent with Rosie brought back the joy.

We went for walks through Holywell Dene, looking for signs of spring that were appearing everywhere. She plodded through the mud by my side in her wellies, taking delight in the many puddles and making sure she missed none of them.

'Mumma splash,' she said, and thought it was hilarious when I jumped in a puddle with her.

We built towers with her wooden bricks and sculptures from grocery boxes. We made cakes for 'Daddy coming home' and left the mess for 'Daddy coming home' too.

Late afternoon we snuggled together and read story books, falling asleep and waking to Peter arriving home with little treats for us, - a bunch of pink tulips for me and a comic for Rosie, or sometimes our favourite chocolate bars or a cupcake each.

And then the morning came that I was awakened by a familiar ache and realised today was the day my baby would make an appearance.

Our second daughter was born upstairs in our home in my own bedroom. I was attended by two jolly, cuddly midwives who made me cry with laughter between the bouts of piercing pain.

Afterwards, I lay tucked in bed holding my daughter who was now cocooned in a tiny cotton nightdress, and cried tears of relief and joy.

Anna Rachel had joined us and our family was complete.

CHAPTER FORTY-SIX

Everyone loves a new baby, we were inundated with visitors and Anna and Rosie were showered with gifts. Having a new baby in the house is such a special time and each morning I woke with a delicious excitement and opened my eyes to see my beautiful Anna lying in her Moses basket next to me.

Our families were a great support, as they had been when Rosie was born, and I was grateful to have such lovely relatives.

Rosie relished her role as a big sister. She scampered about fetching the changing bag and Square Bear, and explained to Anna about family life and the world in general. It was adorable to see her gently stroking her sister's head as she related her favourite stories and sang nursey rhymes in her sweet, if not always tuneful, voice. She also announced that as she was now grown up she wished to be called Rose rather than Rosie, to which we complied.

I settled into a routine much more quickly than I had when Rosie, - Rose, arrived. Somehow a second baby is less of a shock to the system.

Nine days after Anna's birth, Rose turned three and we had a small party for some of her playgroup friends.

Six three-year-olds make a lot of noise and mess and I was glad to be able to escape at intervals to feed and change Anna, leaving Peter and Lorraine supervising games. I was relieved when it was time to send them home with party bags and birthday cake. Rose had a great time and went to bed happily, with three new Barbie dolls and a Barney dinosaur.

Lorraine stayed to help me clean up and I told her I was planning to visit the shop the following morning. I was yearning to get back, partly to catch up on what had happened during my absence, but mainly to show off my new little daughter.

'Are you sure?' she asked. She didn't sound keen and I felt a bit hurt. 'You know how busy we get. Why not come in on Saturday with Peter?

'Well I could,' I said. 'But Aileen and Nadine won't be in and I thought they'd want to see Anna.'

'Ah, they can see her another time,' Lorraine said.

'But I really want to come in.'

Lorraine sighed. 'Okay then, but make it after two when it's not so busy.'

I felt a bit downcast when she'd left. I remembered when I'd returned to work after my maternity leave with Rose, lots of our customers had forgotten me, and many new ones assumed me to be 'the new girl'.

I thought about Lorraine, Aileen and Nadine together in the shop, working and joking without me. They'd probably have changed some of our routines and they'd have 'in-jokes' I would not understand because I had not been there for the spark of the joke. They'd have more productive methods of working now I wasn't there, fat and cumbersome, wobbling about, faffing my way through the day.

Anna whimpered, her sign she was hungry, and holding her to me, I glowed with a surge of love and protectiveness. I supposed I should let the shop go for now. I was the mother of two girls who I loved more than life itself - surely it was enough for me? I was eternally grateful for my beautiful, healthy baby girls.

But still an ache kept surfacing, a longing for my old way of life, for my role as a cog in the machine that was Nutmeg.

Lots of women would love what I have been given, I chided myself as I changed a nappy. I thought in particular of Amy, a customer who wanted nothing else in life than to be a mother, a wish nature had cruelly denied. I had seen the heartache in her eyes as the years passed and no child arrived.

To be honest, I loved all the 'new mother' jobs. Feeding, bathing, dressing, undressing, lulling... I knew it would not last for ever and I cherished it.

The washing, ironing, shopping, cleaning...not so much. Peter did as much as possible to help but often by the time we'd eaten and got the girls bathed and tucked up in bed, it was all we could do to stay awake in front of the television until bedtime.

I was also aware of the boring companion I'd become. I watched the clock as Peter's return drew close, listening for the sound of his car engine and fiddling about switching the kettle on and off, trying to time it so I'd have a cup of tea ready for him when he walked in. The relief of having an adult to converse with activated an outpouring of the minutiae of my day, each of my accounts as dull as the last.

Peter would be delighted to be home with us, but my conversation revolved around feeds and nappies and the route of our daily walk and when he related his day, I felt mine to be mundane in comparison.

I changed into pyjamas and arranged Rose's birthday cards on the mantelpiece while Peter made us a cup of tea.

'I'm going to the shop tomorrow,' I yawned, flopping onto the sofa.

'I'm not sure that's a good idea,' Peter said.

'Why's that?'

'Well, it's early days. It will be such a hassle with the two of them. Why don't you wait until Saturday and I'll take you in?'

'I'll be fine. I can handle a baby and a toddler. I'm not useless!'

'I know you're not, I just thought it would be easier to wait and we'll go together in the car.'

'No,' I said. 'I'm going in tomorrow afternoon.'

'Okay, please yourself.'

'I will.'

The next day, I changed my mind about going several times. Maybe they were right. It always took me a ridiculous amount of time to get two children and myself ready to leave the house. No grabbing a bag and keys and shooting off for me. A huge amount of apparel accompanied me; pram, rain cover, parasol, changing bag, spare clothes, juice, snacks, toys and of course Funny Bunny and Square Bear. Then there'd be the palaver of getting on and off the Metro. And if I did manage to get there with us all in one piece, I'd probably interrupt the flow of work and be in the way which would make me feel even more out of the loop.

I busied myself with the usual tasks; vacuuming, laundry, feeding and nappy changes whilst entertaining Rose at the same time.

At midday, I fed Anna then put together a plate of Rose's favourite finger foods, and she sat happily eating fingers of toast with cubes of cheese, chopped cucumber, carrot, grapes and apple at the kitchen table. I made myself a sandwich and joined her. A shaft of sunlight warmed the kitchen, and I felt a desire to be outdoors. Pale blue sky showed above the green-stained fence outside of the kitchen window, and I could see daffodils and crocus that Peter had planted in pots with Rose in the autumn. After the long, grey winter months, the colours looked fresh and revitalising.

I suddenly decided that I was going to go after all and told Rose we were going to see Auntie Lorraine in the shop.

'Hooray!' she yelled, which cheered me and made me feel I'd made the right decision. She'd love the ride on the Metro and she always liked to visit the shop and see Lorraine, mostly because she knew there were so many good things to eat there. I tidied the kitchen as Rose danced and sang. I watched her and smiled. How lovely to be three, I thought. To feel such joy so easily.

'Let's wash your lunch off your face before we go,' I said. Rose struggled to avoid the flannel I aimed at her face. I managed to brush her hair as I chased her about but it immediately sprang back into its usual unruly curls. She insisted on putting on her coat herself, which she managed to do upside down so the hood hung down over her bottom.

'Let me put that right for you darling.'

'No! Me do it.' Eventually I decided it was not worth the struggle and left it.

Next she fussed about her shoes and insisted on wearing her new tartan slippers my mam had bought for her. By the time I'd persuaded her into her shoes, Anna needed a nappy change and by the time I'd changed her, Rose needed a wee. After chasing Rose back to the bathroom to wash her hands and then back a second time to watch her do it properly, Anna was grizzly because she was hungry again. I decided to give her a quick feed before leaving.

281

Meanwhile Rose took the opportunity to remove her shoes and put her slippers back on.

'Get those shoes on now,' I told her. A familiar smell wafted to my nose and I went to get the changing bag.

'I'll help,' Rose said as I lay Anna on her changing mat.

'No, get your shoes on.'

'I'm hungry.'

'You've just had lunch.' I reached across and grabbed a banana from the fruit bowl and passed it to her. 'Here, have a banana.' She wandered back into the kitchen with it while I got on with the nappy-changing process.

I tucked Anna into her pram and went to dispose of the dirty nappy in the outside bin. I returned to find Rose helping herself to cereal.

'I said a banana,' I told her, but gave her a spoon to eat her cereal while I swept up cornflakes from the floor. As she ate, I removed the slippers from her feet and shoved them in the cupboard under the sink.

The phone rang and I deliberated about leaving it, but my fear that it may be important took over and I answered it, only to regret my decision as I fobbed off a company cold-calling about insurance policies. I ended the call as swiftly as possible. Rose had finished her cereal but was still shoe-less.

'Right. Where are your shoes?'

She smiled sweetly and shrugged, so I had a quick search and found them behind the lavatory. I retrieved them and pushed them onto her feet ignoring her protests as she wriggled about on the floor. It was like trying to put a pair of tights on a cat.

'Keep still!' I yelled. I managed to distract her by pretending Funny Bunny was singing in a funny voice and took advantage of her being incapacitated by giggles to slip her feet into her shoes and quickly buckle them.

I managed to get both the pram and Rose out of the front door and had locked it behind us when a man's voice startled me.

'Windows darlin'.'

'What?' I jumped.

'Window cleaner, love. You owe four weeks.'

'Ah. I'm on my way out, can I give you it next week?'

'If you don't mind, love, I'll take it now. Like I say, you haven't paid for four weeks.'

I gritted my teeth. I'd been busy having a baby and missed a couple of payments. It wasn't like I'd robbed him of his life savings. I fished in my bag for my keys.

'No problem.'

I unlocked the door, silently cursing Peter as to why we needed so many locks on one door. Although the window cleaner looked fairly harmless and I'm sure he was, I unstrapped Anna from her pram and lifted her out. It became apparent she was not happy about this, having dozed off with a nice milk-filled tummy, and set up a raucous yelling. Rose joined in.

'That noise not nice, Mumma,' Rose shrieked. 'I NOT LIKE THAT NOISE!'

'I'll just be a minute,' I yelled above the din and taking Rose by the hand took the two of them back into the house to search for change. I remembered there was some in one of the kitchen drawers. The banana I'd given Rose lay on the kitchen table, the end mangled where she'd tried unsuccessfully to peel it.

'Ooh, narna,' Rose said and reached for it as I counted coins. Still holding Anna, I took the banana and managed to peel it, then went to pay the man.

'Right, are we ready?' I asked. 'Let's go.'

'Look my hat,' Rose giggled.

I removed the banana skin from her head and grabbed a piece of kitchen paper to wipe a piece of mushed banana from her hair. I scrubbed at a piece on her coat too. It left a stain but it would have to stay there.

Rose waited until I had strapped Anna into her pram and locked the Yale lock and the two mortice locks before announcing she needed another wee.

This accomplished, hands washed, shoes retrieved (this time from inside the laundry basket), we finally got out of the house and down the front path.

'Right. Let's go to see Aunty Lorraine at the shop.' I smiled down at Rose but she was grimacing.

'Poo-wee!' she said dramatically. 'Mumma, baby has a poo-bum'.

CHAPTER FORTY-SEVEN

We were a one-car family in those days and because Peter needed to drive to work, most of my journeys were by Metro and bus.

Our local Metro station was about a twenty minute walk away, however, at the thought of toddling at Rose's pace along with her habit of stopping to examine anything interesting we might pass, like a cat, or a gate or a discarded crisp packet, I decided to get the bus to the station.

Getting on a bus with a pram and a baby and a toddler is tricky, but Geordie bus drivers are notoriously lovely and when he saw me struggling, he switched off the engine and left his seat to come and collapse my pram and stash it in the luggage rail before guiding us to a seat. Likewise, a few minutes later, he carried the pram off the bus and waited until I had Anna safely tucked in then waved us off.

On the Metro, we sat near the door so I could park the pram next to me. Rose sat at my side, feet swinging as she carefully observed everyone in the carriage. She loved to chat to people and would scrutinise each person carefully before choosing her prey. Once she'd caught a person's eye she would begin by yelling 'hello' and a barrage of questions would follow.

'What your name?' 'What your dog's name?' 'Where you going?' 'Why your hair is funny?' 'You like my shoes?'

Most people didn't mind and enjoyed chatting with her, usually with others joining in or at least smiling. But today she chose a man of around twenty with a shaved head, tattooed face, multiple piercings and a hostile expression.

'Hello!' she yelled. The man glanced up and scowled, first at Rose then at me.

'Hello man!'

I looked out of the window desperately trying to see something to distract her as the Metro rattled through scrubby wasteland.

'Oh look at the... telegraph pole.'

'Hello, man! Why you face dirty? Why you drawed on you face?'

The temperature seemed to increase and I unfastened my coat and pulled my scarf away from my throat. I told myself I should not judge by appearance but he did not look child-friendly. Or even just friendly.

'Look Mumma, look at the man with the funny face, hahaha. Look at him Mumma.'

Houses began to appear as we left the vicinity of the station and I nudged Rose and pointed.

'Look at all the houses. Look at the lovely gardens. Let's count them. One, two, three...' I cringed with embarrassment, although I could see people smirking, obviously enjoying Rose's remarks.

'Look at the funny man. Look!' Rose pointed and giggled hysterically.

The man turned and stared at us, clenched his teeth and make a sound like a low pitched growl.

'Why you sad, man? You face sore? Aw, never mind.'

In desperation I burst into song.

'The wheels on the bus go round and round, round and round...' I felt hot and uncomfortable and I could feel my heart beating.

'Why you sing Mumma? Why you sing wheels on a bus?'

'Because you're going to get us killed,' I hissed. I pulled her onto my lap when I saw the man stand and make his way towards us. He gave us a last glower then muttering under his breath, ambled off to the next carriage.

'Aw, the funny man gone. Bye bye. Bye bye man.'

At our station, I pushed the pram into the lift and as the doors began to close I spotted a woman with a pram heading towards us. I put my hand on the door to stop it and shuffled my pram across to make room. My pram was a standard Mother Care model that had been on special offer, hers a Silver Cross limited edition that retailed at nearly two thousand pounds. I knew this because Peter and I had seen one for sale and had joked we could buy the girls a car each for that price.

It looked like it was on its first outing - mine was mud-splattered from our daily walks through the local dene and grubby at the front where Rose would sometimes sit as I pushed the two of them home.

The lift door closed and I peeped into the woman's pram.

'Ah, she's beautiful,' I said. 'How old is she?'

The woman turned and looked at my pram, then at me and finally at Rose.

'Seven months.'

I smiled, expecting her ask about my baby but she didn't.

'Hello, lady,' Rose said, and as the woman turned away and ignored her my heart ached at the sight of my beautiful daughter, smiling and innocent with her windblown curls and her coat on upside down.

'My name Rose.'

The woman gave a wry smile. She continued to ignore Rose but addressed me.

'Rose?' she sniffed. 'Now that doesn't surprise me in the least. Such a common name at the moment. Poor thing.'

For a moment I was speechless. Tears of anger and hurt sprang to my eyes and I struggled to think of how to respond.

'We chose Edwina.' She looked into her pram with pride. 'We wanted something sophisticated. A name that not every Tom, Dick and Harry would have.'

'Well they wouldn't, would they, if they were called Tom, Dick and Harry,' I spluttered.

The woman tilted her head towards me.

'I'm afraid when she starts school you will find she'll be one of many Roses in her class.'

The lift doors opened and the woman pushed her pram ahead of us. Rose took my hand.

'That not nice lady, Mumma. I not like that lady.'

'No, me neither.' I said, I said in a choked voice. 'She's what you call a right cow.' I said this loudly hoping the woman would hear.

We made our way out of the station. Rose's smile had now disappeared and she looked about to cry too. I think children pick up on how you are feeling and Rose was a compassionate child and knew I wasn't happy.

I lifted her onto the front of the pram and she sat in front of Anna who was still sleeping. I shook off my foolish tears and forced a beaming smile.

'Did you know, my Rose and my Anna are the best girls in the world and I love them to the moon and back?'

'Moon and back,' she repeated and her lovely smile returned and she giggled, singing 'moon and back' in a tuneless song as we made our way to the shop.

By the time I approached the shop I felt drained. The journey had worn me down. I decided I'd stay for a quick chat and if I deduced I was getting in the way, I'd make my excuses and leave.

I crossed the zebra crossing and something on the shop door caught my eye.

A sign pinned there read ' It's a Girl!' and beneath it a banner pronounced 'Welcome Anna Rachel Kenworthy'.

'Look!' I said to Rose, and she turned and laughed with delight at the pink balloons tied in bunches along the shop windows.

CHAPTER FORTY-EIGHT

The shop door jangled open to reveal Lorraine and Nadine standing with arms wide and almost wider grins.

'SURPRISE!'

Nadine handed Rose a pink balloon and she beamed with delight. The shop was crammed with smiling people, many holding gifts and flowers. I was hustled inside to cheering and cat-calls and was enfolded in a huge hug from Lorraine as Nadine took control of the pram and wheeled it behind the counter.

'Oh you're awake darling,' she said, and without hesitating, unclipped the harness and lifted out a sleepy Anna, covering her face in kisses.

Rose ran to Aileen, arms outstretched, and delighted, Aileen lifted her up and hugged her.

'Hello Rosie Posie. Did you come on the Metro?'

'Yes and I seed a cow.'

'You saw a cow?' Aileen looked at me and I shrugged.

I looked around, overwhelmed with emotion. Pink balloons were tied to the shelves and bunting above the counter spelled out 'Welcome Anna Rachel Kenworthy'. I was greeted and hugged as friends came forward to congratulate me and give me gifts.

I mumbled my thanks, overcome with their kindness and trying to take it all in.

Georgina and Nige were there, and Maureen was perched at the counter, her shopping bag – presumably holding Billy – at her feet.

Tomas and Hanna presented me with a basket of flowers and Hanna said something in Polish.

'My Hanna would like to be holding baby please,' Tomas said and Nadine placed Anna in her arms. She gazed at Anna for a moment, smiling happily then spoke again.

'She says having own baby very soon,' Tomas translated, then the meaning of his words struck home and he gasped, beaming at Hanna and although I did not understand his words, I knew he was showering her with endearments.

Aileen gave Rose a carton of juice and she sat on a stool behind the counter, sucking at the straw and telling everyone she was the 'shop lady', pressing random buttons on the till until she hit lucky and the till drawer sprang open.

'Ooh pennies,' she said grabbing two handfuls of coins.

'No you don't, cheeky Charlie,' Lorraine told her, taking the coins from her and closing the till drawer. 'Come and have something to eat with Mammy.'

I was led to the kitchen and given a glass of something fizzy by Georgina which I sniffed cautiously, remembering another time Georgina had given out supposedly non-alcoholic drinks which turned out to be heavily laced with vodka.

'It's grape juice, I swear,' she said.

Nadine placed Anna back into my arms and she was immediately taken from me by Aileen. She was fawned over and admired, as she was passed from Aileen to Lorraine and then back to Nadine.

'You've had a hold, it's my turn,' a woman joked, and I recognised her as the assistant from the Post Office.

The women clucked and cooed around Anna and I laughed to myself at how some women, however level-headed, turn to mush at the sight of a baby. I was the same. Babies, puppies, kittens, ducklings...I couldn't resist

Georgina didn't ask to hold Anna, I was aware she wasn't a 'baby' person, but she gave me a gift of a hand thrown pottery mug, painted with poppies, perfect for a child's small hands.

'Glad it all went well for you darlin',' she said, and kissed my cheek.

Nadine, still holding Anna, urged me to have something to eat as she ignored several pairs of outstretched arms, desperate to be next to hold the baby. The kitchen was laid out with a buffet and Nige was already in there picking at a bowl of crisps. He handed me a paper plate whilst Maureen, who'd been hovering near the kitchen took this as a sign the buffet was open and shuffled behind me.

'May as well try and have a bite to eat,' she said, loading her plate with sandwiches and a slice of quiche. 'Although I'll probably end up with indigestion.'

'You blaming our cooking Maureen?'

'No, not at all, my pet. It's this stomach of mine. Never been the same since I had the gastric flu in 1974.'

Nige turned to me. 'Congratulations, flower. She's lovely. Another little beauty joins the Nut Shop.'

'Thanks Nige. I have to admit I'm so relieved she's here and safe and it's all over.' Suddenly feeling very hungry, I filled my plate with food and stood where I could keep an eye on both Rose, who was tucking into a huge piece of carrot cake, and Anna who was gurgling happily in the arms of Nadine.

Aileen, who'd been serving customers, came to congratulate me. 'Isn't nature wonderful?' she sighed. 'To be able to create a tiny baby in your womb. It's a miracle!'

Nige's face stiffened.

'Not such a miracle having to heave it out through your foof though,' Georgina said. 'Mother Nature played a blinder there. I'm sure there could have been a better plan.'

Nige held up his palm.

'Eating!' he said, and Georgina laughed.

'Wait till she tells you all the gory details.'

Nige put down his plate.

'I won't!' I told him. 'And anyway, it's not that bad, Georgina.'

'I did it once and that was enough. Anyone who does it twice must be some sort of masochist.'

'You have a child?' Aileen asked, surprised.

'Yes I have a daughter, Skye. She lives in Greece, I don't see much of her these days.'

'Wow! That's amazing,' Aileen said. 'Although I suppose lesbians can have children through other means, can't they?'

'I'm sure they can, Aileen, although I'm not a lesbian.'

291

'Oh...I thought...' Aileen scuttled off up the steps to the sink area red-faced and mumbling about making a start on the washing up, though Georgina was not perturbed in the least.

'So how has it been without me?' I asked.

'Great,' Lorraine said and I gave her a slap. 'You know we've all missed you! Hasn't been the same. I don't think you realised how worried we all were. We're all so relieved Anna has arrived healthy and beautiful.'

'Me too. I can't believe I'm now the mother of two beautiful girls.'

'Me neither. Must get their looks from Peter.'

'Cheeky.'

Lorraine poured me another drink. 'Actually, I was wanting to ask you something,' she said.

'Yeah?'

'How disappointed would you be if you found out that Nick didn't fancy you after all?'

'Not at all,' I laughed. 'It was you who tried to convince me that he did! Why do you ask?'

'He asked me out for a drink,' Lorraine said blushing. 'I think it was me he liked after all.'

'Ah great! And are you going?'

'I don't know. I thought I might.'

'Go for it, he's gorgeous!'

Maureen came to replenish her plate and patted me on the arm.

'Congratulations, you poor bugger,' she said.

'Thanks, Maureen...I think.'

'Eeh, your body will never be the same.' She looked me up and down. 'It's a sad fact of nature that women have to give up their figures to create new life.' She pondered on a veggie sausage roll then stuffed it in her mouth.

'What happened to yours then?' Georgina asked. 'Too many pies?'

'What a cruel thing to say,' Maureen said, taking another couple of sausage rolls to console herself. 'You know I haven't been blessed with the joy of having a child.'

'So I'm right, it was the pies,' Georgina said.

I thought it was time to change the direction of the conversation.

'Had any interesting insights Maureen? Anything good on the horizon for us?'

Maureen sucked in through her teeth. 'Oh I don't want to burden you with all that. You're going to have enough on your plate these next few months. But all I'm saying is there's always trouble ahead in some form or other.'

'As long as the price of pies doesn't go up we'll be okay, eh Maureen?' Georgina said.

I gave her a stern look and she drifted off with a plateful of food. I don't know why she had to constantly goad Maureen. She referred to her as the 'Grim Reaper' or the 'Voice of Doom' and constantly sniped at her. We all knew Maureen erred on the side of pessimism, but apart from that she was a good soul and we were fond of her.

I mingled and chatted and was showered with presents. There were tiny baby clothes, a soft woollen blanket, a musical mobile and all sorts of toys. I was especially pleased to receive some beautiful children's books. Although I had lots of Rose's hand-me-downs and they always shared toys, I wanted to Anna to have some special things of her own and a collection of books was a great start. (Little did I know, twenty years later her collection would have amassed to nearly a thousand.)

Derek had brought me a basket of fruit. 'Congratulations, love,' he said. 'Nowt more special than a new little nipper.' He had six children himself and although he complained about them costing him a fortune, he was a loving father. 'Now that's good old-fashioned healthy fruit, that is,' he said as he handed me the basket filled with bananas, apples and oranges. 'There's none of your fancy foreign rubbish in there, kiwis and mangos and stuff.'

293

I was tempted to ask him where he thought bananas were grown but I refrained.

Anna from Richardson's Travel gave me some Freesia tied with pink ribbon.

'I'm called Anna too,' she told me.

'Yeah I know. I saw it on your name badge. It's such a beautiful name, I had to use it.'

'You mean...she's sort of named after me?' she beamed.

'Yes, I suppose she is,' I laughed.

Anna was thrilled. 'That's amazing!'

Poll congratulated me and asked if I was breast feeding, at which Nige gagged on his crisps and moved off out of earshot while we discussed our experiences. She'd brought me a bag of old baby clothes and an activity toy that clipped to a pram. I enjoyed chatting to her, I was glad for her advice, she had six healthy, well behaved children and I was keen to get some tips.

Presently, Aileen came and put a squawking Anna into my arms. 'I think she needs her mammy.'

'She'll be hungry.' I took her into the office to feed her. I settled myself on the office chair, Anna nestled in my arms, and listened to the hum of voices.

I felt so at home here. The smells and sounds were so familiar and comforting. Yeasty fresh bread, piquant herbs and spices, heady essential oils. Voices interspersed with laughter, the ping of the till and the louder trill of the shop door bell. Nadine's and Nige's voices were distinguishable above the rest, joking about how heartbroken they'd been since Take That had split. Nadine made some quip about Robbie Williams and they giggled together. Georgina was chatting to a customer about how the upside of Mad Cow Disease was that it had promoted vegetarianism and someone was singing along to the music. I heard Anna telling someone that she had the same name as the baby and I could hear Derek explaining that there was nothing better than spuds, carrots and cabbage for your Sunday roast.

A wave of happiness bubbled through me. I belonged here, it was my place.

I heard Rose squeal excitedly, followed by Peter's voice greeting her and he appeared in the office, bending to kiss Anna's head.

'I left early,' he said. 'You okay?' I nodded happily and he took Anna from my arms. 'Go and join everyone, I'll do the nappy change.'

I always found breastfeeding hungry work and I returned to the kitchen and put some bread and pate and couple of samosas onto a plate.

Aileen was making hot drinks and I accepted a cup of tea from her.

'Give me one for Peter too, please, he'll be down in a moment.' He returned with Anna asleep on his shoulder. I offered to take her, but he was reluctant to hand her over, diving into the food one handed as if he'd never been fed for days. I showed him the gifts we'd received and he nodded appreciatively while he munched on crisps and pizza.

People kept calling in to congratulate me, I was moved by all the good wishes and gifts. Several told me how well I looked, and although I suspected they were just being kind, I accepted the compliments gratefully. Even people I'd never met who'd called into the shop for the first time congratulated me and were given a cup of tea and an invitation to help themselves to a bite to eat. Several asked me when I was due back to work but I could only answer that I wasn't sure.

'When do you want to come back?' Lorraine asked when we were alone.

'I'm desperate to be back now, I'm really missing it. But I don't want to leave the girls. Rose starts nursery next month and I want to make the most of the time with her.'

'So why not pop in and help when you fancy it?' Lorraine suggested.

'Wouldn't you mind? I thought I'd have to commit to definite hours.'

295

'Don't be daft. We can do what we like, we're the bosses! The whole point of being self-employed is that we can please ourselves.'

'Well in that case, once Rose settles in nursery, I'll drop her off and head straight here with Anna to help for a couple of hours and take it from there.'

'Great. And I'll keep an eye on you to make sure you don't overdo it.'

'Aye, I bet you will.'

Tomas had never left Hanna's side since her revelation that he was soon to be a father. His face beamed as he sat with a protective arm about her.

Rose was having a great time, singing and dancing and generally showing off in the way little girls tend to do. Lorraine turned up the music and when I heard 'Baby Love' come on after 'Isn't She Lovely?' I realised the tracks had been specially selected.

'I've just realised the music theme! So when did all this happen?' I asked Lorraine.

'We've been planning it for a while. It was going to happen on Saturday, a big baby-shower, except you decided to come in today and we had to quickly change plans.'

'I tried to put her off,' Peter said. 'But she wanted to come in today.'

'I thought you didn't think I'd manage the journey with two children!' I said to him.

'Don't be daft. I'd never think anything like that. You know I think you're Wonder Woman.'

'Ugh, that's a little fantasy you can keep to yourselves,' Georgina said.

'And I thought you didn't want me to come in,' I said to Lorraine. 'I thought I'd get in the way.'

'Shurrup man,' Lorraine said. 'This business wouldn't be here if you hadn't bullied us all into it.'

I laughed and gave her a hug. 'Thanks for this. It means a lot.'

'And you mean a lot to me,' Lorraine said. 'You all do.'

Nadine, who'd overheard, smiled. 'You're a lucky girl.'

I looked at my lovely sister, my two beautiful girls and my gorgeous husband.

'I am indeed,' I said.

38932822R00168

Printed in Poland
by Amazon Fulfillment
Poland Sp. z o.o., Wrocław